THORNAPPLE

THORNAPPLE

CHRIS HUNT

First published in May 1989 by GMP Publishers Limited
PO Box 247, London N17 9QR, England

Copyright © 1989 Chris Hunt

British Library Cataloguing in Publication Data

Hunt, Chris
I. Title
823 .914

ISBN 0 85449 104 X

Distributed in North America by
Alyson Publications Inc.
40 Plympton Street
Boston, MA 02118, USA

Printed and bound in the European Community by
Nørhaven A/S, Viborg, Denmark

TO D.

ONE
The Pedlar's Tale

I

I AM the pedlar man; you know me.

After all, one pedlar is very like another; we are to be found on any roadway in all seasons of the year, solitary travellers bent beneath our pack. All pedlars are the same. Cunning. We know how to look after ourselves. We last out the Winter knowing the cheap inns or the friendly hearths; or maybe we have holes in the grounds like rabbits. We understand the network of old ways that winds among the heath and forest and sometimes threatens the unready traveller. We do not seem to starve in hard times, and when Spring comes we are back upon the road, approaching your village with a taste of romance.

You have bestowed on us this gift. Tied as you are to the land, your village duties and obedience to the lord of the manor, you see in us a free spirit, a man without burdens or responsibility. Where may we have come from? That is anybody's guess, and we would not disappoint you: Venice, Bordeaux, Toledo, or simply Stourbridge Fair – mere names to you, I know, but I may have walked those Venetian quaysides. And as for the thrills I have for you hidden in my pack, you have only to gather round to be delighted and amazed. Gemstones, ivory toothpicks, pins, needles and thread! Buckles, brooches, little blocks of salt, coloured ribbons, oriental spices! Combs and scented lotions! Lucky people – see how I bring some colour into your lives! All I'm asking in return is a little money.

It's odd the way you never wholly trust me. What is it about a wanderer – is it that owning nothing I have nothing to lose, and therefore freedom to do as I please? Unlike you, of course: the lord would soon hear of any misdeeds. Those little lies, those sudden

5

sicknesses on the days when you should be working his fields – you're never quite sure, are you, even in your clumsy falsehoods? Some neighbour might cheat on you to gain the lord's favour. And that reeve is always breathing down your neck.

Whereas I could get away with petty pilfering. By the time it was discovered I could be miles away from here. And though I were as honest as the morning, who would say so in my defence? I have chances for whatever you suspect me of. All pedlars are the same.

Those of you who have never travelled – and which of you have? — suspect the road beyond your village, a highway to the unknown. Sometimes you've trodden a few miles at the order of the lord, hedging and ditching on the waysides, carting for him, holding his horses. But that's nothing; that's not travelling. A turn in the road hides the way and what it holds. You are glad enough to return to the village. How then can you understand the nature of a man who travels by choice, who daily does not know what the journey will bring, who risks the company of thieves and wastrels? Rather than be knowing, you back off.

For you I have always been a pedlar: I was never a child. I have my own place in eternity. There was never a time when I had a choice; there was never a town where I had birth. The lines of my face will merge into a general outline. You were listening to a pedlar. Which one? A pedlar. They all look the same.

But I know what you want of me and I won't let you down. Ballads, verses, I have them for all occasions, and stories come as easy as the selling. So I give you *Aucassin and Nicolette* and *King Florus*, and leave you happy. And no one looks beyond, always content to see what they expect to see, hear what they expect to hear.

There is a lad tending my horse and packing away my wares, his face hidden in shadow, his hair masked by his hempen hood. No one pays much heed to a servant. If you but knew it, the tale I could tell of him outmatches all the old romances. But it deals with that which must stay secret: dark things can be remembered, but are best left untold. And this strange tale is not for the open fireside and the merry gathering, containing as it does much which could get me into trouble. Yet it is always in my thoughts...

I never went back to Cortle. I doubt that we would have escaped her ladyship's wrath a second time. Yet in those old days Cortle drew me. I went there often, and only partly because of the herbs for my trade.

When I left London they thought I was mad to put behind me the cheer and excitement of a town decked out in its bravery for the Yuletide revels. Certainly it was merry there, and in its packed and bustling streets the smells of cooking and the sounds of gusty laughter were inviting, and there was just about everything a man could need inside those walls if he had the money. And if I were telling my tale by a tavern hearthside I'd be hearing the knowing smutty sniggers now – everything a man could need, eh? That's the stews in the backstreets, where the lusty girls are lurking – yes, we know! But they'd be wrong. It was a boy I took, a hard-eyed city lad with small firm buttocks, who gave me a good time and tried to rob me afterwards. That's how it is in London, all commerce and thievery. It's a town that holds no charm for me, a place of business only; and if I could search out some cheap new bauble from a foreign merchant to add to the stock in my pack, that was all I asked of a visit there. And a boy to satisfy the itch of lust.

I'd have done well to have kept to what I knew, the ragged lads of wharves and alleys, but I'd stepped outside my proper place and had paid the penalty. I cannot help it: lust knows no boundaries. Juhel de Bracy was a creature such as minstrels sing of, with butter-coloured hair and mischievous endearing ways, and an odd fancy for the low life, hence his taking up with me at all. But he was Norman. He lived in a house at the river's edge, a great stone stronghold with its base in the water and its front gates opening onto the slope of a street where traders and servants trudged to and fro in the service of his family. It was not stupid of me to sell my wares inside his house – his eagle-nosed majestic mother bought up most of my ivory – but it was stupid of me to stay on when invited by him. My weakness for yellow hair overcame my good sense. I went back again and again under cover of selling my wares, and I daresay even the most bone-headed dullard could have guessed there was more to it.

They had a little room leading off a stairway where they stored clothes, a dim airless hole where time and again I made love to the beautiful youth.

'No one will come in,' he assured me as we pressed against tapestry and fur. Dust and the scent of lavender and southernwood rose from the hanging garments as our bodies moved together in the musty gloom. He was always eager to take off his clothes – a most attractive weakness – and I was able to glut myself upon that slim young body to my heart's content, remaining dressed for a quick getaway. His mother's silks and furs caressed his naked skin, vying

7

with my lips that feasted hungrily on that rich fare. I could taste coriander as I licked his nipples, guessing that he overlaced his baths with herbs. He was almost like a child – so clearly pleased to give such pleasure, thrusting now his jutting prick and now his rounded arse for my delight, half disappearing in the ropes of fur and swathes of silk, to re-emerge laughing.

One day I left the house as usual, and in the street outside his father's men were waiting, and on orders from Hubert de Bracy set upon me with their fists against the house wall. I was flung so hard against a passing cartwheel I felt pain from neck to wrist; and I ended in the gutter with the street muck, in a pool of blood from nose or mouth or both, and with barely wit enough to roll clear of the cart.

De Bracy towered above me, a strutting hawk-faced lordling, seeming ten feet high. 'And if I ever see you near my house again there will be worse for you, much worse.'

I could have got up but deemed it best to appear all beaten down; and with my knees close to my chest and my arms about my head, I put up with the final couple of kicks that seemed to leave them satisfied. An oddly honest boy had gathered up my scattered wares for me, and though of course some were missing, I was still in business. I stacked them away in my pack, dripping blood onto the leather.

Back in Jug Yard, where I was staying at the time, Rahere the bone-gatherer advised me to leave town.

'I was planning to,' I answered him.

'Now you have more reason.'

'I wouldn't go just because of that.'

'Wouldn't you? I would! Anyway,' he added, squinting at me curiously, 'what had you *done*?'

I shrugged. 'Nothing. Normans just don't like Saxons, that's all.'

But I reckoned I was lucky to get away alive, and I took Rahere's advice. A couple of days later I was on the road.

I set out bravely enough northwards and eastwards. I followed Ermine Street until it joined the Icknield Way somewhat south of Cambridge and then took this road into East Anglia.

All the way was busy with the usual mess of Christmas travellers; I was hardly ever alone. They were mostly going towards London. Some baron with his whole household hogged the road in passing, the pack horses laden till they nearly sank in the mud – it amazed me what they had found to load them with. There was all the baggage his lady brought with her, stacked in waggons with vile wheels that could have crushed your feet to pulp. And a gang of noisy men-at-arms to make sure we humble folk kept a proper distance. The nobility love a chance like this, of course, when they can jingle past in splendour while the peasants stare in spite of themselves at the sumptuous display. We all moved out of the way for them to go by, which meant stumbling around in the sunken cart ruts and deep winter mud, which is how peasants are supposed to behave anyway. They watched for any signs of protest on our part, but of course nobody protested.

As the clinking harness and clattering hooves turned away down the road, we clambered up again on the hard surface. Hard surface, I say – well, parts of it were. It was in fact the crumbling remains of the stones the Romans laid so long ago. But now they've been whittled down to a poor skeleton of what they used to be. Some of the old paving stones are still there but too many have been lifted away to build other things, leaving gaping holes that fill with rain and mud. But none of this is unexpected: we travellers are mostly bound together by a grudging acceptance of discomfort. Near the towns and villages the roads are better, but once past these, you are out on your own again to flounder along the highway.

Perhaps it was the Norman baron who made me feel sour. No; I always thought thus on my travels in wintertime. Everywhere I looked I was aware of poverty and lack. It was as if with the falling of the leaves the outlines of truth were laid bare. This feeling is never so strong in the Summer when the land is green and the barley is ripening, and when the folk in the fields are working so hard that either they honestly love what they do or are too tired to see the twisted scheme of which they are a part. But Winter is a dead season. The sowing of wheat and rye is long finished. The skinny cattle have been killed off and salted, and now they hang above the fires, wizened carcasses partly preserved by the smoke.

The faces of you peasants looking out from your hovels are lined and drawn. A curl of foul smoke wisps out of the doorway, along with the smell of animals that snort and snuffle inside. Living has dwindled into a losing struggle to keep warm; your bleak eyes look out from tattered rags and sacking, anything that can be twined around a body numb with cold. Goatskins and filthy fleeces blur the shapes of folk returning from the forest, hedging and wooding, hunting in the short cold daylight for rabbits and any bird they can trap for the watery stew. There's the prospect of a leaden time now the hunting's done, when a man repairs his tools and fixes his knife

9

handles, fills up the cracks in his walls, and carves out eating bowls from the wood he hooked.

The world has always been so, you say – Winter is a lean time. But we have grown used to the cold. We have cheerful sayings to pull us through the bad patches and our hope is after all in Heaven. Our Lord was poor, and we think it no shame to toil with our hands and take what we can from the land. All seasons were created for a purpose and as for Winter, the earth sleeps to wake refreshed and we too find solace in the quiet time. Spring will come again, and Lord knows we shall be busy enough then.

But I could tell you, anyone who travels further afield sees more of the way of things. Why should it be that men who came from overseas and took our land by force should hold high places and lord it over us? Like a crusted skin over a living body they leech upon our land. What angers me is that you villagers are Saxons, some of you born of good old families. Your meekness gnaws at me. Don't you know the way the Normans live? Haven't you seen the meat, fruit, white bread, roast swans, pastries and wine? Where is your pride, your knowledge of times past?. Does no old crone tell you of the days when the lords of the land were Saxon?

It is over a hundred years since the Normans came to plunder and pillage our land. Some of our brave men resisted. Look at Hereward the Hero. But freedom soon came to an end. The old ways were crookedly twisted, and all ranks of Saxons were bundled together under the names of villeins and churls, all owing allegience to the new master. Chains seen and unseen held you in the place wherever you happened to be. Your own land you now held through the say of the overlord and you worked your soil to his demands.

All that was long ago, you say in your defence, and things are easier now. To be sure, ours is a cramping way of life, but we have food to fill us, ale to cheer us, and the Saints to watch over us. If we are suffering now it will be over soon and we shall reap the benefits of Life Everlasting.

And is my lot so much better? you say. Am I any luckier than you, plodding the land with a pack upon my back?

I reached Norfolk some ten days after I had set out from London. I walked into a village church where they had a fair old statue of Saint Blaise, the patron saint of sufferers from sore throats. I was feeling somewhat cold. Moreover, my shoulder, where I had crashed against the cartwheel, was causing me a most odd pain. All down my left arm I could hardly bend it. Unlike the body bruises it

10

seemed to be getting worse, and now I could not lift things with my hand. With every day the fingers grew more stiff. I told myself it was the cold, tomorrow it would ease; but I was troubled.

'Saint Blaise,' I said, 'I hope you'll stop me falling ill before I get to Cortle.'

He reminded me, as if I didn't know, that my steps would soon pass Alkanet's cottage.

'True,' I said. 'Thank you anyway.'

He looked cold too, in his narrow stone niche, his hands all bare.

'Saint Blaise,' I said, 'all's not well with the world, is it?'

He looked at me very severely.

'And what are you doing about it, pedlar man, besides grumbling?'

II

I WAS alone in the wetness of the wasteland.

Since leaving the main track I'd blundered down an old drove way and needed all my wit to see me right. For all my complaints about the condition of the road, I felt it led somewhere and I was rewarded at all times with signs of life. At the approach to a village there was bustle and business. Yapping dogs would run to meet me. The men cutting in the forest would be coming back, their shoulders bowed under a sheaf of branches; chattering children were seeking green boughs to hang about the houses; villagers pointed travellers to the inn. Beyond the village the encroaching forest was always cut back several yards on both sides and I could go onward quickly in the added space and light. As darkness fell they set lanthorns in the church towers and sometimes the priest rang a bell for a while to let travellers know that a haven was nearby.

Between leaving one village and arriving at the next, I got a feeling of companionship, for the road was rutted by tracks of carts, and that meant men passed that way. I went several miles in the company of carters and we gladly exchanged news. Talk followed which I daresay was taking place all over England.

'How goes it overseas? Is Normandy still safe? Is the French king still after our lands?'

'Yes, indeed – he has set his heart on grabbing Normandy. There has been fighting there all year. And then King Philip decided to lay seige to the mighty fortress of Château Gaillard...'

'Shatter who?'

11

'Gaillard. In our tongue it means a merry castle. He has been there since last August.'

'Ah, he'll never take it. *King Richard* had that castle built.'

'True. He may have had his faults as a monarch but he knew all about building castles and the skills of warfare.'

'Besides, that French king is no soldier. Not like King Richard was.'

'That's right. I have heard that Philip Augustus is fat and bald and worn down by the pains of ruling France. Didn't he turn tail and hurry home from the Crusades?'

'They say he only dares ride quiet horses!'

We chuckled contemptuously at this French buffoon, squatting his bulky shape astride a placid nag, gawping up at Château Gaillard, the pride of King Richard. There since August! How he must be hating those impregnable walls!

'Who holds Château Gaillard?'

'Roger of Lacy, a good leader. He'll hold King Philip off for us.'

'What do you think, then? Will we lose those lands? We heard a ballad singer joking about the other castles we had lost. Some gave in without a fight. They said even King Philip was scornful about our poor resistance.'

'But King John is back in England now. He is to spend Christmas at Canterbury. Would he do that if he was anxious about the state of things abroad?'

Carters can be good companions and then again there are travellers who look askance at you, morose, full of misgivings. I travelled some way with a priest, but he didn't speak and seemed to eye me with suspicion. But that's how it is with priests.

When on the road I would sleep sometimes at inns, sometimes in the homes of people who remembered me from before. One place I was always well received, the little house where Alric lived with his mother. I felt some guilt about deceiving that good dame, who always made me welcome. Plump and kind, she'd bustle to and fro ladling out bean broth and eager to hear what the ladies were wearing in London. I sold her the odd trinket cheap to ease my conscience.

'I tell you, pedlar, you are welcome to sleep above while I sleep down with Alric. It's warmer, drier in the loft. You're such a good man, you don't like causing any bother. Time and again you sleep down there with Alric and the animals; I hope they don't disturb you. Alric, don't you be a bother now, and see the pedlar has all he wants.'

'Yes mother, I'll do that.'

Alric was a tousle-headed lad with tangled yellow hair and eyes as brown and placid as a cow's. His strong young body was all muscle, sunburnt, weather-tanned, his thighs were thick and firm, his arse a lively handful. With him there was no need of words to get what we both wanted. In the darkness, close against the goat, three shuffling sows and several cackling hens, we would lie in the earthy straw and take our pleasure. A night with him and I'd feel mankind had no spirituality; I felt no better than the goat. As I went along the old drove way I thought back to the last time I had stayed there. Roping my hands round Alric's warm sinewy flesh, I had gripped his hairy bum; I twined my legs about his heaving thighs and drove my cock inside him.

'Are you warm enough?' his mother called.

'Thank you, yes,' we panted.

'Lord, how restless those animals be tonight – such a grunting!'

'No, don't stop...' moaned Alric in a whisper. 'Deeper...more...'

I held him tight and did as I was asked. A hen flew squawking up the ladder. 'Come, my pretty,' said Alric's mother. 'You *are* frisky tonight! What's got into you?'

'I never told!' Alric whispered, lying in my arms. 'I never said what it is we do. Nobody knows, just you and me. I'm so glad you came back.'

'I said I would.'

'You do it so well. It's lovely what you do.'

'Your body makes me good.'

'I'll do it for you now. D'you see how big my cock is! Look!'

'Surely you are not still awake, Alric?' called his mother. 'Remember you have work to do tomorrow. And that poor pedlar needs his rest.'

Alric grinned close to my face and rolled onto me. 'This kind of work I like.' We set about it silently. Straw shifted as we moved. His mother turned upstairs; the cross beam creaked. 'I like it so much better with you, pedlar,' Alric told me thoughtfully, 'than when I do it with the goat.'

But I was not always so lucky and it looked as if tonight I would fare ill. The track I'd taken in mistake led me about out of my way, and when I'd picked it up again the hour was late. I could well believe I should be sleeping beneath the stars this coming night.

I remembered where the way to Cortle broke away from the main highway, near Thetford, and I took that path. There was a

13

charcoal burner's hut along there where I would be welcome. This pathway was a lonely one; although I knew it led eventually to Cortle, I could have believed it led to the edge of the world. It plunged between the brushwood, uncared for, uncut, so that branches grew high on both sides and hung down overhead. Underfoot there was a path; not, I think, a Roman way, but a way of local tread and very old. A cart might just about pass. A horseman would be pestered by the overhead branches. For a single traveller it was not too bad as long as you did not fear being alone. Large processions must sometimes have taken this way, for people did come to Cortle. It's somewhat out of the way, but once there a traveller finds it pleasing and bustling enough. Audran de Bonnefoy would have taken this path with his noble procession when he left Cortle for the Crusade. (If we were in luck, an infidel would lay him low.) Oh yes, we have a castle at Cortle, built on an old Saxon mound, as so many are.

Because of the overhanging trees the stumbling block was not the slimy mud and gaping stone-holes of the path, but the dismal wetness of the thick, deep grass. December without snow it was, dampening my clothes and spirits, the moisture drops seeming to dangle in the air all around me. From those trees which still bore leaves came the ceaseless sad sound of trickling water, following its whispery trail from bough to twig to undergrowth. From time to time a sudden splash would make me feel somebody was near, only to realise that several of these rivulets had joined to finish their journey together. My steps forward made the grasses swish and twitch. Sometimes a bird would fly up with a cry further on in the wood, and there were other rustlings on the ground, where thickets hid the animals from sight.

The darkening sky was cut across by the black shapes of tall, gaunt trees. Here and there the path widened a little and the trees stood back. In the wet hollows made by the heavy wheels of a cart, green sedge grew creeping. But the damp stillness was no threat to me, and I was never afraid of silences.

When I reached the forking of the ways I rested for a moment against the cross there. This solid landmark was put up in a bygone age as a recognition of the loneliness of the spot. Many a traveller must have been cheered to see that firm-hewn symbol of the saving of mankind. It's possible to believe yourself the only person in the world at times on these forest paths, and to happen upon this sign of the work of Man in the cause of God is a heartening sight.

Cortle was still some way off, but somebody had come out from its safety to mark this crossroads and tell the wanderer that he had not far to go. I leant against the firm stonework and looked about me. Three paths there were; the path I had come, the way to Cortle, and the path to the north. Even as I watched I heard the sound of somebody approaching down that northern path. Slow cumbersome movement it was, with the stamping and snorting of a slow-moving horse. Around the curve of bush and briar came a figure on foot, hooded against the weather, a rough stick in one hand and in the other the halter of a small packhorse. Admiration and envy crossed my mind; I could have done with such a tidy little packhorse myself. The traveller was a salter; I recognised the salt panniers strung across the animal's back. You see a lot of such on the roads in the Autumn when the meat is salted, but they're always about selling the stuff in between times.

We greeted each other and spoke about the weather and the state of the roads. He had come down from Lincoln, and then across country along paths with which he was not too familiar.

'I'm a Cotswold man myself,' he told me. 'I can't abear the fenlands with their treacherous paths and sodden rushes and screeching wildfowl. Fogs like I've never seen...It was a nightmare crossing the Wash, paying over the odds to squint-eyed fishermen to pick you a way across the swampy sand...'

'Ah, but Lincoln's a fine city,' I said. 'I know it well. I was there that Autumn when the King was there and the old Bishop Hugh died. Must be three years ago now.'

'Bishop Hugh...a saint if ever there was one.'

'The King thought so too. They say he put his own shoulder to the old man's coffin. They were building a new minster.'

'They are still building. So you saw the King, then?'

'He was as close to me as you are now.'

'What was he like?'

'Short, and he struts somewhat...The scabbard of his sword near scrapes the ground. He wears a trim beard and he's got bright eyes, full of fun. He's good looking, plumpish. He dresses like one who enjoys his clothes. Bright colours.'

'You liked him, then?'

'I did. I have heard little spoken against him. He is held to be kindly to the poor and loyal to his friends, with a great respect for law and justice. Also I find it in his favour that he likes his wine as the old Saxon kings liked their ale, and he is not over pious.'

'He cannot but be an improvement on his brother.'

I agreed. 'King Richard was a lout.'

15

'And never here! Always in some foreign land.'

'Good only for fighting – harsh and cold of nature – '

'I wasn't sorry to hear he'd died.'

With so much in common, then, and the salter being clearly a man of good sense, you would think I would be glad of his company. He asked me if he were on the right road to Cortle.

I pointed along the path which had led me to this spot. 'There lies the way to Cortle. You should make it by nightfall.'

'I thought it to be more eastward,' he said, not disbelieving me, just a little surprised.

'No,' I assured him. 'I've just come from there.'

'Well,' he said, 'I'd best be on my way then. I don't want to get caught out here in the darkness.'

'I'm sure you're right,' I agreed.

I wished him well and Godspeed and watched him plod away towards the midlands and the south. You have to look after your interests in a wicked world. I had salt in my pack and they'd be very glad of it in Cortle, even up at the castle. What chance would I have stood against a seller of salt on such a grand scale, who would have lowered his prices on that account? No, my trade is more important to me than the chance of company along the road.

I reckoned I would reach my friend the charcoal burner's hut at the closing in of night. With this cheering thought I went on my way. Over my head the daylight waned and the murk of early evening softly gathered, the sky's grey melting into the colour of smoke. The forked branches blackened, fading into sky, as that black cloak spread itself slowly over all. It was hard to see the path now, but I knew I was not too far from the clearing and I hurried on as best I might.

Then I got a shock: the path widened, the grass was flattened, but there was no hut; I'd almost walked out of the clearing before it came to me sharply that this was the spot and no other, and the hut ought to be there. I paced all round the dim clearing, bewildered. I found where the hut had been, the square which had housed his few things and where I had thankfully slept in other times. It was hard to see what had happened. That, of course, was not my problem. I was out in the night with nowhere to sleep. A hardened old traveller like myself should not have made such a blunder.

I sat down on the ground and took off my pack. I could feel then an ungrassy mess which I recognised as charred wood. Seemingly the hut had burned down. Well, that was likely enough, but no help to me. I considered my plight. I could raid my pack for a candle and plod on hopefully through the night, but this would be a careless waste of candle when the daylight would do the same job for me in the morning. And it would be foolish to continue walking the forest path. I was not troubled by tales of demons, fiends and Will-o'-the-wisps, I told myself; no, it was simply that in complete darkness it would be madness to try going forward. A traveller could leave the path unknowingly and stumble about like a blind man, and come the daylight he could be anywhere, lost and helpless in a world of leaves and undergrowth.

I would have to stay where I was.

I made myself as comfortable as I could in the ashy wood left by the burnt shack, and tried to go to sleep. I must have done so, but something woke me: a noise in the forest, a rhythmic beating sound, like wood on wood, which I could not place. I sat up quickly, wide awake now, for there was worse. Across the clearing a moving light, a speck of fire was bearing straight towards me through the darkness, like an eye without face or limb.

III

BEFORE TRUTH struck me, I admit I feared it was a forest spirit come to hunt me down. They approach like this upon the lonely wanderer and in fleeing from them he falls down some pit or drowns in a mere, and it is said of his corpse that the foul fiend drove him to his death. I crouched there gazing at the light, spellbound, but waiting for knowledge to click into place. Behind the light loomed a vast and ghostly figure, a shape of darker blackness than the night and taller than a man. Since it was coming straight towards me and I would soon be lit by the moving light I decided to make myself known.

'What traveller are you?' I said loudly.

The light hovered. It sought me out.

'Is there someone there?' said a voice.

'I am a pedlar. Who are you?'

As an answer, the shape lifted the lanthorn upwards and downwards. I saw a pallid hooded face, black circles about the eyes caused by the light, a tall pointed hat which gave his outline unnatural height, and a long black garment patched with whitish shapes. In this setting I would almost have thought him a wizard of the old sort, but commonsense had returned. The poor wight was a leper.

17

'Well, stay your ground, friend,' I said. In common with many, I had a sympathetic feeling towards these unlucky folk, fated to a traveller's lot through no choice of their own. As long as he didn't come too close!

'Sit down,' I suggested, grateful to him for not having been a forest fiend, but only too sadly human. 'Tell me where you're bound.'

He sat down a little way off.

'You know what I am?' he said.

'You wear the gear,' I said.

'And you still ask me to sit down? That's very Christian of you.'

'I hope so. We wanderers should stick by one another.'

'Well, pedlar man, I've come from London and am on my way to Walsingham.'

'To be cured at the shrine,' I supposed.

'That's right. As I'm obliged to travel, I thought I might do so to some purpose. I've heard tell that all kinds of miracles happen there.'

'True, true,' I said; and unfortunately my nature and trade struggled to the surface. 'But why trail all those miles?' I said. 'You're lucky to have fallen in with me. Why, right here in my pack I've got just the thing for you – a splinter from the staff of Saint Peter himself. Most carefully wrapped. I bought it from a pilgrim who travelled the greatest holy path of all, to Our Lord's very birthplace. There he was able to see the staff itself which the saint held in his hand. He swore it was a wonderful thing. Heavy! You'd never believe a man could lift it. Glowing! It was brighter than the moon. And right here in my pack I've got a splinter from that selfsame staff taken from where Saint Peter plunged it into the ground, just before he was arrested!'

'In Rome, I thought?' said the man gently.

'In Rome?' said I, taken by surprise. 'Well, no, I meant by the fireside where the cock crowed and he thought he might be arrested. Now, would you like to see it? I wouldn't ask half what it's really worth.'

After a silence the man said: 'It's not that I don't trust you, pedlar, but I have set my heart on Walsingham.'

I felt a bit mean then, trying to trick a fellow in such misfortune.

'You're right,' I said. 'For all I know the man I got it from may have been lying his head off.'

I asked how long he had been afflicted and was surprised when he said only a few weeks.

18

'I have a cookshop near Saint Paul's. It's a good little business. Open day and night and never refused a customer. I was an honest dealer. One day I began getting these crusty spots on my face and they began spreading. Somebody said it was leprosy, and before I could hardly turn round the priest was in there with the black pall and the Office of Seclusion.'

I made sympathetic mutterings.

'There'd been a lot about,' he went on. 'They say the Crusaders picked it up in the east. There'd been some in our street – I sold one a pie. Felt sorry for him. Of course, somebody had seen me do it and remembered, so they all agreed I'd caught it then. I had to get out; I'd have lost my trade.'

'Who minds your shop?'

'My helper. I wasn't going to sell out. I'll be glad of it when I'm cured and I go back again.'

'Yes,' I said doubtfully. I wasn't much impressed by these holy relics, but why dash a man's hopes? 'Well, you're on the right road for Walsingham.'

He was, too; it was beyond Cortle, out the other side.

Then it struck me that old Alkanet might know something about remedies for leprosy. I wouldn't have put anything past that old woman. Woman? Ancient crone, I should say.

'Look now,' I said, 'I've had a thought. When I'm in these parts, I always go to this old woman who lives near Cortle. She's a foul old hag and enough to frighten the bravest, but she can fix all sorts of things. Everybody goes to her. I know she could, if not cure you, at least help you.'

'What does she do?'

'She has a weird herb wilderness. There must be every herb in creation there, growing since before the Romans came. She knows them all. I wouldn't tell you if she wasn't a wonder far and wide.'

'Well, if it wouldn't be out of my way...'

'No. Nor mine. I often call in there on my way back to London. She knows me. I will gladly take you there.'

'That's most kind of you. She wouldn't turn me away? Some don't like to come too near.'

'I should think she's seen it all. She's not the kind to be squeamish.'

'Does she live on her own?'

'Except for some halfwit boy.'

19

It was dawn when Jusson the leper and I drew near to old Alkanet's patch.

His dwindling lanthorn led us through the dim shades, the black forest lessening to grey, until pale daylight came smoky-rose over the tops of the trees. Outlandish indeed had my companion appeared when distorted by night, but the light of day did little to change that. Even if they had failed to hear his clapper, nobody could fail to see at a glance the poor wight's condition, his tall crimson hat, his long black cloak scabbed with white patches.

There was an open stretch of bushy scrubland as you drew near to Cortle, a rough sloping heath where bracken and sand sedge grew and sheep were brought to graze. Our path skirted this ground, bordering the edge of the forest and then winding down to Cortle village. But the little path to Alkanet's cottage turned away from the open, plunging like a swimmer's path straight into the undergrowth.

I was thinking back a bit as we trudged beside the heath, about Alkanet and her woodland den and the quiet young lad who lived with her. Half-witted, as I remembered, a secretive and silent figure, with a little pointed face; a shadow in the background. Where had the boy come from? Was he a grandson? The thought of the old crone dealing in love, however long ago, seemed unbelievable. Surely she could never have been comely. What then was the secret? A baron's bastard? No, that was my fancy running away with me. The child of a peasant family, perhaps, left as a babe for Alkanet to save.

His name, I knew, was Marel.

As we were plodding along the path beside the heath, there came a great flurry of hooves, the splash of a scarlet cloak and a noisy brash laugh – all of which so clearly betokened a Norman lord that, guilty thoughts provoking guilty actions, I scuttled quickly into the undergrowth on the edge of the forest. Jusson did likewise, perhaps thinking I had some unusual knowledge, and being obliged himself to keep back from the gaze of men. We could see the Norman was of some hunting party, out after deer. What a fierce contrast it presented, to see a Norman lord in a winter landscape! All kitted out in scarlet, he was, very good quality stuff, warm and heavy; and he had a glossy look about him which I much begrudged. Two things then struck me. First, it was Audran de Bonnefoy, baron of the castle at Cortle; and second, there was some unfortunate beside him, between his horse and the forest edge, trying to hurry by and not being allowed.

As far as I knew, Audran de Bonnefoy had gone off on Pope Innocent's Crusade. I thought we had seen the last of him. I never myself saw him leave, but I heard all about it. Everybody knew he was going, and all the village spoke about it and tried to pretend they were awe-struck at his bravery and sorry to see him leave. Which was not easy, but if anyone let on they were delighted someone might tell Azo the reeve, and then there would be trouble. So everyone was monstrous pious, drinking his health and discussing his chances and loudly applauding his honour. I do believe his lady wife praised him the loudest of all, and what that means can perhaps be guessed. And he really did go. There was a ceremony at the castle gate with his wife handing him a good luck stirrup cup and everyone else looking on; a fanfare too, I think he had. And there sat the great gawk lapping it all up and vain enough to think they meant it.

So what was he doing here in Cortle woods on an early morning, molesting this peasant? It seemed to be a youth, slim, small and hooded. I guessed he'd had the bad luck to cross Audran's path coming away from Cortle, and the baron on his way to the castle. Empty-handed from the hunt too, unless his friends had got a deer and were going on ahead of him. He was having a good time teasing his victim, letting him go a little way, overtaking him, hustling him with his horse, seeming to move off, then closing in again. At last, fairly close to where we were hidden, he wedged him against a tree and leaning from the saddle, barred the way. Then he flicked off the boy's hood and we saw he was a lad of most burning beauty.

I nearly whistled. You don't often see such fairy-tale good looks in peasant guise, and on a boy at that. I know about peasant lads – I've fancied a good many, and they range from apple-cheeked and buxom to lean and stringy with hair like tow. But this one was eerily beautiful, like an angel in a church with golden hair and sunbeams raying outward from its head. It must have been the hair, which was long and sleek and glossy, not at all thatchy like peasant hair. His skin was so fine and pale, his lips smooth and full, not rough and chapped with cold, and his eyes so bright and sparkling. Poor and ragged his clothes might be, but the figure within was graceful and lithe, slight of build...I could not place the age exactly – fourteen maybe – a squire's age. Any knight would have been proud to hand his gear to him.

But what was Audran's interest? This paunchy buffoon was well known for his pursuit of wenches, and he had a lovely lady wife. So did his interest stretch to boys as well? Or just this boy? Had they

21

met before? I sensed that this was not the first time Audran had barged upon the young lad's company and teased him thus. I was baffled, and unworthily excited. I confess to the stirrings of a base and barefaced curiosity, a desire simply to stand there and watch the outcome unfold before us.

Audran leaned forward on his horse and spoke a few sardonic phrases, but they were in French – he had never bothered to learn the language of his menials. The boy pressed back against the tree, shaking his head, revulsion written clear enough upon his face. I felt uneasy then.

'No!' said the boy, plainly enough.

Audran laughed, and drew a dagger from his belt. He gestured callously towards the bushes, and barked a command.

Jusson whispered urgently: 'Pedlar, we must stop it!'

'Christ above! That's more than our lives are worth!'

'But he means to kill him!'

I looked at Jusson in surprise. That wasn't how I interpreted it. But it is true that some men possess a certain – not innocence, but it never crosses their minds that some men desire pretty boys and intend to take forced pleasure from them as is done with females. I supposed Jusson was of this unsuspecting kind. To me, Audran's intention looked perfectly clear and murder was not it. I was galled by the fact that the lad would have to give in because Audran had mastery over the villagers of Cortle. Submit or lose your ears. I just hoped the boy would be able to get some pleasure out of what must now happen.

Jusson, however, was made of sterner stuff. He began to move.

'Leave him alone,' I urged. 'You'll get us both into trouble.'

'No, I cannot stand by,' said Jusson.

I groaned. All my trade in Cortle; all my dealings, all those herbs I wouldn't be able to collect...

You know, for a moment I had completely forgotten that Jusson was a leper. He came out of the bushes like a sleepwalker, as if he were in a procession. His wooden clapper sounded its warning note, and Audran de Bonnefoy turned round in astonishment.

'Unclean! Unclean!' wailed Jusson, like somebody from a tale read in church, bearing down towards the gaping lord.

'Be gone! Be off with you, foul thing!' spat Audran.

But of course an ignorant peasant like Jusson couldn't understand, but simply came nearer and nearer, his crusted hands outstretched as if he would beg for alms or – God save us! — some lepers believe the touch of a noble's robe can heal them.

Poor Audran was faced with a hard choice. He gawped at the leper as if he couldn't believe his bad luck. He glanced at the quivering golden-haired boy before him, and then back at Jusson approaching with all the inevitability of the grim reaper. I bit my lip, wondering what would happen next. But he didn't let me down – poor Audran, even his manly vices were in the wrong order. Fear overcame lust, and with a bellowing curse he turned his horse and was soon galloping away down the path to Cortle.

I emerged from the bushes, a little ashamed I must admit.

'Jusson!' I cried, awed, and unthinking I thumped him on the back. 'Why didn't you tell me you were a brave man, a hero?'

But he turned towards the boy. We both had some thought of a hero's thanks, a prayer of gratitude for the timely coming of his saviours. But seemingly the sight of us was the final terror – I like to think it was mainly Jusson, of course. The boy gave us a frozen stare and turned on his heels and ran at great speed away into the forest.

We both wanted to follow, and with a start of pleasure I saw he had taken the path that led to Alkanet's cottage. By now it had dawned on me, though slowly, that the lad was none other than young Marel, the halfwit boy who waited on Alkanet. I struggled to make sense of the two conflicting pictures – the quiet, shadowy boy and the lovely youth. Had I been uncommonly stupid? Alkanet had always hustled the boy out of the way when I visited the cottage. A poor misbegotten halfwit, she'd told me, so I'd paid no heed to him. Such is the power of suggestion!

'It's Marel, the boy from the cottage,' I said.

'Oh?' said Jusson.

We followed at an ordinary pace, catching from time to time a glimpse of the fleeting figure, fair hair flowing behind, slim and elusive like a forest creature. I felt my eyes were suddenly opened. I was most eager to see the boy again. I remembered him drooping against the tree. But more than that – his running through the rustling leaves had a mystic touch to it. I saw moving lights about him, slivers of daylight shafting through the trees, pallid beams of wintry sunlight in dancing shapes and patterns. I felt he was leading me forward, into events which would bind us.

IV

THERE WAS something very odd about the approach to Alkanet's cottage. It was not easy to say where the commonplace bushes and grasses turned into herbs; there was no landmark or stone. But suddenly as you drew near, you were aware of an outlandish plant, a group of them, and then every plant about you was so. They seemed to have crept up on you, like Moorish traders in a London market. Some I recognised: the long pale leaves of alecost; black lovage and grey sage; dusky silver-sided rosemary and evergreen hysop with its bladed leaves; bright green coriander; rough white borage stiff with shiny hairs; creeping sunkfield, tangled fenkel and wild thyme. You might find them in any cottage garden, sparse and neat, obedient to the housewife, but not as they grew here.

Old Alkanet controlled them, or so she said, but what a struggle of wills there must have been! These woody bushes had grown vast and broad; those that were inclined to height had soared above the stature of an upright man; those that were by nature creepers had pushed their tunnelling roots far onward, much farther than you would have guessed from what was above ground. It was as if there were an enchanted circle around the old crone's house, as if those shaggy bushes were forces of power disguised as mere leaves and held down by the strength of the hag's magic. It is easy to use the word magic about something you don't understand, but with herbs there is some reason. What creatures are these who, posing as bushes, deal out not only food and flavour but health and life! A man could be brought to Alkanet dripping blood the length of the way. Yet with the right potion she could close the wound and restore him to strength.

What is there to fear from herbs like these? As well as their healing properties, as well as the food they provide, think of all the other wholesome uses for these elegant beasts. The floors of rich rooms are strewn with wuderove, rosemary, basil and southernwood. Some make wine; some flavour ale. Soapwort's lather washes our clothes; flax and nettles make thread; moleyn makes candlewicks. Who then might not believe that there is magic in herbs, and that she who controlled them was something of an enchantress?

Even in Winter, supposedly the dead season, the herbs seemed only lightly asleep. Scents seemed to hang in the air, or was it simply that I remembered the Summer? The meadowy smell of wuderove, the potent fragrance of southernwood, and the sweet ones that

24

perfumed the hand that brushed them: basil, balm, alecost, bay and marjoram. Not only scents, but colours too were hidden in the leaves and roots of those disquietening servants. Blue from succory, yellow from agrimony, purple and red-brown from marjoram, from elderberries blue and mauve and from tansy a clear yellow-green.

But there were other herbs growing in Alkanet's garden; and that was why the old woman was treated with suspicion, because she had the power to use those other herbs.

So we approached Alkanet's den, Marel running ahead of us. Her cottage looked to be a growing part of the forest; the plants had curled and twined their tentacles about the little dwelling like the hair of some great monster. In Winter, with evergreens upon it, it was like a green mound of living leaves. In the Summer...well, in the Summer it was paradise, for there were also flowers, and so many scents that they lay as deep as water. It was hard to believe that the cottage could ever have been built by human hands – it seemed to have grown out of the earth, hollowed from amongst the roots of enormous trees.

The little doorway was a black square like a missing tooth. Now from the dark within came the shape of Alkanet. She stood eyeing us. She was even older and uglier than I remembered; her brown face was shrivelled, creased into many wrinkles. Her pointed chin stuck forward and her beak of a nose hung down; between them, her thin lipless mouth was drawn into a grimace, showing no teeth but wizened gums. She wore her unkempt grey hair loose, down to her waist. She was hunched and bent, in a dark shapeless garment and a tattered cloak; a twisted stick was grasped in one hand, and the other raised a crooked finger and beckoned us to approach.

'Ah,' she cackled, 'it's the pedlar man. I know you.'

She managed to say it in such a tone that I felt everything she intended. She made it clear she knew more about me than I wished to show – my character, my history, my thoughts. I am sure too she knew I lusted after my own kind, and all those past times had kept the boy purposefully out of my sight.

'And who is that with you, pedlar?'

'Jusson the leper, from London.'

'Ah, London is it? Leper, are you?'

Squinting at him for a moment, she then seemed to dismiss him from her thoughts.

'Now, what's all this?' she said, gesturing to the cottage, into which Marel had fled. 'What's this garbled story? Were you there? What happened?'

'We came upon it by chance,' I explained. 'Audran de Bonnefoy coming back from hunting. He was having a little sport with Marel. Then Jusson stepped in and frightened him off.'

'How?'

I was surprised. 'By his appearance, of course.'

She snorted. 'Then he's easily frightened. Tricked out in that silly scarlet and black. An insult to the quiet colours of the earth. He ought to have laughed you to shame. But it follows. That's a nobleman of the worst sort, a joke, a fancy feather easily blown away. Jusson the leper, you were a fool. You were lucky he didn't strike you down.'

Jusson shrugged. 'I know. But often I find my disease is such that nobody wants any kind of touch, not even that of killing. There is disgrace in the slaughtering of a leper. It is altogether degrading and polluting, and you would risk a rebuff at the Day of Judgement for such a misbegotten act. I supposed he would feel thus and I guessed he would run.'

'You're too good for this world,' she said scornfully. 'Too good by far.'

Then she turned on me. 'But you, pedlar, you're not. I've heard no part concerning you in this tale of brave heroics. You leapt forward, did you, fists flying?'

'No,' I replied.

'What a surprise!' she jeered. 'Or perhaps you were waiting for the pickings? So we have this leper to thank for the timely rescue. Blast the hide of that nobleman. Nothing that moves is safe. And blast him if he has given *you* ideas.'

I assured her he had not.

'Liar,' she said. 'But it will do you no good. And now,' she went on, dismissing that subject, 'pedlar man, you look very red and blue; the winter weather is not to your liking, I think.'

'I'm frozen,' I admitted.

'Go inside. I'll fix you up.'

Gentle and soothing she was not. I hesitated in the doorway, wondering what she would do about Jusson. She peered up at him and pulled the hood from the side of his face with her clawy hand.

'Jusson the leper,' she croaked. 'Let's have a look at you...Yes, I told you that you were a fool. You are even more of a fool than I thought. Let me see your arms and hands. Now tell me, who was it said you were a leper?'

'Well, dame, it was the people round about, and then it was the priest.'

'Then they are all fools in London,' she snapped. 'That's a very good crop of skin blasts you have there, as fine a crop as ever I saw; but you are no more a leper than I am, or that gawping pedlar over there. So off with that silly hat and come inside, and I'll fix you up too!'

And so it was with great pleasure that we bent and entered her cottage.

The dim room was surprisingly large. The floor was of beaten earth, of course, but strewn with a wealth of dried herbs. Others, in bunches, dangled from the low roof, and from a small window overhung with ivy trailed a greenish shaft of light. A sturdy table was covered with heaps of dried plants and some earthenware pots and plates and spoons. A fire burned, to which we straightway hastened, and it was a joy to smell it. Unlike most fires it was not foul and smoky but gave off a very sweet perfume from its oddly-coloured flames. There was a door at the back which I knew led to a tiny stone-floored recess where the concoctions were made and the distilling done. A ladder led up to a loft where they slept.

We spent a day and a night at Alkanet's cottage. Although the old crone had the face of a twisted tree-whorl and the tongue of a snake, she was grateful to us and repaid us with her skills. I was made to sit at the table with my head under a cloth sniffing a bubbling moleyn stew. When she let me up, I praised its powers.

'Yes,' she said spitefully, 'slugs like it too.'

I drank an infusion of elder blossoms sweetened with honey. I sat at ease beside the fire, and it was a haven of rest after the days on the road.

'Tell me,' I said, leaning forward. 'The cold and all it brings I am well used to. But I have trouble with my arm. At first it was sharp pain and I could barely move it, nor could I carry anything. Now these last few days it has grown numb, but not entirely. Like as if a string pulled it taut from neck to wrist.'

She asked the matter that had led to this condition, and I told her of de Bracy's men and the great wheel spoke that had dug into my shoulder.

'What a life of action some of those amongst us lead,' she sniffed, her bony fingers prodding and poking the length of my arm; she even put her ear to it. The touch of her bristly hair made me shudder.

'I hear nothing,' she said thoughtfully.

I snorted. 'What is there to hear? My bones move silently enough,

27

I think!'

'Oh believe me, I would hear if there were things to hear. I cannot help you, pedlar. I tell you what I think. I think that when the Mother is ready, She will release the trap. Till then you will have no feeling. All usefulness will go, even to each finger. As useful as a hand of twigs. I will pray to the Mother. If She so wills, you will be cured one day – maybe soon, more likely not.'

'But is that all you can tell me?' I said dismayed. 'I had supposed you had a greater skill. The Mother? What business have I with mothers?'

'Are you holy?' she asked then, fixing me with a narrow stare.

'Oh!' I snapped, now angry. 'All come pray to me and I work miracles!'

'I pray to the Mother,' she said calmly. 'But you, even you I suppose own some godhead as the fount of goodness. Even your dark heart must sometimes look for guidance.'

'There is only one God, as you well know, and I do pray to Him.'

'Then do so, pedlar. Find a shrine and make your offering and say your prayers.'

This dismal consolation was all the healing for my arm I got from her, and as much as I trusted in Almighty grace, my views on shrines were not those of the devout. 'Visit a shrine?' I marvelled gloomily. 'You say that to me, who have in my pack twelve separate splinters of the Holy Rood which I myself picked from a hawthorn tree in Kent!'

For Jusson she was sure of a cure, but one which would take time.

Hot leaves of lovage steeped in bacon fat were placed upon every scab of his skin, then a poultice of comfrey leaves and southernwood paste. As she hovered over Jusson she began to mutter. She muttered both into his ears and at the back of his head. I heard some of the words; it seemed a meaningless chant.

'...from the power in me and by right of the Lady...I Her servant do cast this poison far beyond the skies...the fields grow green, the waters spread, the season takes away the scum...'

'Hey,' I said. 'He doesn't need the chanting.'

'He'll have what he's given,' she said. 'And it won't work without it.'

'Heathen practices,' I said.

'Watch your tongue or you'll be sorry,' she snarled, and I was silent.

We saw very little of Marel. He stayed in the loft, and when he came down Alkanet sent him to work in the other room. She

watched him like a gaoler with a prisoner. I certainly felt she had
sensed my quickened interest and was making sure I had no chance
to let it grow. Quietly I marvelled at the change in my awareness of
him. In truth there was no difference in Marel from all the other
times I had called there. He was as ever quiet and shadowy, closely
hooded, busy about his tasks. But now I constantly sensed his
nearness, longed to talk closely with him. To think I had ignored
him as a halfwit when all the time he was an angel. It was
chastening not to have discovered this for myself, but only through
Audran's lust.

'That boy is not a halfwit, is he?' I said, thinking aloud. I was for a
moment alone with Alkanet.

She glared with squinting eyes. 'His wits are no concern of yours,
pedlar, nor anything else about him.'

'No, but I remembered you told me he was halfwitted and I find
myself amazed.'

'Then you had best stem your amazement if you want the herbs
I've prepared for you,' she said. 'He's no halfwit, no, not in the sense
some are. But he's as innocent as a little green shoot in a bed of
hemlock, as unknowing of evil in the world as a new-born babe. If
he has idiocy it lies in a trusting nature, which makes him prey to
any evil schemer who crosses his path.'

'Then had you better not enlighten him?' I said, quite alarmed
for the lad. 'It isn't natural for a boy to be like that. If only for his
own good he should know how to fend for himself. A little shepherd
boy knows about the wolf. Warn him about the world. Teach him
some skills. He ought at least to know how to fight. And one day,
even,' I said daringly, 'he may fall in love.'

'Love?' spat Alkanet scathingly. 'We'll have none of that serpent
here!' Then she relented, paused and thought. 'I haven't the heart,'
she said. 'That boy is the only thing in the world that softens me, the
only thing I know which is innocent and good. There's not a wrong
thought in that boy. I've brought him up like one of my own plants.
I've kept him safe. I've kept him hidden. I've passed on to him all
my knowledge. I count that as one of the good things of my life. I
could not now stain him with knowing about the kind of things you
mean. Let him bloom unseen and ignorant of evil. As long as I'm
alive I'll see to that.'

'Nobody can stay innocent. Since Adam sinned, that is our
burden. A boy knows things without being told. You think you have
done a good thing, but you will be proved wrong. How you have
raised him will lead to trouble.'

'And I suppose you think you could provide the answer, pedlar man?' she snorted. 'I haven't brought him up to trudge the roads of England behind a packhorse. So watch it, I'm on to you.'

I tried not to look like somebody whose guilty secret had been discovered, and went back meekly to my medicine.

During the day, Alkanet had some straggling trade from the village. None of it was suspect. She treated her callers in my sight and chatted to them grumpily as she patted them and peered at them. One came with a toothache. Walther with rheumatics I recognised from before. A thin pale girl, Alys, came because she was unhappy. I remembered her for the dark sullen way she took everything in, seeming to miss nothing, suspicious yet inquisitive, watchful, as if there were a trick in it. Walther's plump daughter Hawise came for a spell to let her see fairies. To each one Alkanet gave her treatment and accepted in return a couple of eggs or a fresh baked loaf or a garden tool. I wondered whether the old crone believed in all her remedies, but whether she did or no, her face told nothing.

But in the evening came somebody who was treated differently.

An urgent voice whispered Alkanet's name from outside the doorway. We were sitting about the dying fire before sleeping, Jusson, Alkanet and I — Marel had gone to bed. The room glowed with a mauve twilight and seemed like a deep cave, warm against the Winter's cold. I jumped up and went towards the doorway.

'Get back!' hissed Alkanet. 'Go you two into the herb room and stay there till I call you.'

We left, looking over our shoulders at the doorway, and closed ourselves in the other room, which was dark and chilly. We did our best to eavesdrop, but the caller was there on secret business all spoken in whispers, so we heard not a word.

When Alkanet called us in, there was no trace of anybody else. We went to sleep, Jusson and I beside the embers. I wondered who could have come to Alkanet in the blackness of evening, on business so secretive and mysterious. For I had seen a girl's face, well hooded as she stood outside the doorway; and beyond her, holding a lanthorn, the dark, cloaked figure of a lady on horseback, waiting in the wood.

NEXT MORNING the weather was cold and crisp, and I set off to Cortle feeling much heartened. The sky was like white fur faintly tinged with yellow and rose; and a light cover of silver frost lay over the crumpled grass and the hardened earth, making creations of great beauty from simple heath plants. For movement and purpose you could hardly believe the path was the same I had been lately following. Once I had left the hidden way that led to Alkanet's cottage and was back on the main track that skirted the scrubby heath, I saw many folk abroad that day.

The first fellow I met was a young swineherd with his crew of bony pigs that munched the weeds and roots among the bushes. I knew him from before – his name was Ulf – and as I greeted him cheerfully I thought what an unkempt sullen-looking fellow he was. He said nothing to me, but eyed me blankly, his mouth half open. I wondered whether a life spent driving swine might addle a person in time; then reminded myself charitably that he was cold and hungry, and the company of the fierce little beasts he kept was not uplifting.

Then I overtook a merry company of entertainers travelling to the castle for the Christmas celebrations, and continued on my way with them. Two musicians there were, leading an old nag over whose thin flanks were carefully strung gitterns, clokardes, flutes and nakers, that nudging against each other made a strange disharmony of sound. With them was one who had chosen to make his living as a buffoon (unlike Audran de Bonnefoy, who was one by nature) with his fool's cap upon his head, its jutting, bell-tipped prow knocking the low branches at the wood's edge. Also a juggler who, now he was not standing upon his hands, could almost be taken for an ordinary mortal; and a wizened old man with a performing monkey. That monkey was better provided for than his master, for it was wrapped up like a baby in all kinds of clothes with its funny little face peeping out. No wonder, for its owner depended on it for his bread. In the party were two women, dancers I was told, but walking to Cortle wrapped in old furs they seemed cold and unenticing. Their names were Gold and Silver, and their care-worn, weather-beaten faces and all-knowing eyes told me they had long since lost touch with whatever names their parents gave them. A boy there was as well, who bounded on ahead, and an older fellow, Simono, who carried a pack with everything they needed to transform themselves by torchlight into mystery. I hoped I would see them perform.

Both the girls and the youth paused to eye me and I returned the gaze. The girls to me looked worn and tired and were not in the best of humour, complaining heartily about the bitter weather and their chilblains. The boy on the contrary looked full of life and spirits; his hair was black and thick, his eyes a sparkling blue, his manner very lively. His neck was thick, his shoulders broad, his movements graceful, and even his travelling garments could not hide the slim hips, muscular thighs and dancer's arse. Just as my interest was quickening, Simono fell into step beside me, almost as if he would insert himself between and lay a claim.

'Whom do you admire?' he asked. 'Them or him?'

'All your troupe are most pleasing.'

'Yes – but it is he who takes the fancy, is it not?'

'Believe me, I am no judge...'

'You don't fool me, pedlar. Everywhere we go they love him. Women fall on him: rich ladies, matrons, all find him irresistible. Ladies who should know better. And if it's not the women, it's the men. Wherever we go...and here it will be no different.'

'But that should please you. It's all coins to the cap, isn't it? You have a real asset there.'

'Sometimes,' the other muttered, 'I could wish him ugly.'

Simono was drawn and haggard, somewhat past his youth, as greying hair and wrinkled skin showed plain enough. Though he was by no means ill-favoured, there were lines of bitterness upon him that worsened such good looks as might be his.

'I picked him from the gutter,' he confided to me. 'Italy he comes from. I was with a dance troupe – we had a green and yellow cart with bells along the shafts – of course, we were a bigger company then. Singers, dancers, jongleurs. Three of them caught leprosy in Taranto. I took Pietro to replace one. Brought him to London, taught him all he knows. I taught him the language; and now how they love his broken speech – they find it adds to the charms he has already. I thought to do us both a favour but I make a rod for my own back and a burden heavier than this pack.'

I felt sorry for him. 'He doesn't treat you as he should...'

'Wanton!' he grumbled. 'He sleeps with everyone, for money or for merriment, and never seems to tire! Just those first few months we had together, no more, no less, when I was teaching him and he needed me – ah, when we first came to England he was such a baby, so helpless. Promises, all promises, all eyes and arse, he lived to please. Have you been to Italy?'

I nodded. He looked disappointed. He had wanted to tell me about

32

the blue skies and the brilliant sun.

'Just those first few months,' he told me again. 'That's all I had. And now the world may have him. All it has to do is beckon.'

'You are still together...It's a good life, travelling the roads.'

'For the pain he causes me I wish I could leave him in a ditch...'

'Pedlar,' called one of the musicians. 'Do you come from London?'

'I do.'

'Have you the latest songs?'

'If I had it would do you no good – my voice is like a crow's!'

'What good are you to us then? Is the selling of baubles the sum of your talents?'

'Sometimes I tell a good story.'

Our journey passed quickly and at Cortle our ways parted, for the entertainers had no interest in the village and the simple there, who would think anything was marvellous because it was new. They went off to the castle, to be well paid, housed and welcomed as befitted them.

Cortle lies in a little valley on either side of a river. The heathland slopes down to it, and so you see the whole of the village and across to the castle tower and the green edge of the wood on the far side. Coming down into it, it's the church that catches your eye – stone built in the middle of the green, with a pointed tower topped by a cross – and the houses hump about it haphazardly, loosely packed athwart the single street. It's an ordinary enough little place, with its cottages and shacks, vegetable plots and dungheaps. The fields lie just beyond it, everybody knowing his own patch of land of course, and the castle looming up complacently to remind them it has the overall say as to when the folk can work their own land. Some might talk philosophically about the simple needs of Man; it might ring truer if there were not always nearby a thriving castle where the simple needs of Man seem to be so much more.

And there is always the village reeve to make sure you don't shirk your duties. In Cortle he was called Azo, the most unliked man there. The worst thing about him was that he was Saxon like everybody else. He started off as a serf and learned reading and writing at the abbey school, choosing to go over to the side of the powerful, so now he had a foot in both camps. The lord told him what duties he wanted, and Azo trotted obediently round letting everybody know. He saw through the excuses and ferreted out the secrets. I was thinking about Azo as I walked towards the church – I meant to say a few words to the statue of Our Lady before I made myself known in the village; I like to do things in the right order. I wondered how it felt to be so disliked.

I put Azo from my mind, for he did not bring calm thoughts. And straightaway into my mind came the image of Angilbert, a bigger slur than Azo. It was dreary to be standing in the silent church looking towards the statue of Our Lady and thinking about Angilbert. For a few moments I had the painful picture that She was a fair damsel from a story, tied there in Her stone niche unable to protect Herself from the rampages of oxen like Angilbert. Somebody had taken a lot of trouble over the carving of Her features, and I felt a knightly irritation that it was Angilbert who was Her legal protector, the one who might come in here at all times and chat to Her whenever he wished.

The church was dark, even in the mornings, but this dimness only served to heighten the brilliance of the holy vessels. The altar cloth gleamed with gold and jewels, the chalice caught the pale sun's light, and the two silver candlesticks stood very proudly. Nobody came in to steal them. The cost of these rich things would set up a peasant for life; but he would never take that advantage. I suppose that by so doing he would risk his immortal soul, but truly I think the motive was a nobler one.

From the corner of my eye I half glimpsed the great wall painting in the shadows. The red and writhing naked souls tumbled into the flames; dark scrawny demons pursued them with their pitchforks, kings and peasants alike, to answer for their sins. Majestic as a monarch the Devil waited for them on his fiery throne. I never liked that picture and turned my back on it now and thought about God's mercy, not his justice.

The quietness of the place was soothing. Perhaps since my last visit a change had come upon Angilbert. He might have become more holy. Perhaps he no longer gabbled the scriptures unintelligibly or threatened people with excommunication for being late in paying their tithes. Perhaps he had even started the practice of preaching a sermon sometimes, and had hit upon the idea of counselling his flock wisely and well, supporting them through troubles, cheering them of their despairs, reminding them of Christ's enduring love. Perhaps he was not so often to be found sleeping in the tavern. Or was it unreasonable to think that because a man put on priest's garb he should become an example to us all and give up those blights that mar an ordinary fellow? I am afraid that Angilbert had gone beyond surprising his flock. He was so unpriestly as to be comic. He was not just a bad priest; he was

34

vigorously so.

There is enough that is strange and beautiful in the seasons of the church to understand why people don't want to criticise too heavily a man of God. His knowledge of Latin is enough to make some afraid, though the way Angilbert used it, if he were casting a spell to raise demons nobody could tell. To hear the mumbling of this tongue, mingled with the chilling ideas of Christ's blood and broken body and the ascent into Heaven, is disturbing even to the cool-headed. And Angilbert was very sure of the horrors of Hell. He left you in no doubt as to what would happen to you if you were not good to him. A short and stumpy figure, even he assumed an air of mystery dressed in his priestly gear, his hands raised in mystic salutation. He wasn't wicked; in another trade he would have been a merry companion. He simply wasn't holy; and I wished for Cortle the best of every kind.

I was standing looking at the shafts of light upon the candlesticks when I heard the heavy door swing open behind my back. I turned round to see Angilbert scurrying towards me.

'Ah! Pedlar man!' he said. 'So you're back!'

His tone suggested I was as welcome as the blight upon the crops.

'Yes, I'm here again,' I said.

'I saw you come into the church,' he said accusingly. 'What did you want?'

A couple of crude replies suggested themselves, but I was very restrained and only said: 'To have a look.'

'Well,' said he, inserting himself between me and the candlesticks, 'you've had a look now. There isn't much to see, as you will observe. And moreover,' he added meaningfully, 'I am always nearby and I always see who comes into the church. Nobody could get in without my seeing them. Nor could they come out without my seeing them either. So I would always notice if they were carrying anything.'

'Cortle is lucky, then,' I said, 'with such a watchful priest.'

He put himself at my side waiting to escort me out. I let him. As we reached the door together I said: 'What a very fine pair of candlesticks you have there. Silver, by the looks of them. I'll have to come back again to have another look at them.'

He gave me a sour look and we separated, he to the tavern and I to get about my trade.

I soon had a crowd about me: housewives and menfolk were glad of a diversion when there wasn't so much to be doing of a winter morning. They were eager enough to look at everything and bought some of the cheaper things. I sold all the salt. I wondered how far that salter had got by now. I also sold pins, ribbon, some combs, a buckle and a couple of razors. But as for the mirror, dainty and set in a carved ivory frame, they looked at me reproachfully and asked how I thought they could afford a bauble like that. And I knew that was the thing they really wanted and I felt sad for them.

Then I went on to the tavern along with several of the fellows I'd been selling to, and spent a noisy and agreeable time there. It might not have pleased a townsman but everybody here found it warm and welcoming, though the fire was foul and smoky and the ale was watery and sweet. Benedict the innkeeper was a big stout fellow and a good friend to travellers. At the benches and trestle table leaned several drinkers, one of whom was Angilbert, already red-faced and rompish. Everybody made room for us latecomers, and we settled down for the afternoon.

All being of Saxon stock, there was a good deal of riddle swapping.

Ralf told this one: 'Two wooden legs have I that touch my hands; yet feet have I that halfway up my legs walk upon air and twig. As tall as trees I am, though not a tree, and yet in part a tree, and I will make you wonder.'

The answer was a Man on Stilts.

Walter told this one: 'He called forth from the hidden depths that which is red and black. The cut of the blade did cause it, and all which never yet was seen or known did show itself to the great harm of he who owned it and was much loth to lose it. In losing, he lost all, which once he hardly knew he owned.'

And the answer was Blood.

This was the one that Angilbert told: 'Upon a smooth surface intricate marks of incredible blackness and glittering gold. Swiftly flew the maker of those marks and he who drove them worked the work in silence, knowing in advance the path that they would take.'

Nobody could guess it, which delighted the priest, and when he said it was a monk writing everybody said it was unfair, because they had never used a pen and had no idea about glittering gold, though some had heard of manuscripts in abbeys being gold painted.

'Surely,' said Angilbert, 'I saw many myself. You'd hardly believe such richness, such skill...'

'You were very lucky to see them, Angilbert,' said Walter.

'And what use are they?' grumbled Wilfred. 'To him or anybody.

What can you do with a manuscript? I'd rather have my hands upon a plough than on a pen any day.'

'You wouldn't know a pen if you saw one,' scoffed Angilbert. 'I daresay you're as wooden as any plough. That's why you can manage one so well.'

'And you're glad enough of the results,' said Wilfred. 'That pen of yours would be no use upon a bare field of hard earth.'

'We each have a part to play in the Almighty's great scheme of things,' said Angilbert comfortably. 'Everybody knows that each man has his own place in God's arrangement. Some rule, some fight for the peace of the realm, some promote the Almighty's great purpose by their prayers. And some sweat and toil. Those who fight and rule are the Hands and Arms of the body of our land. Those who pray are the Head and Tongue. And those who sweat and toil, of which you all belong, are the Feet.'

Much indignation followed at the position assigned to those who drank there, till Ralf, doubling up at his own wit and daring, asked: 'And who is the Cock?' and turned it all to mirth.

'Think what you will,' said Angilbert tipsily. 'But there is only myself who directly serves the Lord. I am the flower that blossoms in the sunshine; you are the roots that grub into the earth.'

Some there muttered or hooted; but some agreed in silence; then Angilbert was overcome by a spasm of stomach ache which bent him double and removed him from the argument.

'Judgement,' whispered somebody, laughing.

'He often gets it,' said Walter.

'Why don't he go to the old witch?' said Ralf, and he was vigorously silenced with nudges and loud talk.

'I wouldn't go to her if I were dying on my feet,' muttered Edith, Benedict's wife. 'I've got herbs enough out the back to deal with any common trouble, and I don't mutter spells over them.'

'Enough, dear,' said Benedict, and asked loudly for a story.

I told them the story of the Famous Battle. We all knew it but we liked to hear it again.

'In the olden days, the good old days of the past, when a man served his lord through love and the realm was Saxon and therefore free, the enemy of the folk were the Norsemen. These fierce sea robbers came plundering our coasts when the nights were calm, to the dread of the folk about the shore. Now Byrhtnoth led his thanes and churls against these foes. Each side of the bridge they stood, in sweet meadowland near the sea. The Norsemen shouted their challenges

37

and the sun glinted upon their war-weapons. But Byrhtnoth, though old in years, cried: "Never while I live shall an enemy take this land. And if you wish to cross this bridge it shall be with the river running red with your blood and with ours, for peacefully you shall not pass. Those are my words."

'So forward came the Viking horde mighty in weapons and many of number. Bravely did we Saxons receive them, sword for sword, clash of blade upon helmet. There was no thought of life or limb, for every man in loving bondship to his lord felt scorn to do other than lay down his life.

'Onward and forward came the fateful foe till at length through force of numbers the noble Byrhtnoth was struck down, his sword still clenched in his failing hand. Even as he lay dying he cried good cheer to his men and called upon the Lord to receive his hopeful soul.

'None fled the field. From the highest thane rich in ring-gold to the honest churl who simply loved his lord, the great sadness forged into a fierce will to fight on, to lie that night beside their lord. For such was the bond of love that Saxons one another bore, that none would suffer the shame of leaving the fray, his lord dead, but rather prayed for the honour of a death beside the beloved leader. So Eadward was slain, and Leofsunu and Offa, and many another nobleman and warrior, and many churls too numerous to count.

'The Viking horde advanced, hewing all down before them, with many losses, great in weaponry and numbers but in valour and faith as nothing. For in their battle victory they had not the glory that those slain Saxons had, and the story of that heroic day will endure in holy pride while we have breath to tell it.'

When I had finished, we all sat back in reflected glory. What heroes they were, our ancestors! We felt breathless and elated, as if we had fought the battle ourselves, only with a different ending. But what a land! The lords were noble, the thanes heroes, and the churls bound to their lords by love! Who would have felt like that about Audran de Bonnefoy?

'A golden age...' murmured Benedict.

'Oh, had we but been there!' sighed Ralf.

'We'd have given them what for.'

'We'd have pushed them back into the sea.'

Exhausted we sat back in a reverent and beery silence. Then a new voice spoke up from the doorway. It was Azo the reeve, who had come in unnoticed at the end of the story and was now surveying us all as a captain might survey the poor dregs of a straggling army.

He clapped his hands slowly, like tired applause.

'It breaks my heart to spoil your merriment,' he said sarcastically. 'It really does.'

He was a big man, muscular and swarthy. He had shaggy black hair and a black beard, and moved like someone who knows he can beat an opponent.

'And fancy,' he went on, 'it's the pedlar man back with us again. It seems like only yesterday we had the great joy of your company. I might have known it would be you in the middle of a seditious gathering, mischief-making with your tales of brave renown.'

Some looked uncomfortable at this interpretation of their enjoyment of a story glorifying Saxon heroes.

'It were only a story,' someone said feebly.

'We didn't mean no harm.'

The humble phrases trickled out.

'You should know better, pedlar,' said Azo, 'than to fill the minds of these layabout good-for-nothings with ravings of glory. Who knows – it might make some of them discontented with their lot! It might stir them up and teach them to nurture wicked thoughts about their betters.'

All this was delivered with a great scorn and a most threatening brow, as he glowered at each separate face as if to fix upon every one there the satisfying hopelessness of their thralldom. Some were suitably chastened and mumbled their devotion and humility. Some scowled back. It was almost funny. The grim thing was that this man had the power to ruin them all.

'Next time,' he warned me, 'we'll have a story about good King William, or failing that a tale with a moral such as simple minds may understand, about the evils of discontent.'

'I'll see what I can do,' I said.

'Meanwhile,' said Azo, ignoring that, 'I want every one of you for log carting and I want you now. Outside, the lot of you.'

They shuffled to their feet and went outside. Angilbert was of course excepted, sleeping now with his head on the table.

Azo glared at me, as if he were itching for the power to order me along with them. But he had not, and my kinship of soul did not extend to willing toil.

It was very quiet now, where before it had been so lively. I sat for a while, warm and lazy, looking into the embers of the fire.

When my grandmother was alive, she told me tales of ancient

Cortle and our place therein, mingling the centuries with one another so that it was both yesterday and a long time ago. When I arrived in Cortle I used to go straight to where she lived, down by the stream, a reed hut put together much as a basket is woven, long since trampled down; and she would sit, white-haired, bright-eyed and toothless, small and bent, receiving me with unsurprise as if I had come in from stick-gathering, and not from a journey which had taken me to the shores of the Mediterranean Sea and visions of the world that she would never know. The world within her ancient memory was more real to her than mountains capped with snow, or boats with pennants at their masts and dealers in foreign markets, merchants at the Champagne fair, and many, many dusty roads.

'I was thinking just now of Sigbert who lived outside the law...Wufnoth the singer, who became a monk...my father Ine who went overseas...Aethelflaed who was more beautiful than the Queen of Heaven...Aethelhere who was a great healer...Aelfgar – but you remember, I have spoken of him – and Ulfcytel, the father of the father of Cenred...but that was in the days of King Raedwald, when we were most powerful...'

And only afterwards, in the clear cold frost-bright air beyond her little hut, would I remember that these living people had been dead these many years and that King Raedwald lived over five hundred years ago.

'The night before the Battle of Hastings,' said my grandmother, 'King Harold went to pray at Waltham Abbey. It was his own abbey, which he caused to have built. It lay within the heart of a great forest. It has a Holy Rood all covered with silver which works miracles. Do you know, when Harold was a boy he had a numbness in an arm and all his wise men gave up hope. But this Holy Rood cured it for him. So Harold went to pray there the night before the battle. He spent all day in prayer and when he bowed to that cross, the cross bowed in answer.

'Staying at the abbey on that same night was Aethelflaed the Lady of Cortle, she who was so beautiful. In the morning she set out from Waltham Abbey to return to her home. Within the year, nine months to the day, she was delivered of a fair son. You come of that stock...'

'Come, pedlar, stop your dreaming,' Edith said. We were alone now in the quiet tavern, and she had brought some wool to card beside the fire. A little heap of soft grey fleece lay by her and I watched her fingers tease the uneven thread. She was a fair-haired woman, no longer young, freckle-faced and with a ready smile.

40

'It's true; I was far away.'

'Are you going up to the castle? Or will you be staying here for the night?'

'I was planning to go to the castle, when I can bear to stir from the fire.'

'You've heard, have you, that's he's back from the Crusade?' said Edith cautiously.

'Why was that?'

'They say he was taken ill. They say he never even crossed the sea. Mind you, I don't think any of us ever expected that he would. What do you think? I'd always heard that Crusaders were brave fellows. Well, they'd need to be, wouldn't they, with all they have to face?'

'His lordship was never famed for his bravery hereabouts,' I agreed.

'And all that farewell ceremony we gave him,' laughed Edith. 'All the village out in strength cheering, and her ladyship at the gate with a goblet of some brew to keep up his courage. What a joke!'

'He's not going to try again?'

'I think not. I do hear that he doesn't please his lady wife. It's said they don't get on at all. He drinks heavily and he's cruel to her. And he's bountiful with his favours, if you see what I mean.'

'Who tells you all this?'

'Oh I know some of the women who work up there. They get to hear things.'

'Well, it is more lively when the lord and lady of the manor are wayward,' I said.

She looked a little hurt at my amusement.

'You may see for yourself,' she said, 'if you're spending some time up there.'

I reluctantly left the fire and picked up my pack.

The afternoon had worn away without my noticing. The winter air was bitter and chill. In the oncoming dusk the houses were dwindling into shadowy shapes, but down the road ahead of me the black bulk of the castle looked solid, firm, everlasting.

41

VI

GREY DUSK lay over the land as I drew near to the castle. I passed the last straggling cottages and the open fields lying stiff and hard each side of the road. Here were other folk, some hurrying to their homes, some travelling to the castle from far away, some castle servants returning from errands in the village. Ahead the drawbridge was down and the gateway open to receive us.

It was a sturdy, well-built fortress. The beaten earth track led straight to the drawbridge, its heavy chains clanking with warning power as the weight of iron-rimmed cartwheels trundled over the wooden slats and into the courtyard. Two pointed stone towers housed the workings of the bridge, standing like sentinels athwart the dark rounded archway, a gaping mouth that could mean safety or threat. Everything the castle contained was bounded by a vast wall of stone that rose up out of the banks of the moat.

In the daytime the courtyard was a bustle of activity, for all the outbuildings were there. In thatched shacks the blacksmith plied his trade, the cooks dished up the meals, the cheese and butter churned; and all day long these servants crossed each other's paths, chasing hens for the pot, leading horses to the farriery, unloading carts, with the poor kitchen folk running with covered dishes to the great hall, leaving trails of cooking smells in their wake.

Now, at evening, there was torchlight and the movement of Yuletide preparations. A steward shouting for more logs, a cart weighed down with brushwood, lights in the kitchen house, and hot flustered faces coming out for air; horses snorting, visitors directed to the hall, lazy servants clouted, and guards to check that all was well in hand. For now everything was plentiful and the doors were open to all. The festivities were beginning, and for the next fifteen days nobody would be expected to suffer. Anyone might come into the castle and share in the merriment; and at night the floor of the great hall was there for you to lie upon curled in your cloak.

We crossed the courtyard to enter the keep, and made our way to the great hall, a vast room of immense height with a raised dais at one end. It was full of people, warm from their bodies and the huge fire. Ornamental screens had been set up to keep out draughts, but it was still chilly in the farthest corners. Trestle tables and benches were set in the main body of the hall and they were generously laid. I was the same as anybody else: I settled down to a holiday given over entirely to enjoyment and the pursuit of pleasure.

I met up again with the travelling entertainers with whom I had arrived at Cortle; they were having a great success. And I was right, the women now looked enticing and lovely in the bewitching gloom of shifting torchlight. It set me thinking about falsehood and truth, and willing disbelief in the face of known things, which happens often in this life. Gold and Silver I now saw as good names for them, for they had false hair, silver and gold, long and glinting as metal does, and their skin was painted so it glistened in the torchlight. Their eyes were made up to look like faery folk; they were not of this world.

The minstrels played for them strange, disturbing tunes which I believe came from the Saracens or from the land of India. Pietro also danced, almost naked, and I certainly gazed my fill there. He had smeared his dark lithe body with an oil that made his muscles gleam, and every leap and stretch showed lines of sinews taut and smooth, rippling the length of his body so that his thighs almost changed their shape with each different movement. And his buttocks were bare, two quivering rounds of flesh that drew the eye and dried the throat and tugged at the prick. Simono did not dance but watched, and I watched him and sighed for his sad lot. What sweet and wretched torture for him, gazing on that perfect form that once had been his alone and now was flaunted for the common sight. He would not care about it if afterwards the boy would come to him and bring true love; but to his pain was added that wormwood, the knowledge that Pietro would take his perfection to whoever pleased him for a night, whoever caught his fancy for that moment, caring nothing for the grief of his one-time master. It was not easy to love a lovely boy when you were older, wiser and besotted.

Amongst the dancing, eating, drinking and merry-making I caught sight of Audran de Bonnefoy and his lady wife. They took their places on the dais and graced us by eating the best portions of the best food, delighting us with the sight of their elaborate furs, gently reminding us that the rich were entitled to be warmer. I watched Audran curiously, remembering the last time I had seen him. He was a broad, fleshy man with blond hair and the paunchy look that comes with over-indulgence. His fingers sparkled with rings; around his neck was a gold chain, and his carefully made clothes were edged with dark fur. His eyes were small, his eyebrows fair, and his face pallid, with thick lips now slobbering over his goblet. His whitenesss seemed effeminate – or perhaps with my tanned and windburnt face I was simply envious.

Berenice de Bonnefoy was a very beautiful creature. She had a dark, mysterious look that made me curious to know all about her. She was slim, with slender hands, and she ate daintily, a fact alone which distinguished her from the others at the table. She wore a dark blue dress edged with white fur, and her hair was dark brown. Her cheeks were unnaturally red, and she had the same glossiness as Audran. A cultivated rose, I thought – attractive, yes, but I wouldn't have trusted her an inch. She looked secretive and cunning.

At the other side of Berenice there sat an older knight to whom she was paying a courteous attention, a figure with greying hair and the bearing of a seasoned soldier. At the other side of Audran sat a lady of equal age to the knight, presumably his wife. Age did not sit so pleasingly upon her, and Audran was paying her no social politeness as Berenice was. Instead he was vigorously flirting with a fancy painted young morsel who sat next in line and was busy receiving his compliments with obvious glee. The poor lady in between was ignored; the couple stretched across her to touch each other and whispered and nuzzled behind her back. I wondered how Berenice was taking it, this gross display, or even if she had noticed it. Yes, she had. You could see she smarted even though she smiled. It was nothing to do with sadness or pain, but mostly annoyance, which she conveyed to Audran with a keen glance from time to time. There were plenty of other guests along the table, so I suppose it was for their benefit that she would have preferred an appearance of wedded bliss. She certainly would not have expected the peasants to notice or even care.

I had been so busy watching those on the dais that I was a little startled to notice that one of them had been watching me. I suddenly caught her eye. It was a lady-in-waiting. She was not so richly dressed, and had that look which maids have who are obliged to spend their lives several paces behind and at the beck and call of another woman, who may or may not in truth be better than they. She was a pretty little thing, with red-gold hair and merry eyes, dressed all in green. It may surprise you that any lady living at a castle should cast an eye upon a pedlar, but perhaps you forget I am a figure of romance – even apart from my natural good looks. I've noticed this strange thing before; the more walled-in a lady feels, the more attractive does a travelling man appear, a man who may come and go as he pleases, like wind and weather. I was quite arrogant enough not to be surprised by her interest.

The more I looked at her, the more I felt I had seen her

somewhere before, and suddenly it came to me. It was with the flickering torchlight and the shadows it cast upon her face. It reminded me of another darkness, another glow. She was the girl who had come by night to Alkanet's cottage before the old crone had sent Jusson and myself out of the room. If that were so...I looked then at Berenice, smiling coolly at another of her guests. She must have been the dark lady in the long cloak who waited outside on horseback. What business could she have with that old woman that her castle herb garden could not provide?

Now though for me it must always be a boy when lust and carnal stirrings come into play, I have always been able to share an affectionate tenderness with a girl when so needed. A travelling man – and a good-looking one – is eagerly received by women whose lives are bounded in by four dreary walls, and there were more than four at the castle. If that young girl were after some romance, I daresay I could help her; not of course with the ultimate pleasure, but with those little things that pass a winter evening pleasantly. It was a crowded place the castle hall, for all its nooks and shadows, and what was connived at between man and maid was like to cause horror and disgust if the lovers were man and boy. The other aspects of this were not lost on me. I saw pages I fancied waiting at table, but I was too wary to risk that kind of tangle. You can't trust Normans, especially pretty ones; I didn't want another Juhel de Bracy and another angry father.

And so if Berenice's maid had any plans for me, here I was, I made that clear enough. But it was not the maid that interested me, it was the lady. What was her secret? What could she want with Alkanet's magic?

A minstrel was singing to the party on the dais. It was a sad song, about Guinevere and Lancelot, and the melody was well attuned to the words. It brought a feeling of roses and stone walls warmed by sunlight, and spring flowers and secret places under leaves, and lovemaking in Summer; and along with it all the sadness at the passing of things. I stole a look at the maid-in-waiting then, and was pleased to see her looking wistful. But it was only a fleeting mood for her, because she gave a quick grin when she saw my look. No, it was Berenice who had been taken by the song. She was silent and spellbound, gazing at the singer and unseeing of her guests. She looked sad and beautiful and I thought briefly that she saw herself as Guinevere.

The song ended and a second minstrel sang. A seller of songs myself, I make it my business to know the words in both tongues:

> 'De mil sospire ke je li doi par dete
> ne me veut ele un seul quite clamer
> ne fausse Amors ne lait ke s'entremete
> ne m'i lait dormir ne reposer
> s'ele m'ocit, mains avra a garder
> je ne m'en sai vengier fors au plorer
> car cui Amors destruit et desirete
> ne s'en set ou clamer...

A thousand sighs I owe her and she takes them all. False Love keeps me from sleeping. If she kills me there will be one less in bonds. I avenge myself only with tears, for Love destroys me and I know not where to turn...'

It set me thinking about Love. Could such Love be? Such Love that suffered from afar, never rewarded, feeding on itself until the lover wasted away and died of it? These days such Love was the matter of all our songs. Those troubadours from southern France had brought their music northward and stolen the hearts and sense of minstrels and listeners alike. For what was life if you did not love? You know how it goes: you sing the praise of your lady; her beauty heals the sick, cheers the sad, brightens the night. You would gladly suffer pain from her than joy from another. Your voice trembles in speaking of her. Simply knowing about her has made you whole; now the world is changed for you – Winter is like Spring, a desert is a meadow of buttercups. If she does not love you in return, you will love her still, for Love is strong and will overcome all hindrance. But if she does love you, you live only because she has favoured you, and you will sing her praises wherever you go. It is a passion that rules your life.

I have never found Love so.

Once more I felt myself watching Simono and I felt uneasy.

> 'Amors es mout de mal avi;
> Mil homes a mortz ses glavi;
> Dieu non fetz tant fort gramavi.
>
> Love is of foul stock;
> He has killed a thousand men without a sword;
> God has not made a more terrible enchanter.'

Inevitably Audran had not been touched. His affected chortling still broke out, and the high giggling of the girl he was amusing.

46

They had heard nothing. I felt sorry for the minstrel; but perhaps he was hardened to it over the years. They ask you to perform; they don't promise to listen. Suddenly Audran leaned back and bellowed:

'What a lugubrious melody! Hey, minstrel, I don't reward you to render my guests miserable! Don't you know any jovial songs?'

'Certainly, my lord.'

'Well then, give us an amusing one. Something we can all participate in – a drinking one with a noisy refrain. Or better still...' He leaned forward, crooking his finger as one about to swap an intimate secret. 'How about one to make us feel a little bit excited? Do you know that one about the raping of the nuns?'

The minstrel did his best; the rollicking thing he came up with seemed to please Audran, and there was a lot of merrymaking around the table till the party retired to their bedchambers.

At night we settled down to sleep where we sat, pulling cloaks and straw and rushes about us, warm amongst the strewn herbs and body stench, old leather and goatskins.

I was wary when Simono came and sat beside me. I had seen Pietro disappear with somebody else, and a night of moaning and self-pity I could do without. Other people's woes only pall when there is no answer to their problem. But I did him wrong. He was in the mood to be cheered.

'You said that you knew stories...'

'What would you like?' I said, as if I could not guess his drift. 'I have *Aucassin and Nicolette*, *King Florus*, *Gugemar*...'

He made a sound of irritation. 'What good are those to me? What do I want with tales of whimpering maidens with breasts as white as hawthorn blossom?'

'Moslem maidens, then?' I teased. 'I can alter the colour of their breasts at will, such is my power. And Moslem maidens must be converted and baptised, so there is good opportunity for stripping the wench as she gets into the bath, and a slow lingering on her charms. That goes down very well, I find.'

'You know what tale I want!' said Simono, lying back upon his elbows. 'A story of a boy, with raven hair and speedwell blue eyes – Italian, if that can be arranged – and love, much love, such love as we have heard in the songs tonight. And suffering, and fidelity, a thing that *some* have never heard of. And plenty of lust. If there must be a lingering on bare limbs, then let them be boys' limbs, and – if you could arrange it – quivering arse flesh. You know the sort of thing...'

And though the tale I told was not the tail he would rather have had that night, I think it pleased him.

I told him of a boy – much like Pietro, dark and beautiful – who went as squire to a knight – by chance the mirror-image of Simono, and very wise and just and masterful – to fight the Saracen in the desert wastes beyond Constantinople. This sweet boy fell in love with his master, but in true courtly fashion never told his feelings. It was enough for him to be close by; he never dreamed that he might ask for more. His master grew to need him, but he never thought to call it Love, for his heart was set on high ideals, as conquering the Paynim. I threw in one or two adventures that bound the two together; and for good measure I added a wicked Saracen who saw the boy buying food in a market and swore he'd have him for his own, and sent swarthy rogues to abduct him and place him in his pleasure garden. A Christian boy, perfumed and painted, at the beck and call of some all-powerful Turk! Half-naked by a scented pool, where eunuchs prowled and palm trees quivered – such a monstrous fate! But then his knightly master, understanding at last how much he needed his young companion – how much, indeed, he loved him! — stormed the Paynim palace with his men, and found the boy and claimed him for his own.

'This is the boy I love!' he told his men. 'Henceforth we shall never be parted!'

And now they roam the world together, sleeping beneath the stars, sure of each other's love and well content.

Simono gave me silver, and laughed indulgently and with some melancholy.

'Why do I give you money to tease me with false hopes and further fan the flames of my desire?' he said. 'Why is it we need stories to torment us when the truth is so much other?'

'And yet we do, I think.'

'No boy would be that faithful – no knight would risk his reputation so! Courtly love – ideal love! Love is never like that – it's one grief following another. Look at that boy who fills my waking thoughts – faithless, reckless, stupid; cheerfully uncaring of the way I feel. And still I love him!'

'Your case is not so rare!'

'I'm so tormented by the demons of suspicion and jealousy I never know a moment's peace. Sometimes I wish he were dead and I the one to do the deed. That way at least I would be sure of him. It is a shameful thing to confess...'

48

'No,' I soothed him. 'I have demons of my own. I know...'

'You?' he said, in some surprise. He laughed uncertainly. 'It's funny, pedlar, but I had not thought of you as one with any kind of passions – merely as a pedlar, one passing with his pack – here, then gone.' He mulled the thought over. 'I can't believe you are the prey to demons such as I know.'

'Ah...mine is the wishing that the world were other than it is. That is a larger demon than the passing pains of Love. And one without solution.'

By the glow of torchlight the dancers entertained us; but it was the beautiful boy beloved by Simono who captivated all. He was somehow disturbing, like a creature from the Otherworld; and not just in the brilliance of his dancing but because, near-naked, he painted his skin with eldritch green or blue, which mingled with his sweat in the half-light to give him a weird and waxy sheen. The great ones on the dais watched him too. I could not help but notice that wherever Pietro slept at night, it was not in the hall.

That pretty minx, my lady's maid who'd eyed me at the table, appeared one evening by my side; and half before I knew it she was snuggled in the crook of my arm, setting the pattern of the nights to come. Her name was Ghislaine. A pert little thing she was, who made up to me shamelessly. When we gossiped about Pietro she agreed he was good-looking but she said he was not manly enough for her and far too full of himself, and that she liked her lovers rugged.

It was to find out Berenice's curious interest in old Alkanet's witchery that lay behind my Yuletide friendship with this girl, and as it turned out, she was most forthcoming.

In those dark nights lit by the dying fire and bewitched by the shadows rising and falling on the high walls, I learnt many things about Berenice de Bonnefoy. I half began to understand her and, so help me, Norman though she was, to care what happened to her. She would have been appalled at everything I knew about her when she finally sent for me. It was on Ghislaine's advice that she sent for me at all, and I have to thank the girl for that, because Berenice paid me very well. I had a lot to thank that sweet girl for – her warmth and welcome and the entertainment of her company. Before I left the castle I gave her the mirror that nobody in the village had been able to afford.

I thought I had been clever and crafty teasing secrets from Ghislaine. Which serves me right for dabbling in intrigue! If I had guessed at the time where Berenice's interest in me would be leading, if I'd had half an inkling of the mess she'd land me in, I'd have warded off Ghislaine's affections like the plague, and slept against the old man with the monkey.

TWO
Ghislaine's Tale

I

IT IS the most ridiculous thing in the whole world, but it seems that I, Ghislaine, am in love with a pedlar!

He is far below me in rank, but that is all to the good in the kind of love that I envisage, for now he may look up to me as a courtly lover should. He has all the correct qualities necessary in this situation; I considered all this before I set out to entice him. He is a wanderer, a figure of romance – ma foi, if he is to be believed he is last in a line of ancient lords, a prince in exile one might say. He cannot sing, unfortunately – I asked him and he said so – but at least he can tell stories, which will have to do. So he can speak of me in words instead of music – no matter, my fame will be bruited abroad that way, an Heloise of our own time.

He is very good-looking. He is above common tall and lean of build. His hair is brown, long to his shoulders, combed back from his brow – which is almost noble. He has greenish-grey eyes, long lashes, sandy eyebrows, and a fine moustache such as Saxons wear on the old tapestries. He has very good teeth and a wide smile, and a little scar above one eye where he was set upon by wicked guards in London. Eleven there were, and he fought them all off single-handed.

He wears a brown leather jerkin and a hempen shirt, his stockings bound about with thongs, his boots well-caked with mud. He has a cloak and hood, and at his belt a knife in a sheath. 'For killing men?' I asked with a frisson of horror. ' For skinning rabbits,' he replied.

He does bend his shoulders somewhat; I suppose that is because he carries a pack, but even without the pack there remains that stoop. It does not spoil his attraction – indeed, I would expect no less from one who travels; it shows that his life is hard, that worldly

51

troubles bow him down. Within these castle walls he can forget those cares for a while. I hope I may do something to help him there which will certainly make my own Yuletide more interesting, for it is very pleasant during the festivities to be in love.

This Christmastide the fashion at the castle is Love, Love and more Love. We are all singing songs of Love; we listen at night to minstrels who play more love songs; we try to compose our own. Our hero is Bernard de Ventadour, Queen Eleanor's troubadour. We study the stages of Love – aspirant, suppliant, suitor, lover. (The pedlar is I think at the third stage already.) We talk of Love's courtesy – *joie d'amour*, that first glowing excitement; *valor*, to be worthy of the beloved; *cortesia*, pleasure in the pleasure of another; *mesura*, love's wisdom and self-mastery.

I saw the pedlar looking at me as I sat at table near my lady. I was wearing my dark green velvet. I returned his gaze – at that distance one should make one's intentions clear, and time is short. That night I crept down to the hall to further our acquaintance with some converse; but I could not approach – he was in the company of a traveller, some grey-haired fellow off the road, and deep in talk, and so I stole away. I knew there would be another night and so there was.

I thought about him as I attended to my lady, combing her long dark hair which was so beautiful and abundant. Berenice sat upon the edge of the bed, wrapped in black fur. In the bedchamber above the great hall we both felt a certain relief to be out of the gaze of strangers and free from the obligation to play a part. A small fire was burning. We spoke in quiet voices.

Berenice said: 'Is any woman happy, married? I would be glad to hear of one.'

I waited. In truth I had expected some such discourse; the evening had been exceptionally difficult.

'Do you cherish fond dreams?' said Berenice. 'You can have no illusions from what you see within these walls.'

'I like to hope that all will be better one day,' said I, sage as a confessor, 'and that anyone who is unhappy will find happiness soon.'

'Not myself,' said Berenice emphatically. 'Not with Audran.'

'But when the love potion works...' I reminded her, supposing that this hope would cheer her.

But instead she shuddered and said wanly: 'Yes, then things may be well.'

I began to think about that love potion. It was rare for a

52

châtelaine to believe in such things, but I knew that Berenice's situation was such she would try anything. We had heard about the old witch in the woods from Agnes the blacksmith's daughter. I knew all the manorial servants, and my lady was content for me to go among them as it enabled her to know all that went on in kitchen, barn and village.

It had been on just such an occasion as this, a few moments solitude away from the blundering antics of his lordship, the quiet chamber, the torchlight and firelight...I let my thoughts stray back to that time, now many months ago.

Then I had thought Agnes' credulity amusing.

'But she assured me that the potion worked,' I had laughed, 'and ever since then he has been utterly faithful, even courtly.'

'One of the men-at-arms? I don't believe it!' was my lady's mocking reply.

'It's true. Apparently he was quite a brute before, and now – amorous, attentive, docile...'

'But how does it work?'

'Oh my lady, I don't believe she knows herself. The old witch didn't say. But Agnes supposed there was caraway in it. They do say that caraway binds a lover. And there was five-fingers in it, for she saw some on the table.'

'Five fingers?' giggled Berenice. 'Not real ones? Is she so primitive?'

'Oh my lady!' I protested in mock horror. 'It's a plant!'

'And how did Agnes hear about this witch?'

'I believe she is well-known in the village,' I shrugged.

'Is she really a witch?'

'Agnes calls her a witch,' I said doubtfully.

'But is she? Does she cast spells?'

'Oh I don't know about that...Agnes is not very worldly and would probably be nervous and easily impressed.'

'Would *you* be?' asked Berenice thoughtfully.

I went into a panic. I suddenly saw the direction of her thinking.

'My lady! You don't want me to visit her?'

'I confess to a certain curiosity,' said Berenice. 'Would she come here?'

'Oh let us not meddle,' I said in agitation. What a hornets' nest was here! 'She might do us harm.'

'Oh, your sophisticated words,' mocked Berenice. '*Agnes* might be nervous?'

I felt confused. I had had no idea that she would take my silly gossip so seriously. It had been meant only to divert.

'We should not ask,' I said anxiously. 'No good can come of it.'

'I should like you to find out all you can about her,' Berenice had then replied. 'And tell me everything.'

The old witch was called Alkanet. She lived in the forest. Not everyone knew about her, and of those that did, not all approved of her. She cured sicknesses, she made love potions, she was old, ugly and mysterious, and nobody would admit to knowing whether she cast spells. People were afraid of her because of her power. She had magic herbs at her command, not the common ones that grew in gardens, but wild ones, old ones, with ancient roots and ancient strength.

That conversation, when my lady's interest had become aroused, had taken place a long time ago, before my lord Audran had gone off on his abortive crusade. My lady and I had visited the old woman several times since then. We were familiar now with the secret path to the house in the forest. Each time we had gone at night, and each time Berenice had told me to wait outside, holding the horses' bridles. I considered it most strange that the lady of the castle should believe in these things, but it seemed to provide a diversion for her, an adventure. Berenice is a mysterious person, given to impulses and attracted by the unusual.

For myself, I found these night-time expeditions terrifying. It was eerie to be out in the dark, unattended, on the silent forest paths. The light from our lanthorn illumined a little circle about us, but only increased the contrast with the black trees on either side. In truth we never saw a living soul on any of our visits, but the darkness led me to think of worse things. Countless tales returned to me – fiends so dark they merged unseen with the night, and wood spirits who carried off travellers to their hidden lairs. The forest would whisper and rustle as though there were people walking in it, always nearby, stopping when we stopped, never showing themselves. I felt sure there were felons and robbers who, outlawed for terrible crimes, had nothing to lose and would spring out and kill us. I marvelled that Berenice could go forward so quietly and serenely, seeming unafraid. And all for a love potion!

Myself I did not think it was worth it. Not to keep the affection of Audran de Bonnefoy! All the time I had been Berenice's maid I had known that their rapport was very bad. Loveless marriages of convenience were habitual, of course. But with my lord and lady it had become destructive and unhealthy. Berenice's icy dignity seemed to reduce Audran to idiotic fury. Audran had always been pompous and boorish, and Berenice obstinate and wilful. But what else could she do but tolerate him?

Now, as I combed her hair, Berenice said reflectively:

'I wonder what drove Guinevere to infidelity. They say Arthur was a gentle loving knight.'

'But unexciting,' I suggested.

'Must love have excitement, then?'

'I think that the sweet and gentle love that Arthur gave could pall for a lady who loved adventure...What would you wish for, my lady, in the ideal courtly knight?' I said to cheer her.

Berenice responded gladly, giving it her full attention, like someone in a game.

'Someone from outside, someone new! Someone exciting with stories to tell. A handsome face, thin and dark, as unlike Audran as he could be; wicked eyes, daring in conversation, powerful in charm...'

I smiled in ready sympathy. 'So would I, my lady! That's just what I would fancy.' I thought happily of my pedlar. Maybe I would be more fortunate than she. Of course I blamed the influences down in the hall. With so much talk of amour courtois, songs of adoration and longing, amorous glances across the laden tables, kissing in the shadows, how could she too not be infected, even a great lady like herself?

But songs of love were no consolation to her. She groaned and sighed. 'What use are these fantasies? In reality I have a striding, strutting buffoon; my pride will not let me look up to him.'

Berenice was too miserable to say more. She asked me to draw the bed curtains and she curled herself into the covers. The bed was vast and ornate and when the curtains were drawn it made a small private room. She had hardly settled herself when the curtains were pulled clumsily back on the other side and Audran appeared with a girl he had been favouring at the table. Blanche Pertigan – not even a beauty! Both were rosy and laughing and half-undressed; it was disgusting to behold.

Berenice sat up angrily.

'How dare you, Audran? Not in here – have you gone mad?'

'Oh don't make such a fuss,' grumbled Audran. 'Where else is there? I thought you'd be asleep. If you make a commotion everyone will hear and I'm sure you don't want that. Just lie down again and look away; there's plenty of room in here for three.'

He settled the girl in beside him and Berenice heaved a coverlet and went to sit on a small stool by the dwindling fire. I watched it all, ashamed for her; I could only guess her thoughts. How I'd be fuming if it were me! But my lady showed no feelings. Eventually the curtains moved and Blanche slipped away.

'Berenice,' called Audran. 'Come back to bed; it's ridiculous to sit there. Don't bear grudges; it's all over now. You know it's you I love – I can't help my little acts of foolish wantonness. I know you forgive me at heart...'

Berenice went back to bed. I could hear Audran talking on in a wheedling tone as I crept away down to the darkened hall,

In the morning their voices within the curtains sounded clearly to all who cared to listen.

'I have to ask you,' said Berenice icily, 'much as I hate to ask anything of you, but this I do ask, that you be less of a fool today. It does no good to your position here if all the world should see that you are recklessly wanton and a boorish drunkard. Have you no dignity? Don't you care that they whisper and sneer about you? You must try to keep up an appearance of authority. You must be respected. Lord knows how, but you must try.'

'Don't preach to me,' snapped Audran. 'It's not your place to pass any judgement on me.'

'I don't want to. But every day your follies are greater. How they must despise you, servants, peasants...'

'Any peasant who murmurs against me knows I'll have his head. Have no fears about that.'

'I have none. I know that you combine brutality with your everyday stupidity.'

'I do? Then what do you think of this?'

There was a sharp smack. Berenice parted the curtains, her nose pouring blood. She asked me to bring water.

'And perhaps that will teach you not to whine about good behaviour to your lord,' said Audran sulkily. 'I should have your love and support, not perpetual criticism.'

I set about attending to Berenice's bruised face.

'What can I say to people?' she said despairingly.

'Tell them she's indisposed,' belched Audran, climbing out of bed. An attack of vomiting seized him. In his noisy distress his oaths and abuse were alarming. I summoned servants to attend him.

'Another pleasant day begins,' observed Berenice.

She remained in her chamber while the others and Audran went riding. As I busied myself around the room I wondered what solution could ever be found for her plight. It grew daily more impossible. I have no doubt that the blame was Audran's. He might find his wife irritating, but his was the behaviour of a boor. I could imagine with a different kind of man Berenice could have been happy. I was fond of her and wished things were otherwise.

'My lady,' I wondered, 'would you wish to have his love again?'

'He'll never change,' said Berenice bitterly.

Surely she had not forgotten about the love potion that we sought together in the dark forest? A very strong wish must have been in her heart to enable her to face the unknown darkness, a very deep belief in the old witch's remedies. A belief in Love, even?

'Have you any of the old witch's potion left?' I asked, thinking that perhaps a very large dose all at once might be what was needed. But Berenice went pale and stared at me.

'What potion?' she demanded.

'Why, the love potion, my lady, that you obtained from the witch,' I said in surprise, alarmed by her haunted gaze.

'Ah yes, the love potion,' she replied, and laughed. 'Oh, I've given up that idea. No potion would be strong enough for my remedy.'

'Then what can you do? If his bouts of violence increase, you may be badly injured.'

She shrugged. 'He's driven by a sort of weakness. He seems to need to vex me in order to prove he is stronger. I feel that he is to be pitied.'

I strongly disagreed. 'Ah! If only he had not returned from the Crusade!' I cried.

'Ghislaine!' said Berenice sharply. 'You must not say that. It is a wicked wish.'

'Forgive me, my lady,' I said contritely. But I wished it all the same. We had been very cheerful together before Audran had departed. We had concocted him a drink of shepherd's needle with wine, to promote fortitude. We had sewn him a pillow full of herbs, some from the castle store, some from the old witch. Berenice had spent a long time sorting out the herbs and putting them into a little bag. There was gillyvor against fevers, betony to drive away bad dreams, marjoram against earache, and a whole host of sleep-inducing mixtures, and thyme to keep up his courage. And they had all proved to no avail, for within a month or two he was back, not a blow struck against the infidel, having been taken ill with pains in the head a little while before they were due to embark.

As well as the despondency induced by his return, Berenice had felt shame that he could do nothing right.

'I had even felt pride in him,' she said, 'seeing him prepared to fight in a noble cause. For a moment he was a splendid picture in my eyes. 'But even that was to be denied me.'

II

A LADY of the castle may give any order she pleases, and Berenice gave order that the boy dancer should come up and dance for her upstairs.

Not that there was anything particularly secret about the arrangement, for I was there; and when they heard about it several of the guests meandered carelessly in the direction of our chamber and asked if they might join us, all female, the wives and daughters of the men who were out hunting. Shameless Blanche was there, and the ladies Anne and Eleanor, and even the grim-faced sour old Lady Guillemette, married to the grey-haired soldier Sir Hugh who fancied Berenice. We sat on the bed and on the floor, and one musician played upon a pipe and Pietro danced. With so many of us watching there was little space for dancing – but no matter! We knew it and the boy knew it – he had been brought here for us to ogle. He knew well enough what was expected of him and obliged with relish. To begin with he would slowly remove his clothes – not all of them, no, we did nothing that one might call lewd – and then he moved about with sinuous gyrations to the music. We gazed and giggled and ate sweetmeats, and since the boy was handsomely rewarded I don't think any of us can be blamed.

The trouble was that men have suspicious minds, and when our fun was discovered the husbands did not like it. And that Berenice should find enjoyment naturally did not please Audran. Another argument ensued. The three of us alone, he strode about declaiming.

'There's no more to be said. Your behaviour was disgraceful and entirely unworthy of your high position. Sending for that bare-arsed boy to squirm about here in your room. The other women were no better, but you should have set an example. Well, there's an end. I forbid it. We'll hear no more about it.'

'Oh how ridiculous you are!' seethed Berenice. 'That something so harmless should concern you. I hardly see why I should pay attention to your ravings.'

'You don't?' said Audran, stopping short and rising to her foolish bait. 'I'll tell you why. Because I am your husband, that's why, and because what I say goes. And because you respect my judgement you will obey it. And you do respect me, don't you?'

In the short silence he sprang at Berenice and gripped her arm. 'You respect me,' he insisted. 'Say it! You respect me!'

'I respect you,' she said, and he let her go.

'I want to hear you say that you will do as I have told you,' glowered Audran.

'Very well. I shall not ask the boy to dance before my friends and me.'

Nor did she; she invited him when no one else was there, and without the music, so no tell-tale signs came forth. It happened when Audran was out, and since he rode and hunted every day that was quite often. I hated it because I had to keep watch on the stair outside, and I felt such a fool, flitting about with a gong and stick to bang if anyone came by. She was quite safe of course, because I could see down the hall from where I was; a passage ran round all sides of it leading to the other chambers, and windows gave on to the hall below. I would have ample time to warn her, but I never needed to and she was not discovered. But I was so uneasy in this role I tried to convince her what a dangerous game she played.

'If he ever found out,' I whispered, 'think what might happen to Pietro!'

'There is no way he could learn of it,' she answered, looking in my eyes with a menacing intensity. 'Who could possibly tell?'

And I was left to marvel at her liking. For I was sure she could have Sir Hugh, who was dignified and rich and meticulously clean, who sat by her at the table and was so polite. And yet she seemed to want this boy, no better than a gypsy.

One morning, as I sat alone with Berenice the riders came back early from the hunt.

'Already?' said Berenice, at first surprised, then wary. 'What can it mean?'

The first indication of Audran's ignominy came when a servant entered muttering: 'Trouble again. Apparently he fell off his horse.'

'Oh my lady, did you hear?' I wailed despairingly.

'Of course not, child,' said Berenice tersely. 'I don't listen to the mumblings of servants.'

But I knew that she was anxious. We supposed that he would come striding into the bedchamber. We waited nervously; Berenice picked up her sewing.

Audran came stomping up the stairs, his boots thick with mud and his manner aggressive. I found him monstrous. He could have been some wild marauder bursting in upon some hearth or chapel, so fierce and savage did he seem, he who was the castle's lord and should inspire respect.

Berenice looked up pleasantly, as if all was as it should be, but her face showed just a somewhat foolish smile. I knew how it would look to him. He glowered down at her, and me I was so apprehensive that I backed away and cowered amongst the bed-hangings.

'Are you laughing at me?' he bellowed to his wife.

'Why should I?' she demanded.

'Oh don't ask me to believe that no blabbermouth servant hasn't passed on the merry tale. It's too amusing not to relate. The lord of the manor falling off his horse.'

As he spoke Audran punched the tall standing candlestick, sending it thudding across the floor.

'Oh have a care,' pleaded Berenice. 'I have heard nothing of it, and I am sure it was not your fault...'

'But it was!' shouted Audran. 'I was not even dragged off by wolves or encircled by robbers. The cursed animal took a ditch and threw me. And the idiots all laughed. Oh you'll be hearing all about it, be sure of that. Well, it's fortunate that here at least I am not a figure of fun. You certainly won't laugh, Berenice.'

He seemed to be daring her. The pathetic thing was that he looked so droll, standing there with his feet apart, big and stupid, in his mud-splattered clothes. I had to press my knuckles against my lips hard not to burst into peals of inappropriate laughter myself. My lady looked at him with profound indifference.

She shrugged. 'There is no need for this performance, Audran.'

I knew at once it had been the wrong thing to say. Audran had been clearly taking delight in towering over her. He must have felt important, dominant. Now with that tone of voice she had spoilt it all, and made him feel an imbecile. Her cool attitude infuriated him. She didn't have to laugh; her face expressed her habitual contempt. He lost his temper. He pulled her to her feet and shook her, and beat her with his great riding glove. I squealed, and servants came running.

It was frightening to see somebody so frenzied. It would be impossible to keep this from the servants and the guests. And then would come the comedy of eating down there in the hall, putting on a sort of show, as foolish and entertaining as the jugglers, and not so skilful. All sensed that this would be so. We looked at each other swiftly, we who watched, not knowing what to do.

Audran went stamping off, shouting for wine. I went to Berenice. Her dress was torn, her long hair had been shaken loose. I had never seen her look so furious. Her eyes blazed with hatred. I drew back.

'What I cannot bear,' she said, as much to herself as to me, 'is not that he hits me, but that he is ridiculous. People must feel such contempt for me. I won't tolerate it. Anybody else would have found a way out. I am beyond even pity; it's too ludicrous for that. This clown, he makes me ridiculous by association. No, I cannot bear it. And I won't.'

Truly I could find nothing to say. I sensed that Berenice had reached a point where resignation had turned to hate.

I was full of apprehension and dismay.

I suppose it was my fear that made me garrulous. To talk about it to my pedlar was helpful to me and his obvious interest encouraged me still further. Each night after I had seen my lady to bed I stole away down into the hall and sat with him, wrapped in his cloak, and it was just as I supposed – he found me fair and showed a great tendresse. He said sweet things and paid me compliments and kissed me several times, and all around us others did the same. He did not talk much about himself. Now I come to think about it, I know very little of him at all. He said I had lips of honey and cheeks like roses, but I do not recall that he ever spoke directly of Love. Perhaps humility kept him silent.

I told him things I should not, things my lady would be horrified to learn had reached the ears of another. But she would never know – his fate was not likely to be linked with my lady's, so where was the harm? I daresay none of us will ever see him again.

Will I be sad? I do not think so. Amour courtois is curiously unsatisfying; and I suspect that the pedlar is not very good at it. Even his careless boast of being descended from an ancient line of lords was nothing to be proud of, as it seemed.

'If someone said that he came from a line of Saxon lords,' I mentioned to Berenice, 'what would it mean?'

'That he was a lunatic,' shrugged Berenice. I admit that I was disappointed, and she laughed.

'Besides,' she added, 'those old Saxon lords lived like pigs.'

The pedlar knew no love songs, and seemed as fascinated by what I had to tell him about Berenice as by me myself. He asked no searching questions about my background, life and thoughts, and only spoke of romance when I prompted. And to be honest, his kisses were not passionate. They did not stir me at all.

Out of the kindness of my heart I mentioned him to Berenice, thinking that she might buy all his goods and be munificent to help him on his way. I know that he has pretty things within the depths of that great pack he carries, because he gave me a gift from it before he left, a mirror in a carved ivory frame – nothing special, but pleasant enough.

I asked the pedlar if when we parted he would be sorry. He said he would. I asked if he would think about me as he roamed the land and he said yes. Adore me from afar? Yes, he promised. Keep my image in his heart? He told me that he would. I felt a certain pity for him, for of course he could never achieve me. I am too high-born for him, and also Norman. I can be only as a star he sees on high. It cannot but be dismal for him, travelling the land remembering my charms that never will be his to possess. But then, that is the lot of the courtly lover.

One night towards the end of Yule I was awakened by the sound of whispered voices. Now that sounds strange, I know, but somehow I had learned to sleep through noise, the moments when his lordship staggered in from the pursuit of lust in other regions of the castle. I'd hear him swear and stumble, clumsily undress, heave back the bed curtains, and I could close my ears to Berenice's jibes and accusations. But this night was strange. They did not usually think it necessary to disguise their conflict from me, even I suppose enjoying the participation of an audience. I lay there frightened.

Within the bed were Berenice and Audran, whispering. I could not hear the words but I could sense the urgency, the force they used to keep their voices down when surely both most strongly wished to shout aloud. Then Berenice began to weep, and Audran growled and told her in an even tone to stop.

She slid the curtains open. 'I swear,' she gasped, 'it wasn't me. What more can I say? I don't understand it...but I swear it wasn't upon my account.'

And then she wrapped herself in fur and sat in the chair by the embers, and looked straight ahead and silently composed herself.

'Come back to bed,' said Audran several times; but she would not; and finally he muttered she might go to hell then for all he cared, and maybe that would teach her.

I knew that if she needed me she would call, so I said nothing, and she did not ask for me. She sat there in the chair till dawn, with Audran rolling in the bedcovers and snorting like a pig.

I must admit there is always some relief when the festivities are over and the common people leave the castle. I know that we must open our portals to the poor for the Seigneur's sake and share our warmth and food with those who have less. But those who have less, to compensate do smell the more and leave a mauvaise odour where they were, and we know nothing of them. They could be felons every one, for some do surely seem to be so, ragged and savage, with brooding eyes and sullen faces. And I even include the travelling musicians and the dancers and the man with the monkey – yes, even the beautiful Pietro, whose unsettling presence caused me the inconvenience of keeping watch on the stairs. So I was glad when the troupe departed, even though it was so sudden. Berenice said they were rogues and malcontents and none of them to be trusted and we were well quit of them. She said so sharply and I guessed she spoke in pique.

So as I say, it's no bad thing to see the celebrations end, and peasants back into the fields where they belong. The pedlar too I think will be no loss.

Indeed, I do not think what we shared was Love at all.

THREE
The Pedlar's Tale

I

THE LADY of the manor does not usually send for a pedlar. When Ghislaine told me that her ladyship wanted to see me, my first reaction was one of guilty panic. Any offences I might have committed, could she have got to hear of them? Perhaps she was angry I had taken up with her maid. Ghislaine assured me that Berenice knew nothing about that. I still felt very uneasy, and angry that Berenice had such power that she could ruin my trade, just as she and her husband could ruin the villagers.

'But why are you looking so morose?' Ghislaine demanded laughing. 'My lady isn't a monster. Why should you think she wants to do you harm?'

'Ladies of her rank don't ask for pedlars,' I said. 'They send a steward. I haven't got anything that would please her.'

'Don't be so modest,' Ghislaine teased. 'Anyway, don't you know your courtly stories? Ladies at a whim may do as they please. She may wish to raise you to a prince and ask you to live with her in regal splendour. All the best noble stories lead to such things.'

'I wouldn't know; I only deal in crude ballads,' I said sullenly.

'Go to her and discover,' said Ghislaine. 'I think you'll find she simply wants to see your wares.'

Feeling most uncomfortable I followed Ghislaine out of the great hall. She led me up a stone staircase. It felt cold there after the animal warmth below. Through a narrow window came a whiff of chill January air. It reminded me that it was time to be moving on. The walled-up warmth of the castle Christmas was over, and all would go on again as usual. I would have to travel on, to stock up my pack, and collect Alkanet's fine country herbs to sell to the ladies in town.

64

We reached the end of the stairway and stood before the heavy door. A bored man-at-arms straightened himself and let us through.

Berenice was sitting in a low chair beside the fire. She was wearing a wine-coloured dress edged with black fur. Her face looked somewhat pale but her cheeks were reddened with a false colour, and the lids of her eyes were painted too. I thought her very beautiful and, probably because of her gilding, dishonest. I felt uneasy, and suspected it was because she was rich and powerful and I was, in spite of my conceit, poor and vagrant.

'My lady, the pedlar,' said Ghislaine.

'Thank you, Ghislaine,' said Berenice. 'There is no need for you to wait on me now. Please withdraw.'

Ghislaine looked disconcerted and somewhat rebellious. But she had no choice than to do as she was told.

'Come here, pedlar,' said Berenice. She had a lovely low voice. 'Unpack your treasures and let me see what you have to sell.'

I knelt in front of her and unpacked everything that I had left, the more costly things. All the time I was puzzling about what she could want and why she had sent Ghislaine away. There was no one else in the room at all. I found it hard to keep up the patter. She could not really be interested in these things.

'My spices come from Arabia,' I said, 'across deserts of sand. Camel trains carry them to the markets of Alexandria and dark-skinned sailors steer them down the mighty Nile. The sights they have seen, if they could only talk...Pepper now, ripened in the sun on the hillsides of Asia. Wild beasts lurk in the grasses there and so the tribesmen burn the undergrowth to frighten them off. That's why the pepper seeds are black.'

'Indeed,' said Berenice smoothly.

'Yes,' I continued stubbornly. 'Ginger, from India the mysterious, from the swampy reeds...cinamon with its strange scent, teased from the bark of a beautiful tree...'

'Incredible.'

'Galingale, my lady, its sweet root to enrich the flavours of the cooking pot...thyme and coriander...'

'I have those in the castle garden.'

'Of course. Then I have sorrel to cure rotten gums and prevent bad breath, and comfrey to ease boils and ulcers.'

'I thank you, I have none of those things,' she said, looking pained.

'No, of course not, my lady,' I squirmed. 'Succory, for gout ...brooches, ribbons,' I rambled on. 'But I can hardly expect my lady to be interested in these things; they are so very inferior to what my lady is used to.'

I must have shown my wonder at her wanting to see anything I had. She smiled, and asked me to put aside a pound of galingale.

Then she said quietly: 'You have been spoken of by Ghislaine as being honest and reliable.'

I was surprised. I waited.

'Tell me something about yourself,' she said.

'I am without history,' I said. 'There is nothing to tell.'

'I'm pleased about that,' she said. 'And I wonder if you can assure me that to others you will be as discreet. For instance, I would say that you have already forgotten where you spent Christmas. Perhaps you would feel that what's past is past, and has no account now.'

I did not feel that, but I said: 'I am happy to fit my thoughts to your ladyship's wishes.'

'Have you a home?' she asked.

'The road is my home.'

'Friends?'

'Anyone who gives me a roof.'

'Would you be prepared to help me?'

She looked me full in the eyes and to my amazement I saw no haughty Norman lady, the villain of my tales of policy, but only a beautiful and unhappy woman.

'I would be honoured,' I said.

'It is not much I ask,' she said tremulously, 'but I need it done well. I have to put my trust in you.'

'My lady,' I assured her, 'of course you may.'

I surprised myself. What was I about, behaving like the lovers in the songs? This was a Norman lady with wealth and power whose castle stood on the place where ancestors of mine had given orders in the days of Raedwald when East Anglia was great. I ought to hate her and I ought to wish her ill. I could at least have shrugged off her request for help. That would have been satisfyingly spiteful and I might have felt appeased.

I blame it on the love songs. Night and day, all Christmastide, those songs had sounded in our ears till we were singing them crossing the yard, reaching for our dinner, taking a piss. I had one such in my head as I knelt there:

> 'Au comencier la trovai si doucete
> ja ne cuidai por li mal endurer...'

which has a sweet insidious tune; I blame it all on songs of Love. I am not a courtly lover and I have no patience with the idea of worshipping some woman – nor man – from afar and thinking about her for no better reason than because it is expected of you as a lover. Either you think of a person or you don't; it happens. But shut within those castle walls, penned up with love songs, playing games of devotion with a wide-eyed lady's maid and never walking twenty miles a day, a man acts out of character. It seemed entirely natural upon my knees before the lovely lonely Berenice to promise her – what? What was she after?

'Hold out your hand.'

She filled my palm with silver. I tried to look careless, but I had never held such wealth.

'You understand,' she said, 'it is your secrecy that I am buying; your silence.'

I waited, hoping she was not already regretting the generosity of the amount.

'I know that some people would be glad to abuse my trust,' she said. 'There is nobody in the castle that I could ask. I would be afraid they would let my husband know. Our servants are not dependable in loyalty. You cannot know how difficult...sometimes...how alone one feels...'

She was near to tears. I was completely softened. I saw the point of courtly love. When in love an ordinary day would be a journey of the heart; plain homely tasks an expression of devotion. Thinking of the beloved would put a spring in the step, a lightness in the heart. Would I die for her, as the minstrels sang?

No. I still had a long way to go, as a lover.

'Will you help me, pedlar? Will you be as anonymous as you say? Will you be an unknown face, now here, now gone, travelling as inconspicuously as the wind, a man I can rely on?'

'My lady,' I said. 'I would like to say that I am all those things. Because I value your trust in me I must say that I can only be as much as is possible in my position. I have never seen myself as heroic; I find the world too funny and too sad. Given this, I will be your servant in any way I can, but in a real way, not an ideal one.'

'Of course, you are quite right,'she said, 'just as I am unable to be the lady of the castle without being Berenice as well. But nonetheless I know you are the best, the only person who can serve me in this matter. It must be a travelling man, with freedom to come and go, and no particular loyalties or ties. Will you do your best?'

'Your ladyship has only to command.'

'No, I don't do that,' she said quickly. 'I have no rights over you. I ask for help because you can do something for me which I cannot. I want you to fetch me something. You go to London, I think.'

'Yes, in time.'

'And you will return here?'

'Again, in time.'

'Well, although it would please me to have you return as quickly as possible, I only ask that in your travelling you include an errand for me.'

'Certainly, my lady. Anything.'

'You may think this is a strange request,' she said a little hesitatingly. 'But do you know where to find an alchemist?'

'No, but I can easily seek one out.'

'You would not be afraid?'

'No.'

'Well, I have here a note. It is a short list of some things I need. An alchemist has them. Simply give him this. I have sealed it. There is no need for you to read it or mention to him who it is that asks for these things. Then bring them back to me as speedily as possible, hidden in your pack. Bring them privately to me, and there will be gold on your return. Have you understood?'

'Yes my lady.'

'Good,' she said relieved. She handed me a small sealed parchment and watched me put it in my pack.

'Shall I see you then, in the Spring?'

'Yes; I will return in the Spring.'

I packed away my spices. I got to my feet and she asked me to leave. The heavy door shut behind me. I went down the staircase. Ghislaine was waiting impatiently.

'Well? What did she want?'

'Just as you thought,' I said. 'To see my wares.'

She looked disbelieving and disappointed. 'Is that all?'

'She bought some galingale.'

Ghislaine gave me a scornful look and I at once lost her interest as a figure of romance.

'I'm leaving today,' I said.

'Then God speed you,' she replied. Such was our fond farewell.

As I crossed the great hall it seemed to me that the Yuletide garlands were already drooping; the rosemary, the bay, the mistletoe, the holly and the ivy were hanging their heads. I left the castle without much regret, for the festivities had been enjoyable but I had had enough; my feet itched to be on the road. Too much company and the closeness of people now irritated me, and I was looking forward to hearing the sighing of the branches of the trees, and meeting with whatever might befall me on the highways.

As I crossed the courtyard a couple of castle servants I knew came running up and fell into step beside me.

'Pedlar, have you heard the news? There's been a murder done – and hushed up after!'

'The boy dancer, Pietro...'

'Knifed on the dark twist of a stair...'

'No one knows who or why...'

'They say he must have been going up to the rooms where the nobility sleep...'

'Simono and the rest are fled...Gold and Silver, all. No one knows where they went.'

I murmured shock and horror, and moved onward.

I could wish him dead, Simono had said to me, *and I the one to do the deed*. So – his demons had got the better of him at last; I pitied him with all my heart. Thinking back to my encounter with the Lady Berenice I despised myself for a fool in thinking courtly love had any place in life. Was not Love pain and rage and jealousy, a 'terrible enchanter'? I said a prayer for all who found it so, and I resolved to keep my feet firm on the earth, my fancy free and my thoughts clear.

But when I left the castle that fond love song with the sweet caressing tune still hung about my head and plagued me.

Even as the green and noisy festivities of the old year were falling away like crackling leaves to the earth mould, the new festivities that betokened hope and faith in the future were taking place. A procession was crossing the village street led by Angilbert, beaming and rosy and looking very much as if he had celebrated well. In his hands he carried the gleaming processional cross. The villagers followed him; they carried sticks decked with ribbons and the ploughs were decked with ribbons too. Angilbert was taking them on the well-trodden way around the fields in the age-old ceremony of asking the Lord to bless the bare ground and grant us a good crop and fair weather. I stopped and wished them good luck and I did so with all my heart; a hard season lay ahead of them.

Benedict the innkeeper stopped a moment to speak to me.

'You'll be off then, pedlar?'

'Yes, back on the road.'

He said quietly: 'Will we see you at the place tonight?'

'Tonight, is it?' I said.

He nodded.

'Well,' I said, 'it would be a shame to miss that.'

I had suspected that Alkanet's celebration would take place on that day. I hoped that under cover of it all the old hag's watchfulness would be eased and I would have some chance of talk with Marel. For all my mingling with the doings at the castle I had been constantly plagued or blessed with that image of him running through the woods, covered with light and shadow, and I could not bear to leave Cortle without getting closer to him and letting him know something about what was in my mind.

II

THE GREAT bonfire burned in the secret clearing in the forest.

Nobody could have found their way there without first knowing the path; its existence was shrouded from those who were not in that knowledge. An ancient well was there, a dark mouth lipped by stone. Upon the stone was carved a line of mystic numbers. Long ago in old times our ancestors had prayed there. There was a deeply felt holiness upon the well, and though the ceremonies had changed, the reverence continued.

It was strange to think of them, people who lived here not knowing about Christ and His suffering for us, which would have given them so much more gladness than the stone. But as they knew nothing about God, it was good to think they had the stone which God had sent them in the meantime, before He was ready to let them know about His Son. Yet even when the missionaries had come and the great promise of eternal life laid open to them, they would not desert the stone. They never left it lonely. Even when they worshipped at the church in the village they did not forget the church in the wood.

What would they have thought about the ceremony now taking place? I suspected they might shudder in their graves. There was not much religion about it now; no, in these later times the old ceremonies were mostly used to cheer the cold spirit in the dark days and nights. They were rollicking and tipsy, those villagers who came to the fire, and many would have looked blank if you had asked them about the Old Religion. They had come there for a good time. Oh, they knew Angilbert wouldn't like it if he found out, but they would be hard put to explain why it was so, or which part of it was wicked.

Alkanet's hunched figure was bent over a bubbling cauldron which hissed and steamed. Marel was beside her, but so hooded that nobody could see his face, and so intent upon the stirring and the handing out of drinks that anyone could be forgiven for supposing that he was an old crone of like kind. No one paid him any attention, for the story was about that Alkanet had a halfwit servant, and the bad spirits that attended on such were not pleasant to be near.

I had met up again with Jusson the leper, though I should now say Jusson the cook. I hardly recognised him. He had an ordinary sort of face now, rough and creased and still marked with pitted scars, but nothing to what he had been, and he told me Alkanet had promised he would improve even more in time. Now he was amongst the dancers. All dressed up in skins they were, some in antlers and horns or with reed masks over their faces with slits for eyes and mouth. There were women too, as merry as the men. The drink made everybody cheerful, and those who could play a tune gave out a good sound on pipes and tabors; and some sang and chanted, and some rolled upon the grass, and it was all in fun and good humour. It was heartwarming to watch, to think that for a time they could be free from their hard life and toil, and forget the cold and sadness that Winter and the land cause to the peasant. It was thwarting to me, to be so near to Marel yet well within Alkanet's all-seeing gaze.

'What's in that stuff?' I asked Alkanet as she handed her brew to one and all.

'Nothing that they can't take,' she said grudgingly. 'There's goose-tongue for flavour, a spot of angelica to cheer away their glooms; there's fenkel and gillyvor, very cheering together; corian-der – that's a love helper – plenty of alehoof; enough bay but no more; and borage.'

'They are all wholesome,' I said.

She snorted. 'What do you think? Would I want to poison a whole village?'

I guardedly supposed not.

'No,' she said scornfully. 'Oh, I've got the wherewithal, pedlar, never fear. I've got plants in my patch so potent that to brush your hand against them and then to sniff your finger would have you cold on the spot. Don't think I haven't. But I am mistress here. I hold those dragons down and bend them to my will. They crouch

71

there snarling but I hold the chains.'

'Doesn't your power alarm you?' I wondered.

'Not at all,' she cackled. 'Why should it? It's nothing at all when you know your business. I know mine and I've passed it all on to Marel here. There's plants that scream out a warning even to the simplest, you know. Even you, pedlar, would be wary of the henbane. Jagged leaves and streaky flowers and a nasty stink. But it has its good uses – like a person it can be helpful or wicked. Take some poor girl giving birth; the child don't come, but the twilight sleep of henbane fools her into a trance, and when it clears she's through it – the child's born or dead, and she couldn't tell you how.'

Slowly she stirred her brew. 'Then there's hemlock,' she went on. 'Higher than a man in height, with scabby stems and those crafty white flowers and a stench of decay. But hemlock's a joker and pretends to be sweeter than he is. I've known folk die thinking the leaves were parsley and the fruits were caraway. But when you know, yes, once you know, you can't be fooled. These plants are safe in my hands.'

'But surely you know that some call you a witch. Don't you risk that by your knowledge?'

'What care I for their silly fears?' she snapped. 'They believe what they want to believe. I can't help it if they're stupid. What'd you have me do? If some youth is a dolt enough to come to me for an ointment made with a mix of southernwood to bring on an early beard, why should I tell him to leave it to nature? If they come to me for fenkel to block holes and cracks so demons can't get in, why should I tell them to overcome their fears instead? No, pedlar man, I'm not what you mean by a witch. The witch is their own dread and their own belief. I am the means, that's all, the way they can get their desires. If they believe it hard enough then my help is of small worth; their hopes do the rest. I'm not an evil force. I have power, yes, but the first move comes from the one who comes to me. I never go to them. I never start the magic. I am on their side; I want for them what they want themselves. And I like the payments they bring. Marel and I never go short.'

'So you see yourself then as a power for goodness,' I said.

'My army of plants do as I tell them,' she replied complacently. 'People they are, with goodnesses and badnesses like us all.'

Marel suddenly looked up. His eyes were a startling blue. He said: 'Thornapple has no goodness.'

Alkanet darted him a look of crafty malice.

'Be quiet, foolish child,' she said, perhaps as angry with the boy for having caught my attention as for what he said.

'Thornapple?' I said.

Alkanet looked shifty. She had been enjoying the picture of herself as a benevolent dame. She shrugged.

'Some people are wholly bad. Some plants are wholly bad. Thornapple is one.'

'Why?' I asked, looking at Marel.

'I fear it,' he said.

'Thornapple is the felon of our patch,' said Alkanet. 'We have to keep an eye on him. If he were to escape we should have nothing but trouble. He's tethered by a group of sturdy guards – don't worry, pedlar man, he can't get out. He can't run wild.'

It came as no surprise to hear of evil plants there. I never trusted that old crone. A force of goodness indeed! She could be good when it suited her, no doubt, but she knew about the absence of goodness all right. I watched her, crouched over her cauldron, her bony hand grasping the ladle, her twisted shape outlined against the glowing fire. I could believe anything of her. And this was the guardian of the beautiful Marel. What thoughts was she putting into his head – what wrong ways of looking at the world?

Then I remembered what Alkanet had said about the magic. 'I never start the magic; the person comes to me.' And I found myself wondering about Ghislaine and Berenice. What magic had she done for them?

'Is it magic?' I persisted. 'What you do, is it magic?'

'We are very curious tonight, are we not, pedlar man?' she jibed.

'I am taking advantage of your good humour, dame,' I said.

'Magic?' she said. 'Well, what's magic? The only things I do that I believe in are the cures. There's no magic in them. That's just the good earth healing her own kind. I only lay on the ointment. As for the others, the curiosities, they work sometimes. But in all honesty, I never know whether it's me or luck. There, pedlar! I wouldn't admit that to everybody. I must say it suits me very well to be known as a powerful old woman. It keeps them coming. Oafs! The good thing about you, pedlar, and there aren't many, is that you go away. Of course, we have to put up with it when you turn up again, but at least in between times you have the goodness to disappear.'

'I do it entirely to please you,' I said graciously.

She snorted, but she was still in as good a humour as I had ever seen her. Perhaps it was the result of the brew she was stirring. I wondered if I would be able to coax my way into her favour. She didn't exactly dislike me. Perhaps in time she might grow to see me as a protector for Marel, somebody to instruct him in the world's ways, in the sort of thing a young boy ought to know. Careful not to let my happy imaginings show, I turned from her and watched the revellers.

'You have worked a wonder with Jusson,' I said. I was so fawning it was sickening to hear.

'Nothing,' she said scornfully. 'Absolutely nothing.'

'The love potion in your brew works,' I commented, watching a couple kiss. Then I wondered: 'But will her ladyship's?'

'What ladyship?' sniffed Alkanet.

'Our lady at the castle,' I replied, smirking at its holy sound.

'You're talking riddles, pedlar.'

I suddenly found my interest awakened sharply.

'She came to you for a love potion,' I said, lowering my voice.

'She did no such thing,' scoffed Alkanet.

'But she did,' I insisted. 'I know she did.'

'I'm surprised you know anything about it, pedlar,' she said suspiciously. 'I would have thought she had kept it to herself. I can't believe you're privy to her thoughts, a travelling layabout like you are.'

'She came to you,' I said again. 'How I know about it doesn't matter.'

'Aye, she came to me,' said the old dame, 'but for a potion of stronger magic than you seem to know.'

I felt puzzled. 'Before he went off to the Crusade, she visited you one night with her maid.'

'That's right,' she chortled. 'She came to ask my advice and I gave her some basil.'

I could find no particular meaning in that. 'Whatever for?' I hardly imagined Alkanet would tell me, but she did.

'You know what basil is for,' she said, enjoying my puzzlement as if I were a somewhat stupid pupil.

'You eat it?'

'You eat it, do you, innocent?' she mocked, and nudged my arm, a gesture which I found repellent. 'And you know what happens when you sew it into a sleeping pillow, along with all those other sweet herbs, those gentle ones that do you good?'

We turned away from Marel. He could not hear what the witch was saying.

'What happens?' I whispered.

'Sniff the basil,' she said. 'That breeds a creature in the brain.'

The words sounded evil and chill, and struck me cold in spite of the brilliance of the fire and the nearby revelry.

'Nonsense,' I said stoutly.

'Nonsense is it?' she sniffed. 'Who came back from the Crusade with pains in his head?'

There was too much here for me to take in. 'Natural causes,' I persisted.

'Maybe. Who can say? But he had basil to sleep on. He laid his fair face upon it.'

'He seems well enough now,' I said, refusing to believe the implications of what she told me.

'At the moment, perhaps,' said Alkanet. 'But she's been to visit me again, the lady in question. We're being a little more cunning this time.'

I hoped she would say more. I was in luck; she was relishing it, her tongue no doubt loosened by the drink.

'My lady is too delicate a person,' she sneered. 'So tender and careful. She couldn't do a crude straight action if she tried. Not for her the spoonful of thornapple in the goblet, oh no, nothing so vulgar. My lady is a deep and tangled creature. My lady wants a spell.'

'What, you are casting a spell for her?' I gasped.

'Am I?' she said. 'What is it to you?'

'Have a care,' I said urgently. 'You will get yourself into trouble. All very well to play witch with simple village folk. But have nothing to do with Normans. They're too powerful. If anybody finds out, you risk being driven away or worse. And more, you'll bring trouble on Berenice. Her husband would kill her.'

'Exactly,' she said. 'Either he will kill her or *she*...'

'Hold your tongue!' I said angrily.

'I seem to have got you worried,' she said, her crabby face creasing into a grin. 'Don't tell me you admire her. I would have thought that you, pedlar man, of all people, would have been glad to see her brought low.'

It had been so, up until now. I had always hated the Normans at Cortle. Alkanet knew that. Was this to be the way of destroying the de Bonnefoys? Was Audran to be bewitched to death, and Berenice accused? I was uneasy; it seemed laden with hazard.

'What plans have you?' I asked anxiously.

'I never plan,' she cackled. 'I told you, I never start the magic. I am the means. It so happens I know of a spell. She asked me for something which would do the work without blame to her. I was glad of it. I have her now. If she succeeds and becomes the widowed

75

lady of the manor, I shall have all I want from her. She needs my silence; she shall have it, at my price.'

'You're a stupid old woman,' I said angrily. 'You fool yourself. She's more powerful than you are. She can have you turned out. She can do anything.'

'No,' said Alkanet comfortably. 'I know her sort. She's weak. I could frighten her into stupidity. She may hold a high position but I can deal with her. She'll make a fool of herself somehow. I shall win either way.'

I feared that Alkanet was right. Berenice was desperate and lonely and, I believed, the sort of woman to lean upon a man, not the kind that defends a castle at the head of her soldiers. I had longed to see trouble come to the castle, but not especially to Berenice.

'What kind of spell is it?' I said.

'Nothing you need trouble your head over, fool of a pedlar man,' said Alkanet cheerfully. 'Nothing that concerns you in any way. The spell is made with sulphur, and she'll need some dark signs that magicians brought out of Arabia, with other things that I could tell you, if I chose. I told her that this mixture can be found at any alchemist's. How she gets it is her own business.'

III

ALKANET'S WORDS seemed to burn a hole in my pack and lay bare Berenice's letter in a circle of flame. Did she know I was the messenger? I could credit her with any cunning.

I was too confused to talk to her any more, and I left the celebration early, spending the rest of the night at the cottage, and sleeping badly.

In the morning I got ready to set off. Marel sat in a corner of the room, as quiet and grave as he always had been. I could guess nothing about his thoughts from looking at his face. But Alkanet watched me.

'Sit you there a while, pedlar,' she said. 'Build up such faint strength as you have. I will go and pack up your herbs.'

She went off into the herb room and allowed the door almost to shut behind her. I was amazed. I stared at the door as if it was a ghost. She had left me alone with Marel. I jumped to my feet and took a step towards the boy. He looked up at me, startled.

'Listen, Marel,' I whispered. 'It isn't right that you should be

76

living here in the back of beyond, with this weird old woman. A boy should be out in the world – you need to know about life – handle a weapon, ride a horse, see folk, learn their ways. Come away with me – I can teach you all this, and more, and I swear I'd make you happy.'

He stared at me so blankly that it crossed my mind that perhaps he truly was half-witted – not that it would have made any difference to my feelings. He was so beautiful that just to look at him gave me the greatest pleasure. All that sleek fair hair that I longed to twine around my fingers, those wondrous blue eyes, the flawless skin, the boyish jaw. I had never been so close to him before.

Then I supposed – with remarkable understanding considering how overwrought I felt – that he had never been so close to me either. He looked wide-eyed, like a forest animal, or one who watched the world as if it were a picture, not taking part himself. And now a figure he had grown used to watch had come bursting out of the frame. I could have kicked myself for being so brash and clumsy; it was just that I couldn't believe my good fortune, and thought the old woman would come in at any moment and I had to make the most of it.

'Did you understand what I said?' I asked.

'I must ask Alkanet,' he said.

'No, no, don't do that!' I said. 'Just tell me whether you believe what I say and could come to trust me. I want to look after you. I'm a friend to you. I would help you to be a friend to yourself.'

He looked very puzzled as well he might.

'I can't leave this place,' he said.

'Of course you can,' I said. 'Why ever not?'

'I belong here,' he said. He spoke softly, like someone in a trance.

'No,' I said. 'You could be happy anywhere. I'd make you happy. Come away with me. I love you!'

He shrank back. I felt thwarted. It was too much to have all that sweetness so close and so unresponsive. I put my hand on his cheek and forced his head up and kissed him hard. It was lovely – like plunged into crushed herbs, the ones you have to bruise to set free the taste and smell. When I let him go I found my discomfiture had only worsened, especially as along with the pounding in my ears I could hear Alkanet shuffling about in the background, and in she came with bundles of herbs. Marel sat there quietly, looking at the ground. I took the herbs and packed them away.

'Jusson is to return with you,' said Alkanet.

Jusson was outside in the little clearing. When I was ready I joined him. Alkanet said she would bless our journey.

'What do you know of heavenly protection?' I asked suspiciously.

'Who said anything about that?' she cackled. 'I said I would bless your journey.'

'No, dame, you shan't mutter chantings over us,' I said.

'You'll do as I say,' she threatened. 'Or I'll wish you ill and then you'll be in trouble.'

So we stood there, somewhat cowed and sullen. She raised her horny hand and peered upwards, crying: 'Against heaviness and badness and the dark spirit and against the pitfalls of the way, a protector, a charm. Words I offer, prayers that no pain come by you, no sting, no evil threaten you. Preserve you against terrors, shield you fair, completely keep and save you, all working for a favourable travelling. And forward go.'

It was not clear who was to keep and save us, and I secretly made a cross with my fingers. Then Alkanet came very close to me and peered up into my face. I wondered into which age the thread of her life led back.

'You need my blessing, pedlar man,' she said. 'For all that you are a rough and scruffy vagabond without a home in this world, you are acceptable to me. In some things I have had to alter my old thoughts. You are needed to return to Cortle. I must have your safe return. There will be something for you to do here when the time is right. Go now, but you will return.'

I wanted to ask what she meant, but I felt that she herself didn't know. I would have time enough to puzzle out her meaning in the long days that lay ahead of me.

'Well, thank you for your blessing,' I said awkwardly.

Jusson thanked her again for his miraculous cure; she waved us away and scuttled back to her woodland den.

So now we were back on the road. Away from Cortle we went, along the path where Jusson and I had first met. We struck up a fair friendship; he was easy to get on with and it was agreeable to have a companion on the road to London.

When we came to Alric's village I fixed it for us to sleep in different places, so that Jusson did not get to know of how it was with me as regards boys. I had my night in the straw with Alric as I always did. A good boy he was, that one – he would allow me all I would. When I lay upon him we were like two rutting snuffling animals there, hair and flesh, panting and heat. I could never behave so with a girl – I thought briefly of the fair and delicate Ghislaine – no, I liked the feel of muscle and those parts which

78

females could not supply.

But when I lay satisfied, straw in my hair, and sweat upon me, I felt a sudden emptiness, more than that of being drained of my seed. How would it be, I wondered, if one could join the sweetness of woman and the passionate lust of the male! What perfection that would be! And I thought: Marel – if only *we* could ever lie like this. And I pictured all his golden hair and I tried to imagine him naked, his slim body next to mine, and I groaned at the torment I endured. If only I could be the one to awaken him to love! And my hard common sense told me that chances were if I did so the boy would go straight off to look for a woman, and I'd be to blame for arousing him.

Although dreams have no place on the road, I knew well enough that Marel would be travelling with me in my thoughts for much of the way.

It was cruel weather. The skies were always beautiful, full of light and shadow, sometimes looking like satin in folds that caught the glint of firelight. The cold sun lay in these folds, a dim golden blur that tinted the white and grey sky in the day and set in spilt gold in the afternoon. One evening it delighted us with a rich scarlet, and set blood-red; and such were the shapes of the clouds that day that there seemed to be in the sky a giant plumed bird plunging into the sunset, its breast mottled grey and red, and behind it the sky almost green. Well, that was the sky. On the ground it was a different tale. The road was hard, of rutted frozen mud, rough to the feet and dangerous to carts. We came upon several broken beside the road, with angry grim-faced drivers cursing as they wrenched at the shafts. In the mornings the grass glistened white beneath our feet and crunched like stones as we walked over it. In the great ruts old rain had turned to ice. When we passed throught the villages there was not much movement, but cold faces peered at us from doorways where they were trying to keep warm inside. In the taverns we ate bacon if we were lucky, and black bread and vegetable soup; we drank ale. Jusson bore it all without grumbling but he was longing to be back in London where the food was better and he could cook it himself.

In the fields the men were labouring, carting marl and lifting muck. They were spreading out the hardened mixture of dung and straw, their breath coming in frosty wisps as they hunched over the clods to break them up. It looked a back-breaking task.

Our journey southwards was slow. We were in no hurry, and we warmed ourselves at any fire we were invited to. Early mornings and late afternoons were bitterly cold, and we travelled mostly in the middle of the day. There were others on the road as cold as ourselves, and there was not the good humour that goes with some happier seasons. It was a grim time of year, the Yuletide games all past, and a long time till Spring. People were grumpy, and all grievances seemed nearer the surface.

Now we were passing near the country where Hereward the Hero grew to fame, the fens of Ely, with their secret paths and hidden islands, where the folk gather osiers to make eel traps and baskets, and thatch their houses with rushes. In these reedy waters you can find an abundance of fish, and birds roost here that you never see in other places. They come from the sea, up the rivers that feed the Wash – Witham, Welland, Wellstream, Ouse – and there are many abbeys hereabouts, whose monks helped Hereward in his time of revolt. He was a noble Saxon, Hereward, driven from his home by Normans; so he became an outlaw, living rough, a reward offered for his capture, every day a danger to him. But he lived a wild and merry life, for he had the love of a good woman, Torfrida, and a band of honest followers, and a deal of good adventures. I was telling some of them to Jusson as we walked, when into our path stepped a monk, as suddenly and silently as if he had appeared from Heaven, and uncannily as if he had been in my story.

'Kind travellers, I need your help,' he said, and led us off the path around a hawthorn thicket, with a tale of an injured horse trapped in a ditch, an abbess taken ill, companions distressed, and much beside.

A group of monks there was indeed beyond that thicket, but monks such as had never sang *resurrexi et Adhunc tecum sum, alleluia* in church, for they had hefty staves in their fists and not a tonsure between them. Briskly surrounding us they cleaned us out of all the money we possessed, except Berenice's silver which I had sewn into one of my boots, and rifled through my pack, taking everything except the herbs, which they strewed carelessly among the grass clumps. They pulled their cowls about them and took off down the track towards Brandon. We retraced our steps to Elvedon, told our story, and joined some men from Elvedon to go after them. We caught them all, drinking in the inn at Brandon; I got all my goods back and there was five shillings for me and Jusson as reward.

We don't live in the days of Hereward now.

In the company of pilgrims on their way to London, for Canterbury, we came south. As we approached London, Jusson's

80

spirits rose and mine fell. It was not so much the noise and stink and the press of people, which was at least offset by the shelter and familiarity and the colourful doings therein; no, it was that I would have to face up to the niggling problem which I had tried to keep out of my mind, the errand for Lady Berenice. It was simpler to forget about it, merely putting one foot in front of the other and keeping warm and knowing where to spend the night. But the smoke of London grew nearer every day and its dirty outskirts hugged us in. Clanging bells sounded through the cold air. The gutter smells rose to meet us; the stench hit sharply after so much forest air. The meadows outside the town walls which in summer were so green and festive were hard and crusty, with ice still in the furrows of the marshy northern moorland.

From a distance London is all towers and spires – there are over a hundred churches. The old Roman wall that keeps the city in is tumbledown in places, and the houses cluster round about it, straggling into the fields. It curves north from Blackfriars above the River Fleet to New Gate, thence to Cripple Gate and Bishops Gate, where the roads lead up to Lincoln and away. Down to Alders Gate the wall goes, to the Tower of London. Streams and rivers wind about – the Hole Bourne, which becomes the Fleet, the Lea, the Wall Brook the Ty Bourne. Two miles upstream of the Thames you can see the great palace of Westminster; a mess of houses lie between it and the city.

My old feelings crept upon me as we drew close. London sucked us in, a great maw that took in all comers. Good and bad were here, pleasure, danger, wealth and poverty, joy and sorrow, piety and lust. You put yourself into the path of all these things by going in.

IV

WE ENTERED through the portcullised gateway and the tall houses closed about us. The narrow streets were busy and crowded; it hardly mattered here whether it was Winter or Summer, you could barely see the sky beyond the overhanging gabled roofs.

We made our way along twisty streets whose level rose, fell, sloped, sunk; we flattened ourselves out of the way of carts with murderous wheels. We passed rows of shops marked with their symbols – the vintner's bush, the cordwainer's boot. Noise racketted on all sides, from the crowds of folk shoving and pushing, from

81

alleyways with the sounds of work, hammering, sawing, shouting; the loading of casks, the grinding of wheels, the metallic ring of harness and hoof. Travelling tradesmen bellowed their wares and pestered us for custom, beggars cried for alms.

With a sudden soar of spirits I noticed a pretty apprentice with an arse to drive a man mad. Ah yes, there were sights to see in London, and I'd been a fool to forget the fun that could be had of a dark night. The visit need not be so bad after all.

We sloshed our way through the filth underfoot where wandering dogs snuffled and the hooves of horses splashed it up on to the cloaks of the unwary. It was all somewhat sickening after the roadways, where the hazards are natural ones. The surprising thing was that within a week you took it all for granted and thought nothing about it at all.

Jusson had decided that he would not return to his shop until his face had recovered itself, though he did ask me to go and spy out how his little business was doing. It flourished still, a friendly little place, and the assistant had acted like no story knave, but was merely carrying on the trade and keeping his customers happy. For the moment Jusson stuck with me.

When I was in London I sometimes used a little room over a cooper's yard. He let it to all manner of folk, but there was always a space to lie yourself down, and a pallet if you were lucky and the room not too crowded. It was a noisy place, but it was somewhere to go and we met up with other wanderers there, and our first night in London we all went out and got drunk.

Then for many days we simply joined in the teeming life of that town. We caught up on the gossip, heard what the king had been doing, and what songs were new; who was dead and who was pregnant.

We learnt with no surprise that Château Gaillard still stood firm. and had kept the Frenchmen out. We heard that a force of ours had tried to relieve the siege but had been unsuccessful and badly beaten – something to do with the currents of the River Seine and not the skill of the French – with losses so heavy that the river ran red with blood. We heard that King John was undeterred and even now preparing to return to Normandy himself, that he was hopeful of the outcome and that supplies were being sent across the sea to our allies in Normandy, and that the king was sending hounds and falcons over for his hunting when he began his fresh campaign.

We went down to the river and watched the swans floundering in the half-melted ice and sea birds standing cheekily upon the hard

82

glossy surface; we walked along the quays where ships were giving up their cargo – Venetian velvet, wine from Bordeaux, oranges, lemons, spices and oriental silk. We watched the workmen building the new London bridge, which was nearly finished now, a vast thing built of stone, with many sturdy arches, leading over to Southwark; and I noticed once again that workmen always seem attractive, half-stripped and broadly muscular, lifting and stretching, most manly in their bearing; and when they bend they jut their arses up all carelessly with legs apart, as if they'd no idea how tempting they become by doing that.

Here I was pleased to see Henry the Sailor at his trade. No sailor at all, but he had a boat; how he had come by it no one knew, but it was his livelihood. He had no use in his legs, and like a duck was cumbersome on land, scrabbling about by means of two round blocks held in his fists, enormous power in his shoulders and a neck all straining sinews. His face was dirty bronze and sparsely bearded, with a great gold earring in one ear, and teeth as black and spiked as nails. He worked with a boy, one Sparrow, a scrawny mite with flighty eyes and stringy limbs, light as a twig and slippery as wet fish. Henry rowed his little boat between the great ships' bulks, like a piece of river garbage, picking from the water scraps that fell from the beaky prows and bustling decks above him. Patient and sharp-eyed he made enough to live on, sometimes netting a true treasure – money in a purse, a jewelled weapon, kegs of wine – for which the boy dived, fearlessly, beneath the shell-encrusted hulks. At night when chance presented, Sparrow climbed aboard and pilfered daringly from the deck and below, and Henry waited in the boat, a little bobbing shadow fading into darkness with an oarsplash faint enough to be an echo and no more.

Whores of the wharves hung about the doors of beery taverns. Some of them I knew and would have stopped to gossip but for Jusson's dreary disapproval. He was so plainly ill-at-ease we came away.

I stayed well clear of the better parts of town and went nowhere near the house of Juhel de Bracy. But I often slipped away from Jusson, whose company now irritated me, for when I grew to know him I found out he was a prudish fellow, a man of narrow ideas which did not tally with my own. Now I was hungry for the company of the thieves and scoundrels I knew well who hung out in Jug Yard.

Home again! I leaned against the crumbling wall of that low hovel where, for all these men were pickpockets and pilferers, I could lay down my pack and know it would remain untouched. A cellar it was, scooped from the bowels of some high pile above us, storehouse for merchandise, so near the river that you could hear the water lap. The ceiling hung down low, all warped from barrels piled too heavily overhead – we heard them rolling noisily down a ramp outside. Beneath, we were as safe as foxes. A floor of earth thick-packed with straw and stolen furs and hides begrimed with mud was underfoot. All manner of wild fellows hid their pickings here and no one ferreted amongst what was not his, unless he had grown tired of life and cared to risk a knifing.

Henry and his boy lived there at the time, and Tyb the one-eyed thief with his two women Mag and Ella, and Rahere the bone-gatherer, with Dickon who wore women's clothes and was more fond of fripperies than the women, who from years of fighting for their place had grown tough and sly as men. I don't know why, but far from scorning Dickon for his funny ways the men who lived there took great care of him and brought him gifts back, as if it was a matter of pride with them that each must prove his manhood by the better bauble he provided. The same was not true of Guy and Osbert, two boys who lived by peddling arse to sailors. Tyb could not abide them, Lord knows why, since they were pleasant enough lads and free with their earnings too and always buying ale to share. When they stuck their heads around the door they'd ask if Tyb were there and if he was they went away. In every other way Tyb was most reasonable, and went with whores himself, so where's the difference? Yet to him there was, so contrary some men are. A loud-mouthed dicing bully was Tyb, murderous when he was drunk, but that was how he was, and treated right he was a good strong arm and loyal to his friends.

Rahere was thin and small and mouse-like, quiet of manner, shifty, his fingers always dirty from his trade. His trade? He gathered bones from graveyards. He went out by night with a bag of digging tools, returned as ghosts do, before cock-crow, with a sack of bulging bones, and in the day he scraped and whittled till the flesh was off, and some he burned over a little fire, with a foul stench which has been known to cause the hardest felon to spew his meat forth. Then carefully he would choose his saint, and wrap the bones in cloth.

'This one shall be Saint Lawrence, well-roasted from the gridiron...this a knuckle of Saint Paul...a thigh from Nicodemus...This the finger of Saint Cecily, put to death in her bath by steam...poor maiden, eh? I often wonder if she was a big comely

84

wench all lying there without her clothes...This little bone looks like a virgin martyr, wouldn't you say? Saint Catherine? I'll find a bit of velvet for it... Ah, which of you is that sniggering and smirking? You think I won't be able to sell this trash? Have you been to Canterbury? The pilgrims mob you there for relics, poor fools. I could sell Saint Lawrence twenty times over, and I've done so!'

We passed a flagon round.

'So – King Pedlar's home then! Bastard son of Harold's line he is. When are you coming into your own to lead us all to riches?'

'Ah, you don't believe that story,' I said modestly.

'Why not? *You* do!'

'Well, if we must have bastard ancestors why not aim high?' I shrugged.

'Like he who shot that arrow that did for him?' Rahere chuckled. There was no ancient pride of race in Rahere.

'I see I am among oafs, just as I thought. Don't you pay heed to anything I say? I have told you often enough, King Harold did not die at Hastings. That story was put about by his enemies because they could not find the corpse.'

'I have not heard that story.' It was a young man unknown to me – sallow of skin, short of stature, with ragged brown hair and a shaggy moustache. Sharp lively eyes he had, a traveller no doubt, and one that sang and played, for he had a battered gittern and knew bawdy songs, with which he later entertained us for a meal.

'Pedlar, meet young Wulfstan, who tells more tales than you – and better.'

'You are Saxon?'

'These days we are all English, are we not?' cried Wulfstan. 'Those old words must go. I choose to forget my origin and mingle with what belongs to now.'

'We never can forget – how can we? Deprived of our birthright – '. The patter tripped easily off my tongue.

Wulfstan spat. 'What birthright? I was born under a hedge. I daresay it was not much different for you!'

'Treason!' Henry guffawed. 'Throw him in the river. Don't you know the pedlar comes of royal blood? He'll have you in the Tower for that!'

'Aye, the pedlar keeps us on our toes,' said Tyb. 'He'd have us all believe we could be heroes and rise up and send the Normans packing. The tales he's got in his head of them old Saxon leaders. In days gone by the likes of you and me would have worn furs and velvet like the Normans do today.'

85

'But the past is nothing,' Wulfstan said. 'What good is it to fill your heads with wishes and regrets? None of us remembers Hastings. Let it go, I say, and deal with what we have today.'

'That isn't much!' said Dickon grumbling.

'Well, it's better than dreams and making up a tale of what you wish had happened.'

'It's true as I stand here!' I cried.

'You sit!' laughed Henry. 'And I say there's too much thinking here tonight and not enough drinking. Sparrow, see to it.'

'So,' said Wulfstan, squatting down beside me. 'Who was it chopped to pieces at Hastings if not Harold? Who did they bury on the cliffs to guard the shore?'

'Gyrth,' I answered. 'His brother.'

Wolfstan snorted.

'True!' I maintained. 'When they brought in Edith Swan's Neck to recognise the battered corpse she told a lie. This is what happened: the night after the battle a peasant drove his cart amongst the slain dead. He was looking for the pickings – rings and gold and weapons. He saw a strange unearthly glow that hovered over one of the bodies on the field. He crossed himself and trembled. Then he saw the man was living. Upon his finger was a ring of such magnificence he guessed that it must be the king.

' "Sire, are you alive?" he gasped.

' "I am," said the king.

'So the peasant carried him into his cart and hid him there and took him away. With all his best thegns dead and England lost, King Harold went abroad, and he became a pilgrim. Long afterwards he yearned to see his native land, the places he had known as a boy, and he returned to England. He lived a hermit's life, ten years in a cave near Dover, always looking at the sea whence so much trouble came. He died at Chester, very old. No one knew who he was; he wore a hood, so no one ever saw his face. But on his deathbed he told all, and when the hood was lifted it was seen that he was scarred about the face, and one eye gone, the flesh all puckered up and shrivelled, much as if an arrow wound had caused it…I have this from the monks of Waltham. Every word is true.'

'Do you believe him?' Wulfstan asked Rahere.

'I surely do,' he said with a great guffaw, 'as much as I would believe anyone who picked splinters of the One True Cross from hawthorn trees along the Canterbury road!'

Wulfstan sang us bawdy ballads then and some joined in and Henry most of all. He sang a lot, did Henry, bearing no particular

86

grudge against the Almighty for making him crippled of limb, nor against Life for making him poor. From his massive chest and throat his deep voice came, a pleasure to himself but not to anyone nearby, for he never knew the words and tuneful as a bull in pain he sang what he remembered, horrible snippets of French love songs whose meaning passed him by, made into English gibberish. In his boat this singing carried from one bank of the river to the other; in our small space it gave torment bad as any penance from the Church. Happily, as night drew on, those who worked by darkness left. Henry grasped his wooden blocks and dragged himself outside to where his boat was tied, Sparrow with him. Tyb took a swig of ale and fixed the ragged bandage round his eye and handled the three daggers that he wore at his belt, never saying where he went. He would return at dawn, with chalices, slim golden crosses, jewels.

The embers of our little fire burned low. Respecting Wulfstan as a fellow tale-teller and traveller I asked him: 'As a Saxon then, are you not troubled by what you see on the road? The beaten down villagers, the Normans in their silks and furs? And to remember that it was not always so, that Saxons ruled the land, Saxons whose land it was by right of birth, before these foreign raiders stole it from us – destroying all we had? We had laws, we had heroes, we had wonderful songs of thought and war, manuscripts, carvings, stonework...They had nothing – they were pirates, no more...'

'You think it was a Golden Age, do you, the time of Aethelstan, of Aelle?'

'It was! All men were bound by the Bond. You know that, surely? Master and man, a bond of love?'

'Yes, I know that. I know the old poems. But I know more. I know it was not so simple. Moreover, I know it was a hundred and fifty years ago. Isn't it time we moved on? Who remembers it now? Those old ghosts are long since gone.'

'Walk the field of Hastings,' I cried in quivering tones. 'See if that is so!'

'Pedlar hates all Normans,' Dickon explained patiently, patting his hair. 'More so since he was done over by Hubert de Bracy and hurt his arm. And all for cuddling in the pantry with Hubert's pretty son.'

'Ah – you favour boys?' asked Wulfstan with interest.

'What's it to you?' I said looking shifty.

'No more than a monstrous curiosity to know all I may about my fellow man and weave it in the tales I tell.'

'H'mm,' I said grudgingly. 'That's reasonable enough. But you won't find any tales about Aucassin and Nicholas, or Lancelot and Gawain. Even though there always have been lads who love each other, and always will be.'

'Then we have to tell our own,' smiled Wulfstan like a plotter.

'Boys with yellow hair...' I murmured comfortably. 'A golden-headed boy has caused me trouble and will do again before my time is through. You have a story?'

That night by chance, with Tyb away, Osbert and Guy called in and stayed awhile by the fire. And so it was that four of us at least were lovers of men, for lust or money, Dickon being there, his hair all braided up in coils of stolen pearls, his grimy dress of faded burgundy.

Of those that dozed, Rahere, Tyb's two women, and some scabby beggar in a cloak, they cared not one way or the other, and dozed on. When Wulfstan bought his night's lodging by a story, some listened, some did not, and throughout the tale there was the sound of Rahere chipping bones, scraping with his knife, and making little heaps of saintly fingers, which the embers picked out grey and rigid where they lay.

'I tell this story for the pedlar,' Wulfstan said.

A little north of Pevensey, said he, there was a farmstead, Twineham, where a Saxon and a Norman lived in harmony. He had seen them for himself, he swore it! What a rigmarole he told me! How they fell in love with each other in the peaceful days before the conquest, Edwy a Saxon with golden hair, Gilbert a handsome Norman. They had met at Harold's coronation and swore undying love there, while the thunderclouds of discontent around them gathered, and then they had had to part, Edwy to his farmstead, Gilbert to the service of Duke William. Then came the battle, and we all know what happened there! And afterwards it befell that Gilbert's men took Twineham and made Edwy prisoner. Then followed such a rambling story – how they fought and loved and hated and loved again – with much life-thought thrown in, about the power of Love and Fate (or as we Saxons call it, Wyrd) which has the greatest power of all, for it is blind and deals out fortune or despair with balance awesome in its carelessness.

And Wulfstan would have me believe that this was true and he had seen it with his very eyes. 'Yes! There they live, down in the south, in peace, and farm the land together, knowing that the land must come first, before the petty squabbles over kingdoms, before pride of race or private wraths. And Love is their reward, for at night they sleep in one another's arms in the bower of that farmstead.'

'And you have met them!' Dickon marvelled.

'Yes; I heard it all from their own lips.'

'And Edwy still has golden hair?' I said.

'As buttercups!'

'And Gilbert, still handsome?'

'As an angel.'

'And yet he fought at Hastings. Strange indeed are the workings of Wyrd!'

And I laughed heartily, and so did Wulfstan, for it is well known that Saxons are poor reckoners of time.

'It could never happen,' I declared.

'It did not; it's a story,' Wulfstan said.

'A Saxon and a Norman in harmony – never!'

'It must be so. There is no other way.'

'And what do you suppose would happen when they died? The Normans would walk in and take the farmstead anyway. Someone like Hubert de Bracy would take it over.'

'You know my views – they are in the tale.'

'I can't agree with them.'

'I didn't ask you to. But if you can weave them into your own life you will not be so bitter.'

'How can we not be bitter, with the state the country is in? Such injustice, so many wrongs?'

'I see I might have saved my breath...'said he, shrugging his shoulders and moving nearer to the fire.

V

SMALL-FRY DEALS of my own account kept me busy on the London streets. I had a profitable arrangement with a chandler; I brought him samples of Norfolk beeswax and flax for his candles. Mere tallow he could get from the slaughter yards but fine beeswax gave his candles quality, and he provided for many rich houses and the Church. Flax he needed for his wicks, and the flax I traded on behalf of growers in the east was the very best, smooth silken strands, like Marel's hair, spun, woven and well-plaited. I bargained an order for packs which would be delivered later, saving the costs of merchant dues and earning me a tidy fee.

On a like venture I had rabbit pelts to show a felt-maker for his hats and shoes, and moleskins, and a load of inks made from bark and oakgalls to interest scribes. A bundle of stuff made out of horn – caskets, drinking-horns, spoons and combs – I sold these myself from a tray, up and down Cheapside.

So much for work – but there was much besides...

There are certain parts of London where the law-abiding never go, no, not even men-at-arms on dark errands for their Norman masters. You find these places down among the wharves, humpy unpaved alleys winding between old heaps of sagging houses shored up by worm-eaten buttresses of mouldy timber, where thieves and beggars and the dishonest poor eke out a living. In every weather somehow underfoot it's always puddled, slimy, stinking with the rare and curious flavour of the riverside – foul water, rotting fruit, stale fish, a sudden whiff of spices, rank old ale, dead carcasses that jut up stark and twisted from the mud; and piss that stains the walls and slithers slowly down the mucky runnels.

Amongst this motley was a tavern with no name, and here one night a good time was had; and yet it started with calamity.

Up from the river with their night's pickings came Henry the Sailor and young Sparrow, the one bellowing and swearing, the other squeaking and squealing, and both dripping wet, slabber'd and sost, and very wroth.

Blinking from our slumbers round the glowing embers of the fire in our warm den we listened to their tale of woe. Sailors on the deck of a ship had witnessed their thievery below and threatened them and shouted at them, and our two had shouted back and swapped so many curses that the sailors had pursued them. Henry and Sparrow rowed off at speed, but some of the sailors came running down the gang plank and followed them along the bank. Thinking themselves safe on the water, Henry and Sparrow had been boastful and triumphant but had so enraged the sailors that they ran as far as London Bridge and waited where the workmen were, and when the little boat drew alongside, up they jumped and hurled a hunk of stone down into it, which sank the boat and split it in twain. So Henry and Sparrow swam ashore as best they could and scooped up whichever of their pickings floated. It had been no easy matter for Henry to scrabble home upon his fists. He slung a great wet white loaf down at my elbow, one that would have made a tasty munch when warm and dry. We ate it nonetheless but river water added nothing lovely to its flavour. We raised the fire to dry their clothes and soothed the two, and later when their bad temper had eased off, Wulfstan sang a song for us about cruel fortune.

That night I went with Rahere the bone-gatherer to the tavern, and sat with him in some dark corner where at first we put our heads down and talked business over ale.

'Make me a dozen fingers of Saint Catherine,' I decided, giving it some thought. 'And I'll have two or three jaws of burnt teeth – Saint Lawrence has always been popular in the villages. Saint Catherine's fingers, very small and dainty,' I added, 'and well-polished and clean. I've got some little velvet-lined casks – purple velvet – for the single bone to go in. Purple sets off a bone to its best, I find.'

'Twelve Saint Catherines,' muttered he, 'and thirty Lawrence teeth...it shall be done.'

Rahere grew more than common thoughtful in his cups. He eyed me with his bright rat's eyes and said: 'I daresay you think me a hard man, pedlar, to do what I do; I mean the trade I follow. It isn't so. I'll tell you something. You know how when they dig up the body of a saint – I mean a real saint, not our sort of saint; I mean for instance when they found the relics of Saint James, or when they opened Cuthbert's tomb – a smell of violets rises. That's how you know it was the body of a saint. Well, let me tell you, when I dig about for bones in shallow graves they don't smell pretty. I've got used to it over the years I do daresay, but still I know it isn't very lovely. But sometimes, pedlar, in the dark there, with my fingers in the soil, and thoughts of demons in my head, and fear of being found there doing what I do, what keeps me going is the thought that one night I shall scrape the dirt aside and from the skeleton beneath will rise the scent of violets and I'll know I've found a saint. I'd like that. Yes, I really would. I wouldn't touch what I had found; I'd put all the earth back in place as gently as a bedcover. I know holiness when I see it. You might say,' he said reverently, 'that my whole life has been the searching for the smell of violets.'

Now the tavern filled up. There was music playing, and some whores came in touting for trade, and there was some kissing and larking about. In our dark corner we were pressed into the wall by crowds, so we shoved those nearest to make space, and standing found a merry sight to see – two dicers at a table and a gathered group roaring encouragement, laughing and nudging. With good reason. One of the dicers was none other than my one-time golden-headed weakness, Juhel de Bracy, that luscious simpering lad who'd let me have my way with him amongst his mother's velvets, and then cost me a battered arm. No great surprise to see him here, for the foolish youth liked to flirt with danger and be among the low life of the town. But what gave spice to the present moment was that his opponent was Liam the Demon Dicer. You have never seen such a friendly affable face as his – the face of a kindly monk, you'd say, or an honest breadmaker – a warming smile, plump cheeks and pleasant eyes, a broad brow faintly strewn with grey-white hair; and leaning forward with his dice as one would lean to say: tell me your troubles! He worked with weighted dice, and what he'd do, he'd let a young accomplice beat him at the game in full sight of all, and then challenge some newcomer and wipe him clean. Well, certainly I was curious to see the outcome in this case!

A pile of silver lay between the two on the rough stained trestle. I heard young Juhel wail: 'But I have no more money!'

'Win it back, lad – your luck's bound to change!'

The silly boy believed him, and in true gaming fashion diced away his cloak. An interest quickened, of a bawdy sort. Then Juhel lost his jerkin. The whores came wriggling closer for a better view, and so did I. We wanted Liam to strip him and we pressed about to see it all, and Liam would not disappoint us, as we knew. Smiling sweetly and encouragingly he won Juhel's boots and belt.

'No more,' began that unhappy boy. 'I'll have to call it quits.'

'I wouldn't let you go like this!' cried Liam. 'It would be unkind. No – I shan't let you go till you have won some money back. Try one more game! You still have your shirt to play.'

'No – I think not – ' Juhel protested politely.

'I said I shan't let you go,' said Liam pointedly, and rattled his dice.

Juhel looked about him, beaten. No way would he be allowed to leave, unless by some wild chance he could win all back; his fate was sealed, and when he lost the next throw the lovely red-lipped women helped him from his shirt. The fiddler and the piper hustled nearer and played merrily and loud, and some began to dance, a curious jig, full of suggestion, lust in every writhe.

My throat went dry to see Juhel sitting there bare-chested, bare-armed, in his trousers. One more throw would do it. Rahere, squeezed up against me smelling vile, had his lips drawn back like a panting dog. Perhaps I looked the same. I licked my lips.

'One more throw?' said Liam apologetically.

Juhel nodded dumbly. The music stopped. Somebody hiccoughed, somebody laughed. A dice got lost under the table. One of the whores retrieved it, grubbing between people's legs, and got her skirts lifted – this distraction parted some onlookers for a different

sport, but I stayed where I was. The dice were th␣
groan of pleasure and a cheer from all. The music starte␣
Liam stood and bowed. All turned to Juhel. Foolishly he
to resist. Two seized him by the arms from behind, an␣
grasping hands pulled off his trousers. Wild yells of deligı
knew he would be pretty! Now I was beside him, protectively
nobody wished him ill – sport, that was all, and he deserved it for
folly and for being such a gem.

They lifted him about and pushed him to and fro, and tweaked
his pretty cock and chucked his dimpled chin. The two whores
kissed him, drenching him with their big bodies. He was surrounded by laughter, whirling red faces, gappy teeth and mudstained
leather. Grabbing hands reached and slapped his tempting arse.
But that was all. All! you might marvel; but I tell you, for being
what he was and where he was, so far he'd got off lightly.

'That's enough,' I said easily, removing him. I got no trouble; all
they'd have done with him next would have been to sling him out of
doors.

'You took your time!' squealed Juhel at me.

I laughed comfortably. What a sight he was, so rosy, bare and
downy gold, with his face all flushed, his hair dishevelled and
unkempt, his dignity most sadly ruffled and his hands clasped over
his cock.

'Get your clothes,' I suggested. He looked around, then his alarm
grew greater. All his clothes had disappeared, vanished like an
autumn mist. Nobody had seen them go, of course. In answer to his
horrified demands all he received were laughs and shrugs. Some
beggar would go bravely clad tomorrow.

'But – how shall I return home?' he asked me, appalled.

'How did you get here?'

'We came by boat.'

'We?'

'I have a servant, waiting in the boat.'

'Where is your boat?'

He told me. I asked for clearer directions, so I knew exactly where
it was.

'Your servant – he would have a cloak perhaps, something you
could wear?'

'Yes! He would!' Juhel cried eagerly.

'Then we must fetch your servant here, must we not?' I said
briskly. 'Rahere!' My friend was at my side,, grinning wickedly.

'Rahere,' I frowned, 'it isn't funny. Rahere, he came by *boat*,' I aid. 'You heard. You heard where he moored it. Go and find it and bring his servant here. I daresay he'll reward you for your pains, eh?'

'Oh yes,' said Juhel gratefully.

Rahere touched his brow and slipped away.

'And while we're waiting, Juhel,' I went on, 'we will go outside.'

'We?' he gasped. 'But I have no clothes – '

'I said we will go outside,' I repeated. Juhel was not to know that my left arm was as weak as water; my tone was masterful and he obeyed. I only paused to grab two fingerfuls of lard as I went out, and down a couple of steps I led him, into a pitch black yard, where kegs stood stacked upon flagstones cold and slippery and the night air struck sharp.

'Over the barrel with you,' I said. 'Quickly.'

He submitted, whinging about the cold. I parted his thighs and eased my way in. But though he grumbled he moved his bum against me with all the warmth and willingness I remembered from before. We could hear the music from inside the tavern – merry, saucy music, lewd and lovely. I fucked him till I'd had my fill, and all his little gasps and sighs gave me no doubt that all the pleasure I was getting was his pleasure too. I ruffled his hair and we separated; and when I opened the door I saw his servant looking for him. The last I saw of them, they were hurrying away, Juhel in his servant's cloak and shoes, the servant hobbling behind, down towards the river.

I didn't follow them; I couldn't have played along with the game of surprise and shock when they discovered that their boat was gone. If Rahere had read me right the boat was now elsewhere, well hidden out of sight. And after all, what was one little boat to the de Bracys who could buy another dozen? On the other hand, to Henry the Sailor it was his livelihood.

I heard that Juhel and his servant hired a boat from further down the river to get safely home. Well, maybe he would think again before he flirted with the low life for the fun of it.

'A real good turn you did me, pedlar,' Henry told me gratefully. 'I won't forget it. I'll repay you one day when I find the gift that fits. Whoreson good of you to think of me. I'll see you right; I don't know how yet, but I'll find a way.'

'Well, it won't be through your singing!' I assured him, thumping him.

Within a day or so we heard him on the river once again, bellowing his beery ballads like a bull with his balls burning, and rowing a neat craft touched up with paint and tar to look like nothing anyone could trace to Juhel.

Osbert the tart poked his head round the door one day and looked about. Finding only the sleeping beggar and myself and Dickon, and Mag one of Tyb's women, who sat scouring out a pot, he came inside and squatted down by Mag.

'I've got a chance of work in the country,' he began. 'There might be something in it for you.'

They made a sorry couple. Both had purple eyes from bruises got in Tyb's drunken rages. She listened, scraping at the pot.

'A man I met,' went on Osbert, 'has come into his inheritance and goes back to the country to take over his house. He wants some servants, but they must be man and wife. So how about it? Shall we be wed? What do you say?'

'Married!' Dickon gulped. 'I'd say yes if it was me!'

'It isn't you,' said Osbert roughly. 'What d'you say, Mag? Chance for a new start, eh? And I'd leave you be – I wouldn't bother you. It's him not you I want, so you wouldn't be cluttered with little ones, and in return for living in a proper house the only thing you'd have to do is scrub some floors. So how about it?'

'All right,' said Mag, and put the pot down.

I couldn't help but feel that if he'd looked in and found Ella it would have been she to get the benefit of his suggestion. It seemed to me curiously pleasing that upon such freaks of chance lives change direction. We wished good luck to the happy pair. I dug into my pack and gave them some trinket as a present; Dickon gave Mag some ribbons from his dress. We were sorry there was not to be more of a celebration, but the newly promised couple had to flee from Tyb, and Osbert's man friend waited up by Bishops Gate.

When Tyb got to hear of it he went mad, and laid about him with his fists. Poor Guy the other tart made himself scarce and disappeared for days. Wretched Ella took twice as much of Tyb's wrath than before, and if we asked her why she didn't leave him she said she was tired, and living with Tyb was all she knew. Then after his first rages Tyb went into a sad state and gave up going out at night to steal, which meant he was too much with us and spoilt such peace as there was with snivelling and complaining and throwing pots at walls. I left the shelter of the thieves' den to return to Jusson and the cooper's yard. Every man has the right to drink himself to death, but not to rob another man of his sleep. And I had troubles enough of my own.

The uselessness of my left arm tormented me and none of the apothecaries in London could do anything about it; I suffered 'cures' of all kinds at their hands, none of them working, one leaving me with a scar from wrist to elbow. Then there was Marel. Far away in Norfolk as he was, he was always near in my thoughts and he was managing to spoil any pleasure I tried to get.

There was a boy I had down by the river one night, a good-looking scrap with a nicely rounded arse and most appealing eyes. He found us a place in one of the warehouses, up a ladder amongst a nest of wine kegs, where he stripped for me with all the skill of a dancer. I satisfied myself upon his body and we swapped fair words, and I expected to feel contentment, but I did not. And this was a pretty lad, not just a willing arse. But all the time I was pestered by floating pictures of soft blond hair and clear skin, and those wide eyes of cornflower blue. I knew that he now had a hold on me I could not shift, and that I would not be able to rest until I had gone back there and seen him again. I swore at myself for a besotted fool – but there it was, I needed the sight of him. And I could not leave London without performing what I had been asked to do by Berenice de Bonnefoy.

I kept putting it off. But I thought about it so much that I became irritable and morose and a very poor companion. At night I'd awaken in that smelly little room above the cooper's yard, and shift about on my pallet and listen to the snores and grunts from the other sleepers, and think to myself that sooner or later I would have to hunt out an alchemist and do my lady's commission, a spell for a murder.

VI

KNOWING THE meaning of Berenice's errand, I could not rid myself of some strand of responsibility for what might happen. At first I felt protective towards her, as if I might save her from herself. It was understandable that she should wish Audran dead; but if she had any part in his dying she would surely damage her immortal soul – and possibly be found out here on earth! Even if everything went smoothly, it was dangerous for a lady to be toying with magic, and I felt anything that came from Alkanet must be suspect. Of course I could always pretend I had lost the letter; then Berenice wouldn't get the mixture and nobody could cast the spell. But that would mean I could pay no more visits to the castle or wander around Cortle at will. And common sense told me that if Berenice didn't get what she needed from London, her desperation would be such that she'd try another way. There were enough likely murder brews in Alkanet's wild herb patch to succeed. I went round in circles sorting out the rights and wrongs and changing my stance each time. In the end I decided to shrug my shoulders and leave it all to fate – to Wyrd, even.

So I asked around for an alchemist, and one cold bright sunny morning I went along with Jusson to one of the pleasanter parts of town to do my errand. To our surprise we found the house we had been directed to was a fine large structure with ornamental timbered walls, in poor repair certainly, but nonetheless a good-looking dwelling-place, with a yard behind and a garden. The door was opened by a nervous-looking woman dressed in grey, pretty but looking worn and anxious. Behind her were several small children who eyed us with sharp curiosity. I asked if the alchemist were at home.

'May I ask who you are?' she said.

'I am a pedlar, and this is Jusson, a cook.'

'Well, that's all right,' she said, seeming relieved. 'As long as you aren't after money.'

'No, not at all,' I assured her.

'Come in; my husband is in his room.'

We followed her inside. The rooms were poorly furnished and threadbare. We went down a dark stairway with worn old steps, along a twisty passage and down to a low cellar door which the alchemist's wife opened for us. It creaked nastily, and a whiff of foul-smelling smoke drifted out into the cold passage. Jusson and I sensed one another's uneasiness.

There are those who won't go anywhere near an alchemist at work, having a morbid fear of him, believing him a sorcerer; and all that I had heard about alchemists being the Devil's agents came sneaking into my mind as I entered that room. You can never be sure what they can raise by their conjurations, and there are strange stories...Within the world as we know it there is the power of God which is a comfort always; but there is also the Other, and you keep that at bay with wisdom and prayers and don't think about it too much. Deep-down terrors, unseen in the daytime, are uncomfortably recalled at moments like these – fears lurking in the corners of your mind like Alkanet's hagridden roots, making you a prey to demons. Such thoughts plagued me as we stood there on the threshold: it was my own dread that was disturbing me, not the sight in front of me.

The alchemist was standing beside a sizzling furnace, its glow giving his face an odd bright sheen. He was an oldish man with long white hair and a loose robe, a wild unkempt carelessness in his appearance.

There were smaller furnaces attached to the larger ones by tubes and pipes and metal bars, and above each one hung containers and casks bubbling and frothing and hissing, giving off smoke and fumes, coloured air and pungent smells. The white hot embers and blue flames made weird light patterns, so that the room seemed like a strange cave. Upon the benches close by, the instruments he used were lit up oddly, catching glints of amber light. There were heaps of huge old books, and in the further shadows mysterious shapes that I didn't care to probe into. That room was an eerie place and I didn't like it. To me it spelt all the unwisdom of tampering with the unknown.

The alchemist never raised his eyes. But there was another man in the room, a friar, who noticed our entrance immediately and looked straight at us. What I saw jolted me into sudden alarm. It was simply that when a man wears a friar's garb, in spite of Angilbert and others who bring ridicule to their station, you expect to see a benign and welcoming countenance. Even Angilbert had a certain foolish boyishness. But this friar had the most startling unfriar-like face which shocked me before I had time to laugh at my simplicity; after all, a man couldn't help his face, and if he wanted to become a friar he couldn't then develop a mild and saintly appearance at will.

The friar and I seemed to be summing each other up. I could almost feel him thinking: vagrant, Saxon, use in such a way...I was uncharitable, I know, but if ever I took an instant dislike to somebody it was to him. It was not that I had any premonition of the trouble he was going to cause me; it was an animal ill-will, to do with his strong dark handsome face with its black brows and vicious green eyes, and the lean dancer-like form that his garb only enhanced. It was to do with the lurch of my guts as I knew I desired him, and the difficulty I had pretending I didn't.

The woman said: 'My husband Jerome and his assistant Roger Fortunatus. Jerome, here are two people to see you.'

The alchemist looked up briefly. The brews hissed and gurgled as if they were alive. We were of no interest to him; he could barely focus upon us. We must have seemed unreal. He peered irritably in our direction and made a vague bow.

'Roger can see to them.'

I looked hesitantly at the wife.

'It's quite all right,' she assured me. 'Roger is like one of the family. He knows everything about my husband's work. He's very diligent. He'll help you.'

Roger came towards us. 'You can trust me,' he said, gripping my hand in a strong firm grasp.

'You put me at a disadvantage,' I answered. 'I have a commission for an alchemist and plainly you are not he. I wonder if I should give it to you. It's not for myself; I wouldn't like to make a mistake.'

Roger laughed. 'Very mysterious. You've succeeded in arousing all our interests. But fear not; I can help, whatever it is. In truth, I'm more reliable than Jerome, who is so engrossed in his Great Work that he would certainly give you something else by error. So what is it that you seek?'

'Go on,' said Jusson. 'Give it him; it doesn't matter who takes it.'

I handed over the sealed letter. It was all out of my hands now. I'd done what she asked.

Roger read it thoughtfully. I watched him. He wore the clerical tonsure but his hair was very long for a priest, and thick and dark. His robe was Benedictine black – how well it suited him! Upon his forefinger he wore a gold ring shaped like a snake, twined round an amber stone big as a carbuncle. No priest's ring, that! With us all waiting there, and nobody speaking, the throbbing sounds of the dark experiments filled the room uncannily loudly, and Roger's face became part of the writhing shadows, chalky white, hollowly black, like something supernatural. I had to shake myself from crazy fancies; after all, I must have looked the same, and I didn't feel at all supernatural, far from it.

'Well, this is straightforward enough,' he said. 'I can fix these for you. Would you like to come back for them later? I have to prepare them first.

Jusson fidgeted somewhat quickly towards the door; he was as ready as I was to be gone. There was money in the letter, and Roger gave it to the alchemist's wife. She looked very grateful, and I felt that we were henceforth welcome. We agreed to return towards nightfall.

Instead of simply receiving a package, we found that when we returned to the alchemist's house we were treated like guests. The wife had prepared for us a good meal, and she urged us so kindly to stay and eat with them that we were happy to accept. At the table were the woman, whose name was Marget, Roger, Jusson and myself. They made a great fuss of us as if our goodwill was important. Jusson at once unwound and settled down to return their friendliness. Even I found that animal suspicion only goes so far, and I began to half forget what it was about Roger that I found so disquieting.

'Doesn't your husband come to the meal?'

'Oh no, you'd hardly believe it if I told you the seriousness of his dedication. He never leaves his room. He even sleeps there! He feels that one day the breakthrough will occur and we shall be rich.'

'He is after the Philosopher's Stone, I suppose,' I said.

'Indeed. And what it has cost us already is immeasurable,' she sighed. 'You've seen the children – barefoot; you've seen the house – threadbare. Would you believe it, we were once fairly well off, respected and respectable. Our neighbours were glad to visit us. Now see us – all our money has gone into his experiment; creditors hammer on the door, and as for ourselves we are totally ignored by him. It's terrible to see him eaten up so, a man who was once clever and useful. If it were not for Roger I don't know what we'd do.'

Roger looked diffident and changed the course of the conversation.

'Do you know what's involved in Jerome's work?' he asked.

'A little. Something about four elements.'

'The learning comes from Asia Minor,' he explained. 'And the four elements you've heard about were discovered by the Greeks. All matter is made up of earth, water, fire and air. All substances are of four qualities: hot and damp, cold and dry. By certain processes it becomes possible to change the composition of matter. As you know, cold wet water can be changed into hot damp air. Alchemists know the secrets of more significant changes. They believe they can break down each substance into its essence – all they need is the right agent to effect the change. The master agent is called the Philosopher's Stone. Using that, base metals can be transformed into silver or gold, common matter turned into the elixir of life. The possibilities would be endless.'

'But could it be done?' I said.

'I begin to think not,' said Roger. 'I have stood beside Jerome this long while; the work seems to lead only to dead ends and disappointments.'

'Oh, don't say that!' begged the wife. 'You told me you had some faith in it. Our whole future depends on his success. I couldn't bear it if all our suffering was to be for nothing. As for Jerome, he'd sink into despair.'

100

'No,' said Roger soothingly. 'After all, he isn't merely seeking an easy fortune. He's wanting to understand the parallel between mankind and the physical world. He will be satisfied by knowledge even if it doesn't entirely turn out as he expects.'

'But isn't alchemy dangerous?' I wondered. 'Some people have a deal of fear about it.'

'Well, some people are fools,' said Roger bluntly. 'It's true that there is much about learning which alarms the superstitious. Some people don't even feel happy about the use of numbers simply because they come from the Orient. It's the same with astronomy. It has nothing to do with magic or devils, yet some people get very alarmed by the signs and symbols, things that are not strange when they are understood. They're merely a language whereby one magus communicates with another. And if people are silly enough to fear such, then they are fools, I say.'

'Yet they do,' we agreed.

'Well,' said Roger cheerfully. 'Some fear it; but others seek it out for their own benefit, and that's something we're often thankful for. We've had many a good meal out of someone's credulity, haven't we, Marget?'

She looked uncomfortable. 'Perhaps you shouldn't say,' she began.

'Oh these two are not shockable,' said Roger confidently. 'They know enough about the world's shifts not to be surprised if we look after ourselves. Our wrongdoing is very mild. It's just that we have taken a little gold from people who were ready to give it, believing it'll be popped in the pot with the bubbling lead and will all turn into shining wealth. Of course, we did tell them it may take some time, and that it may not work at all. It's been a bit tricky when they've wanted to see the brew, but we've been all right so far. This is not Jerome, of course,' he added. 'Only me.'

And he plied us with good wine; and Marget withdrew, and it seemed we were all getting to be great friends. I had given up wondering whether I liked him or not. He would come out with a remark of careless callousness, such as boasting that he deluded men into parting with their gold: a trickster, I decided. But his traveller's tales impressed me for I do admire a yarn, and he'd met Blondel de Nesle in a low tavern in Paris and learnt magic from an English magus in Toledo. Then he said nobody knew who really had lain with Christ's mother, and I despised him for his childish wish to shock. Then he said all Normans were unscrupulous land grabbers, and I agreed with him; then he said that people's weaknesses should

101

be played on by superior minds, and I mistrusted him greatly. Then he said I must have led a merry life and that I interested him as being not of common stock – and then I liked his good judgement. All of which showed more about my tipsy confusion than Roger's character.

He asked me to talk about myself, but I would not, and suggested instead that he talk. He was very happy to do that. I think it might have been his favourite matter; there was a strong feeling of vanity in the things he said.

No, I did not like him, over all.

VII

IT SEEMED that the entire town could talk of nothing else – Château Gaillard had fallen to the French!

That great bastion built upon a mighty crag, so lovingly cherished by King Richard, was lost to us, taken by King Philip Augustus, that fat Frenchman who only rode gentle horses. How could it have happened? It was said the French had dug a hole through the wall of the keep and weakened its foundations, and then battered the wall with siege engines till they forced their way in, with hand to hand fighting all over the courtyard. We had been quite wrong about Philip Augustus; he was not a buffoon at all. Suddenly he assumed an alarming new importance. To be sure, he left the Crusades early and Richard stayed to fight – but who was dead now and who was alive? It seemed his whole ambition was to drive us out of Normandy and take that land for France. Now he had Château Gaillard – surely he would make for Rouen next. And then what? I forget who it was first said that from Normandy it would be but a small step to conquer England. After all, it had been done before! Rumours quickly spread. Had Philip Augustus set his aim on England? Were we to see another Hastings? In our own time?

And while we marvelled and doubted and listened to every traveller who had news, the Winter crept away, and Spring came to the town.

I have said that in a town the sky makes no difference; the house tops hide the seasons. Of course, this is not true. It was the remark of a cold and footsore traveller. The approach of Spring is always wonderful. If, in the town, it is not so apparent by budding leaves and new little flowers, it shows itself by the light in the air, the

102

warmth on the cheeks, and the smiles of people no longer numb with cold.

It was plain enough to see that Roger Fortunatus had grown tired of the alchemist and his wife. The arrival of Jusson and myself was welcome to him, and since he was lively company, we were glad enough to pass some time with him.

One holiday we went to a fair in the Smithfield meadows outside the city walls. I was in good spirits because I was going to buy a packhorse, and fairs are much more fun if you have some money. I owed it mostly to Berenice's silver, but saving, small-time cheating and gambling had helped. It wasn't one of those big fairs that go on for weeks and are full of foreign merchants; but there was a lot going on besides the selling of everyday items – jugglers, fortune tellers, wrestling and archery, and of course much pickpocketing.

We were looking forward to playing a trick. Roger had got himself up as a magician, in a weird outfit, a long robe with stars on it, and a tall pointed hat. His tonsure was quite hidden and his long hair flowed down his shoulders. I was startled and impressed by his appearance. He reminded me of someone, some picture I had seen, but I couldn't place it. I suppose the setting wasn't right, for the thing I had in mind was certainly wicked although I couldn't remember how; and I knew this mysterious figure was only Roger.

There were so many people there that I thought the whole of London had turned out to the meadows. We found a good pitch and then I began to call out and shout to the people that a miracle was about to be performed. The crowd was in good humour; the day was warm and sunny; we had an audience circled about us in no time. Jusson was wearing a white hood over his head, with slits for his eyes. Since leaving Cortle he had been attending daily to his face with Alkanet's potion and now he was smooth-skinned. No beauty, but greatly improved!

'You all know this man,' I called. 'You know his fearful story. Jusson! Jusson the Leper!'

They gasped and shrank back. Some of them knew him, and those who remembered his leprosy muttered amongst themselves and passed the story around.

I called for silence. I introduced Doctor Radulfus from Arabia, who had read the Lost Books of Ancient Lore in a mountain pass beyond a fiery desert. Roger looked frightening. He raised his arms in the air, and in the uneasy silence he spoke in a beautiful vibrant voice. He told them he had travelled the world by ship, on horseback, by camel train; and he had learned healing from a master who lived as a hermit in a faraway country. He would lay hands upon Jusson and he would be whole.

They were drawn. They watched Jusson kneel at his feet, and Roger laid his hands upon Jusson's head and murmured an incantation. It must have been Latin. It sounded much like what Angilbert said at mass. I do know it made me feel uncomfortable because it sounded so true and holy, and of course it was a trick. I could well imagine him as a priest. His voice was fervent, intense and sensuous. He could have made church services sound sacred. I felt credulous and simple; I had to remind myself that it was only Roger.

At last he gently drew off the white hood and raised Jusson to his feet. Spellbound, the crowd gaped and gasped. Jusson turned to them, a foolish look of joy upon his face.

'I am healed!' he shouted.

Then he flung himself at Roger's feet, kissing his robe and blubbering thanks. Roger revelled in it. He stood there tall and splendid, accepting the homage. I began to find it loathsome.

Before the afternoon was out he had been urged to drive out an evil spirit, had prayed for rain, blessed some water, cursed a demon, promised good fortune, and arranged for all sorts of small illnesses to be gone by next week. In each case he had been grateful to receive a payment, and promised we'd drink well that night.

I bought my little horse, a strong sturdy beast entirely suitable for his purpose. Comfrey I called him, for my mind was never far away from things to do with herbs, and like that plant my horse was useful, rough and shaggy. I arranged for his stabling and met up again with Roger and Jusson. We had a good evening out, and went back to the alchemist's to sleep.

Roger had a bare little room under the eaves there, and the three of us went up the stairs somewhat the worse for wine. Marget, standing with a lanthorn and looking out for Roger so she could lock up, gave us all a withering look. I had the feeling we were not much welcome in her house now.

As we sprawled out to sleep, the only light a wedge of moonlight from a window-slit, there was a restlessness about us brought about by that odd stirring which in springtime lets a man know he had best be moving on.

'I shall go back to my shop tomorrow,' said Jusson. 'Ha! When the news of my cure gets around I'll have a deal more trade than ever.'

'And I'll be off to Cortle,' I said. In the corner of the room, wrapped in a little package, the ingredients Berenice had asked for lay gathering dust.

'Ah – the mysterious mixture,' said Roger, uncomfortably guessing my thoughts. 'What's in it for you, pedlar? It's a commission from a lady?'

'What's in it for me? I'm to receive gold from the lady's hand when I deliver the package,' I said lightly.

'What's she like?' said Roger curiously.

'Norman.'

'Yes, but more than that. Is she young, beautiful, happy in wedlock?'

'She is the first two; not the third.'

'What kind of beauty is it? Haughty, cold, perhaps, unfriendly?'

'Not at all, no, though she tries to be. I see her as warm and passionate if only she could find a fellow worthy enough. Her husband isn't he. A big pale bloated lout he is, much hated, scorned and laughed at. But she is lovely, though somewhat over-painted. Dark and slender and sad.'

'In all points a lady from romance then!' Roger laughed.

'Yes indeed,' I agreed. 'A knight would do very well to win that one.'

'And I never saw her,' complained Jusson. 'Still, I mustn't grumble about the time I spent at the old hag's house after what she did for me, and I suppose I did have the boy to look at; and he was quite as pretty as any girl.'

'What's this?' Roger teased. 'Is it a Paradise up there? Beautiful women – beautiful boys?'

'Nonsense, Jusson,' I said quickly. 'There's no one there as beautiful as the lady Berenice.'

'Well, I may be a man of simple tastes,' maintained that well-meaning idiot, 'and I know you can't compare a young lad to a lady of the castle. But you forget, while you were up at the castle admiring your beautiful lady I was stuck there with the old woman, and I had plenty of time to see this boy. A sweet and innocent lad, he was, as clear and fresh as a daisy, with hair like spun gold, and gentle ways. I know she kept him hidden away and hooded most of the time, but I couldn't help but notice he was fair. Ah – and nor could you, now I remember! When they had that ceremony, when they wore the antlers, you were all the time beside the boy – I can see you now chatting with him and the old crone beside the cauldron.'

'A ceremony?' Roger asked. 'With antlers? This is all most

intriguing.'

'It's nothing at all,' I snapped. 'Jusson, you are raving.'

'I am not!' protested Jusson reasonably. 'It was the strangest sight I ever saw.'

'Well, that's enough,' I muttered. 'You could get those good people into trouble if the Church found out. They were only having a good time, keeping warm and trying to forget about the Winter.'

'Oh Christ!' said Roger wearily. 'What do you think I am? I'm the last person to go bleating to the Church. I'm all for the old ceremonies. I know something about them – from the books I've read. So! Your villagers know something about the old ways, do they? What do they do? Do they worship the Goddess? Have they rituals to make the crops grow?'

'No,' I said abruptly. 'They're all good Christian people and they go to church.'

'And why are you so cagey about it, I wonder?' Roger said. 'What is this obscure East Anglian village to you?'

I gave in grudgingly. Attempts to put him off only seemed to rouse his interests further. 'It's just a place we visited on our journey,' I shrugged.

'Where the folk follow the old ways.'

'Really it's nothing like you think. They only go to drink the brew and have a laugh.'

'Do they tie scraps of cloth on trees, each cloth a prayer?'

'Oh, nothing so skilful!' I protested.

'But they dance?'

'After a fashion.'

'In a circle?'

'No, all over the place.'

'And embrace?'

'Some do.'

'But not as an old ritual?'

'Of course not.'

I was becoming annoyed and defensive.

'They simply have a good time,' I said.

Roger then laughed.

'But what a waste,' he said. 'They have all they need for the true magic and they don't use it. Like having a tool you can't understand and therefore you miss the benefits. Do they drink aconite and belladonna?'

'No I don't think so,' I said. 'Alkanet did tell me; but they were mostly wholesome herbs to induce wellbeing without harm.'

106

'But they don't know what they're missing,' declared Roger. 'It would be much more satisfying with the potent herbs. Heady sensations, floating, wonderful irresponsibility, excitement. Bats' blood, I've heard, added to it.' He drifted off, presumably picturing it all. I said nothing. I didn't like his interest in Cortle.

'Bat's blood?' Jusson sniggered sleepily. 'This is all too much for me.' And he noisily dozed off.

As we settled down to join him, Roger said quietly: 'Pedlar, do you know what you have in the package for your lady of the manor?'

'No,' I said.

'You have the ingredients for a very ancient spell. A murder spell. The victim is to die by wasting away. Do you still want to take it to her?'

'I must,' I said. 'She was very unhappy and I told her I would come back.'

'It's for the husband, presumably?'

'I suppose so.'

'I wondered whether you knew what she was asking for,' Roger continued. 'You were somewhat secretive when we met. I must admit that it aroused my interest, and I very soon recognised what her list meant. There is much in her situation to draw a person.'

'Yourself, you mean?'

'I suppose you would not permit me to take the package?'

'I ought not. She commissioned me, and I need to go again to Cortle anyway. It's a place I know well; I stock up with all the best herbs there to sell in the southern towns.'

'Would you allow me to come with you?'

I knew he was going to ask me that. I felt that it was quite beyond me to foresee what effect the presence of Roger would have on that giddy situation. I wondered whether perhaps he could do some good for Berenice, maybe. It was, after all, in Berenice that he seemed to show his interest. He had not seemed much bothered about Marel.

'Why do you want to come?' I asked.

'I'm bored with Jerome and Marget. I'm bored with London. I want to breathe some country air, and see whether the lady at the castle wants an errant knight.'

'After all, it is Spring,' I agreed. 'I don't mind your coming. I would prefer a promise from you that you don't meddle with the villagers' interests, and confine yourself to what's going on at the castle.'

'But of course it's the castle that interests me,' he protested. 'A sad and beautiful damsel, an idiot husband, the cruel walls that bind her, the desperate plot...these call to me like the substance of an old romance.'

'I was thinking of leaving tomorrow.'

In the middle of the night, sleeping restlessly, I was jolted out of sleep by Roger calling out and sitting up, wild-eyed and dishevelled, with the moonlight on him.

'What's the matter?' I asked, alert at once. He was shivering, covered in sweat, and eerily white in that firm glow from the

'I had a dream,' he gasped, quite unlike his usual swaggering self. Cold and shaking he grabbed my wrist.

'You've no idea,' he whispered. 'Sometimes I am so scared. God will punish me. I feel Him after me, demanding the fulfilment of the vows I made. In the night I'm afraid He'll come and claim me, and make me do in the afterlife what I won't do now. With punishment and revenge.'

'Oh no,' I said. 'God isn't cruel.'

'He is, he is,' groaned Roger.

Well, I stroked his hair, spoke gentle words, and comforted him as best I could. And suddenly I remembered what it was that Roger had reminded me of – the wicked image, the disturbing recollection. It was the painting on the wall at Cortle church, the painting of the Devil, which disturbed me every time I saw it, for I guessed the artist held a sneaking regard for that dark personage, and had created something of strange beauty – green-eyed, black-haired, and handsome, though his mouth was cruel, his manner terrible.

And then I laughed uneasily – for what was Roger but a man with troubled dreams, who now lay in my arms, whom now I soothed to sleep?

FOUR
Roger's Tale

I

BORN ON the festival of Imbolg, in a God-bereft village over in the west, I, Roger, was the son of a woman with long black hair whose way of worship was the way of the Goddess. The rituals of the Goddess have to do with fire and water and the moon. Too young to understand their meanings I remember instead the heat of the leaping flame, the white and nubile glow of candles embedded in moist earth; the eerie moon – Maid, Mother, Crone – who watched our celebrations, silvering the surface of the mere; the sky the underbelly of a great raven; the forked trees black as burnt parchment; and the darting bats that brushed against the bending bodies of the folk within the conjured circle.

My mother by day worked in the fields, a thin and dirty peasant, ugly even, for she had buck teeth like a hare and she was very dark; but she possessed that strange and inexplicable fascination that those who do not comprehend must call magic. Hedgerow potions gave her powers. She smelt of herbs. I thought her beautiful, and others did also. Gifts were brought to her, some of them rich and exotic – these came from the castle: carved ivory boxes, rings and furs. Such things were brought by men on horseback. I ached with envy for their arrogance. Their horses' hooves trampled our plants with superb carelessness, splendidly unaware. They circled about the vile hut where we lived, till the springing leaves were flattened in a mire of mud; their horses drank from the butt where we collected rain. Sometimes I was lifted up and sat astride a lofty strutting horse, never questioning why it was these gleaming giants should show an interest in a scrawny peasant lad, but well enough aware that the distance between horse and ground was the distance between power and penury. After such visits there would be gifts left – meat, white bread, wine, hoods of beaver – and in the aftermath my mother would clutch me to her, saying: 'Never fear, the Lord shall not have you; you belong to the Goddess and you are Her child'; and we would cut cloth scraps to tie upon the tree within the grove, and circlets of oak leaves and holly.

By day I picked stones from the soil, up and down the furrows in all weathers, endless flints and jagged pebbles into heaps to make the plough's way easier; and I threw stones at flocks of birds that dropped upon our crops. It would have dawned on me soon enough that this was not the life I wished to lead. However, others thought so too, and I was spared the necessity of running away at an early age to what would certainly have been a life of equal hardship.

One day the lord came back, dismounting from his horse to find us sitting on the ground inside the hut. He pulled aside the goatskin and let in sunlight which fell on me warm and dusty. How we must have seemed to him, as we squatted there in the dark, picking at bits of rag, twining shreds of straw, binding cloth upon a sheaf of oats to call Brid to come amongst us!

'This must stop,' he murmured gravely. 'This cannot be for him.'

'No!' shrieked the woman, understanding what he meant. 'He is given to the Mother. He will never be the Lord's.'

But he took me away nevertheless, and I went unresisting. I knew well enough that his way led to the castle, and though it was not wealth as such that I yearned for, I understood where lay the power. The ways of the Goddess were the shabby ring of huts, the rags tied to the tree, the backbending toil of the fields; and so I chose the God. This meant I must break my links with the village and never go back, at first because they told me not to, and then because I did not wish it.

I have no feeling for the land. I have always lived in the present. I bear no grudges to the Saxons for having overrun the Celtic lands. No one owns the land; she owns herself. The old races were weaker and withdrew; the new settled in their place. What's that to me? I wasn't there. Why add to suffering by dwelling on what's gone? My early years were past; I looked to what was to come. It was the urge for wider knowledge drove me; that is a greater issue than who owns the land.

I lived at the castle on an uneasy footing, taking readily to the word of the Lord as taught me by a worthy monk named Hubert, along with the skills of literacy both in French and English. Always cherishing a strong feeling of my own worth it seemed reasonable enough to me that castle folk should suddenly wish to nurture and

110

educate me – cleaned up, I was a personable brat, dark-eyed and eager, not at first comprehending why the sons in wedlock took against me so. I survived several fights with this wholly Norman pair, but when their sister began to take an interest in me of a different nature it was judged best to think once again about my situation.

Elise was her name, a big pale fair-haired maiden, and she'd stand behind me as I studied Bede's *Lives of the Abbots* till the plaits of her long hair brushed the sides of my face and the warmth from her body raised the hairs on my neck, and she told me I was going to be very handsome when I grew to man's estate. That she was right was deemed no justification for such forward mien; and still at an early age I found myself in conversation of a sober sort with that great lord who now I understood to be my father.

A heavy grizzled knight, he came one day to the little sloping table where I was copying out *The Dream of the Rood*. That I was very young and in a state of innocence can be surmised as I reveal that it was May and that the warm breeze from the window arch that stirred the parchment's edge brought me no thoughts of Love and eagerness to be out in the fields, no, merely was I taken with the Love of the Cross for the Hero whose body he bore; in those days I was constantly aware of matters spiritual.

'You are happy in this kind of work,' my father said, a certain dubiousness belying the conviction of his statement.

I assured him that I was, the fervency in my voice assuaging his remaining doubts about the wisdom of his coming proposition. What did I know of anything? That fervency was born of gratitude for his having taken me away from stone picking in the frost-hard furrow.

'Very well,' he murmured nodding. 'Then it will be for the best.'

A swathe of fox fur from his trailing sleeve brushed across the parchment, lightly smudging all that I had written. For the powerful and worldly, learning in itself has little beauty, other than a symbol or a means. He did not notice.

'There can never be a question of inheritance,' he told me. 'You shall be a monk. Hubert will take you to the abbey. You'll learn Latin, live in peace and stillness and illuminate fine manuscripts. You'll understand the finer skills of learning. You think that we have works of knowledge here, but no!' Convincing himself rapidly he warmed to his theme. 'There is much more in the libraries of the Church – all that has been discovered since the written word was passed about amongst us.'

111

I don't recall that God was mentioned; but the finer skills of learning tempted me and I needed no persuasion. Relieved, I suspect, he smiled and patted my shoulder.

'In later days,' he said benevolently, 'you'll thank me, for the world has nothing to offer an illiterate Celt who prays to scraps of rag on oak trees.'

There is some truth in that, would you not say? The certainty of that expunged the guilt he surely should have felt as he condemned me to a life of celibacy before I had experienced stirrings of a carnal kind or knew the words for what my body would one day discover. This act of seeming kindness now seems to me comparable with many acts of cruelty I have witnessed since, for he was a man who revelled in the consolation of the flesh, and knowing its delights consigned his son to do without, and cast him to the barren winds of purity.

I ran eagerly to embrace them.

A Benedictine abbey it was, far off and farther south, pleasant and enlightened, the kind of place that makes austere Cistercians rent what hair they have; and for the next few years I swear I was devout.

I was given with all ceremony to the Church, brought to the altar, and my right hand wrapped in the altar cloth. Brother Ailred received me on behalf of the abbey and made the sign of the cross above my head. Then I had to have my hair cut and I was sprinkled with holy water. Psalms were sung and I was given a monkish habit and cowl. It was a good way of life and it was the one I wanted, the life of the scholar. I wasted no time over sadness for I have always been one to understand when a way of life was over, and as easily as any little worm I cast the old one from me like a shrivelled skin for which I had no further use.

In cloister and in chapter I was taught with other boys. We were taught with an intensity born of the fact that learning was a jewel to be both jealously guarded and to blaze in its own illumination; therefore as recipients of its richness we were blessed indeed. Nor was there any scarcity of beatings for any laziness or lapse – the brother who instructed us used a birch rod to bring home his meaning, and for our offences it was *vae natibus* – woe to the buttocks! At night we slept in the dorter under the benign rule of the Master of the Boys, brother Ailred who first received me. I never understood why we were forbidden to touch. We had to sit with space between us, and in the dorter masters with impeccable

112

reputations and dull characters lay between us boys and made sure each one kept his distance. No matter, all my leanings were towards the spiritual. The discipline of the abbey and the discipline of God blended for me in a manner that satisfied. The way of the Goddess I found easy to abandon, for rather than a religion it seemed the primitive outpourings of the unkempt.

Yet now it is only with some disbelief that I recall that we would rise two hours after midnight and live a day that framed itself within the services of the church, and three of those before daybreak. It seemed to me that those grey walls enclosed all that was needed for a rich existence – the love of God, the pursuit of learning, the fellowship of brothers. In seeking harmony of spirit we worked together in activities as diverse as making books and keeping bees and growing crops, and we read all that we could lay our hands on.

The books we had there were a joy to me, not only for what they contained – the words of Saint Jerome, the Blessed Gregory, Boethius – but for the vellum on which they were written, with its own particular smell, handled lovingly for more than a hundred years. The north wall of the cloister was our place of study, where a row of little carrel niches housed a bench and desk and precious solitude.

In Summer I would sneak off to the haymeadow and read books I had hidden in my sleeve, while bees droned in the clover heads. Then as each new truth dawned upon me I would feel as if I were a traveller in some small bark on an enchanted sea, discovering golden islands ringed with translucent clouds, each one a place of wonder, each one seeming to be a haven for the hungry soul, but proving always to be merely a stepping-stone towards the world's horizon, other islands beckoning.

In Winter I would sit over some manuscript, a heap of candles burned to flattened stubs of tallow. One January night I was found weeping by that kind old brother Hubert who had first brought me here.

'There isn't time...' I snivelled. 'All that has been thought about the world and written down, all that has been discovered, and which I must understand... a man's life is not long enough...'

'I know, I know.' he soothed me. 'Look,' he said in vexation and caring, 'you are near frozen solid.'

Nor could I move. Unnoticed, snow had blown in steadily and fallen on one side of me so that the cloth of my robe had stiffened into points as hard as wood. Meticulously he rubbed my limbs till I could walk and muttered over me and shook his head, marvelling that anyone could suffer so for the sake of learning; but for me it had been the pains of love.

I had no difficulty deciding that this was the life for me, and took my irrevocable vows of poverty, chastity and obedience with no misgivings.

It is so long since I have been an innocent that it seems strange to contemplate a time when looks or touch or cynical observation would have passed me by. If I was ever desired I did not know it, and if there were hints or references made at any time I did not understand them. What I did not know was that Ailred the brother into whose hands I had been given had marked me for his own, and with a curious purity of intention, had nurtured me through boyhood till we might meet equally as men who knew each other's mind. Prospective advances from other sources he had staved off with his influence. I supposed him merely a thoughtful mentor, sleek and dark, cultured and highborn, and with a natural elegance; he was all those things.

Those demons that made us fall asleep in church or sing off-key or over-eat, which may be labelled merely Sloth or Gluttony, are nothing to the demon with no name who comes and shows us wasted opportunity, deeds done too late or early through unknowing. That demon lay in wait for me, a mischievous dancer behind the cloister arch, beyond the shadows of the steep, cold night-stair, and in the silences of the stone-rimmed moonlight.

There came a spate of visions, an outbreak rife as any communal digestive upset after pork. No doubt the first were genuine. I myself had visions – mine were very dreary: voices telling me I was a chosen instrument, and pointing fingers showing me a straight and narrow path; indeed this heavenly prompting was a direct contribution to making my complete commitment. But several brothers started to see women.

'Naked she was – her clothes had been torn from her – they lay in a little crumpled heap, a white shift and a yellow gown. Five soldiers were about her, each one with a sword in his hand, the red blood dripping from the blade. The nearest soldier seized her by the hair. Thick flowing hair she had, and very shining. I saw the sword lifted up. And I awoke to pray.'

'You have surely seen a virgin martyr!'

'Who could it have been? Saint Catherine? Saint Winifred?'

There was much discussion. Unfortunately that brother could furnish no more details, but within a day or so a luckier dreamer saw

Saint Cecily, and he knew it was her for the poor soul was in her bath, the bath wherein she had been put to death by drowning. And would you believe it, she was as naked as the other! He saw each luscious breast – round as rosy apples, he explained – indeed all her charms were visible, for, strangely enough there was not much water in the lady's tub. How white her skin was, yet how dark her maiden hair...He likewise woke to pray.

In the morning it transpired that several of the others had had visions. Suddenly sleep became a mysterious excitement, for we knew not what awaited us there. We seemed to have developed a curious facination for what Saint Bernard of Clairvaux called 'the dungheap of the flesh'. Next day, in garden and in cloister the word would go about as to who had had the vision last, and we would go to hear it, and in telling us the dreamer would elaborate all he had seen, almost as if he knew what we required and would oblige.

'But her waist was small?'

'I could have spanned it with my two hands.'

'And yet her hips were slender?'

'Like a reed.'

'I would have preferred them wide.'

'They were wide! I had forgot. She was at first in shadow, but then she turned, and, yes, the hips were wide. And the buttocks large.'

'Yet firm, not pendulous at all?'

'Indeed, very firm. In no way pendulous. One might have patted them and felt no heaviness at all. And if she were to bend, there would be a certain tautness. A handprint raised in chatisement would have left a neat clear mark, upon skin so very white, and flesh so delicate and smooth.'

And then there came a startling aberration. Brother Ranulf had a vision of a youth! The interest quickened. We all must hear.

'Slim and golden-haired – hardly more than a boy – his chest all smooth – the muscles of his arms straining in his bonds – his hands were bound behind him, on his face a look of anguish...'

'He was naked?' (We must know this important fact.)

'Of course he was naked!' Brother Ranulf said in mortification. We breathed again.

'And there were soldiers. Roman soldiers, driving him with bloodied swords. A thin trickle of crimson, the colour of the holly berry, marred his white skin.'

'And his hair was gold?'

'As the sun. Yes! *All* his hair was gold!'

115

We digressed, ascertaining whether it had been Saint Florus, who was flung down a well, or Saint Sebastian, who died transfixed with arrows. It was not Sebastian, for next night Brother Ailred stayed asleep long enough to see the arrows and the tree, and thus no time was wasted in mere speculation – Sebastian was not golden-haired.

'He was dark and slender, and his eyes were green. His arms were bound above his head, his back was arched. His lips were parted in a cry of pain. He was above common handsome. He was in looks not much unlike Brother Roger...I would have thought them cousins.'

I did not miss the curious gazes that now followed this revelation. That night I indulged in what the church calls 'intentional pollution' with myself, and found it very satisfying.

Visions followed thick and fast, both male and female. Retaining still some innocence I was not blessed with one myself, but I was happy to hear the accounts of others. And now my choice of reading matter never was philosophy and history as before, but always Pagan literature, which in that abbey we had in some profusion – *Dido and Aeneas*, *The Trojan War* with the story of Helen, and Ovid's *Art of Love*. I knew that Saint Jerome said that the songs of the poets were the food of demons, but this was the food I relished. Visions of virgin martyrs I did not have, but I had very troubled dreams, and woke in great confusion, not always to pray. I fell in love with Dido. At all times of the day, in circumstances when my mind should have been on the Scriptures I pictured her – her loneliness, her beauty, her passion, her despair. I imagined comforting her. If only I had been there... if only she were real.

It was not long before the demon waiting for me put it in my head that outside in the world were women much like Dido, and they were real enough. In towns, in villages, in England or in France, in castle and in market square there were women, women such as had been seen in visions by the monks, with breasts like rosy apples and tiny waists and full ripe hips and long lush hair that one might twine in a handclasp; maidens in meadows, merry girls in green gardens, lonely wives awaiting consolation; and for personable youths of marriageable age a wealth of opportunity lay wasting. But not for me, for I was there within the abbey, destined to devote myself to God.

How well the ancient writer so described it! 'The sirens have the faces of women because nothing so estrangeth the heart from the love of God as the faces of women.' Faces? For there was more to women, was there not, than faces! And other monks than I had known the secret torments I endured, as could be seen from rules laid down to deal with them. 'He who intentionally becomes polluted in his sleep shall get up and sing seven psalms and live on bread and water for that day; but if he does not do this he shall sing thirty psalms. But if he desired to sin in sleep but could not, fifteen psalms; if however he sinned but was not polluted, twenty four; if he was unintentionally polluted, fifteen.'

Sustained by vivid imaginings of myself and Dido – taking ship to Italy and lying on the sunny deck in long embraces, hand in hand till we sank down in the many-scented flowers, in a bed beneath a blanket on a winter's night – I daresay I might have survived this metamorphosis and grown to placid equanimity in time. But further trials awaited me to fan the flames of my burgeoning desires. Three new monks joined us. Brother Peter and Brother John were sons of a rich man, sickened by the excesses and artificialities of the outside world, young as myself, yet world-weary already, satiated with the pleasures they had known and longed to relinquish. Brother Tobias was an older man, a reformed philanderer, who had savoured of excesses all his life, and now intended seeking his salvation while he could.

I was drawn to all three. I found them spellbinding. The sun upon us, we would sit against the wall within the cloister, and I would glean from them the tales I yearned to hear.

The two youths answered with unnatural disgust.

'Oh! Do not ask us, Roger! If you only knew the filthiness of this vile world...how blessed are you in this holy place! Here there is only the sound of the church bells' sonorous chime, and the buzzing of bees, and the mellifluous voices of the choir. Out there is the din and racket of the streets, the yells of the pedlars who cheat you at every turn, and the garish musicians with their raucous music, and the girls in the doorways, with hideous whorish laughter...'

'...tempting you with the thrust of their bosom, the curve of their thighs, their scarlet painted mouths – Jezebel and Lilith are in abundance, dragging you down as the tenuous water weeds reach out for the solitary vessel...'

I gasped. 'And have you ever – ? Did you – ? Were you tempted?'

'That has been my downfall. I remember the first time I lay with a whore, a ramshackle bed it was, in a dark little room, and a villainous blackguard at the door to take my money and hurry me away so that others might follow! And she, with hair as black as old rope, all tangled and crawling with lice, her cheeks fat and brown, and her body a big warm thing where I drowned in her sweetness, her foulness...' Thus Brother Peter. And John, stirred by the chords

117

in his own recollection, continued: 'My first was no street whore, but the wife of a friend of my father. Twice my age she was, and considered a beauty. Yet much of that beauty was false, for she painted her face; and her wonderful hair so praised of many was twined about with hair from another that cunningly joined her own with strands of beads. Her eyes were all-knowing, with the secrets of the earth in them. She was tired of her old husband and I was a virgin boy, clean-limbed and fresh. We were alone one winter afternoon in a chamber in the castle. I could not go riding for I had hurt my back in a fall, and I lay resting, she with her tapestry. She eyed me as a vixen might a rabbit. Then she came across to me, sat down beside me, fondled me. She stroked my brow and said sweet things to me. She placed her hand upon my privities and so manipulated my shaft that it grew stiff and hard, yet I myself grew weak as water. Then she made us both lie down, and she showed me where to put my hand to please her, which I did, and of a sudden then before I knew it I was in her, taking and receiving pleasures – yet I swear it had not been my intent. And thus I say, mistrust women! For my good sense told me that she was old and false, and yet she so magicked me that she could do with me as she would and I was helpless. Thus was Adam tempted and I well believe it. You are fortunate, Roger, to know nothing of the snares of womankind!'

'But how was it?' I stammered urgently. 'Was it so wonderful? Was it akin to Paradise?'

'I am ashamed to say it was.'

Brother John's reply in no way eased my yearnings. Then Brother Peter sniggered: 'And it did not help your backache, I daresay!' and they laughed together, as two who know what lust can do.

Then they saw my staring crestfallen face and took some pity on me, understanding.

'You have given up nothing,' Peter reassured me. 'Women are nothing compared to the Love of God. How can they be? God speaks to our soul, our spirit. We become as angels; we become as we were meant to be. A woman is of earth, with all the earth's vileness. Earth is decay and change and filth, putrefaction, dung. In consort with a woman you become as she – a rotting beast that wallows in the stinking mire of his own lusts. Only in conjunction with the spirit can we attain to purity. This must be the aim of every man, for thereby he becomes a portion of the Father.'

I shivered. I suddenly recalled my mother then, the only woman with whom I had been closely bonded, many years ago. I was long

118

since ashamed of her and never spoke of her to anyone. Peter's words were symbolic, and the beast, the rutting, and the stinking mire were nothing actual; yet to me they were, and to my horror I recalled the fetid hovel where I had spent my early days. I saw it clear as if it was around me still: the pigs that sheltered with us, the stench of their excrement, the bare and dirty thigh of the woman, that brushed against my shoulder as I crouched there in the straw. I pressed my fist into my eyes to be rid of the hideous remembrance. Purity! Yes, we must seek purity, the whiteness of the Father, the radiance of his glory that would wash us clean.

'Woman is Lilith,' John agreed. 'Lilith was created before Eve. God made her out of slime. From her body came that which we know as demons. She is the night hag, mother of succubi. She sucks the blood of men who sleep alone, she comes to them in dreams, and in her lewd embraces all their manhood withers.'

'But Dido..' I protested. 'Dido was not so. She was a queen; her love for Aeneas was the sacrifice of self. Surely her love was pure – great and worthy, comparable to the love a man might feel. Surely no man need feel ashamed to return that kind of love?'

'Aeneas left her, did he not?' shrugged John. 'He knew his destiny. Had he remained with Dido, lost in luxury and lust he would not have fulfilled his purpose nor gained fame. A woman saps the strength and holds the hero back, emasculates him, makes him corpulent and soft. The steel of manhood is never tempered in the silk of a woman's embraces. Ugh! I almost vomit when I think of it!'

What did I know of women? The only other one to make impression on my youthful recollection was Elise, the smiling sinuous half-sister at the castle, who had pressed her breasts against my back, and draped her flaxen hair about my neck, a threat so tangible that I had been plucked from her presence and eventually sent here. What power there thus must be in woman's lust, that it should be so feared!

II

THE THIRD monk, Brother Tobias, as a big tall handsome man, much decayed from over-use and somewhat older than myself. His hair was very fair and silvery, his face square and sallow, weak about the chin and fleshy where the skin sagged into jowl. His eyes had a lewd gaze that suddenly glinted when he laughed or lusted, and I saw him do both. He took a fancy to me, I knew it. His skin was roughly pitted, showing the waxy bloom of unhealth. He had a bodily misfortune that caused swelling in his ankles and his fingers. He ached in every part, he told me.

'You see me in decline,' he said. 'Such is the destiny of flesh. I was a handsome figure of a man – '

'You are yet!'

'No – ' he shook his head. 'I'm paunchy now, and yellow – look at this.' He tapped his ample stomach. 'I've lived well and now I'm paying for it. I've travelled. I've lived off the fat of the land. Women – yes, I've had women – Roger, you wouldn't believe the number of women I've had! Or how easy it is to get them into your bed – or beneath a haystack, or behind a barn!' he guffawed. 'There's a great abundance, Roger, of women trapped in castles. Lovely ladies with time on their hands and the itch of lust in their bodies. Their husbands go off to the wars, or maybe they're old men whom policy takes away from home, leaving wives behind them. There they sit, like plums on a tree, ripe and smooth and sweet and moist, awaiting the man who can reach out his hand. They're not the stupid things some men like to believe them, you know, women. Some of them are thinkers, in their way. They're wasted there and they know it. They long to hear of journeys, events, danger and foreign lands. Spin them a story and they're yours. They long to give themselves to a hero worthy of their longings. It's so easy, Roger. It's so easy to win them. You wouldn't believe how easy it was...'

He sank into a reverie, a dream of women, women like plums, dropping into his palm. I looked down at my hand and opened it and cupped it till it made a space whereon a plum might fall; and I too dreamed.

'You see, I was particularly handsome!' Tobias assured me firmly. 'Six foot tall, like King Richard, and my hair the colour of spun gold. I could fight, ride – I was the very devil with a sword – and I could joust, wrestle. Feel that muscle, if you can, through this whoreson cloth.'

I gripped his arm; he groaned and laughed. 'It's but a shadow of what it once was. You would have thought me made of iron when I was your age! Stripped I was a hero. Aeneas – Hector – Lance-lot – I was all three! And – ' his eyes took on an intimate mischievous smile, 'my prick was ten inches long, and that was in repose!' He chuckled, nudging me. 'You don't believe me.'

There we sat, our backs against the sun-warmed wall, the cloister arches mellow in its light. Brother Tobias rolled his robe above his knees, and further.

'Someone might see!'

'What if they do? I was picking lice out, wasn't I? That's all I'm doing. Now – take a look at that, boy. Is it not magnificent, even in its sad state of degeneration?'

'Yes. I've never seen one so big.'

'Quite so. You should have seen it when I was in my full-blown manhood. They told legends of its prowess. They made songs about my potency. Women feared and loved it. Women! Why am I always telling you about women, when after all we have none in here, so what use is that? I've had boys as well, you know, and they are just as good. In some ways,' murmured he, tapping the side of his nose, 'boys are more pleasing. I have travelled, as you know, and I have found the dusty wayside strewn with peasant lads who, for lack of any to instruct them in the intricacies of life's finer propositions, are – to put it briefly – not too clever. So as for little bouts of transitory love they need no persuasion. They do it among themselves, you know; it's natural to them. They know no better...'

There was no question but he had aroused my curiosity, and we both knew it. Henceforth we saw to it that we were together for our tasks about the place. It was the springtime of the year, and warm, and for the first time in my life I felt those rising earth tides as a force within my body. Tobias and I planted seeds in the garden, and hoed and weeded, the sun on our backs, and he watched me with his narrow glinting gaze and wicked grin and shook his head.

'However did you come to take the vows?' he marvelled. 'If ever I saw one whose limbs were framed for love, that one was you.'

'Ignorance sent me here, ignorance on all levels,' I said bitterly, attacking the clumps of earth with the tip of the hoe.

'And what have you learnt?'

'I don't deny the value of my learning. Where else could I have read what I read here – where else could the ideas of civilised man have reached one who was born in a wattle hut? Unfortunately now I begin to learn that I have unwittingly condemned myself to the lack of certain other kinds of knowledge, which now appear to be more needful.'

I drove the hoe so hard against a stone I broke the tool.

'And it's not even permissible to curse it!' said Tobias sympathetically.

'Yet I do not necessarily desire to turn my back on the abbey,' I said, frowning. 'The life of the scholar is one that sits on me easily.

But now I feel such urges in my body that if I do not satisfy them I am like to lose my wits.'

'I would be doing you a kindness,' said Tobias contemplatively, 'if I eased your need.'

'What could you do?' I asked him, wide-eyed, hopeful, disbelieving. It was, I think, the last remark I ever made in innocence.

What could he do? Well, he could lead me to the barn and find us there a nook amongst the hay where sunlight did not reach, and mice and rats went scuttling to their dens, and hopping insects quivered on the rye-grass and the old dry flower-heads.

'This will be my final foray into fleshly pleasures,' said he in the tone of one who made a vow. 'I swear it. After this, pure celibacy ever more. And therefore it must be most special.'

With such a generous preceptor to instruct me I could not fail to learn the ways of love, and without boasting I may say I took to them with brilliance and alacrity. All that may be assayed between one man and another we performed. I learnt to savour the taste of male seed upon my lips and to put my face against the musty warmth of secret hair, while my tongue discovered the delights of close proximity to the dark and unseen places of the body. And I knew what it was to lie against a man, beneath a man, above him, mouth on mouth, while tongues played lewdly in a slavering kiss. And he would prise apart my arse cheeks, teaching me to open to accommodate that awesome prick. Afraid at first I soon lost all my trepidation, and then bold I found a wealth of new sensation richer than the dreams I used to have of Dido, richer most of all because of their reality; and this was what I learnt most sharply under the ministration of this teacher – that actual things are better things than dreams, and then I knew that I would no longer be content with merely dreaming. And so the raucous beauty of my sexual revelations was greatly marred by dread, for I was never one to endure a situation I was eager to cast off.

Sometimes I watched him by the shimmer of many candles, on our knees at prayer in the church. Next year's crop of innocents pursed their youthful lips and sang in sweetness and sincerity: *Sit semper illi gloria, laus et honor. Nos, quesumus, conservet in hac sacra solemnia, canentes – eia! eia!* Brother Tobias knelt there, framed in an aureole of light. His shaggy head now bowed, his massy shoulders hunched, he was every inch a penitent and I do not doubt his prayers were holy. What havoc he had wreaked within my ordered mind! Had the flesh such power then? Was it by the pull of my loins that I would be drawn away from calm and contemplation? Should I not resist it? The ancient saints subdued their flesh by trials, solitary, ascetic, in the crags around the rocky shores, their cells of boulders weather-washed and cold. They stood up to the neck in icy pools until their limbs were beyond sensation, beyond pain, and all the while they uttered psalms. They did this to subdue the recalcitrant body, and I likewise ought to be subduing mine. I should confess my wayward thoughts within the chapter house and do my penance – endure a beating – for Sin was always punished with a beating here. I scowled at Brother Tobias as the root of my confusion; and what was most confusing of all was that I felt suffused with gratitude. God in Heaven, the old goat showed me how to love.

Beneath the church at the base of a dark stairway there lay the crypt. A low-roofed vaulted place it was, formed from blocks of Roman stones, each slab a welter of ancient markings, as if a comb had been drawn across it, and here and there a Latin scrawl, not always of a holy nature. The glimmering of a single candle lit this place with shifting shadow-light. Brother Ailred, himself a shadow disengaging itself from the wider dark, was waiting for me.

'What is this of Brother Tobias?' he hissed. 'Tell me from your own lips. Is it true?'

'What have you heard?' I whispered back. We were alone, but private converse always went in whispers – the angels and demons that sat perched upon carved capitals would soon betray all they might overhear.

'That you and he – it is too vile to mention.' Nevertheless, my fastidious friend mentioned it. He grit his teeth in effort. 'That he has known you carnally!'

I knew that to admit it would be to risk denunciation in the chapter house, and penance, yet a curious recklessness was in me, which I did not understand. I have noticed this strange effect with others also – that if carnal knowledge has been good, the need to share it – even boast about it – overcomes restraint and modesty.

'It's true,' I replied carelessly. 'He taught me pleasure, in the barn.'

'What – everything?' cried Ailred, that serene and dignified monk all suddenly a prurient youth who meets his fortunate friend on the morning afterwards.

'Yes, everything,' I answered with slow satisfaction. 'He has a truly vast – experience.'

'Oh!' Ailred wailed, as if calamity had come to Egypt. He wrung his hands. 'Cruel – cruel truth – '

'On the contrary, a kindness. I certainly have no regret.'

Ailred siezed me by the arms. His fingertips gripped to the bone. 'How could you, Roger?' he whispered, his face close to mine, distorted in the agile dancing of the light. 'He is a sinner of the vilest kind – debauched, depraved – and ageing – you must have known – that *I* – that *I* – '

' — was saving me for yourself,' I answered him with a sneer. My first, I think.

To hear the words so baldly stated disconcerted him, and he became immobile, staring. I released his grip.

'It doesn't matter, Ailred. We can yet be friends. The one does not preclude the other. For you are right – you are a more attractive man than he. So sleek and smooth, so highly born... your skin must be like polished parchment.'

I reached up and touched his face. Lightly I drew his head toward mine until our mouths were touching. I sucked him to me with a kiss. His hunger gratified my vanity. Years of long-smouldering desire were in his response. He clawed my lips with his till his teeth bit. I was excited. I held him hard against me. Such passion was aroused between us that there was no other course than that we must be satisfied. We fumbled in our robes and thrust and struggled in a fierce embrace. But even our groans and gasps were all in whispers, absorbed into the depths of stone around us. Then we drew apart.

I leaned against the wall, impressed at lust's intensity. But Ailred was distressed.

'You do not understand,' he wept, and even his weeping was in whispers. 'This is not what I wanted. I wanted innocence. Love. I nurtured you from boyhood. For higher things. I wanted our love to be pure.'

'I think that you delude yourself,' I said, with reason, for my mouth was bleeding from his passion.

'No!' he quivered accusingly. 'You are not what I first thought. You are not what you seemed. You tempted me like Eve in the Garden. You are the spawn of Lilith. There is the Devil in you.'

Self-loathing made him speak so. I was but an instrument whereby he understood the grossness of his flesh, a man who had thought himself all spirit, who now must bear the burden of his harsh discovery.

'We can be more gentle next time,' I suggested.

He spluttered incoherently before he finally possessed the gift of word.

'Are you asking me to sin?' he then said coldly.

Was I? 'Yes, I suppose I am,' I answered.

'Then you are an evil youth, for in full possession of your faculties and knowing what you say, you answer me thus.' He was restored now, speaking evenly, sure of his ground. 'And there are punishments for such as you.'

He turned his back on me and bent his head to go out through the archway leading to the stairs. I heard him rustle his way up towards the nave, and I was left alone. I had been bold; but now, in solitude, beneath the massy edifice of pillared stone, I felt the whole weight of the Church above my head.

III

IN THE chapter house on the east walk of the cloister the monks met each morning, and after psalms and collects and the abbot's sermon there would follow lists of misdemeanours and confessions and then punishments. A wide low room it was, with little windows, plain and sturdy pillars supporting the arches of the roof, and stone seats in niches all about the wall, and a raised seat for the abbot.

All that Spring of burgeoning desires and ripening confusion there was fine weather, and the dust motes floated in the sunbeams as the business of the day began.

I was not surprised when Ailred reported me as one who had sinned. Sin was an interesting term. A brother who had fallen asleep at Nones or guffawed in the munching silence of the refectory would have his abberation mentioned by its name. Sin was another matter, and was always followed by a beating. It did not occur very often – whether through chastity or through not being found out, one cannot tell – but it cropped up regularly enough for the ritual to be a familiar one, and on this day my eyes were truly opened.

When a brother sinned, and confessed to that sin, he stood before the abbot and in consultation with the others it was then asked: 'Naked or clothed?' and there would be a brief muttering and a decision made. The penitent then knelt to take his punishment, hands clasped, head bowed, some six or ten strokes of the birch rod dealt out to his back. Now in my innocence I had always assumed that the severity of the sin dictated the variety of the retribution.

Foolishly I thought that those who had sinned most wickedly were beaten on the bare flesh, and those who had sinned lightly were allowed to keep their clothing.

I admitted to having sinned – I was not asked to specify what I had done – and stood before the abbot, who surveyed me sadly, in reproach, for I had never sinned before and maybe he had high hopes of me. Brother Tobias was not called to account; the day before he had been taken ill at Compline and was now in the infirmary. The usual question asked, it was decided that my sin required the removal of my habit, and I began disrobing. Enlightenment came to me. Suddenly I understood the truth behind this procedure; it was the young, good-looking monks who had to strip; the old and ugly kept their clothes. Swift as a lightning flash the recollections of those monks I had seen beaten for their transgressions tumbled through my mind – all young, all persona-ble; dainty buttocks, lissome limbs – how perfect a picture as they flinched beneath the rod – virgin martyrs for our inspiration. And all was done in the name of holiness, all sanctified by church decree, permissible, correct, for the improvement of their souls and the edification of the observer.

I sensed the tension and anticipation in the air as I took off my clothes. Though all had seen me naked washing, dressing, this was different, was a ceremony, almost as if I would be seen now for the first time. For me also it was new, undressing to a swathe of eyes, as a pedlar might unroll the contents of his pack to an expectant crowd that waited in absorption, and then in that panting silence the clamour of my nakedness.

While I knelt there Ailred prowled about me, making speeches.

'Saint Basil says that it is through this sin that the enemy has kindled the desires of many and then handed them over to eternal fire, hurling them into the vile pit. For fifteen years they should be denied the solace of Holy Communion. Cummean in his Penitential says that sinners must fast and sit apart and dine on bread and water, doing penances for seven years. Pope Gregory considers a penance of ten years more apt, and pronounces that the wrongdoers should be beaten with rods, for it is necessary that the crop which had brought forth bad fruit be cut down.'

I felt that he was inciting the others to imagine me about the act of sin. I fidgeted about uneasily; the stone floor was very hard. That this was Ailred's private spite was clear to me, for no mention was made of Tobias, nor did I mention him; and I would not demean myself by telling anyone that Ailred also was not entirely without reproach. But when I saw Ailred closing in upon me with the birch rod I resisted.

'Not Brother Ailred,' I stipulated, knowing well enough that at his hands I would be lacerated. He glared at me, the recollection of our encounter in the crypt a hindrance to his impetus. With a poor grace he passed the rod to Brother Hugh, a lad of undisputed honesty, and at his hands I took the beating.

There I knelt, head bowed, but seething inwardly with a mass of thought. I knew that I would be the stuff of vision to those who felt pleasure in the contemplation of a naked youth in enforced submission. Nor was I Saint Sebastian who took his arrows calmly with a heavenward gaze, and, in the inferior representations of his passion, with the look of one who has dined well on pheasant. No, I found the birch a most painful teacher, and I could not help but writhe and twist about nor stop myself from crying out, and even as I groaned I heard the sound and knew that it was somehow curiously provocative.

My punishment did not endure for long. I crawled up, throbbing, fumbling for my clothes. My body was on fire, my mind alert, curious as to the effects of pain, analysing its neutral sting that gives off heat yet none of wholesome warmth's invigoration. By that devious route I learnt that sometimes flesh in pain has the power to excite the onlooker, and I felt disquiet in belonging to a way of life that worshipped saints in torment.

In consequence of that event I received propositions from brothers who had not previously suspected that I sinned, and I enjoyed some couplings in the fields with them. And there was an odd little occurence with old Brother Bernard, who was half-witted. A chubby, toothless man, he tugged my sleeve and chortled full of meaning until I would accompany him inside the church. He led me to the choir stalls, where beneath each wooden seat was a misericord. He lifted them up and down, reminding me what lay depicted underneath: the scenes of daily life – butter-making, harvesting, woodcutting, thatching, and so forth; and the other things – the dragons' heads, the centaurs, castles, goblins, saints, all carved with care by craftsmen. Then finally we came to one which showed a naked female being beaten by what must be supposed to be her husband; he held her by the hair, which was long and thick, and in his other hand he held a broom of twigs. All this was carved in wood and perfectly explicit. Brother Bernard jabbed at it with his finger and giggled and covered his mouth with his hand as one who knows that he is naughty. All my years at the abbey and though I knew there were misericords I'd never noticed that one. I found it odd to come across it within a church, and it disturbed me, positioned as it was between a mitred saint on one side and a sheaf of wheat upon the other.

Brother Tobias died that Spring, and I was with him. He died in the infirmary, with singing from the adjacent chapel to see him heavenward. The last days of his passing were much troubled with his fears. Would three months of a life of penitence – and those not quite as penitent as could be wished – suffice to atone for some thirty years of wayward living? All the brothers reassured him, and the abbot sat with him and gave him peace, for there was never any question in that abbey of God's mercy, and our abbot liked to think that spiritually and physically all his monks were comfortable; he himself certainly was. But when the end came for Brother Tobias it was repellent, for afterwards that of which the body is composed burst forth and with it such a stench that made me run from the room, full of admiration for the ones who stayed and did what was required. But I sat in a huddle in the sun outside and thought much on the transitory nature of this life, and how a body loved by many women and some men had come to this in time, as must we all. And afterwards I found I could not talk about it, and took small consolation in the words of Holy Writ. I knew that I must leave this place. But how?

I sinned no more, but grew lazy, sullen and rebellious. I did not see why I should rise at two hours after midnight when the bell for Matins rang and my body wished to lie abed; or be silent when we dined – if a thought came to me then, what harm to tell it fresh? The framework of relentless religion oppressed my spirit, and that place – not one of the most austere of abbeys – seemed to me burdensome and grim. Besides, the new millennium was now underway. Did I want to see this new century from within the walls of an enclosure?

Abbot Guthlac applied himself to my problem with tolerance and care. His lodging was more like a house of the secular persuasion. He received me in a room which had fine tapestries on the walls, combining holiness with practicality, for they showed the lives of the Saints and kept out the draughts; and although it was a warm spring day he had a fire in his hearth.

Elderly and placid he seemed untroubled by his obvious love of comfort. He ate as well as any lord, and this room was furnished

128

with more than mere necessities of life. Every surface that could be decorated was so, the window niche with paintings and with crucifixes set with jewels, not with tormented Christs; the shelves with chalices of silver and reliquaries glittering with gemstones; a coffer covered by an altar cloth embroidered all over with fine gold threads; a gilt-edged book that lay half-open on a little table, with a bowl of sweets beside; a chair made comfortable with cushions. And upon his fingers he wore rings: a ruby, which we understood he wore to symbolise Christ's blood – but the emerald and the amethyst?

His sybaritic tendencies did not shock me. I have always admired those that can turn their circumstances to advantage.

Abbot Guthlac handed me a goblet of wine, and spread himself into a chair. He bade me sit down, but I was too restless, and I stood and paced. He studied me and sipped his wine.

'Now this is more than mere accidia,' he surmised. 'Am I wrong? I sense a strong divergence from the chosen path. But leading to where, I wonder? Where is it, Roger, that you wish to go?'

'Away from here,' I said ungraciously.

'The learning which you once professed to love no longer satisfies you? The books we have here – ?'

'I have read them all,' I grumbled.

'What – all?' he marvelled, smiling – for some were very dull.

'All that interest me.'

'But learning itself yet draws you? I hope that this is so, for you are above common gifted.'

'I love all kinds of learning. But there is not enough here. The books lead me so far, and then refer to other books, which we have not. And many questions are left unanswered.'

'Let us be clear about this. It is the restriction imposed upon your study by the confines of the abbey walls that irks you – nothing more?'

'No, nothing more,' I answered uneasily, not entirely convinced of the honesty of my reply. 'After all, I am a monk.'

I looked curiously at the abbot. What could he come up with? What possible solution was there for my situation? I knew that such a one was unlikely to prescribe a list of penances and self-mortification – 'Your restlessness is caused by demons; they must be subdued. Hair shirts for you henceforth, and constant prayers and supplications' – and I thought instead he might suggest a pilgrimage. This was an accepted way of solving personal confusion. Several of our brothers had gone off to Walsingham and come back with their wanderlust dispersed, glad enough to draw the abbey's old security once more about themselves. But this was not what the abbot had in mind.

'I wonder whether you might like to try a term of study at a school of learning,' he suggested. 'The beauty of this notion is that such would suit your present needs and cause you spiritual development.But also, familiarising yourself with the curent state of learning you could bring your knowledge back and teach your brothers your discoveries. That would be an ornament to the abbey, and of benefit to you. Indeed, there are things I would like to hear...Then, you might devote the remainder of your life to writing down what you have learnt, making a new book for the abbey library.'

Half speechless with delight I blurted out my gratitude. And where was I to go? I knew so little of the schools of learning – were they not across the seas? He told me I should go to Paris; France was the leader of the world in philosophy, courtliness, thought and languages. I nearly swooned in my excitement.

Until the time came for me to go, I felt agitated and jittery, afraid that something would occur to prevent my leaving – illness, earthquake, death, war, a change of heart from Abbot Guthlac. I lost interest in my books, and it was all I could do to keep up the appearance of being a dutiful monk. Yet the days did pass, the time arrived; and in the Summer I set out, I quit the abbey and turned my back on it.

Much had been offered me by way of warning and advice, much had been murmured to me concerning books and learning and the pursuit of knowledge. But as I rode away that full-blown summer morning, with all I needed in a saddle-pack and the wide world ahead of me, my thoughts were of the ladies in the castles who would drop into my palms like plums, and the eager boys who waited by the waysides, and knew no better.

IV

ALTHOUGH I turned my back on the abbey, it was merely the cage of the buildings and the bonds of its rhythms that I rejected. I did not question that there was any other way of looking at the world than as the creation of God the Father in his wisdom. Yet soon after I set out I discovered one who saw things differently.

Let it not be thought that I travelled south alone, tipped out of the abbey to fend for myself – no, I was with a large group of pilgrims also on their way to Southampton to take ship for foreign parts, some to the shrine of Saint James in Spain, others to Jerusalem. Nor was this my first excursion to the outside world, for I had been on errands for the abbey concerning farming matters and the sale of sheep, and thus was not obliged to gawp at every tree and village we encountered. I had seen before the peasants toiling in the fields, the shepherds with their dogs that herded flocks of sheep along the dusty tracks, the pedlars with their packs, the splendid horses of the travelling barons, and the cumbersome carts weighted down with timber, straw or cheeses. More startling to me was the sight of a man disfigured for a crime, his arm a stump and badly mangled, for you may be sure I kept well clear of the ugly sights in the infirmary when anyone was brought in from outside. Nor had I heard other than the music of the Church until a band of minstrels joined us for a while, and entertained us as we went, with tabor and shawm.

The weather being fine, the route direct and all of us eager to be on our way, we drew near to Southampton at the end of the second day of our journey. The first night had been passed at an abbey known to Abbot Guthlac; the second night we expected to put up at an inn. Our course had taken us through leafy woodland and all without mishap – no fallen tree, no swollen river blocked our path, and no wayside robbers troubled us, for we were a large and merry party by the time we reached the town, and looked about us for a place to spend the night. Indeed, our size was like to prove our disability, for the inn we found was small, and in the street outside we circled about aimlessly, our horses restive, while it was decided who should stay and who should look for other lodging.

On the opposite side of the street was a row of fine houses, tall, narrow and timbered, merchants' houses it would seem, bespeaking wealth and stability. To my surprise a manservant was sent from one of these, with the message that there was shelter there for the young monk that night, should he so wish it. Indeed I wished it, and I said farewell to my companions without regret. Their envious and inquisitive glances burned my back as I crossed the street. My horse was stabled and I went into the house.

I entered a small square hall with a low wooden ceiling and steps leading upward, and beyond, a lean-to kitchen. I was received by the lady of the house whose name was Gytha. She took both my hands in hers and invited me most courteously to share her roof that night. To be thus warmly welcomed by a person of her looks and standing made my heart leap in a silly hope that I had struck lucky this early in my travels, and that my most treasured dream was come upon me far more speedily than I could ever have suspected possible.

The lady was a little older than myself. She was a merchant's widow, comfortable in means and sought in marriage by many; but she had decided to choose carefully and in time. Meanwhile she was relishing her leisure, which she spent in good works amongst the poor, and in the studying of her husband's books. Two servants saw to her household and slept at night in the hall.

It had not escaped my eager eye that Gytha was a very comely woman. Her face was oval, with small shapely lips and frank grey eyes, her eyebrows finely curved, her cheekbones high, her neck pale and slender. Her hair was hidden in a fold of white linen beneath a little cap, but it seemed to be abundant and of a chestnut colour. She wore a blue dress woven in with silver threads, the throat laced lightly over the cloth of her shift, the sleeves tight at the wrist, the skirt low-waisted, hanging in brocaded folds which she lifted as she walked upstairs. The rustle of that dress caused me a quiver of the heart.

Above the small hall was a solar, with a fireplace and table, stools and cupboards, and a great coffer carved with aspects of the changing seasons. A small window set into the gable gave us light. I saw her bed beyond a small partition. A ladder led aloft; at the top was a space beneath the eaves with no window, but a paliasse and candle, and a bowl and a pitcher full of water; here I was to sleep and wash the dust of travel from me, and then come down to eat.

When eventually we sat each side of the table for a dainty meal and wine in silver chalices as fine as I had seen in church, I could not hide my wonderment. I hardly liked to ask so charitable a lady why I had been chosen, why so singled out. She must have seen me from the window when she sent for me – but for what purpose?

She laughed at my confusion. 'Poor Roger,' she teased me lightly. 'I understand. The reason I asked you to be my guest today was so that you might grant me a kindness. One that will surprise you, and amuse you also.'

'Anything!' I gasped. 'You have but to say.'

'My husband was a learned man and since he died – ' she paused in pensiveness. My hopes soared, only to be dashed immediately. 'Oh Roger! How I miss his conversation! I need to talk – dispute – exchange ideas...'

I took my disappointment with good grace and ruefully undertook to satisfy the lady. That evening we discussed the Sabellian heresy, which questioned the divinity of Jesus Christ; and the Nestorian heresy, which maintained that the Holy Virgin could not be called the Mother of God since She gave birth only to the human aspect of our Creator. We queried Saint Cyril of Alexandria's right to sainthood, for his behaviour was exceptionally vile, and chief among his crimes was the instigation of the hideous death of Hypatia, a learned woman and a mathematician. She was dragged from her chariot, stripped, and torn limb from limb. We discussed what made a saint. We lost ourselves in the Consolation of Philosophy; and went to our separate beds with something of a headache.

In the morning she asked me to stay.

'Just for a day or so,' she pleaded. 'There are always ships for France...'

In the day she took me riding in the forest beyond the town. The manservant rode with us, a little way behind, and when it was time to eat he served us a meal set on a fallen tree, and while the birds twittered above our heads and the flowers bloomed at our feet, we talked of learned matters. We returned early so that I could help her with her Latin. This was not the view of womankind that I had been led to expect. I said as much to Gytha.

She looked up from her writing, quill in hand, and eyed me thoughtfully.

'And what did you expect, I wonder?'

I dared not tell her about Lilith and the demons.

'Many of the monks were blessed with visions,' I murmured, 'all of virgin martyrs.'

'Virgin martyrs?' she enquired quizzically.

'Naked and praying, with the bloody swords of soldiers round about them and their heads bowed in submission. Saints every one of them.'

'Yes,' said she, with some asperity, 'it would suit many men if women were thus, virgin martyrs ringed with soldiers.'

'I did not have such a vision,' I pointed out, implying I was not of the common herd.

'You are a jewel,' she observed, but somewhat too tartly for my liking. Yet she held my gaze for longer than was comfortable, and I thought that I sensed invitation there.

I lay upon my pallet in the warm night, prickled by straw and Love's sharp stings. Nowadays of course I would have gone down the ladder and risked all for the chance of satisfaction; then I was unsure. Did she desire me? Would she welcome me? Then discipline spoke sternly: what of the vows I had made, the vow of chastity? Did that then stand for nothing? Was she worth it, a mere woman? Was she worth the breaking of my vows and the self-loathing that must follow? And was this private disputation pointless, dealing with the matter of illusion, since she had not yet asked me to her bed, nor had I made it clear I wished to be there!

Again, the following day, we rode into the forest, ate there, and after many hours of serious converse we began to talk of Love. No good was that to me, for the love we spoke of was the love of other folk – Troilus and Criseyde, Hero and Leander, sweet Dido and Aeneas, all those lovely tales found in the works of Pagan poets. What prompted Love, we asked, where did the impulse lie? Why did Love alter – why was it not fixed and unchanging, as God's love for mankind? Why were the great love stories sad, so often ending in despair and death? Gytha had opinions enough on all these issues. Our path took us beside a cornfield crimson with poppies, and the sun beat langorously down.

Gytha dismounted, and I followed; we tethered our horses. We stood beside the wheat; behind us the forest. It happened that we were quite alone.

'Do you know what day it is today?' she asked.

'I do indeed. I counted every day until I could be quit of the abbey. It's the last day of July.'

'Lughnasa,' she said. 'The god of light; his day.'

'Do you mean Lucifer?' I asked uncertainly.

'No, I don't think so. I believe that Lugh was a god of old times. He knew all about the harvest.' She traced her palm across the wheat ears. 'He would bless this field and it would prosper.' She began to pick a bunch of poppies; there were many flowers in the wheat, but mostly poppies; we gathered armfuls, and wheat also; then we sat upon her cloak between the cornfield and the forest, and there seemed no breath of air; the corn was silent and the leaves were still.

The lining of her cloak was of grey silk. She took off her headgear and let her hair fall and it hung in thick dark brown profusion. She lay back upon the cloak, in her blue dress, with scarlet all about her where we had strewn poppies. She showed me how to unfasten her dress. We both took off our clothes. A couch such as this I never had dreamed possible, grey silk that shivered like water, and the naked body of a woman and the rich crimson of petals pressed against her

134

white skin and the night-black bush at the centre of the flower. I was afraid I would not know what to do, but I found I knew well enough, and never did I lose seed so pleasantly, for it is a most evident truth that the rough blankets of a dorter pallet do not well compare with a woman's thighs. The sun and her soft hands caressed my back, and with the stirring of a sleepy breeze the corn stems rustled and the dancing grass heads quivered with small butterflies. I wished never to leave the place where I then was.

'Come, now we must eat,' she said, and began to move away. I did not see the necessity, but she would have it so. We sat on the cloak and rubbed the rough wheat ears in our palms, blowing away the chaff and tasting the small ripe tawny grains. My head was buzzing with excitement. I needed to examine my feelings, relate them to previous beliefs and olden dreams of Dido; and I looked to Gytha for confirmation of our ecstasy.

'The corn is blessed,' she answered. 'In the name of Lugh, the Mother is embraced, the God of the Waning Year is reborn, and the bread of life is eaten.'

'What do you mean by all that?' I asked warily.

She reached for her shift. 'The harvest will be fruitful now, because of what we did.'

I could not believe this kind of talk from one who had latterly seemed as wise as Hypatia. She had disputed with me on all manner of subjects with more skill and fluency than many of the abbey brothers, and now she jibbered like – I had not heard such crazed mumblings since that of my mother and her cronies, well dismissed as ramblings of a long-since conquered race, worthy to be despised. I stood up feeling dizzy, and we dressed in silence.

Cold and brooding I mulled over what had happened, as we rode away.

'Do you mean to tell me that you lay with me as a ritual act and not out of desire?' I blurted out.

How dignified she looked now, clothed, her wondrous hair invisible, enclosed in linen.

'For a ritual act,' she answered. 'But it could not have worked without desire. I did desire you.'

A fragment appeased, I cried: 'You should have told me what was in your mind.'

'Then you would have resisted. And besides, you believe in the God within the Church.'

I gasped. 'Don't you?' I felt appalled, as if the earth was slipping away beneath my feet. I saw the gaping mouth of Hell awaiting

Gytha, an eternity of doom and dread...

She smiled comfortingly. 'Don't fear for me. The Goddess is kind, and in our after-life there is no pain and punishment.'

'You are quite mad,' I marvelled, sweating. I was icy cold, far more than could be blamed on the trees' dark presence. 'For God's sake keep these thoughts a secret to yourself.'

She looked at me in some surprise. 'Roger, I am not alone in my beliefs, you know.'

'What *are* your beliefs? In all our talk of Scripture and philosophy I never thought to question whether you accepted God the Father.'

'Surely you have heard of the way of the Goddess? Truly, Roger, I had no wish to see you so disturbed.'

'You do not know how much!' I seethed. But why was I so? It was far more than that she had indulged in a kind of moral deception at my expense – for after all, why should I care what her reasons had been, when the result had been so mutually delightful? I attempted to sort out my thoughts.

'Once, when I was a child,' I began painfully, 'I met a woman who practised what you call the way of the Goddess. Tying scraps of cloth on trees, gathering boughs of holly and of oak, conjuring a circle – do you do those things, all that?'

Gytha remained silent, reasonably enough – I must have sounded half distract.

'I thought it was a savage cult,' I said, 'for a downtrodden race, feeble of intellect and easy to conquer – why, the Saxons overcame them, and what were they at first but drunken pirates with a taste for farming? I despised that way of life, forgot about it, thought myself well rid of it. But if *you* believe it...'

'I do,' she answered firmly. 'And you fool yourself if you think it's the ravings of the downtrodden. Rich men, burghers, lawyers, merchants – the Goddess has Her followers in every rank. Even William son of the Conqueror trod that path. This day is the day on which he made his sacrifice.'

'If *you* believe it,' I repeated, 'then that elevates it – that makes it like a true religion.'

'It is a true religion.'

'But how can it be?' I cried angrily. 'It has no philosophy behind it, no written word.'

'What is the most important thing we know?' said Gytha.

'The love of God,' I answered swiftly.

'No,' she replied. 'The earth we stand upon, which nourishes us – our Mother. She lives and we are part of Her. Only in that

136

harmony is anything possible at all.'

'Men have been hounded and put to death for denying God,' I warned her darkly. 'It is called heresy, as perhaps you may recall.'

'To deny the Goddess also leads to death,' said Gytha soberly, 'since She is bread and wine and everything that flows and grows. She is the moon that moves the seas, and the sun which ripens is Her consort. You see,' she added warmly, 'the Goddess never denies Her need for the God; She understands that both are part of the One, unlike your Church which has no love for womanliness. Nor have we ever felt obliged to travel to other parts of the world and kill all people who pray to other gods. To be the child of the Goddess is to know happiness and peace, for She is Life itself.'

'Can Her servants cast a spell and lay a curse?' I demanded urgently.

She stared at me surprised. 'Why do you ask that?'

'Can they? Is it possible? Could a woman have that much power?'

'Tell me what you mean. What kind of curse?'

I would not. The last rantings of my mother, which I well remembered as the Norman lord and I rode to the castle, had seemed mere rhetoric, empty and spiteful and of no account. *He is given to the Mother; he will never be the Lord's.* Guilt certainly I felt for having left her so readily, self-interest prompting my malleability. But now I was afraid. *He will never be the Lord's* – and here I was, just as she foretold, clear of the abbey, discontented in my service to the Father, and already one of my irrevocable vows tarnished with lust. And was the Goddess there amongst the wheat when I made love to Gytha, unwittingly Her priest, fulfilling all the dark designs my mother prophesied? Could her power extend across the years; could my confusion be her doing? But this was idiocy – no woman had that power. Yet that I could even think it for a moment! Power was here somewhere, either at that source or in my own imaginings.

And I ran from it.

In my mind I ran from it. In actuality I rode back to the town with Gytha, asking no more questions about her strange religion, neither responding to her conversation more than mere politeness required. When we returned to her house I packed up my small possessions and made my preparations for departure.

'Will you not stay the night?' she asked.

Like a fool I answered no, but my pride was hurt, and such was my inner turbulence that I doubted whether I could have given her satisfaction even had I wished to do so. From that encounter with

137

the Goddess I emerged defeated.

But never since.

Stabling my horse where Abbot Guthlac had instructed me to leave it, I made my way to the waterfront. It was night, and the wharves were a mass of lights, and all the ships that rode at anchor in the harbour were flecked with light also, lanterns at their masts and prows; and all these dancing brilliances dipped and swayed above the black reflecting water. Some of the warehouse doors were open, and by the blaze of burning brands men worked to stack their goods away. Swarthy foreigners, swearing at the weight, rolled cumbersome wet casks across the slatted wood and left trails of slimy water; and sailors staggered over straining ropes to reach the warm and sweaty taverns that lined the water's edge, with their promises of girls and songs.

I made for one such place. An inn sign painted with the image of a leathern bottle creaked above my head and I went in. A barn-like place it was and crowded, steamy warm, no air within; instead an ale-drenched stink that passed for air, diffused with acrid smoke from a hearth where meat lumps turned on spits and cauldrons swung from iron chains, and hags in rags stirred brews that passed for food.

It was a place where had I been wiser and more cautious, I never would have entered, given that the rich, the weak, and the religious might be a mite at risk. But I suspect my bravado or naivety was mockingly admired, for I was treated to no worse than jibes, as:

'God has come amongst us!'

'What'll it be, bishop?'

'Find a nice wench for his grace – find Inga.'

A hooded old woman brought me a bowl of broth, a hunk of leather which she'd have me believe was bread, and a drink that looked and tasted like the water wherein red cloth has been boiled and dyed. I was too much a curiosity to be left alone, and on the bench beside me I soon had assembled two or three that found my presence inexplicable.

'What are you doing here, a monk?'

'Eating and drinking, as you are.'

'On the run? Stole the abbey silver? I know a man who'd give you a good price.'

'On the run – yes, I suppose I am. But without silver. Perhaps if I'd known there was a market for it I'd have been more practical.'

'Will you sleep here?'

'Is that possible?'

'There's a room upstairs. But – ' and here there came some throaty laughter, 'a woman goes with it.'

'Which one?' I enquired, finishing the brew.

Delighted guffaws greeted my collusion. With shouts and catcalls they produced the recommended Inga, warning her that this one was a priest.

'So what? I've had priests before,' she boasted, and there she was before me in all her tawdry splendour. 'A priest he may be,' she observed, 'but he's young and as fine a piece of meat as ever I laid eyes on.'

I looked up from my ale to see this female – spiky, sandy hair, and smuts of grime upon her cheeks and the allure of rotting apples in the gilded sun of Autumn. She was a woman of the kind whose breasts you notice first, the rest a short while afterwards, and the face hardly at all. Her rough gown had a slit from neck to waist and was barely tethered by a ragged cord; her hips were wide, her arms bare and her manner challenging yet comfortable. She leaned towards me, hands planted on the table, breasts an inch or so from my face.

'Well then, do you want me?' she asked.

I nodded; and a chorus of approval greeted my decision. We were accompanied to the ramshackle stairway with all the pomp and bawdry of a country wedding, and near thrown bodily into the room above, till we had to shove the onlookers away by force, so eager were they to observe the miracle of a ruttish monk who made no secret of his humanity. Yes, from the first I was the kind that gives the clergy a bad name!

A vile and stinking tallow gave us dingy light; I saw the knotted wood of some great rafter, and the pitted daub between, but where we lay was no bigger than a store space, with a bed of straw and blankets.

I had scarcely time to look about me before Inga had stripped off her clothes and got to work on mine. To be naked before this gross whore had the effect of rousing my prick like a divining rod; I never knew it could get so big and hang out so – a bird might have perched on it, no, three or four! And when she praised it I was as foolishly proud as ever I had been when Ailred praised my decorative letters. I gazed at Inga hungrily, comparing her to Gytha. Gytha was all clean and white and soft and gently swelling; her breasts were little handfuls, she was in proportion, delicate and wholesome. Now I saw her as a woman, not a symbol; now I could

139

have fucked her. Inga's breasts hung big and pendulous with nipples like a yellow bruise. She stood with thighs apart, her tawny bush inviting me. She pulled me to her, till her hands were everywhere and all my skin ached to be in her and I tumbled down with her into the bed of straw. Free from the burden of intellect I took her as a beast might, knowing only the sensation of the pounding shaft and all the slippery warmth of limb on limb, belly against belly. Between her wide-splayed legs I felt a great release – this was womankind and it was not disturbing or frightening to me; I was myself and in control. Woman was Lilith as the monks had said, conceived from slime and mud and never any threat to Adam. If only I had dared to treat Gytha so! That would have put the Goddess in Her place. If only this was Gytha! Well, there would be other times and other Gythas, but I understood it now, and I would use the knowledge.

Woman was Lilith, and the world was back in balance.

I took ship at Southampton on a vessel of conveyance, one that hugged the coastline on its way to Dover, anchoring along the way to pick up cargo from the southern harbours – deer hides, beaver furs and bags of soft grey unspun wool. I slept on deck amongst them. Other travellers were with me, and an old musician who sang playnts to a sweet-sounding harp. I found those two days aboard ship most agreeable. I read Boethius and watched the sea birds wheeling, while the wind creaked in the sail and the blue-green sea made waves beneath us, and fair weather all the while.

I watched the sailors playing dice and set about to learn the skill; the sailors knew a wealth of gambling games and by the time we crossed to Calais I was good at all of them, and richer than when I set out. In the town I bought myself a dagger.

My links with the Almighty wearing somewhat thin I found a church and I attended Mass and prayed for protection on my journey. In halting French I bought an ambling nag and set off in the direction of Amiens and Beauvais. I had thought to travel as direct as possible and alone, but that night I learnt something I had not previously realised.

Do not the figures of romance sleep beneath the stars? Well, this I tried, in a bower of bracken and coarse grass which I constructed in the dusk against a little drystone wall. My nag and I had both well feasted, and she stood nearby with all the appearance of contentment. Having taken the precaution of commending my soul to God I settled down to sleep.

I woke in the night in a sweat-streaked panic. But why? Were there robbers about? No, nor was there storm, nor demon, nor wild animal, nothing which might reasonably cause my physical distress. Yet there I sat with pounding heart – I could hear it, tabor-loud, slamming my ribs – awash with cold terror, chattering my teeth. I had to stand up, stride about and take deep breaths, and in bewilderment I asked myself, why? What? Until the truth came rapidly upon me: I could not bear to be alone. Never in my life had I known this kind of solitude. There were no walls about me now, no roof, nothing between the heavens and myself. I was afraid, afraid of the great open sky and the blank empty air between and the intangible darkness. My own company was not enough for me; I did not like it. Without the presence of others how could I be sure of my existence? It is words that make a man alive. I spoke to the dozy nag then; I discussed with her some of the lesser points of early Christian writings; it was the nearest I have got to lunacy. I prayed, but to my horror I discovered prayers were unhelpful. I was ashamed of that night; and I have seen to it that I never got into that pit again.

In the morning, joining up with other travellers bound for Paris I had forgotten the shivering wretch I was the previous night. Around me was the gossiping throng, the mare ambling beneath me, and I was munching bread, my thumb in a book of helpful advice propped open on the horse's withers:

'To a labourer: *Dieus vous ait, mon amy.*
Or: *Dieus vous avance, mon compaignon.*

'To an equal: *Mon Seigneur, Dieus vous donne bon matin et bonne aventure.*'

I could think of no more fitting wish for myself.

V

GO NOW: my husband will be returning soon.'
These words followed me about with the repetitive inevitability of the refrain of a song.

How susceptible women are! Sing them a song and tell them the words are for themselves alone and they melt, they're yours. Never omit to tell them that you love them, for the easily spoken phrase is the key that turns the lock and opens up the door to anything you desire. I came to Paris to learn, and by the fragrant breath of all the saints together, I learnt everything that Paris had to offer.

A year passed, and you would have thought that I had lived in Paris all my life, so comfortable was I in that place they call the Paradise of the World – since there is found the knowledge of good and evil. I forgot the callow youth I had been, the newborn chick with the eggshell of the abbey sticking to my feathers; he was far behind me now.

To be sure, when I first went there I was serious in my intent to learn. I put up at the place the abbey recommended, the home of good old Frère Bartholomy, who spent his days in useful solitude in a cell-like chamber writing a history of the life of Saint Augustine, never emerging except to eat and sometimes not then. My little room was plastered white, my bed was narrow, strung with rope whereon a mattress lay, and all was clean and serviceable, while the sound of bells from the nearby churches reminded me of God and discipline and passing time. From here I walked each day the short distance to the Rue de Fouarre, where from five in the morning the masters held their classes in a small bare rented room up a little stairway or in the courtyard below where we sat on straw bales taking notes.

We were taught in Latin the Seven Liberal Arts – the Trivium, the study of speech in Grammar, Logic, Rhetoric; and the Quadrivium, the study of number in Arithmetic, Geometry, Music and Astronomy. We also dealt in history, philosophy, law and natural science, within the framework of religion, for all learning was a means to come closer to the Creator and to understand His mighty purpose. The works of Augustine figured largely, and Pagan writers were somewhat disregarded. Most of our basic learning originated in Greece, but it was adapted and absorbed into the Christian framework, and therefore it was assumed that we approached the masters humbly and with reverence; we were not expected to find flaw or criticise.

King Philip Augustus was on the throne, nicknamed 'God-given', for it was common knowledge that his father Louis VII (that inadequate saint who could not satisfy the beautiful and restless Eleanor of Aquitaine) had prayed for a son; his prayer was answered – and became Philip. King Philip was considered a good fellow – handsome, red-faced, fond of food and women, with the interests of the city at heart, for he ordered the streets to be paved with stone, which made travel easier.

I loved the work I did, and all my life was roses, for I had enough money from the abbey to live comfortably, and an eagerness to learn, and time between to wander the streets.

Within the city walls lay gardens, churches, brothels, markets, all criss-crossed by narrow wayward streets and bustling squares. Fiddlers and singers vied with cheese sellers and men with mangy bears on leashes for the kindliness of your attention. There were always festivals, processions – holy ones that left the heady scent of incense in the air from swinging censers borne by dainty pink-faced youths; profane ones with wild raucous music, jongleurs, tumblers, acrobats that whined for money, swarthy girls with golden ear rings, dancing, with bare dirt-black feet. Across the Grand Pont lived the rich, the goldsmiths and the silversmiths, the money-changers and the merchants with houses near their trading ships; and here beyond the Petit Pont we students argued in the streets and eyed the women. Rue des Parcheminiers, Rue des Ecrivains – here there were books for sale, parchment, scribes working at their open windows – Place Maubert where buxom housewives bought their bread; and down at the quayside by the foamy silver-grey water of the Seine the *grant orberie*, a vast sweet-smelling herb market, where in amongst the stalls piled high with lush wild greenery you might even find an English pedlar selling lavender from Norfolk.

'*Li tiens es beals, la joie est grant*'; I wandered round the narrow stinking streets – Rue du Chat qui Pêche, Rue des Marmousets, Rue du Pied de Boeuf – and across the open space of Place du Parvis Notre Dame, all in a daze of gladness, for these were streets where Abelard had walked.

Why is it men fear learning? Look at what they did to Abelard – no, I don't meant *that* – I mean the way they hounded him for what he said. 'By doubting we are led to enquire; by enquiry we perceive the truth.' Now what is wrong with that? But how they are afraid, these churchmen! Their power rests on such sand. To keep their flock in proper subservience they keep true knowledge from them. 'A doctrine is believed,' said Abelard, 'not because God has said it, but because we are convinced by reason that it is so.' I very much approved of all he wrote and said so, but it got me into trouble with a master named Girart, for I stopped his lectures every time I doubted; and insisted it was but to satisfy my searching conscience. 'The fathers of the church,' I reminded him, 'and the masters who teach in the Rue de Fouarre, are to be read not with the necessity of believing them but with the freedom of judging them.'

He was only a little older than I was and he couldn't take my constant interruptions. He was from a good family, very well spoken and accustomed to giving orders and being obeyed. He had family retainers at his beck and call, who lurked about behind him, chewing straw and gnawing meat bones while we sweated over Aristotle. He was most unmaster-like – good-looking, with a lovely mouth, and eyes that glittered when he grew intense.

One dark night in Autumn, after he had been teaching late and all the others had gone home and I had been particularly troublesome, he wouldn't let me leave; and his retainers, previously instructed, held me by the arms against a slimy house-wall down some alley close at hand. He came and stood in front of me, not two inches from me, I insist; I swear I could feel the heat from his body. He breathed into my face, telling me I drove him mad, I spoilt his class, he wasn't here to lecture such as me, but those who knew his worth and heard his words in silence. When I protested he yelled at me to close my mouth, and those that held me so twisted up my arms I could not speak if I had wanted to, but only gasped and groaned. And then he said that if I wanted to be Abelard so badly then perhaps I would like Abelard's punishment? And he hoiked up my robe and seized the handful of my balls and pulled a dagger from his belt quite huge enough to skin a boar. Well, I cried mercy, and I swore to be good and quiet; I promised anything! And he looked so surprised – Devil take me; what had he thought I would do else! He stared into my eyes, and then he fell on me, his hand still round my prick, and shoved his loins on mine and became 'intentionally polluted' against my belly. If I had not been scared I would have relished it, but held in place by iron-fisted servants I was not at ease, and have never quoted Abelard in a dark alley since. But at least, thank God, I am still whole.

I left that master then, for contrary to what it may appear I did want to learn. An aged greybeard taught me next, and we pursued somewhat of dialectic, ethics, politics, and much about the world, from the four great rivers of Asia to the serpents that eat deer in Africa. I learnt that there were three

144

evils in the world – ignorance, sin, and mortality, and three remedies for these evils – wisdom, virtue and action. So, well equipped for life's struggles then, I had no difficulty making the decision not to return to my monastery back in those quiet green fields so far away.

The letters started coming, slow at first.

'To our dear brother in Christ, Roger, we greet you well. Spring has come again and we are surprised not to have seen your return. As was well understood, you were released from God's work in the abbey for the duration of five months only. These months have passed . . .'

'To our brother in Christ, Roger, greetings. It is with pain and sadness that we have cause to remind you of your obligations to the abbey which has nurtured you from infancy. We would have supposed by now that the lack of money alone would have been cause enough for you to put an end to your sojourn in Paris, for be assured no more will be forthcoming from the abbey. We remind you once again what was agreed between us . . .'

'Roger, brother in Christ, greetings. We are distressed to have had no word from you. Yet Frère Bartholomy assures us that you thrive and we can see no reason on your part but wilfulness and ingratitude whereby you neither answer our letters nor return to the fold. We look forward to your speedy reply . . .'

'Roger, you have made promises to God. Let me remind you in all urgency that it is not beyond me to punish with the threat of excommunication any monk who lapses in duty and obedience . . .'

After that I opened no more of their letters and I left the old skulking sneak Bartholomy. He was very glad to see me go as we had had strong words when I brought in a poor artist off the street to paint my too-white room a mass of gaudy colours. I'd known all along that I was never going back to the abbey. Perhaps I'd not admitted it to myself, but return to that prison – the notion was repellent!

It was true that the loss of money was an irritant. It was this that led me into the taverns of the *quartier*, where I diced for the wherewithal to buy my bread. The villains who frequented these disreputable haunts were lively company, and I was not the only penniless scholar who took this way out of his poverty. I met there many I already knew, and I kept company with two especially: Alain a scholar, a Breton, who earned his money singing to a cittern, and Remi, also a scholar, no, a vision, who earned his money whoring.

Alain was freckled, short and stocky, with a mild clever face and a serious clumsy manner – none of which was noticed when he sang, for he had the voice of a lark, an angel, and he knew so many songs and stories; he was like a doorway to another world.

Instead of Logic at the schools now I learned *chansons de geste* from Alain: *Gormont et Isembart, Roland, Charlemagne, Guillaume*; and love stories: *Floire et Blanchefleur, Aucassin et Nicolette*, and the lovely langorous tales of Lyonesse – songs to steal a lady's heart. Poems were the sun's rays to the ice of her resistance. I had a good time with women, most of it forbidden fruit, secrecy and danger lending excitement to the passion, even causing it. I hid from Isabelle's husband in a jewel chest, with my knees pressed into chains of gold, my face in torment on the knobbly shapes of emeralds, a silver pendant prickling my ear. I could not help it if my frightened palm closed on a pebble that happened to be a topaz, one that I later sold to the great benefit of myself and my companions. What is one topaz to the rich? An unscrupulous thief would have taken several. I hid in a box of documents in Mellette's house, but a swift perusal showed me nothing worth my while there. I climbed a high wall to the bower of Marianne, by means of vines and roses that near did for me what Girart's dagger did not. I took tavern wenches beside cider presses, and matrons in their chambers, and I never had to work at it.

It seemed that women found me beautiful; this surprised me. Vanity I did possess, but it was of a mental kind – I liked to think I had an enquiring mind and I was not afraid to question all established thought, even that which some considered dangerous, heretical. I did well in disputation, I could take on masters from the schools and talk my way around a problem, arguing any premise, even one I disbelieved, simply for the joy of proving a point, discomforting an opponent. But my face and body I had rarely seen as fodder for desire. I thought it was the unexciting lives that women were obliged to lead, and not my excellence, which made them eager to receive me; and words also they liked. Because I did not value overmuch the structure of limb and muscle that enclosed my thinking mind I caught myself despising those who did. When some fair female praised my eyes I thought her simple. If she believed the words of love I spoke I marvelled at her credulity. I felt amused when the winning was always so easy, the culmination always the same. And yet it pleased me; for it made the world seem in appropriate balance, namely, I controlling, I untouched.

Alain, my fellow student in life and poverty, was sometimes my accomplice, singing love songs out of sight while I embraced the lady. On an evening laden with the scent of roses I made love to Beatrice within her high-walled garden. Her dark brown velvet dress slipped from her white shoulders; the moon shone upon her skin; sweet music ornamented every kiss:

> Amors me tienent jolis,
> Car adés me font penser
> A la douce debonaire
> Qui je ne puis oblier . . .

Alain was a more agreeable companion; but I liked Remi better.

Remi was just so good to look at you forgave him anything. He stole from everyone, he lied with every other word, but when he'd drunk too much and became affable he loved everybody in the world and he let you use his body and forgot who'd had him, a most convenient weakness of which I often took advantage. His hair was fair and fluffy, his eyes ice-blue, his body polished smooth with frequent handling.

In the mornings he greased his anus with oils of sandalwood so that it was always ready, slippery and smooth. I used to watch him do that. It always left me roused. Naked he would bend this way and that, his thighs apart, knees bent and buttocks jutting, and the daylight picking out the tints of his flesh: translucent white along the curve of his spine, smudges of ochre at the shoulder blades, sheer gold as the muscles shifted, shadows of rose about the ripeness of his arse.

I sometimes wondered what it was that made him so attractive, for he was not to all tastes, his features were not regular and neat and sometimes he did stink. But what did draw men to him was that he made observers think of lust; he brought lust to the forefront of the mind, and memories of bedchamber encounters and the wish to satiate oneself in lust's forgetting; and in his company somehow all things led to lust, and if he could not take you at that time it followed that you had to take yourself behind some doorpost, such were the urges he called forth by being there – just by the careless movement of his thigh, the twitch of his plump arse, the spreading of his legs.

Once as we sat together in the dim dank cellar of a ramshackle tavern near the Petit Pont I wondered how it was that someone from good family and with a scholar's mind could live the life he did.

'How can you bear to go with men for money?' I demanded, more curious than appalled. 'Ugly men with pockmarked faces – fat men – old men – anyone?'

'They pay more! And if they are too vile I close my eyes.'

Those same eyes idly roamed the dingy room as he spoke, assessing possibilities. Rough men, rats from the dark holes and corners of the town, sat in the shadows, hunched over their ale.

'But does it never trouble you to ask payment for something which is spoken out against so forcibly by Saint Paul – Saint Augustine – Pope Gregory?'

'And what have they to say on the subject of fornicators?' Remi shrugged. 'And lapsed monks?'

'It's true that my life is imperfectly spent,' I admitted, chastened. 'And I am still a prey to guilt.'

'Your pleasures never seem to satisfy you,' Remi said. 'You go after women, you achieve them, but it never seems to mean anything, only the notching of a score, or a series of victories against morality. You never fall in love.'

Everything he said was true. For all I knew of love I might as well have been a virgin.

I daresay some despondency showed upon my face at that point. Remi put his arms about me. 'Come here,' he told me sympathetically.

'Here?' I gasped with hope and trepidation.

In a moment we were pressed into a corner, hidden only by the dark abutment of smoke-stained oak beam. Hidden? It was not likely. Drinkers on the benches close by observed us, but with no more than a laugh and a shrug – for what did it matter to them, thieves and layabouts with enough sins of their own, and the capacity for surprise and disapproval so abundant in the protected long since worn away.

'Have me ...' Remi murmured, rubbing against me, making bare his arse and shoving me to enter him, turning about, his face against the wall, his buttocks smooth as rose petals. Ardently I sank into him; gratefully I fucked him.

As we drew apart I murmured: 'Do I owe you?'

'No,' said that obliging youth. 'It was a gift. Because –'

'Because?'

'I think you never will be free of guilt. You asked me how I could bear to do what I do. The secret is I like it. You – well, you take your pleasure, but – there is some aspect of you, Roger, which is joyless.'

A man who had been watching what we did now got up from his seat and came towards us, dark and menacing. His clothes were tattered and he wore a low-browed hat that made his face a shadow. He seized Remi by the arm.

'How much did he pay you?' he said roughly. He was a strong-faced, big-nosed man, good-looking in a brutish sort of way, with long hair curled in little tendrils jutting from his head. His chin stuck out aggressively, his lips were thick and sensuous, his shoulders broad, his eyes were hard and calculating. He hung over Remi like a predator.

'Nothing,' Remi stammered. 'It was given.'

The fellow twisted him, and hurt him, disbelieving such a stupid story. A man nearby to save us trouble flung a coin. It landed in the filthy straw.

'Take it, for the entertainment we have had!' he sniggered.

I picked it up and gave it to the man who threatened Remi. He snatched it, spat, and let him go.

We left that place. I feared for Remi; he had never learned to fight. No more had I; but I was good at making myself scarce.

After I had left Frère Bartholomy's place, and with no wish to share the communal hostel where the students slept in dorters reminiscent of a life I was well quit of, I lodged here and there, depending upon what I had in my purse. Most often with Alain I shared a room no bigger than a cupboard upstairs at *La Vâche qui Rit* above the kitchen there, with floorboards warmed by cooking fires; and learnt to sleep through singing, cursing, rattling of pans below. And less and less did I attend the lectures now, and more and more I lay abed and lazed and drank – I found I had a great capacity for liquor – while Alain sang and talked of life; and down we'd go, no further than the inn beneath, to win or lose at dice and hear the gossip of the backstreets.

We thought we lived so dangerously, but I wonder whether we ever truly encountered a villain of the direst kind there, for half the customers were students like ourselves, thinking to experience the bitter richness of the dregs and wallow in a sort of wickedness and call it life; all were from good homes and all were very young. To be honest the most exciting thing likely to happen was for someone to lose at dice so heavily that he lost all his clothes and was tipped naked into the street, and that was only exciting if it were somebody one wanted to see naked.

But there was one incident which I found exciting – though as with all pleasures that truly touched me, it was of a cerebral nature.

One evening Alain shook me from a drunken doze and told me I must go downstairs – Blondel was here! I had never seen Alain so moved, his eyes alight, his limbs a-quiver, and to be truthful I reckoned the occasion justified my being hauled from bed.

Down in the tavern it had something of the flavour of a church. All usual converse ceased, and everyone there – the crowd of familiar youthful faces, strained with the weight of their intellectual prowess and the excesses of their ale – was grouped about the strangers as about the masters at the schools, in pose of disciples.

Four noblemen sat drinking round a table. That they were here at all was to be marvelled at, but that was soon explained; they were in disguise! Like figures of romance they were about to travel south, to Poitiers, without retinue or embellishment, as dust-grimed *vagi*, men of the road. And one of them was Blondel de Nesle, a man of Aquitaine, of the household of Queen Eleanor.

I leaned against the wall and watched him. Blondel! A legend in his own life time, King Richard's faithful minstrel! Some ten years ago when Richard had been captured by Duke Leopold of Austria and immured in the castle of Dürrenstein, Blondel had crossed Europe searching for the imprisoned king. Outside the walls of every castle on his journey he sang songs that Richard knew, hoping to discover

150

where the king was incarcerated. He crossed rivers, mountains, valleys. He grew gaunt and windswept. Devotion kept
him hopeful. Dressed in shabby clothes, an ordinary troubadour, he passed unrecognised from village to village, asking
where the nearest castle lay, and singing to the great
impassive walls. Eventually at Dürrenstein he heard an
answering refrain, the king's voice at a window. His long
search was over.

The king was dead now, killed by a crossbow bolt at Chalus,
and Blondel had passed into song and story. Yet here he was
before us, as if he had dropped in from Emmaus and with
more recognition than received by Christ and adulation from
admirers somewhat more intelligent than Cleopas.

He could not have been old, but yet his thick long hair was
silver-white, and in the sycophantic atmosphere about him it
was not inappropriate to envisage it as an aureole of light.
Handsome he was indeed, with wondrous deep-set eyes and a
fine-chiselled face. His companions grouped about him,
well-dressed, their gesture of anonymity merely the addition
of long all-embracing cloaks, beneath which they were
blatantly wealthy, and in any case each one wore an excess of
rings upon his hands. For someone travelling incognito the
hero troubadour needed small persuasion to sing for us. He
sang *Chanterai por mon corage*, and when they pleaded for
King Richard's song composed in his captivity he graciously
obliged:

> Ja nus hons pris ne dira sa raison
> adroitment, se dolantement non;
> mes par confort puet il fere chançon.
> moult ai amis, mes povre sont li don;
> honte en avront, se por ma reançon
> sui ces deus yvers pris.
>
> Ce sevent bien mi honme et mi baron,
> Englois, Normant, Poitevan et Gascon,
> que je n'avoie si povre conpaignon,
> cui je laissasse por avoir en prixon.
> je nel di pas por nule retraçon,
> mes encor sui ge pris.

Some listeners were moved to tears (Alain was one)
empathising with the memories which that song must hold

151

for him. They asked him about Dürrenstein. He told us it was
on a high hill with a rocky slope that curved down to the river
Danube. He told us of his feelings as he heard the monarch
answer with the words of a song which they had composed
together – his heart leapt with joy and disbelief; his eyes were
blind with weeping. I saw Alain dry a sympathetic tear.
Fawning fools, I thought with some amusement, why don't
they ask him if he and Richard ever fucked?

'And what did you do then?' I asked him bluntly.

'How do you mean?' the hero turned to me, and favoured
me with an enquiring glance.

'Did you enter Dürrenstein?'

'No; what could I have achieved by that?'

'Demanded to see the king. A poignant reunion in his
chamber.'

'The idea was to find him, and then return and tell the
world,' Blondel explained it to me as if I were an idiot.

'Is it not a fact that the world already knew?' I shrugged.
'They all knew where he was. Surely your journey, though
impressive, was also somewhat pointless?'

'I beg your pardon?' A sliver of ice crept into his tone.

'I understood that Duke Leopold informed the Emperor
immediately, and then the King of France. Prince John also
received the information from somewhere, since he rapidly
sprang into action. For whom did you make the journey?'

I guessed the answer even as he said it.

Dramatically he cried: 'I made the journey for myself! For
love, for minstrelsy! For everyone who keeps alive a hope in
his heart against all odds. For courtliness!'

For courtliness! That strange phenomenon that drives a
man to devote his life to the service of his love, with never any
hope of recompense.

His listeners applauded. Blondel smiled. Complacency was
in that smile – the ease of one who senses he has made his
mark on history. He added smoothly with a withering glance
in my direction: 'We understand these things in Aquitaine.'

Then they all began to talk about the south. A wondrous
place, the south. The wine there sparkled more, the women
were more vivacious, the land more beautiful, the climate so
temperate that apricots grew on every wall. The sun shone
for ten months out of twelve, and everybody sang. A Paradise
on earth, slow and gentle, love blooming in the very air.

Troubadours sang songs of love. It was a land of legend –
Melusine – Lancelot – Launfal – Aucassin and Nicolette,
Eliduc and Gugemar; it was a living poem. And in the castles
ladies dwelt, susceptible to song.

I caught sight of Alain's face – transfixed, as one newly in
love. I looked for Remi, but remembered he was peddling his
wares on the Pont Neuf. How could there be truth in
romantic love when at the same time pretty youths sold
arse-flesh for the same price as two gallons of ale?

The courtly party now stood up to leave. Respectfully the
adoring crowd cleared a path, and for a moment I was close
to Blondel in the doorway. The hostility between us bound us
– we must speak.

'Go south,' said Blondel, in a tone half kind, half superci-
lious. 'The sun is warm in Aquitaine. There you may lose that
coldness in your eyes.'

'Tell me,' I answered with the coldness of which he accused
me. 'Did you ever fuck the king?'

His eyes flickered, and for a moment I thought that he
would answer that question to which everybody wished to
know the answer. But a provocative youth dressed as a monk
was not to be the one to pierce that particular enigma, and the
moment passed, and he and his companions were gone.

After that evening I could get no sense from Alain. 'All my
life is wasted! I have never seen the south,' he moaned.

'No more have I. This is the farthest south that I have ever
been.'

'Brittany I know,' he wailed. 'But who can say he lives until
he has seen other countries, lands of legend?'

When Remi came in he too was preoccupied. Thoughtfully,
at the corner of the tavern table he counted out the pickings
from his night's encounters.

'Roger,' he said. 'Do you remember that man who
threatened me, when you and I made love against a wall?'

'I do. A swine of vilest magnitude.'

'I've seen him again,' said Remi, as one who made
confession.

'I hope you ran the other way.'

'No. He saw me on the bridge and came to me. His name is
Ivo. Look, he gave me silver.'

'But he was villainous . . .'

'He thinks that I should go into partnership with him,' said Remi. 'And whatever we may think of him, his purse is full of silver.'

'Have nothing more to do with him,' I told him. 'Come south with me and Alain.'

Then we all fell to laughing, for in that simple way did Alain and I decide to go upon the road.

We sold some books to get money for the journey, we diced for more, and begged in the gutters for the rest. What would Abbot Guthlac have thought of me, I wondered, as I sat with Alain on the paving-stones of the Pont Neuf, my right arm in a bandage stained with pigs' blood, pretending I had lost the means to hold a quill? The sun shone kindly on us, Alain with his crutches, and a bandage round his head, strumming out a melody to show that though he was a cripple he was not downhearted, and passers by threw coins into his cap.

'I used to have an image in my head,' I said to Alain. 'Alms, lady, for the love of God! – I used to think that France was full of castles where the lonely châtelaines sat waiting for a travelling man much like myself, and all the waysides leading to these castles were peopled with obliging youths whom I could tempt behind the bushes. Someone told me this was so, an old reprobate monk whom I dearly loved. I'll tell you, Alain, between Calais and Paris this did not prove true.'

'There have been women enough here in Paris,' Alan said reprovingly.

'True. But the lonely châtelaine is my ambition,' I replied. 'With her, I might even find courtly love. And while I waited for her good favour, if I could pass the time with the credulous boy that old Tobias promised me I would consider myself well satisfied.'

'I do not think that anyone would define courtly love in that way,' Alain told me. 'And why mock something which is beautiful, just because you don't believe in it?'

'Well then, I must settle for mere lust,' I answered lightly. 'And leave courtly love to minstrels – Alms, good master, for the love of God!'

Hustled from our pitch by a herd of silly sheep that crossed the bridge upon their way to market, Alain and I made off somewhat the richer and discussed our plans. We would gain nothing if we stayed in Paris. There were too many students, everyone knew it, and afterwards no work, no patrons. The

154

seething overcrowded schools poured forth excess of scholars – for what purpose? We would be doing them a favour to decamp; no one would miss us; and we were tired of disputation. All around us was a whirling wayward world where we could put our talents to good use and learn what it might teach us.

Remi would not come with us. Ivo, the man who once had threatened him, had taken him under what he called his protection. A questionable kind of safety, this – the arrangement seemed to be that Ivo chose whom Remi went with, and took money from them, some of which he gave to Remi. Yet Remi seemed peculiarly content. Where Alain and I saw merely a pockmarked pimp who had his way by force, Remi seemed to see a man of strength, pragmatic and decisive. And who were we to argue, since Ivo had fists like hammers and a temper like to rise as suddenly as does a dry wood fire?

So I, who did not believe in courtly love, went south with Alain and his songs. And as always must be in a search for romance, it was summer and the fields were green.

VI

IN OCTOBER we arrived in Perigord and by misdirection lost ourselves.

We had by now ceased marvelling at the sights encountered on our way – the churches of Poitiers and Angoulême, the pinnacle of Rocamadour, the wide rivers in the fertile vine-rich valleys, the great soaring rocks, the monastery near Chinon where we stayed for a month to read their magnificent library. But there was nothing much to marvel at where now we were – a forest deep and vast, as enigmatic and perverse as any in the annals of the questing traveller.

The rushy floors of castle halls had been our resting places many times; hospitable households had received us, and we had paid our way with song and story; but never had we won the heart of any lonely châtelaine to whom we were the answer to a prayer. Transitory delights with village girls had been the sum of my achievements; and Alain interested himself in neither maids nor men.

And now the trees were red and gold and it would soon be

Winter. In the mornings by the rivers heavy mists lay on the water meadows, and the dark came early. This was much in our minds now, for neither of us was a seasoned traveller, and if it is true that the forest has much to teach us about the true nature of ourselves, we did not wish to learn it shivering and frozen in a makeshift shelter in the snow.

Suddenly we drew rein sharply as the bushes round about us rustled, shook and parted, and across our path a wild boar plunged, and paused stock still, not three yards from our stopping point.

I never had been this close to a monster such as this. His bristled back gleamed with bladed spines; his hooky tusks leered like a menacing grimace. Sweating and snorting he was running from some foe. His lowering head looked this way and that, the eyes sharp-bright, the breath a rasping growl. What we would have done if he had charged I do not know – we were so stunned that we remained as still as stone. The creature took a heavy breath, then thudded off into the undergrowth.

We listened now, and we could hear the distant sounds of hunting some way off – the barking of the hounds, the crash of bough. I shuddered; a conflict so meaningless seemed to me sinister and inexplicable.

We came into a clearing where the autumn leaves blew down upon a herd of swine. Rough skinny beasts – unappetising fare – they rooted in the beech mast, clumsily unsettling our horses, causing us to yell at them and look to see who was their keeper. There was a swineherd with them, a black-haired youth in dirty peasant gear. Appeased by his apology we stopped to ask him where the nearest village was and where the castle.

Before he could explain, the equanimity of the forest was shattered by the oncoming sounds of the hunt. Noblemen circled the clearing, eight or so, on beautiful horses, colourful in reds and yellows and blues; men with hunting spears – the barbed *eofor spreot* such as Beowulf used to fight the monster – whooping and calling and scattering the pigs who darted off into the brushwood. Cheated of boar the noblemen chased pig. I backed against the shelter of the trees, but Alain stupidly dismounted, with some idea to help the swinehead who recklessly set about to save his pigs, though the horses' hooves kicked the staff from his hand and he stood there with

156

his bare hands staring up at his aggressor.

I stared too. This arrogant oppressor was a vision. His horse reared up, and showed him to us in his glory, golden and magnificent. A handsome face lit up with lust and power, his clothes and jewels glittering in the gilded sun. The image would stay with me for ever – the two sides of myself. If I had never left my village I could have been that boy, black-haired and grimy, herding swine in a nameless glade, and how well I remembered gazing up at splendid horses as they impassively destroyed our harvest; if I had been my father's true born son I could have been that rider, young and masterful, chillingly uncaring. My heart pounded; I shared a passionate complicity – but with both.

A hunting spear beat the boy to the ground; the riders careered around him killing the pig, bellowing with laughter, and the pig's squeals terrible to hear. 'Get up, boy, tie the pig to the pole.'

They obliged the boy to rope the pig by its legs to a branch and then they rode off with it, rustling the leaves, thwacking the undergrowth, and a dozen startled birds flew skyward.

Shocked and chastened to find the slaughter had excited me I dismounted to help the boy retrieve his pigs. Alain also had been hurt by staves and I had not noticed. From amongst the trees now came some other villagers, to stare, to mutter and commiserate. In answer to my questions they replied: 'That was Stephane de Laussel, son of Guillaume, who owns the forest and the village and every soul therein.'

An elder of the village, named Joubert, a greybeard of some authority, invited us back to their settlement, and since Alain's hurt needed attention we agreed. When we arrived, we found the nobles had gone there before us, for everyone was gathered round a water trough which gave the people clear drinking water. It was now dyed a muddy red, the nobles for their sport having slung the dead pig in it, where it bled into the water. Not without cause was Stephane hated hereabouts.

'But you have other water?'

'Oh yes; there is a spring, deep in the forest.'

We lived for some days with these peasants, sleeping on dry bracken in a hut. I saw the spring in question.

Joubert showed the place. When I first saw it I was amazed, for it lay beneath a mossy bank wherefrom a great tree grew,

157

and everywhere upon this tree were rags of cloth tied.

'Every cloth a prayer,' said Joubert, watching me.

'So you follow those old ways here,' I murmured.

'Yes,' he said with narrow hostile eyes. 'And what have you to say to that?'

'Nothing. My mother also . . . I have not seen anything like this since I was a child.'

'Yet you wear a priest's garb.' This shaggy gaunt old man wore a belt about his waist that bristled with hunting knives. His hands were gnarled as wood, his manner stealthy; he could walk a forest path without the breaking of one twig.

'Nonetheless, the truth is I was dedicated to the Goddess.'

He grunted, weighing up what I had said. I had surprised myself when I confessed so much to him. Fear plain and simple made me do so. I felt that I was brought there to be tested. My clothes showed me a man of God to those who knew no better. I think if I had been mad enough to rave about God's laws and retribution that old man would have stuck a knife in me. We were alone. The massy forest surged on us like waves, and no one would have been the wiser. I was grateful to my mother, to the Goddess, that my admission was true. I half suspect that she had saved my life.

The peasants in this village were unnerving. Most peasants are sullen brutes but these seemed menacing, with more spirit than is customary among a people worn by toil, submission, hunger. Did their religion strengthen them perhaps? Unlike those peasants who believe in God and therefore accept poverty and labour meekly as God's will, with Heaven their reward, these followers of another way would not have been so patient. In this religion sometimes spells are cast, to change things. But I saw none while I was there, and only my uneasiness gave me cause for suspicion.

While Alain lay recovering, a mass of sodden leaves packed tight against his bruises – all applied with jumbled mutterings, none of them Christian – I was glad to leave the village, accompanying that swineherd as he took the pigs to graze.

I was attracted to him. He was good-looking, with a suntanned face and wide blue eyes. But more than that, I could not rid myself of the notion that I might have looked like that if I had remained with Celtic kinfolk, working on the land. In him I saw myself untaught, unlettered, knowing nothing except the change of seasons and the lore of earth.

158

Mind, there is more to herding swine than meets the eye, I learnt. I had already seen how fast young pigs could run; it was no joke to try and catch them. If you want to keep them by, you throw a handful of beans down, and the pigs being greedy will group about them and stay together. A pig is stubborn, and if you want him to go forward you tie your twine around his back leg and pull that – then he'll tug forward. Then you must watch to see the acorns are not too hard since they could make a young pig choke, and if one does, you shake him by the heels or stick your fist down his throat; I saw the boy do this, and felt appallingly impressed – of places where one might wish to thrust one's hand down, a pig's gullet does not rate highly. An obscure penance kept me with this boy and his rooting swine. Also, I was sure that Stephane would return.

As we munched vile bread and clods of cheese I learnt the boy was of Italian stock and named Rigord. He did not talk much, and there was about him a subservience to his lot which marked him, I suspected, as a victim to the whims of others. Again I blessed the lucky chance that plucked me from a similar fate. But as to making him a victim of mine I hesitated; being very wary of the influence of Joubert.

Two days later Stephane with a courtly party rode gracefully into the clearing. He was accompanied by another man, a woman, and three servants who ran along on foot. One carried dead rabbits dangling from his fist, and his face was much disfigured. Men at arms followed, with bows and arrows and staves.

Over his shoulder Stephane called: 'Francois, Louise, over here – this is the boy – come and see.'

Francois and the lady rode closer. The pigs shifted out of their path, obliging and inane.

'Come here, boy,' said Stephane. '*Here*.'

Rigord went warily over to the noble lord, and I, lurking by a tree, observed them. With the ebony handle of his whip Stephane obliged the boy to look up at him, and asked him his name.

'And do you know who I am?' Stephane enquired. 'I am your master and I own you body and soul.'

He looked across at me, as if I might wish to query that assumption; I gave a slight shrug. Who was I to argue on a point of principle? God's piss but he was beautiful! His eyes

159

were glittering topaz, piercing, haughty, like a bird of prey, his mouth thin and disdainful. His clothes were gold and black, sewn all over with little jewels, a cold kind of brilliance, like sun on ice. His hair was tawny, cut straight along his forehead and down the sides as if the wind had no power to ruffle it. He could have been no older than myself.

'I shall need respect from you, Rigord,' he said. 'When I find lack of respect I become vexed. Joffrey! Here, animal.' The man with the dead rabbits and the ruined face ran up to him and dropped on one knee.

'Look down at Joffrey,' said Stephane. 'I became vexed with Joffrey. He is always respectful now.'

I am sure that both Rigord and myself determined on a course of greatest respect from that moment onwards.

'The peasant,' Stephane told his friends, 'if you catch one early enough before they coarsen up, the peasant, male or female, has a certain quality, a kind of innocence which is never seen in higher spheres. And it has been my pleasure many a time to enjoy that . . . and to destroy it. But you are right, my dear Louise – the peasant is also a dirty animal, and it takes a certain skill to spot the exception that may prove a delight. I think I have one here.'

And to prove to himself that what he said was true, Stephane ordered the boy to strip and show himself. As peasants must obey their masters Rigord did as he was told. I ached with envy at the manifestation of such absolute and careless power. We watched the boy take off his clothes. He had a pert young body, slim and lithe, with skinny muscular arms and a smooth lean belly, and a bush of curly black hair above a tasty prick; his arse was round and firm; his thighs hairy and strong. There was no one there who did not gaze his fill.

But Stephane did no more than look that day, and laugh, as if to show that he could take or leave the sight before him. Then over Rigord's head he said to me with eyes full of amusement: 'You see the power I have. Unfortunately I do not possess the same domination over the Church.' And he ran his gaze the length of me till I felt I was standing naked as the boy, and for a moment it occurred to me that I regretted he did not possess that power.

When Stephane and his crew had gone and Rigord had gathered up his tumbled clothes, I asked him curiously: 'What will you do?'

160

'Nothing,' he replied shiftily.

'Will you tell them at the village?'

'No; and nor will you.'

'But if Stephane comes back?'

When Rigord said nothing then I looked at him, and knew. God's teeth, I thought, amazed, amused – he hopes it.

At the village around the fire that cooked their food they told us that Guillaume de Laussel had been their lord for twenty years. He drove out the previous lord and installed himself at Gravillac, the castle, and ever since held sway as distant as a god, uncaring of his folk as is the ever-changing sky. Rumour had it that he dabbled in intrigue and played a game of treachery in high places; certainly he was often gone from Gravillac. Stephane, however, was only too much present, and they dreaded he should ever come to power.

'He is a kind of madman,' they believed. 'Ridden by demons, reckless and full of rage, and like to satisfy his lusts upon those he should protect.'

'But never think that Stephane and his kind are fixed and unchangeable, as the stars of the Heavens are,' said, Joubert darkly. 'They came, and they could go.'

But others hushed him up, because they did not trust us.

'Stephane surely is no more than a wayward boy,' I said. 'Hardly a monster.'

But no one had a word of good to say for him.

Alain, later, now recovered, said that he and I had best be on our way; but I suggested he was not yet wholly fit, because I knew that Stephane would be back.

'I cannot understand,' said Alain privately, 'your sudden fascination with swine herding. Is it the boy? You would not be wise to tangle with these people. You've heard them – they are full of hatred.'

'I help him mind the pigs.'

Alain laughed contemptuously. 'Is that what you came to the forest to find? Kinship to a swineherd?'

And I was lucky. It even crossed my mind that Stephane also sensed affinity between us, for when there has been the invisible transmission of messages from eye to eye, those that give and receive it know it; and there had been such messages.

The peasant boy Rigord was not a great talker, and while we sat upon a fallen tree and idly watched the backsides of the snuffling swine, to pass the time I told him stories. But all talk ceased when Stephane rode into the glade.

It was what we had both been waiting for. He was alone, except for men at arms that lurked discreetly by. He was as beautiful as the dawn. He wore yellow, with the glitter of gold threads, metallic, as if the gold ran deep through to a steel within, no weakness of mere flesh.

'It must be clear between us,' he said to Rigord, 'that whatever I do to you is done by me out of ownership, because you are my chattel and I may do with you as I please; and it must be received by you as an object receives the kick or the touch of whoever passes. No other kind of contact is permissible between us, none whatsoever.'

And the young lord made him kneel down in the dry leaves of the forest floor, and he drew his dagger and moved the blade sinuously about the face of the boy, and obliged him to kiss the gleaming metal though the boy's lips were trembling with fright. I went and stood nearby, scared for the boy, but Stephane laughed and put the blade away. Straightaway he put between those same lips his noble prick, all scented with strong perfumes – over-sweet, as the posies that ward off the plague. And he showed Rigord what to do to give him satisfaction. I watched absorbed.

Stephane flung the boy from him and put his prick away.

'Well,' he challenged me. 'That was a sin, would you not say?'

'It is generally acknowledged so to be . . .'

'You shall absolve me.'

'I?'

'You have the power – you wear the garb. You shall take God's part, and pardon me.'

'I have long since ceased to consider myself pure enough to speak on God's behalf.'

'Good! An impure priest shall serve my purpose well. Besides,' he smiled sardonically, 'what I have just done is common practice within the walls of a monastery, is it not? I daresay you have done as much yourself.'

'It's true; I have.'

'Absolve me then; you are the man I want.'

The glittering young lord dropped to his knees before me

and he put his arms around my waist, his face against my crotch, purposefully, till he could feel the movements of my prick. The nearness of his face stirred me, and he knew it.

'I acknowledge my sin,' he murmured comfortably. 'And I demand absolution.'

'I, Roger . . .'

'Roger? No other name?'

'Roger Fortunatus.'

'No mere parent gave you a name like that.'

'I chose it for myself, as an omen for my life.'

'I like it. Continue.'

'. . . absolve you, Stephane de Laussel –'

'Ah, you found out my name,' he said gratified.

'. . . from your sin.' I made the sign of the cross above his head. 'In the name of the Father, Son and Holy Ghost. Amen.'

'Good!' He jumped up. 'I have come to you this time. But I shall expect you to come to me henceforth.'

Then he remounted his horse, and he and his servants rode away. Rigord and I looked at each other, lust for Stephane written on our faces, and we moved to an embrace, with nothing said, all sensed. Traces of Stephane's use of him were on the boy's face; I tasted it.

'You understand,' I murmured passionately, 'I want nothing from you that you do not wish to give. But I do want you.'

He led me where a great tree lay upon its side athwart a running stream, with a thickness of creepers and brambly bushes growing all about, all interspersed with the soft grey wispy trails of travellers' joy. He made his body ready for me, and I took him there against the tree. Dark berries nudged my shoulder. Against the mudstained leather of his jerkin I pressed close, and in him I was so at one with him that I became him, and lost myself in what I might have been, or what I truly was.

'What we did – did it mean anything to you?' I asked him afterwards.

'I liked it, if that's what you mean.'

'It wasn't the first time, I think?'

'No, a boy from the village . . .'

I wondered what his life was like; I guessed it; and I wondered how he could bear it.

163

'Will you stay here all your life?'

'I will. What else is there for me?'

'Do you never dream of travelling?' I asked this in mere curiosity; it never crossed my mind to ask him if he'd like to travel with me.

'I didn't use to. But now I do begin to think about different things, other kinds of ways of living.'

'What do you mean?'

'Well, since I saw Stephane. And since what happened with him.'

I felt a certain curious resentment as I heard him mention Stephane's name. 'Whatever can you mean? What difference can there be for you?'

'It's plain enough. He likes me; he'll be back. And I'll be glad to see him.'

'Everybody knows that Stephane is a monster,' I said angrily. 'You would do well to keep away from him. Take your pigs to a different place,' I urged him. 'He'll be no good for you. He's cruel and thoughtless, that much is perfectly clear.'

Again he did not speak. I found his stubborn silence infuriating.

'He is a nobleman – he is far out of your reach. It is ridiculous that you should think of Stephane.'

Rigord smiled ruefully. 'I know,' he said.

The stupid clod, I thought with savage scorn. That I should have ever thought myself allied to him in some unaccountable and mystic manner! The idea was repulsive.

VII

ALAIN HAD had enough of sojourn at the village. When he insisted that we leave I agreed; but I suggested that we made for the castle Gravillac where if we were fortunate we might spend the winter. Alain was understandably dubious and reminded me in no uncertain terms about his treatment at the staves of the castle folk.

'But that was because they thought you were a peasant. As a minstrel you will be treated quite differently, as well you know.'

'But you are talking about Guillaume de Laussel and his

reprobate son. Have you heard all the stories told by the villagers concerning both of them?'

'No; I would not demean myself to listen.'

Somehow I persuaded him, and we set off for Gravillac.

Guillaume de Laussel's castle was a tall gaunt heap of towers and battlements that soared up from flat fields.

'They hang felons from those ramparts,' Alain told me cheerfully enough. 'Heretics and trouble-makers. Dare you still enter?'

The main gate was open; it led into a courtyard. We went in.

The castle was built around a great hall, a huge round archway of stone supporting a roof of fine timber. Arched doorways led at intervals away, and above them, windows of the same shape, showing a passageway that circumvented the hall on the upper portion of the walls, so that people could look down through them into the hall. Beyond this passage, in the massy thicknesses of the walls were the rooms of the nobility, small chambers set in stone.

Within the hall was constant activity, with servants, peasants, men-at-arms, and dogs – a vast array of these, the mastiff boarhounds, raches, bloodhounds, and the handsome wolfhounds, big and lazy in repose, dozing by the fire, tall as a man when they stood on their hind legs. Visiting nobility with all their entourage were much before our eyes, with brilliant gowns and cloaks that trailed behind them in the tawny thick-strewn rushes on the floor.

We were absorbed into this tapestry; within a week it was our way of life.

I was wrong if I thought Stephane had sought me out and given me precise direction. For a week or so I saw very little of him; but in that time I saw much else, first impressions whose truth was borne out by the days that followed, all the small intrigues that unravelled as we gazed, for very little is secret within a castle's turbulence.

Stephane's companions of the forest, for instance, Francois and Louise, cousins to the family at Gravillac – here it was plain enough that Francois worshipped Stephane's mother, and that Louise liked pretty pageboys.

I saw Stephane's father, Guillaume, or more often the swirl of his cloak as he passed. Often absent from home, whether on matters of intrigue as believed by the villagers, or merely upon business of estate, he was a powerful impressive figure, inaccessible as a mountain peak and too high for his children to reach, at table curt, peremptory and distant. Stephane quarrelled with his father up and down the castle's length and breadth, noisy and querulous, as ineffective as a stone thrown at a battlemented keep. Even when he set fire to a pile of documents to make his presence known it gained him nothing and the flames were doused. Plain enough to all it was that Guillaume had no time for him.

Now with his mother it was otherwise. The Lady Azais thought Stephane dropped from Heaven like a rose from God's own garden. She was a charming woman, soft and beautiful, with hazel eyes and pale complexion, hair of silver-gilt, a joy to look upon in her gown of cream brocade and rabbit fur – and certainly discerning, for she praised me warmly and begged that if I did intend to winter at the castle I would teach her younger sons something of my learning; I agreed. She had seven children, and adored them all; she saw no further than the castle's wall – the world beyond might perish; she had all she needed where she was. She loved Alain's music, and made him as welcome as myself. She thought her household richer for our presence, and she said to me what many said before and since: 'By Jesu, how you ever came to be a monk! Your face and form are beautiful as day . . .'

However, she was thus fulsome to almost everybody, and such compliment was no indication whatever that she was to be the lady of the castle who languished for my love – I cherished that dream still, but now I knew the figure at its heart would be a lord.

Stephane flaunted himself before my gaze, basking in the certainty that I was well aware of him. So conscious was I of his every movement that I believed that everything he did was calculated to tantalise and goad my longing. *This could be yours*, his message was, *if I so chose*. He played the flirt with the ladies at the dining-table, and teased the servant girls – and boys – who carried in the food. Sometimes he came into the room where I taught grammar to his younger brothers, and spoke irrelevently of hunting boar, and castle gossip and the uselessness of study. Then he would disappear all day to hunt. To hunt! What manner of diverse activities that term described! I taught his brothers with my mind elsewhere and watched for his return, with all its possibilities. I positioned myself at the narrow window, where far below among the dun-coloured trees of the waning year might come that sudden bright smudge of colour, Stephane's entourage, with some dead beast in tow that meant their forage had been worth the effort. The ceremonies of the hunt I found abhorrent, and I never grew a liking for the spilling of blood.

It is one thing to explore the hidden reaches of the mind and dare the misty regions of what is called heresy – but to venture the flesh, the body's vulnerability, against a desperate danger knowing the boar is a mighty fighter, to no purpose save the thrill of danger, seemed to me entirely inexplicable. I hid this weakness, for I seemed to be alone in feelings such as these. Here at the castle, boar hunting was sport, quest, manhood, glory, needing all the skill of warfare, and accorded warfare's acclaim. And because of this I knew that in my heart I felt a certain jealously. I half suspected that if I had been brought up as a nobleman I would have thrilled as they did, to the chase, the kill, the awesome lust for blood.

One night Stephane came to where I lay, down in the great hall with a cloak about me, and he stretched himself beside me as if this was most natural.

'What did you think of that young pig boy?' he enquired.

'Which pig boy?' I said carelessly.

'You know well enough.'

'Fine, if you like them rough and dirty.'

'I've been back to see him. I'll tell you what we did.'

We lay side by side, whispering in the dark. Around us other bodies stirred and snored.

'I made him take off his clothes,' Stephane said with his face close to mine. Our mouths were almost touching. 'I made him walk up and down for me. Without his clothes he is timeless. Gods with nothing better to do came down from the aery mountaintops to gather boys like that. They took them to be their cupbearers, but those duties extended somewhat . . .'

'And is that what you intend?' I demanded, hot with jealousy.

'What?'

'To bring him here to be your cupbearer?' I sneered.

Stephane snorted. 'Thank you for your implication that I am a god! But what do you think of me to suggest that? Bring a peasant to the castle? Shower him with all the comforts of wealth – waste good food upon a palate used to weeds and stalks? I should think not!'

'Yet you have the power to do that,' I mused, thankful for the darkness, for his scorn was chastening to me. 'To raise him, to improve his lot.'

'What an odd idea,' said he. 'As far as I'm concerned the peasant is part of the forest, an animal no less. That boy is little better than his pigs. He knows it. I made him go down on his hands and knees. Have you seen his arse? So big and round and coarse – I took him from behind, the little brute, I drove my cock between his hairy buttocks till I'd had my fill of him, and Jesu save us but he liked it! The filthy little dungheap, he relished every moment of it. What do you think of that, then?'

'I can well imagine it. Particularly as I have already taken him myself, long before you did. I do recall the sensation of his ample arse, the sweetness of his warm insides, the tender groans, the pain and joy of satisfaction . . .'

Panting somewhat we lay very close, aroused by memories of Rigord and by the nearness of each other.

'Come to my room,' said Stephane brusquely. 'Follow me.'

I went with him from the hall, past the dozy guards and up the spiral stairway that led to the upper passageway. The room which soon I grew to know so well was then merely a mass of firelit shapes in a dark and musty space, with a bed strewn thickly with furs. Stephane turned to me, excited, seizing both my arms.

'You are to do for me what once you saw the peasant boy do. You watched us that day in the forest – so aloof, so seeming calm, but I knew what you thought, and I decided there and then I'd have the same from you one day – I'd have those learned dignified lips around my cock – a better use for them than singing psalms!'

'I don't dispute that. I'll be glad to give you what you want.'

Stephane sat down on the bed and spread his legs. I knelt in front of him, and put my mouth around the taste of sandalwood and skin.

I slept in his bed that night, and every night henceforth while I was at Gravillac.

I cannot say why it was I loved him. It was clear to anyone that he was thoroughly despicable, heartless, cruel, even stupid. The damage had been done before I came there. A cloying adoration from his mother never filled the hollow where paternal care ought to have been; a childhood lacking affection had warped his nature – but these are no excuse. Suffice to say I was besotted with him and lust was largely its cause. Stephane was as handsome as a fallen angel, sun-bright like they, and arrogant and shining. How often would I kiss his perfect face and marvel at its beauty – the high cheek bones and aquiline nose, the cold topaz eyes with tawny brows and lashes, and the full sensuous mouth, the sleek metallic strands of his pale hair.

His body was lean and hard and lightly smudged with gold, the more so since our love took place in the aureate glow of fire and flambeaux. He was all muscle, taut and lithe and heavily perfumed. Bodyservants massaged him with aromatic oils and bathed him night and morning in liquid coriander. I shared that bath and I had never smelt so fragrant! The scent lay on the skin and lasted all day long.

I told him often that I loved him, without knowing fully what I meant, for after all, what did I know of him? The secrets of his heart were never shown. In him I think I loved an aspect of myself, one that I envied and admired, one that was long suppressed and never could be, the self I might have been if I had been true born. Those winter nights were warm for me. We slept in musty scented sheets beneath a heap of furs. Stone walls twelve feet thick protected us. Far, far below, December snows whitened the forest, and Yule drew on apace.

At the festivities Stephane wore crimson velvet, edged with beaver. His servants laid his clothes out for him in the morning, and brought him a casket of jewellery lined with purple silk whence he chose his rings. His favourite was a stone of amber set in gold, the gold so twined to make the shape of a snake. His fingers were long and fine, a noble's hands. Mine were the same shape, and all his rings well fitted me.

Beyond the stone-rimmed windows snowflakes feathered softly, and down below the castle servants culling holly boughs and bay brought garlands to deck the walls; and every kind of minstrel and jongleur – including Alain – entertained, and Christmas music filled the castle.

Stephane once admitted: 'In taking you to bed I thought at first to fuck the Church. I see now you are more devious than a mere symbol, and besides in no way do you represent a muling priest. The Church! It fails us on every count, and most of all it fails us by denying lust. If lust is of the Devil, then Mankind is devilish, so how can we be saved? We might as well be damned in ecstasy.'

The Church would not be silent, as we found. The music in the hall was holy music – merry, carolling, pulsating, holy none the less. After all, it was Christmastide, the festival of our Lord's birth, and this was rightly to be celebrated. When I lay in bed with Stephane in the swansdown of his mattress we could hear the music wafting up, sacred refrains sung loudly to the tabor and rebec – *de virgine Mar-i-i-a* – *tibi laus* – *tibi gloria* – *laus* – *gloria* – all in the rhythm of fucking. But love could oust religion, and I know we took an added pleasure indulging in the rituals of profanity while downstairs they chanted jocund songs to our Creator. And sometimes when the tabor sounded more than common loud we fucked in time to it, sniggering with the wickedness of what we did, and called each other Holy Stephane, Holy Roger – to thee be all glory and all praise for thou art mighty –

Posuisti super me manum tuam – Alleluia! – you have laid your hand upon me. *Probasti me et cognovisti me. Tu cognovisti sessionem meam et resurrectionem meam* – you have searched me out and known me. You know my sitting down and my rising up.

Tu solus dominus – you alone are the lord.

'Never leave me,' Stephane murmured holding me. 'I have not known love such as this. With you it is the gratification of the beast within me transmuted to the gold of love's pure passion. Stay with me. We may well become true lovers . . .'

'I'll never leave you . . . you are my other self. I couldn't leave you – you are always with me . . .'

'When my father dies,' said Stephane, practical and merry, 'this castle will be mine. I'll never marry. You and I shall rule this place, and fit it to our every need.'

We laughed and hugged each other, comfortable in contemplation of so mischievous a plan.

In January Stephane came in from hunting with a tale to tell that caused a flutter of disturbance round the hall. Some prowling discontented villagers had set upon them with their makeshift weapons. These peasants had been easily repulsed, and Stephane laughed about it now he was returned. Francois revealed it had been most alarming at the time. Stephane decided certain houses should be fired as a punitive measure; men-at-arms rode forth upon this mission of destruction. Stephane's mother fretted, but no one at the castle seemed overmuch concerned and all went on as usual. I felt uneasy, for I vividly recalled the wall of hatred that I had encountered in the forest. But no one feared the peasants – nobles never did – and I allowed myself to share the careless scorn with which the incident was dismissed.

Barely within the week the body of Stephane was brought back from the forest on a hurdle made of knotted boughs. Gored by a maddened boar he met his death in the forest, bleeding into the snow.

A hundred times the story was recounted; how they pursued the mightly boar all day, how they encountered him and lost him, tracked him once again, the biggest of his kind that they had ever seen, a devil in brute form, slaughtering and wounding hounds, avoiding arrows, impervious to spear shaft, enraged by pursuit, cornered at the last. They surrounded him and fought on foot with swords, and drove him to a thicket. Here the telling always faltered, shifted – hounds dead and savaged, confusion, panic, Stephane always heroic somewhere in the midst of it, separated from the others. Shared guilt that they were still alive caused some discrepancy in their accounts, and Francois told me he had seen some peasants running from the thicket and swore it had been they who drove the boar at Stephane. I believed it. I went to Stephane's father and I told him so, and Francois lurked behind me, nervously. But Guillaume, pausing for us on his way across the castle hall, received our news with scepticism. He said it was not possible.

'They hated him,' I cried. 'It was a plot – they must be punished – and their village burned –'

'Here we have Stephane talking,' said his father wearily. 'Twenty years I've had of Stephane's rages, vengeances, perversions of the flesh. The boy is dead now. The boar is killed. Its mort was sounded and the carcase slit and roasted,

171

every wretched portion thrown to the hounds who gorged themselves upon it, and the head brought home upon a pole. Justice is done; and there's an end.' He turned on me a look of great indifference. 'I would suggest,' he added coldly, 'that you take yourself away from here and set about to square your own conscience, if you can, with the God whom you profess to serve.'

His mother meanwhile was in grief's extreme; there was no talking to her; she was witless. Others hovered between shock and curiosity and pretended sorrow. There were many emotions there; but only I had lost a lover.

I took the amber ring from Stephane's forefinger and put it on my own. From amongst his possessions I stole a bundle of things that would be useful to me – a warm cloak and gloves, doeskin boots, jewellery to sell – and I gathered my belongings and went in search of Alain, Alain whom I had forgotten and ignored, and told him I could not stay in this place.

'But it is January,' he protested, 'no one travels.'

'I will travel', I said demented; and because he felt some ancient obligation he came with me, leaving behind the warmth and safety of the castle, and we made our way into a wilderness.

Upon that journey I fell ill, escaping from my thoughts into a raging fever. The light of the snow showed only trees, pale trunks, and ghostly branches shivering in the wind. The wind was loud, a presence, and it rose and fell, sudden gusts coming like a shock, dropping to a low growl, pausing for breath, then rushing forward like the thudding hooves of horses. Whirling trees, rank upon rank of trees, glided past us, scattering ripples of papery snow, only trees as far as the eye could see. How long we travelled I had no idea, nor where Alain was leading us. But when I saw the broad highway and the sprawl of building by the wayside's edge, its gates and windows and the towers of its church, and recognised it for what it was, I recoiled, half dead from cold and weakness.

'Not to a monastery!' But I fainted on my horse, and we were taken in.

The sound of holy orisons wafted round me like a suffocating fume, God's domination clamping its grip on the back of my neck and beating me down with the beauty of its weaponry.

I saw the workings of His hand in this – He whom one denies, abuses, flees, thinking one has won one's freedom, only to understand too late that God is the all-embracing air, the pit beneath, the silent Lord who waits and holds out His inevitable arms.

VIII

BY AUGUST I was in Toledo, learning occult science at the hands of a magician.

The time spent at the monastery I firmly shoved into the sack of unwanted thoughts and threw it clear away. It was dead time and best forgotten.

It had been a Benedictine abbey to which Alain took me, somewhat east of Carcassone, and they received a fellow brother with concern. Not that I knew or cared, since I was out of my mind. A thousand demons trampled me and some of their names I recognised – Fear of God, Ache of Love, Wasted Opportunity, Perverted Talents, Pride, Lust of the Flesh, Ingratitude – enough to damn me many times over, and certainly the pains in my body from no physical root were caused by the pinpoints of their burning armoury.

But three months were enough to right me, and once out of the pit and on firm ground I counted myself clear of them.

'I'm pleased to see you well,' said Alain as we walked together in the cloister. 'How you raved! I feared for you . . .'

'What did I say?'

'You talked of Stephane, and of God – and other more dubious matters.'

'As what?'

'Oh – villagers coming out of the trees, with faces like gargoyles and stones in their hands, blind eyes crowding about you – halfwit ramblings. In particular? Well, that Stephane was a sacrifice, the Green Man of old legend, whose warm blood the earth needed for the rebirth of Spring.'

Alain laughed dismissively.

'And what is wrong with that?' I turned on him aggressively.

'It is a quaint and pagan notion.'

'No,' I said. 'The earth receives him with the Goddess's embrace, a loving union; not like the justice of the Father, which is all punishment and judgement. Stephane waits for me, in a perfect place.'

Alain eyed me strangely. 'I had thought you were recovered – but I believe you think you speak the truth.'

'I know it.'

'Well – I should not repeat such foolishness to the abbot.'

'You should never have brought me here,' I told him passionately.

'Is that the thanking I receive?' said Alain, reasonably enough affronted. 'You were half-crazed and feverish. You owe a debt of gratitude to the good brothers here. Where else should I have brought you to be healed?'

'Where else indeed?' I wondered. 'But not to the Father, who heals with one hand and possesses with the other.'

It was apparent that Alain and I had lost whatever camaraderie there had been between us. He felt his duty to be done now that I was on my feet, albeit a little odd. His consideration to me during the ravages of my fever had been prompted I suspected more by fear of what I might blurt out in the monks' hearing than by affection. But then, we were never more than travelling companions, and I had not treated him well. When he decided to leave the monastery, the weather now fair and mild, I did not try to dissuade him and we parted easily, without emotion. He said he would be going back to Brittany.

Myself, as I sat in the sunshine reading *Lives of the Scholars*, I determined to set out for Spain. I envied and admired those wandering fathers. Adelard of Bath in the last century went off to Syria to study Moslem manuscripts and learning; Peter the Venerable, Abbot of Cluny, to Spain to seek out a translation of the Koran. Gerbert, who became Pope, went south for mathematical instruction, settling in Toledo to study Moslem sciences and translations of Greek texts, and there dabbled in magic. They said he made a brazen head which solved all problems for him by magic means. I intended to do as much as they.

There was just one thing to do before I left. Attending Mass at Pasque I knelt to pray within the monastery church and all about me sang their adoration of the Father – *Pascha Nostrum Immolatus Est* – but I made a deviant oratory.

'I was tricked into this place. Although I thank you for the

174

healing I do not accept the restoration of your rights and when I leave this place I will relinquish once again your hold on me. Here in this your church I say All glory to the Goddess – Maid, Mother, Crone – whose works were in these lands before the missionaries came, and still are here and still shall be as long as forests last and rivers and the world itself.'

Not that I particularly believed this to be true; I merely wanted to offend Almighty God. And after that defiance I felt well quit of the snivelling wretch I was when I had been unwillingly brought into the fold, victim of Winter and the pains of Love. Now I could go forth with a liberated mind.

This monastery was set beside a wide highway, a well-travelled route to Spain, through Narbonne where I sold a fistful of gems from Stephane's jewel box to provide me with the wherewithal to travel. I joined a gathering of pilgrims. We took a coastal road. I saw the dark blue Mediterranean Sea and the brown hills of Spain, where our first glimpse of the natives was a band of brigands who surrounded us and robbed whom they deemed wealthy. By folding my arms inside my sleeves I hid the amber ring I wore; but I need not have troubled. A curious reverence for the Church caused them to spare me; though in the slim twist of leather about my waist beneath my robe I had more wealth than any of them. I took up with a party of scholars then, coming from Italy to study at Toledo; we went on together. I gained the reputation of an ascetic for I did not join in bawdy talk or visit any of the brothels on the journey; but I had a fair skill telling stories on the way. In flaming summer heat we reached our destination.

The city rose upon a tawny rock, shimmering in the heady stillness, floating above a dusty plain, with white villages below and oxen in the fields. The wide brown Tagus circled round about, crossed by a bridge hewn from the same dry rock the tiered city stood upon, a place of mosques and churches and the forging of Toledo blades, the finest in the world, where workmen hammered steel and swore it was the water of the Tagus that gave the weapon its great excellence.

At the school there in Toledo I studied some translations of Greek thought concerning free will and predestination, Islamic drafts converted into garbled Latin, and brought into Spain by the all-conquering Moors. Much hampered by a lack of understanding of the Arabic language, I set about to learn it. A strange infusion of cultures we were there, with Christians, Moors and Jews working side by side in the pursuit of knowledge, all in the fearsome heat that lay upon the city, with a fine white dust along the streets and afternoons too hot to walk abroad. I learnt some further aspects of astronomy, astrology and of alchemy. I often had the sense that what we studied was mysteriously wicked and would be seen in England as pure heresy; this lent spice to my endeavours.

It was an Englishman who taught me such Arabic as I acquired, enabling me to read the sensuous songs of al-Mu'tamid of Seville as they were written and to learn at first hand of the battles of El Cid. This Englishman had severed all connection with his early life and dropped even his name. He called himself Alfonso Alcazar and he lived in a tower with a Moorish dome beside a newbuilt church where once there was a mosque. He wore the Moorish garb – wide trousers, a silk tunic with a sash, a turban on his head; yet he admitted to me later that he first saw light of day in Shrewsbury! All his life he had been a scholar, most of it wasted, he said, in alchemy, in the search for what they call the Philosopher's Stone, the means to transmute base metals into gold – this he did in London; but fortunately he had had the sense, he said, to abandon that cursed path, and now he devoted his attention to the study of Arabic and to the science of the occult.

Lean, gaunt, his face was tanned and skeletal, yet his expression mild and equable, his eyes pale blue, a wispy goat-like beard upon his chin. At first I was his pupil, but he showed a certain fondness to me, and invited me to live and work up in the slender tower where his library was housed.

The room where I worked was strange and beautiful. Its walls were painted with intricate Arabic designs upon a background of lapis-lazuli with silver stars and flowing ornate symbols, and the window where my table stood had scalloped edges painted with gold leaf, most elegant a frame for the sky beyond, azure by day, ebony by night, the waxing moon shaped like a jewelled scimitar.

The books which old Alfonso had were books the Church in England would have burned. Here I learned that the Scriptures were but part of a larger series of holy writings, and that what had not fitted the requirements of those who found them were discarded; and that originally there had been many references to goddesses, but they had all been expunged because such talk did not well accord with the word of God the Father. When he knew me better, Alfonso made no secret of the fact that he was a magician. In his possession were papyri from the land of Egypt containing spells and curses in the name of Isis, Horus, Anubis and Osiris, with instruction for the mingling of bats' blood, toad entrails and ox hair.

176

He had an ancient parchment out of India, with the Saturn square upon it, and the numbers that in sequence have a devastating force. Strange his chosen way, for in his study side by side lay books of undeniable scholasticism with shrivelled crocodile skins and human skulls with gemstones in the eye sockets, and a wand of cypress wood and the embalmed lung of one who in his life had been a prince.

Long into the night we spoke about the Tree of Life of the Cabala, and its ten sephiroth, the unfolding aspects of God , whose names he spoke in Arabic, power centres of which the skilful magician gains control; and the Lightning Path, with those several mystical pathways which lock into that framework, with all their correspondences.

When I asked him to relate it to the philosophy behind the way of the Goddess, he did so; but he was dismissive of earth magic, as he called it, because true power lay with the use of symbols, names and interconnection; the way of the Goddess, he said, was for the simple.

One night I sat absorbed over my books and worked into the dark hours till I fell asleep, my head upon the manuscripts, the candle burnt out; and I awoke to find Alfonso with me, standing there, his hand upon my shoulder.

'What is it with you, Roger?' he said wonderingly. 'So greedy to discover – and so dissatisfied with what you find.'

The moon poured its light upon us, casting a pale sheen on parchment, quills and bulging leather books.

'You have now dedicated your life to magic,' I said. 'You, a scholar, who could go anywhere and study what he would. But magic is a dead-end path. You must see that? You think you will be in control. But ultimately God is in control. Whatever we do, we come up against the workings of His will. If we are on a path He does not like, He blocks us, drives us back where He would have us go.'

Alfonso laughed with some contempt. 'That is your youthful nurture speaking. They told you this when you were still unformed, in that long since abandoned abbey. It's hard to shake it off, I know. But sometimes, in order to pursue a shining light, the light of undiscovered knowledge, we have to dare to question God's dictates. You know that; and you would agree with me if you were properly awake.'

'I am awake,' I said morosely. 'I tell you from my own experience and you can learn from me. I left the abbey where I made my vows to God and I sought freedom of the mind and body, and I so trained myself that I could pass a month at a time without a thought of God to bother me. But He is always there in wait, glowing like the slit eyes of a wolf beyond the brightness of the fire you light in the clearing, skulking till the fire dies down, and then as you cower by the cold ashes out He prowls to sink His jaws in you...'

'God has no jaws,' said Alfonso pedantically.

'All you mean by that is you have not felt them,' I shrugged.

I turned round and looked up at him, and he looked away. For all he had made light of it, he knew well enough what I meant.

'You study magic,' I pursued. 'You think to put yourself in control by working your discoveries to your own purpose. What is the summit of your hopes? What would be the greatest manifestation of the power that you have gained?'

The moonlight showed Alfonso's face a skull wherein his eyes gleamed like cold sapphires – he had a dozen similar in grisly heaps upon his cobwebbed shelves.

'I want to raise up demons,' he said slowly. Carefully he watched my face, to see the effect upon me of the magnitude of his confession.

'Demons!' I laughed weakly. 'I can do that simply by falling asleep...'

From that moment our paths diverged; I could not feel for him the same respect. And then as always happened with me I grew aware of boredom creeping up, and the mysteries of Arabic which had before seemed like a bright hand beckoning now seemed hard work, and I was restless and began to look about me for other ways to spend my time.

I went from forge to forge to study weapons made, and stood for hours deciding which of many daggers was the perfect one for me, for it seemed most remiss to leave Toledo without purchasing a blade, and I gave the business as much care as men do buying horseflesh. I gave my old one to a beggar, and afterwards I wondered whether I had set him off upon a life of crime.

Down at the river's edge below the city I sat and watched naked boys bathing. Very beautiful the boys of Toledo! Their hair so black and curly, their bodies glistening with waterdrops – strong brown arms and rippling shoulders, with curvaceous buttocks, dark lissome thighs, and perky mischievous pricks. Older men in wealthy garments tempted them with coins – some went behind the bushes, and some went further, to a life of self-advancement, the eternal shifting conflux between affluence and flesh. A brown-skinned boy was pleasing to me, and between the sweet cheeks of his ample arse I eased away the pain of knowing that the last time I had fucked had been with Stephane.

178

When a party of pilgrims set off northwards into France that Autumn, I decided to go with them. I parted from Alfonso with affection. He gave me an Egyptian ankh, symbol of life, to wear about my neck on a silver chain, and a letter of introduction to his old friend and fellow student Jerome with whom he had studied in England when they wasted so much time together over alchemy and drained their wealth away in search of wealth perpetual. London? Was that where my future lay? I doubted it.

Alfonso wished me peace and happiness, but with so dubious an expression that I fancy he suspected there was little chance of its fulfilment.

Our journey took us through the Col de Roncesvalles, north east of Pamplona, the very place where Roland fell, a mountainous pass where the flower of French chivalry were slain by a monstrous Moorish army many times their number. In his bravery and pride the hero Roland would not sound his horn for help from Charlemagne, and he died fighting, with his faithful Oliver, betrayed by Ganelon, but passing into legend.

It happened that we were attacked by brigands in the wilderness before we reached the pass. We fought them off, and some were slain on both sides. It was my misfortune to kill one of the robbers myself, one who would have taken my amber ring from me, and I was chastened by the experience. My hand shook as I resheathed the dagger. I had learnt that when anger so possessed me I had strength and will to take another's life – and over what? A piece of stone and metal, an inanimate object – precious to me certainly, but worth a life? In the cold aftermath my reason told me no, but in the heat of rage I saw the question differently. And to my shame I knew that part of me was curiously proud to think I had been worthy of Stephane and my forebears, and had not flinched from what seemed right to me.

When we reached Roncesvalles I marvelled that wherever an event has taken place there follows somebody who starts a shop and turns it all into money. Besides the hostel which had been built there, with its beds and baths, there was a shack where the faithful could purchase treasures from the battle: sword fragments, polished hilts and helmets, shoe leather, and repulsive heaps of bones – hewn fingers, dented skulls, and endless rows of teeth, and all supposed to have been gathered after the great slaughter.

I stood and stared at what was offered to me as Roland's forefinger. It was a finger bone, that much was true. What if it was his? I would have dearly loved to own it. But I could not bring myself to believe it could be so, for all the seller promised me that by all the saints he spoke the truth. I turned away, and went and sat upon a rock and let the ghosts come to me.

The mighty mountains all about me, the great craggy slopes, the narrow defile between the scrubby foothills –easy indeed to picture the sight – *here* it was the hero died, *here* all those brave youths, and Oliver his friend – ah! were they lovers in the carnal sense? If only we could know! A fit of weeping overcame me in that place, to do with death and lovers...

Bertrand, a fellow student from Toledo travelling with the pilgrims, eyed me oddly. 'How strange,' he observed, 'to kill a brigand in the morning, and after noon to weep for men you have never met, who died four hundred years ago.'

Towards the end of the year I found myself beyond Bordeaux at La Rochelle and took ship there on a wine vessel bound for England. A thousand times I wished I had not, for though we hugged the coast it was not a good time of year to make that particular voyage. However, in spite of choppy seas and storms I took some pleasure in it, reminding myself of the voyage of Saint Brendan where natural hardship was made worse by lack of food; and on this ship at least we drank well. The captain was a jovial man and liked a game of dice, and regularly put into harbour when the going proved difficult.

I was pleased to celebrate Christmas in strange circumstances because it made it easier to forget where I had been last Yuletide. We were up by the coast of Brittany by then, and we attended Mass in some obscure village with an unpronounceable name and a strange old church besides some ancient standing stones, and so by chance it fell I said my prayers to God and Goddess both, expecting nothing from either.

In January we sailed up the Thames, the ship dropped anchor in the port of London and I stumbled to the wharfside in a snowstorm.

In seeking out the dwelling where Alfonso's friend Jerome lived, I had no other purpose than to cadge a shelter from the weather on the streets. The door was opened by his wife Marget, and when she ascertained I was no creditor she let me in, and Jerome welcomed me, astonished that I brought news of one whom he had once held dearly.

It must have been ten years since he and Alfonso worked together in the mystic search for gold, and in the meanwhile Alfonso had turned traveller both bodily and spiritually. Yet all that time Jerome had worked upon his alchemy, as strongly possessed as

180

anyone could ever be by demons. It seemed to me a wasted life – but who was I to judge? And after all, what did I know of alchemy in practice? It caught my interest and I sought to make myself indispensable. This was easy, since Jerome was barely in this world and needed every kind of help. And Marget was worn down with loneliness and arguments with creditors.

Inevitably Marget and I were left together frequently and I had much opportunity to study her and wonder at her life. What could God's purpose ever have been for her? Painfully astute, she knew well enough that Jerome's obsession was like to come to nothing, yet marriage yoked her to him, to their unsatisfactory existence, to certain ruin and the destitution of her children. From conversation with her I suspected that she was as clever in her way as Jerome, for she explained to me why his experiment was doomed to failure; she knew all the terminology and formulae. Loyalty bound her, but she was despairing. A chivalrous wish to be her saviour by discovering some kind of missing link in Jerome's calculations was my main motivation for working with her husband.

Of an evening when the children were in bed and Jerome in his cellar, she and I would sit beside the hearth in the dark parlour lit only by firelight. Outside the small high window the slithering slaps of rain gusts sounded.

'It's good that you are here,' she told me warmly. 'It gives Jerome an added impetus. It's been so long since anyone accorded him a proper interest...'

'It's I who should be grateful,' I assured her, with a slight flicker of guilt, knowing, for all my helpfulness, that I was scrounging on her hospitality. 'If not for you I would be wandering and this is no night for it.'

'So young,' she murmured, 'and such a traveller...'

'Oh no, I've not been anywhere to speak of,' I said modestly. 'Adelard of Bath went to Syria...'

'It is not common to have been to France and Spain. Hundreds never leave the village of their birth.'

'I'm just one of the many, I'm afraid. The schools churn out too many scholars with no prospects of employment, so they drift. I don't know if that's good or bad. It doesn't make for stability; on the other hand it's good to see the hidden places of the world.'

'You certainly had the look of a traveller when you first arrived.'

'Dirty, cold and weatherbeaten,' I said ruefully.

'Perhaps. But what adventures you must have had along the way...'

'Why no, it's just a tale of shabby inns and dusty roads, that's all...'

'Do you mean to tell me that you won no woman's heart along the way?' she teased me. 'I am sure you are aware of it, but you're unusually handsome. I can't believe that your beauty was lost upon the ladies you encountered.'

'Oh, I've kept clear of women,' I assured her. 'You see, in the abbey where I was brought up I knew no women, so I was never at ease with them...With you it seems different. You seem so understanding – like a mother might have been...or an older sister,' I added hurriedly, for she was not that old. 'But I never had either...' I paused to let the warm still air absorb the poignancy of my remark. I watched her profile in the fireglow. She must have been attractive in her youth. The cares of her life, and the dull severe clothes she wore, clouded such beauty as she still retained. With someone to make her happy, I thought assessively, she would be good-looking now. 'Yes,' I sighed, 'it's true I've travelled; but love I have not known, nor the soft touch of a woman. I suppose they think because I was a monk I have been taught to hide my feelings. Or that I do not feel at all...it is not so.'

I looked across at her. I did not suppose for a moment that she believed me, but what of that? She was a very lonely woman.

'And I'm so tired.' I looked at her with longing. She held out her arms to me. I knelt on the floor and pressed my face into her lap.

'Roger,' she began doubtfully. 'I am no longer young...'

'It doesn't matter,' I assured her. I almost added that I loved her, but I found that was one lie I could not countenance now that I had known love truly.

'It doesn't matter,' she agreed, as if she had been making a decision; and she ushered us to bed.

I cannot say there was much of desire on either part; it was a mutual need for comfort bound myself and Marget, and I think it was a bargain suited both of us. After a day spent sweating over furnaces and handing potions to Jerome, how very agreeable it was to sink into the feather bed, the downy pillows, and the warm thighs of his wife. I think a woman generates more heat; and I was warm of nights that Winter.

But Winter passes, and one day that same house which had seemed a haven to me suddenly seemed dark and stifling. Instead of helping Jerome with his work I found the idea of descending to that steamy underground den repellent. Even the amusement of cheating the gullible of a coin or two, by promising them gold from a magic cauldron in the distant future, palled in time. I took to wandering the streets where sunlight brightened dreary walls and folk were lively in the fresh new light. I strolled the wharves and looked at ships, and listened to some grizzled sailor bawling love songs from a boat, the words so jumbled and outlandish that they made me laugh; and when he started up that song of King Richard's captivity I'd last heard from the lips of Blondel, I picked it up and went home singing.

As I closed the door behind me as caught Marget's gaze – reproach, resignation. She knew I was restless but she would not form the words for she was wise enough to know she had not the power to stop me if I chose to leave. I gave her a contrite kiss and looked the penitent, and to assure her of my good intention I strode off purposefully to Jerome's lair, and set about making up for lost time by carrying out his instructions almost conscientiously.

Within the hour the door was opened. Marget entered, bringing visitors, a twitching idiot that fidgeted in the shadows, and a pedlar, with a package.

From head to foot that pedlar was a Saxon, straight from the old manuscripts that show us thanes in Harold's day. Tall and lean he was, broad-shouldered, tanned by sun and wind, with shaggy dark brown hair and long moustaches. Suddenly I was reminded that, though learning knew no boundaries, politics were composed of them; and I suspected that his appearance, partly God-given and partly of his own manipulation, was in some way a statement. Amused, I guessed that I knew little of the intricacies of daily life in my own land – the abbey, learning, travel had removed me from them. Where would I fit in, half Celt, half Norman, where a man must know his place?

The pedlar, blowing into Jerome's cage of dreams with all the trappings of the outside world upon him, caught my interest sharply and intrigued me with his startling reality.

I moved towards him, holding out my hand.

'You can trust me,' I told him, perfectly aware I lied.

With satisfying aptness the pedlar dropped into my life just when I needed a diversion. I did not see the hand of God in this, Who only sends me spite and sorrows; therefore I blessed the workings of Chance, whose indifferent company at least gives one a deal of some impartiality.

Jusson I considered a dull fellow and I was glad to lose him to his meat pies and his pastries. But he had unwittingly done me a service.

That evening as we ate I told them something of my life; there was enough to tell to make a merry meal of it and yet leave the most untold. You may be sure I did not mention Stephane, Ailred nor Tobias, nor the boys I had along the way; but women I had known I boasted of, because this makes for joviality, men among men. The pedlar was not equally forthcoming and his silences intrigued me. I was already curious, because he brought a package to me that contained a murder spell, and given to him by a woman.

Who was this personage, this secret beauty, Berenice de Bonnefoy? What private torments had so driven her that she should resort to these despairing measures? Had I found at last the lady of the castle that I had been seeking in a dream amongst the gilded mists of romance? Her presence called me, like a distant throb of music.

But from Jusson's burblings and the pedlar's blatant wish to keep him quiet, it seemed there was more. A beautiful boy who had some dabblings with the religion of the Goddess . . . a boy moreover whom the pedlar had surely marked out for his own . . . a boy that special!

A boy who knew no better, and a lady who might drop into my palms as plums do – those old promises made by Brother Tobias by the cloister wall, promises which had tempted me and wrenched me from my vows to God and led me on the road. Did I not deserve this chance? The justification, the reward, the compensation for my continual flight from the Almighty, the nightmare which would never leave me while I fled the Lord?

The answer was before me, affirmation.

Now it was clear to me that if I was to persuade the pedlar to let me accompany him then he must never suspect I had an interest in the boy. And to be honest (if I can remember how honesty feels) it was the lady that most drew me. Marget had somehow stirred in me that sweet completeness which I would have liked so long ago with Gytha in the crimson of the cornfield. However, it is a careless man who does not hedge his bets, and if the lady failed me the boy would not.

And so I would say nothing of my lust for male flesh, neither would I show it in my words or deeds. I would travel with the pedlar and I would not let him suspect my true intentions; and if I could not have the lady, I would have the boy.

184

FIVE
The Pedlar's Tale

IT WAS a very agreeable journey to Cortle.

Firstly the weather was much improved since the last time I had trod those roads, and secondly Roger was a much more interesting companion than Jusson, who was now safely restored to his cookshop.

We were subject to the usual hazards of Spring – it rained, and the roads were muddy, in some places like little streams. But it was sweet rain, not the cruel snow-rain of the dark months; this was the fruitful rain that hastened the crops to grow. It fell showery and almost warm, and in between times a vigorous sun came hot and strong, so that vapour rose up from the puddles, and the bushes and wayside flowers could almost be seen to grow. The winds were warm and sweet-smelling; there was a freshness in the air, and clear skies of blue, and fat white clouds. The trees on all sides were busy regaining their leaves, every bud was straining and bursting; some were deliciously blossomed, fragile and wind-blown, and the new leaves were a sharp bright green. Birds sang on every branch.

And what an increase in travellers there was! No solitude now. There were trundling ox carts, riders on horseback, pilgrims and priests, merchants laden down with goods, all kinds of people that cold weather had previously kept at home.

Around each town and village the fields were full of activity. Sowers slung with baskets plodded the strips casting corn with a determined rhythm. Others were dibbling beans and planting kale. Boys paced the finished acres frightening

185

off the birds gathered hopefully on the still thinly covered
trees and hedgerows. One place we saw a ceremony of
Blessing of the Planting. Before sowing the first corn the
village priest took it in his hands and said a prayer:

'Our Lady, Our Lady, Mother of Earth,
May Your blessing give us
Fields full and fulsome
Fruitful and fair,
May the Lord Almighty
And His saints up above
Keep from this His land
All evils and the works of witches;
May no witch or man be powerful enough
To counter this blessing,
In the name of the Holy Trinity, Amen.'

Roger thought it was curious how the church was to be seen
imposing its authority upon the ancient ways. These prayers
to the Trinity were intricately woven into patterns of belief so
old that their beginnings were lost in the roots of time. Man's
needs were always the same, and he made offerings and sang
chants to whichever deity he believed was in control. The
priest spoke a mass over a piece of earth, but often it was still
intermingled with old fragments of spells, and the turning
the way of the sun. This Christian man of God might be
shocked to think he was like a Pagan spellcaster, but the
beliefs were common to both, and both prayed for the same
ends. And these ceremonies were going on all up and down
the countryside.

Slowly then we journeyed on, with many stops to see to
Roger's blisters. When we first started out his face fell when
he understood he'd have to go on foot.
'Oh! Must we *walk*?' he groaned.
'If you go with me you must. I'm trudging with a
packhorse, and you'll have to ride at snails' pace if you take a
horse. Perhaps you're thinking better of it already, eh? It
won't be what you're used to.'
'Oh no,' he said firmly. 'If you can walk, I can.'
I felt some fondness for him as we journeyed on; he never
said he found it heavy-going. He had boots of best quality –
Lord knew where he'd got hold of them – it was just that he

wasn't used to walking.

Myself I was much taken with the pride of ownership in Comfrey. When we stopped I'd be careful to take off his pack-saddle to let his heated hide dry off, and be sure he ate no hay with barley grass in it which would have made his gums sore, nor no buttercup that could scab the mouth.

I could not hide of course the trouble I was having still with that left arm of mine, which was in no way improved. It baffled Roger as much as it did me; for you could see no wound or mark or bruise, and yet the feeling in it was now very slight and all my fingers stiff. He often studied it and traced his hands over the muscles, for it teased him not to understand a thing. In villages we passed he asked about for remedies, which he tried out to no avail; he dragged me off to every wise woman we were told about, and crones with not a third of Alkanet's skill were let loose upon me with their pastes and potions, and all to no purpose. Kindliness partly spurred him, I daresay, but I knew his real wish to cure me stemmed from his great vanity – he longed to be the one to unravel the secret cause of things and master Nature. Not that I cared. A cure prompted by vanity would have been most welcome. I doubted I would ever use the thing again.

'A pity some of the skill you have in tricking the gullible does not work for my arm,' I observed sourly, after one more failed remedy.

'The Devil take me, but you're right,' he said. 'Whatever can it be? I hate to be so thwarted!'

We passed a horrid sight along the edge of Huntingdon Forest. That pestilence known as murrain had cursed some wretched village land and all the length of it the hideous heads of the dead beasts were stuck on posts to warn the passers-by. How vile they were, the eye holes bare, the horns up-jutting and the strands of hairy flesh dangling from the bone, flies buzzing, rooks and magpies rooting in the mangy rot. Last week that village would have been a thriving place; now with livestock gone they would be poor and lorn.

'How well that sight reminds us to live while we may,' I shuddered.

'How sharply it recalls God's indifference to us,' Roger added, pale and strained.

'God gives His comfort also,' I suggested.

'God caused the pestilence in the first place, did He not?'

187

said Roger savagely.

'You seem determined to find Him at fault?' I said uneasily.

'That has been my experience,' said Roger.

We crossed ourselves and hurried on.

'You think well of King John then, pedlar,' Roger commented.

'I do. All I have heard of him suggests that he is just and kindly and caring of his people. I know someone who is one of the royal baggage train – he says the king pays well, and always considers the welfare of all, even down to the most humble – even down to the camp followers!'

'Then you haven't heard he murdered his nephew,' Roger chatted pleasantly.

'What nephew?'

'Young Arthur of Brittany, whom he captured at Mirebeau two years ago.'

'I thought he was in France, in captivity?'

'*His corpse* is in France,' Roger said.

'Ah, I don't believe it! Why would he do so? Arthur is no threat to him.'

'In France it is common knowledge. He was killed at Rouen, secretly.'

'Ah, the French – they're always spreading grisly rumours. Every rumour about our kings and queens starts in France; everyone knows that . . . Was he really killed?'

'Ha – you begin to believe it!' Roger chuckled. 'They say,' he added, as one might begin a story, 'that on a dark night the king came to his nephew's cell, drunk like a madman, and he slaughtered him with his own hands! Aghast at what he'd done, the king then caused the body of the hapless youth to be dropped into the Seine, a weighty stone around the neck. A fisherman found it, tangled in his net.'

'I've seen the king, he is civilised and good-humoured . . .'

'But aren't they called The Devil's Brood? Wasn't their ancestress a daughter of Satan, who would not stay in church for Mass? And whose son is he – look how his father used to froth at the lips and writhe on the floor and chew rushes in his fits of rage!'

'Tangled in a net, you say? And with a stone about his neck?'

'In France it's common knowledge.'

'The boy perhaps provoked him? He was after all captured in a treasonous act, besieging Mirebeau in war against his lord.'

'Oh indeed, I do not doubt that young Arthur was an offensive little brat and justly merited what he received. It merely surprised me to hear you had good words to say of John, who after all has none of Richard's physical charms. Richard's ways with boys you must have heard about . . .'

'His ways with boys . . . so you have heard that rumour?'

'Why do you think he spent his life abroad, where boys are bought in street markets solely for the purpose of pleasure! Safely away from the probing glances of his barons and the Church! In those hot climes they make an art of sodomy. He was no fool, our golden monarch, and believe me, he indulged himself!'

'How do you know this?'

I should have guessed.

'In France it's common knowledge . . .'

It almost befell for us as it had for that startled fisherman of Rouen when we skirted Fen country.

We passed through a village where the folk were gathering round a corpse the river had washed up. And all had stopped their work and left what they were doing to come marvel at the sight, for this was no everyday dead body. It was a Norman soldier, as could be seen by the rusty weed-grimed chain mail armour that he wore. But it was not the armour of today, the helmet being conical, such as they wore at Hastings. This was a soldier from a hundred years ago, one maybe who had fought against Hereward and his Saxons, shot with an arrow, who had lain in river mud weighed down by armour all this time. Within his helmet mask he was a grisly skeleton. The villagers said it was not the first, that at other times and in other villages they sometimes had found long dead Norman soldiers trapped by reeds and weeds in ancient armour.

I stared in awe, and crossed myself, and thought much about Life and Time. Only yesterday in a village we had passed, a child had died of hunger in a ditch, and no one had stopped work to come and stare, for it was common. It seems that it is how you die, the circumstances of your death, that cause a stir, not Death itself. I looked for Roger but he was not there.

I found him further on, arms crossed about his chest, and shivering.

'It's horrible,' he said through chattering teeth.

'He has been a long time in the water,' I agreed. 'It spoils the beauty of the fairest . . .'

'No, I didn't mean . . .' He turned to me and tried to smile. 'It wasn't him . . . I mean the fact of Death – I can't bear – I hate anything to do with Death – all that reminds us that we have to die . . .'

'Then you will have a troubled passage through this world,' I answered grimly and with pity.

Up near Swaffham we heard the news that Queen Eleanor of Aquitaine was dead. Now, in April, when all the birds were singing, and the skies were bright, the time beloved of lovers, this lovely lady died.

'But she was more than eighty years of age!' Roger cried. 'She has had five times the span of many. I cannot grieve for her.'

Young and beautiful, with raven-black hair and the dark eyes of those who come from the south, she had been married to the pious king of France. What a trouble she was to him! Her wayward ways distressed him. She even went on a Crusade, and merry wicked tales were told of her. When the king annulled their marriage she wed Henry Duke of Normandy, Count of Anjou, he who had become King Henry II. She bore many children – two of them were kings – and when she grew to hate her husband she fought against him through her sons. At her court in Poitiers minstrels came, and lovers, troubadours sang songs of chivalry and passion. She was adored for her beauty, she inspired countless songs of love. For so long she had been a marvel, an ideal, a Queen of Love. She would never be forgotten.

I could not but be sad to hear that she was dead. With that, and the fall of King Richard's castle – for he too, with all his faults, had been a man of power and glamour – it seemed a time was over.

No one sleeps out of doors unless he has to, and so there were not many times that Roger and I were alone at night in some wild spot beneath the stars. But there were some.

I was surprised how little he knew of living off the land.

190

Simple things he did not know, like how to catch fish in the shallows or where to look for honey in the nests the wild bees make in trees. He had not heard that meat must be cooked straight after you have killed it because if you let the stiffness set in you will never get it tender. Also I noticed that his eyes were not as sharp as mine, and distances he did not see as well as I did. But when it came to book learning he was a fount of knowledge and I knew nothing; so each man has his skills. But he had some funny notions. He had this idea that a forest was like a man's mind, with dark things lurking, and that when you went into a forest you were like to find some truths about yourself. But I just laughed.

'Whatever would my life be like if I risked meeting hidden thoughts each time I took a path within a wood! Your way of looking at it is a townsman's way.'

'I don't deny it,' Roger laughed. 'To plod as you do in all weathers on your own would drive me soon to madness.'

'You are as burdened down with symbols as I have been with pans and baskets!'

'It's true – it's my church training. I have been trained to see the symbolism of all things beyond their simple actuality. Just take a dove, a simple dove. You see an ordinary bird a-pecking at the seeds some wretched sower laid, but I see this: Two wings – two kinds of life, the active and the contemplative; the feathers of its wings, being sky-coloured equal thoughts of Heaven. The different shades upon the body show the changing sea of our struggle through this life. The bright gold eyes as lush as golden fruit show us the light of experience which we attain as we too ripen. Its red feet represent the blood of martyrs, the Church's bitter food.'

'And when it cocks its tail and shits?' I wondered; but this Roger did not know.

That night, in a bed of furze and deerhide in a shelter I had slung together from withy props and brushwood, we awoke to find our arms about each other.

A weird moment! Suddenly both wide awake and staring face to face. We pulled apart. But there had been that moment . . . My heart was beating quickly. If he had said to me then that he wanted my body I'd have given myself and gladly. I thought he wanted me – no, more: I knew it. It was in his eyes – you don't mistake desire. But it had been so brief. Within an instant he had put up a shield between us, making me think I had imagined what I saw. I lay wondering. His talk was all of women – boastful tales of wenches he had known in Paris. He even admitted that he'd bedded the alchemist's wife and many others like her. So I was wrong – it was my own desire which made me see it in the eyes of others. I marvelled at myself for being such a fool.

II

AND SO we came to Cortle.
Although I did wonder what Alkanet and he would make of each other, I had firmly decided to keep Roger well clear of the herb garden. I took him straight to Cortle village and I didn't point out the path that led to the old woman's cottage.

We went into the church, as was my custom, and Roger wandered about it looking at the carvings; and then I sold some items from my pack at the church porch, and everyone crowded round to congratulate me on my little horse and made cheerful remarks about my coming on in the world, which made me glad, because success noticed is pleasing.

Then we went across to the tavern, and as it happened to be towards evening we fixed to stay there for the night. All the usual folk were there, and others joined us as the evening wore on.

I asked whether there was any gossip about life at the castle.

'They are both still there,' said Benedict. 'Not gone visiting now that the weather's better. But I hear that it's because he's not right in his health. No one seems to know what's the matter with him, but different people have said that it's a sort of attack. One day he do seem to be all right and the next he's taken to his bed. And even when he's up and about they say he can be a mite odd. I'm glad to have nothing to do with him. I fear it must be hard on the castle servants.'

'We don't see much of Azo these days,' said Ralf. 'He ain't bothered by that man's oddity. He's taken to living up at the castle and mixing with the castle guard and acting like he was one of them. I bet he'll be changing his name soon – something Norman, to go with his character. Good riddance, I say; the more he's with them, the less he's with us.'

'But what would happen if the lord were to die?' asked

someone, 'Who'd be our master?'

'Well, she would, wouldn't she?' said Walther. 'There's no children. Yes, she'd be our master, and what do you think of that?'

'Well, she's pretty enough,' someone decided. 'But it would seem very odd her telling us what to do. She may be used to managing her servants, but I would think it strange to own a woman as master.'

'It would be all wrong,' said Angilbert decidedly. 'Woman's place is not at the head of troops. Those that know their duty are busy bearing children, and anything else is sinful and wrong. The Devil uses women as his instrument, you know. Remember sinful Adam. If Berenice de Bonnefoy were ever to become our master it would be a sad and dreadful day for us. Apart from which, women are inferior. They cannot hold positions of power.'

Roger said: 'But what is so dreadful about the lady Berenice, priest?'

Angilbert bristled.

'She's a seductress, that's what. She's the sort that uses her charms as an instrument for the downfall of man!'

'Have you personal experience of this?' asked Roger in amusement.

'Of course I haven't,' said Angilbert twitching. 'What do you think I am?'

Benedict laughed behind his hand.

'You are too modest,' said Roger. 'I feel sure that any lady, high born or low, would prove susceptible to the wit and wisdom of a scholastic man like yourself.'

Angilbert was foolish enough to feel flattered. He smirked self-consciously. 'It's true, of course,' he said. 'A wench loves words. I see that you are a discerning man, sir. We men of religion must stick together, wouldn't you say?'

'Surely,' said Roger seriously. 'But I think it only right that we should first resolve our position on the great issue of the day, don't you? To that end, I must know whether you profess to be a Nominalist or a Realist. Otherwise we may quarrel.'

I wished that Angilbert would simply say that he had no idea what Roger was talking about, and ask him to explain. But no, with a section of his flock about him, peering curiously at him, he couldn't bear to lose face. He began to

193

bluster.

'Well, some maintain,' he said, 'and others think the opposite. Certainly the feelings are very strong on both sides. I have often thought about it. But I am never much called upon to expound it here. We are a simple folk. Only the day to day benefits of my guidance are needed.'

'There is no need for them to be deprived of making the choice for themselves,' said Roger. 'You could explain it to them; or I could.'

'Oh, you do it,' said Angilbert grinning foolishly. 'I must say, it is so refreshing to meet with a man of learning like yourself. One feels so isolated in an out of the way village.'

'See this man, said Roger, presenting to us Lambert, a quiet sleepy youth who had no idea whatsoever about the great issues of the day. 'The matter in question is whether he exists. Is he real?'

We felt relieved that the great issue of the day was so easily decided, and also thankful that it wasn't a religious problem. We all agreed that Lambert was real. I don't remember anyone denying it.

'So far, then,' said Roger pompously, 'you are all Nominalists. The problem comes with generalisation. Lambert is real. Lambert is a Man, a specimen of Mankind. Man, meaning Mankind, Man as opposed to objects, Man in general – is *that* real? We cannot touch it or pinch it or even see it in the same way that we can touch or pinch or see Lambert. That kind of man is universal, an ideal. We cannot even picture it. It includes too much. It represents all men, yet it is no man in particular. Can we therefore say that it exists?'

We didn't know. As you might expect, the great issue of the day was not going to be resolved suddenly in Cortle tavern by some field labourers.

But some of us for the sake of argument took one side and some another. I felt safer with what I could see, and being in no doubt that Lambert was real, whereas only imagining and supposing the reality of Mankind, I seemed to be a Nominalist. Angilbert was too.

Benedict said: 'Yes, but God do see Mankind, even though we do not. He must look down upon us all, and in His head He has the full picture of Mankind.'

'Very good,' said Roger. 'And because Benedict can imagine so much, does that not give the notion some reality?

194

So is it not real, just as much as Lambert is?'

'Not quite so much,' we decided.

'Take then mere ideas,' said Roger. 'Justice, beauty, truth. There is no proof that they exist, except in the mind of a man who conceives of them. Or, I must add, in the mind of a woman, for some very great thinkers have been women.'

We let that one pass, supposing it merely a little compliment to Edith, Benedict's wife.

'But if such a man does conceive of them, doesn't that make them real?' I asked.

'But you can't see them if they are in a man's mind,' said Angilbert.

'Do we then only believe what we see?' demanded Benedict stoutly. 'I don't think you of all people should go along with that, Angilbert.'

Angilbert looked confused.

'No, of course not,' he said. 'We believe by faith.'

'You have been tending towards Nominalism so far,' said Roger.

'Have I?' said Angilbert, somewhat muddled.

'What I would suggest to you,' said Roger, 'is that the whole question of our faith is tangled up with the problem. If you are a Nominalist and say that only tangible things exist, then what of the nature of God? How is that a reality? What about the Trinity? How can there be the One God and the three? How can both be true?'

Angilbert stood up, red-faced.

'That's heresy!' he shouted.

'Exactly,' said Roger coolly. 'Outright Nominalists are very suspect people within the establishment of the Church. That was why I was quite surprised, Angilbert, when you said that your own views were undecided. I thought that with the souls of your flock in the balance you would stand strong against any heretical leanings. But now you've reassured me, with your righteous indignation. I can see that you are not heretical at all.'

Angilbert was speechless. All of us who had been pleased to be labelled Nominalists now felt uncomfortable, and hoped that God would realise that we didn't know what we were talking about. But it was worse for Angilbert, who had not only been made a fool of, but had seemed to be flirting with an heretical viewpoint. He was only saved by an attack of his stomach complaint, which had him doubled up, and a circle of helpers about him with advice and supporting arms.

'I know a cure for bellyache,' said Lambert eagerly. 'Shall I tell him? 'Tis this. You collect twelve live snails, crush them between two slices of bread and eat them with milk.'

'I don't think that would help,' said Benedict. 'But I sometimes wonder if we shouldn't tell him about . . . Ah, no, you never know what foolishness he might go and do in the name of religion, and I'd be sorry to see the old ways go.'

Angilbert's gripes broke up the gathering. He was taken home. We sank then into silly talk and riddles – even Roger told one. As night drew on the others left, and Benedict showed us a corner of the room and gave us each a sleeping pallet. I fell straight asleep, with the warm room and too much over-sweet ale. In fact I slept so well that when I awoke I sensed at once that it was morning.

But Roger was not with me. I sat up, surprised. He was gone.

Then a sickening thought struck me. I looked inside my pack, which had lain between us. The contents were tumbled about and the package for Berenice was missing. So, I thought, he stole it. I might have known. I must have been stupid.

When I went out into the street I asked about, and I was told that he had left very early, and had been seen setting off in the direction of the castle.

III

I SAT over bread and ale at Benedict's table and wondered what to do. It didn't take me very long to reconcile myself to the loss both of Roger and of the package. In truth, I was glad to be rid of it. I didn't want to go to the castle and hand it innocently over and receive gracious thanks for evil business. As for Roger, all my old mistrust had been revived. Within my pack lay my livelihood and I didn't like the idea of anyone messing about with it even if they only took one item.

The only thing I was sorry about was that I wouldn't be getting the gold Berenice had promised for delivering the package. That's what I felt most sore about. I even considered going after Roger and demanding it; but of course I didn't.

There was no knowing what Berenice would do. She might think I had guessed her secret and needed silencing; or perhaps she had never intended paying me anyhow. After all, I had done little to deserve it. I'd been very offhand as a messenger, dawdling in London and then losing the goods.

I felt relieved. It was no longer my problem, but all in the hands of Providence. Now I could devote myself to something much more agreeable, a visit to Marel.

So I set off with Comfrey, a real delight in the warm sunny morning, and a very light heart. I left the village; I passed the heathland and found the secret path that led into the forest. The trees were full of birdsong, and lush with new leaves. Woodland flowers grew all about.

I remembered that last time Alkanet had been very kind to me in her way. It made me hope that she would again allow me some time with Marel. I sensed the appearance of herbs now, mingling with trees and undergrowth, and when I reached the clearing again the shock of how beautiful it was struck me. This time the little house was all covered with leaves already thick and luxuriant. Alehoof trailed its tangly stems and bright blue flowers, and fluffy foalswort grew, and the red and blue flowers of lungwort. What a pity, I thought, that Marel was such a prisoner! What an enchanted setting for such an enticing captive! What a fearful old witch it was that had convinced him he must stay there!

Nobody came to the door. I tied Comfrey's halter to a tree and made my way to the doorway.

'Is anybody there?' I called, looking in.

There was a movement upstairs.

'Who is it?' called Marel's voice.

'It is the pedlar man,' I said, suddenly elated to think he might be there alone.

'Oh . . . pedlar,' he said. 'You may come up.'

I could hardly believe my ears. I looked round about me quickly in case Alkanet was returning. I climbed up the ladder that led into the loft. As I came up I noticed an unusual smell which I couldn't place, but it was partly herbs and partly a musty decaying smell which was seeping through the sweeter ones. I emerged into the loft.

Marel was kneeling on the floor. He was nothing like he had been when I last saw him, hooded and subdued. Only in beauty was he unchanged. His abundant corn-coloured hair fell across his shoulders. He turned and looked at me with huge eyes.

At first I thought he was kneeling beside a bed of flowers. Certainly there was a bed of flowers there upon the floor. But what lay upon it so astonished me that my heart began to beat at a great rate, and a queasy feeling rose in me. It was Alkanet, dead, arranged in the centre of the flowers. She was dressed in white, with her hands folded and her eyes closed. She was very grey and small. There were flowers everywhere.

'She's dead,' I said. It sounded foolish, and I had never truly supposed that Alkanet could die. I thought she could fix nature and remain forever master.

'Yes. She died two days ago.'

'How?'

'She simply fell forward and lay with her head on the table amongst the herbs.'

'And you did all this?'

'Yes. The blue flowers are rosemary; I burnt some for sweet air. This is bay. This is tansy; it staves off decay.'

'Ah,' I said, still marvelling.

Then my commonsense returned.

'Does anybody know that she is dead?'

'No. No one has been.'

'She must be buried, you know.'

'Yes.'

'Do you know what she wanted?'

'Yes. There is a piece of earth she kept soft. She told me where. She expected death.'

'If you would like to show me, I will help you do it.'

'Ah, that's kind of you.'

I thought so too! It was hardly a job I fancied, but I couldn't let the boy continue to sit beside the corpse. There was a spade in one corner of the cottage. We went through a curtain of a soft spray of leaves to a quiet hidden place, and there we dug a narrow grave and buried Alkanet and all the flowers and herbs that adorned her. We covered her with earth.

Then Marel said: 'Holy Goddess Earth, Mother of Nature, take unto thyself thy faithful servant Alkanet who used thy gifts so kindly, only for good. Let her be one with thyself in the fullness of thy being.'

'In the name of the Father, the Son, and the Holy Spirit,

Amen,' I said loudly.

'Why did you say that?' asked Marel, surprised.

'I thought that it would give Alkanet a safer passage,' I said.

'Who are the people you spoke of?'

'Do you really not know?'

'No.'

'She should have told you,' I said angrily. 'It's shameful that she should leave you so unknowing.'

So I took him back into the cottage and we sat each side of the table, while I taught him all I knew of God and His son, and all the Saints, and the promise for us all of eternal life. He liked it; he listened with childish pleasure.

'And now, Marel, what will you do?' I asked.

'There is no choice. I shall live here, and carry on her work.'

'Why?'

'The garden needs me.'

'Listen, Marel,' I said. 'Ever since I last saw you, you have been always in my mind. I am better off than when you saw me last; I have a horse now. We could travel the land together, companions on the road. There is so much more to a lifespan than one herb garden. Won't you come with me?'

'I can't. I'm like the herbs – I'm planted here; I have grown here. I would be afraid if I were plucked away.'

'That's delightful nonsense,' I said. 'You are a boy, not a plant. You could travel along with me. See villages and towns. See London. I'll teach you everything I know. What do you say?'

'I have told you. Why do you ask? I belong here.'

'Is it because you don't know anything about me?' I asked.

'Not at all. I know much more about you than you think. I have all Alkanet's knowledge.'

'Not all, I hope,' I said. 'I fear that some of her knowledge was not good.'

'We were talking of you.'

'Yes. What do you know?'

'I know your name. You were named after one of the old Saxon kings. I know that your dealings with Cortle are partly because of old your family lived at the castle. At least, it was not a castle then, but a house, where the Saxon masters lived. And when the Normans came, some of your family were made to leave and became peasants, and some of your family left of their own will, and of that stock came you. The story was passed down, and you think of your ancient birthright when you come to Cortle, and you work against the Normans when you can.'

'All that is true,' I said. 'But I keep it to myself.'

'And so shall I,' he said. 'But I know things about you which are of far more worth. I know that you have visited our cottage many times and have always been kind, and suffered Alkanet's hard words without anger. I know from your deeds today that you are good and kind. Alkanet spoke well of you to me because she knew that one day I would be alone and I could trust you in the days to come. I'm also grateful that you liked me.'

'But you won't come away with me.'

'No. But I shall always be here when you come back.'

'But Alkanet was right,' I protested. 'You'll be alone. You would be at anyone's mercy. You know we saw you with Audran de Bonnefoy . . .'

'Yes,' he said, colouring. 'Since then I've been very careful and our paths haven't crossed. Of the villagers who come to visit here, there is no one who does not wish me well. I shall serve them with cures and all will go on as before.'

'A boy needs to know how to take care of himself,' I said. 'To fight – wield a staff – use his fists.'

'I never needed to,' said Marel. 'With the herbs I have every kind of power. I could kill or weaken whoever I wanted to.'

I shuddered. He said it so easily, with all the simplicity of a child.

'You mustn't say that!' I cried. 'People wouldn't understand. They would call you a spellbinder.'

Marel looked at me blankly.

'I wouldn't use the herbs that way. Everyone knows that.'

I wasn't happy about it. I sat scowling and hunched up.

'Do you plan to stay here tonight?' he asked.

'I had thought to,' I said. 'I expected to collect come herbs and move on later.'

'You can still do that,' he said. 'I will pack up the herbs for you. And you can sleep here.'

I had a dismal vision of myself gallantly stretched out in my accustomed place on the floor, while he lay upstairs alone smelling of flowers.

'I remember,' he said, 'that last time you were here you

spoke words of love. When I say that you may sleep here I mean that you should be with me. I would be very glad of your comfort. I'm very glad that you came here today and helped me. I believe you when you say that there are things I should know. I would like to know them from you.'

I could scarcely believe my ears.

'What do you mean? Do you mean that I may lie with you – in your bed?'

'You said that you had things to teach me, didn't you?'

'Yes – but – are we talking about the same things?'

'Well,' he grinned, 'I'm not talking about quarterstaves.'

So at last I slept in the scented loft.

At first I dreaded that Alkanet's ghost would come back to pester me and affect what I did. To my relief I learnt that Life is stronger than Death, something I did of course suppose.

Slowly, savouringly, I undressed the beautiful boy. What followed was like nothing I had known before. The boy smelt of flowers; and all around us hung the magic. I was like one at a shrine. I knelt before him; he let my lips and hands go where they would. I placed him on the bed. I could hardly believe my good fortune. Yielding and golden he lay beneath me, and I had my way with him, every way.

We lay in each other's arms. Our work had left me exhausted and him thoughtful.

'So,' he said dreamily. 'That was it.'

'I love you,' I said. 'That's how it is with Love.'

'I needed to know it,' said Marel. Then he gave me a mischievous little look. 'I hope you can stay more than one night, pedlar. I am not so clever I can learn it all at once.'

A man might think himself in Paradise to be where I was now.

Like one who goes to sleep in Winter, cold and shivering, and wakes to find a full blown summer day with roses, meadows white with flowers, and sun upon his back, so I woke in the bed with Marel, heart's desire. The very air bloomed where we lay, the bed, the boards, the boy all smelt of such a sweetness you might well believe there never was the filth of roads, the sweat of travel, and the soggy slush of clothes swamped wet with rain.

Beside me Marel lay, a sleeping angel. His flaxen hair lay lush across his face, his boyish arm curved and its pale gleaming hairs lit by sunlight. I touched his warm skin. I

201

gazed at him, dazed, he who had been hooded from me at all times before, now naked, every part of him. I sat up, rubbed my eyes and stared again.

My own long shanks looked rough and hairy by the side of him; I wished I was more beautiful. But he was every whit as wonderful as I had guessed. I traced the slope of his back to the dimpled hollow at its base; I touched the downy golden hair that furred his creamy buttocks and the thicker curls between his arse cheeks. I turned him slightly till he spread out on his back. His pretty cock lay limp beneath the honey-coloured bush of maidenhair, his belly white and smooth; I laid my face upon it.

His hand reached down and stroked my hair. 'If this is Love I think I like it,' said that lovely boy, so adding to my sum of happiness I thought my life could only be a downward path henceforth – I had seen its greatest perfection.

So strangely holy did I feel, it was a great relief to have to go down for a piss, and I was glad to find that Marel also was mere mortal, for I am not at ease in mystic places.

Like a bull at a gate I blurted out what I would say again: 'You've got to leave this place, my love. It isn't right for you. You'll go with me, won't you, when I leave? I long to have you with me on the road.'

He smiled. 'Get dressed. Folk will see you.'

'What folk?' The forest seemed deserted. 'There's no one here.'

'There will be. They come and go all day.'

Cheapside it was not, but he was right. All day he pottered making pastes and potions, and both men and women came, with corns and earache, stomach gripes and questions.

I loved him for his loveliness, and thought to do him a service by taking him with me and looking after him, but now I understood that he was skilful in his own right and I saw well enough that he'd be of great use to me, knowing so much. So wonderful a partnership it would be that I could hardly wait to get back on the road and put it into practice. The garden was no more than a stopping place to me, a haven where you built up strength and came away refreshed. It wasn't real. It wasn't life. Why did it take him so long to see that? Why couldn't he agree with me?

'Don't waste our time with grumbling,' he said of an evening. 'I know you'll go again; I know you're a traveller.

But while you're here, show me some love.'

Heaven clutched at me again. We went upstairs.

How could man know such sweetness and still stand upright? I asked myself this many times as I looked down and saw Marel's bowed head, the moonlight of his hair spread out about my loins, his warm wet lips around my cock, my sense of wonder almost spoiling the joys of mere passion – could this ever be an everyday thing with us, when I felt such whirling happiness? Then his wide eyes grinned up at me as if to tease me for my ecstasy, and I pushed him back down and pressed his head against me with a pleasing surge of power to master him. A lifetime was not long enough to do all we might do.

Sometimes it was enough for me to lie him on the bed and look at him and marvel. He was so perfect in his shape – I could not fault him. I would move him this way and that, lift his arm and study the gold fuzz beneath, touch his small nipples till they hardened to my finger tip, trace the ley line from his navel down, and move my palm across the curly crotch hair and the warm crook of his groin till his sweet prick would jerk up; then I'd have to bend and kiss it till a tiny bead of juice came from its tip. Under his balls were honey-coloured curls; I'd spread his thighs and nuzzle there, thinking: this is Marel – here against my lips – Marel, who was hid from me by Alkanet, and now my face is *here*, my tongue is tasting him.

Sometimes it was enough to look and touch, yes, but sometimes I must show my love more surely. Then he'd kneel for me against the bed, his elbows in the soft strewn herbs, with little flower heads by his face against the meadow-hay, his arse raised up to me; and then I'd part his golden cheeks and slide between his thighs and lose myself in sweetness. It brought me close to tears, this pain of Love's fulfilment. And I'd thought myself so sharp, so shrewd a traveller!

But the garden made me edgy. I itched to get the boy away from this disquieting kind of ideal beauty. I wanted us to be on the road together, watching the seasons change, each side of the fat flanks and plodding hooves of my useful little horse. Odd thoughts, I know, to be mingled with the heady satisfaction of our lovemaking; and his affection could soon make me forget them, and so they did, time and time again. But in his world there was nothing for me to *do*, and I knew there must be a limit to the time I spent there. Meanwhile, we slept together every night and I buried my face in his golden hair.

I had to ask it.

'Audran de Bonnefoy,' I said. 'He has never done more than bother you from on horseback?'

'There was one time,' Marel began. Then he smiled at the expression on my face. 'It's important to you, pedlar, isn't it, that you were the one who brought me to Love's rites? Be calm, then, you are my first and only. But once Audran held me hard against a tree and kissed me, and he handled me – here – and here. When I struggled I felt sensations. I broke free and ran. Afterwards when I thought about it I wanted to understand. But not with Audran. Then I thought of you.'

'And you have not been sorry . . .'

'No, far from it. But,' said Marel firmly, 'I am staying here.'

I groaned. 'How can you say that? You have not had other lovers, but I have, and believe me, you can take my word that what happened between us was very good. How can you let it go to waste?'

'It will never be wasted; we have breathed it in. My magic will be stronger for knowing it, and your thoughts happier.'

'But we could be together,' I complained, as earthy lovers always will, 'having that pleasure every day. Thoughts and memories are not so good as what is real.'

'My place is here,' he said.

'But why?'

'It's all I know. You saw how it was with Alkanet. It has passed on into my hands. It's my trust. I am the vessel of the magic.'

'Oh,' I grumbled, irritable before such talk. 'Vessels – magic – you're a boy, and you could be travelling the land and seeing life.'

'Life is here,' he said. 'I am this place.'

Mystic remarks had no place in my scheme of things. But there was no shifting his stance. I tried to tell him what our life could be together if he came away with me. But he was not the sort of boy that you could tempt with visions of foreign cities nor yet the simple fact that it is good to see what lies around the next bend in the road. It made me gloomy, because I had to ask myself was my life so good anyhow?

204

What could I offer him? Cold and hardship sometimes, living rough, the whiff of danger, aching feet. No wonder I could not persuade him! What it all came down to was that I could not be still in one place but must always be for moving on; it had now become my nature. If that's how you are there's nothing you can do about it – you can't justify it with a string of words; and if somebody doesn't find the prospect pleasing then that's that. Not that I wasn't peeved to think my company itself was not enough to draw him from his wretched herb garden – I was very sour about that!

To eke out my livelihood I had built up a network of small trade across the country and it wouldn't wait. I grew gloomy at the thought of leaving him. I could've hit him for his obstinacy. As for the Earth Mother in the elder tree I didn't see why he couldn't worship Her along the road as we can who love God. She wasn't only in the garden, was She? God's servants know that living is to grapple, and we never could thrive till we'd left the garden, and sought knowledge, with its jostling crowd of joys and pains and difficulties. But Marel said he was the garden; and I had no patience with him.

I promised to return again towards the ending of the Summer.

'First, do you love me?' I demanded.

'Yes. Surely you must know that.'

'And you'll think of me from time to time while I'm away perhaps.'

'Yes; often.'

'And ask yourself whether this lonely life is what you want after all? You'll find it strange, you know, without old Alkanet, hag though she was.'

'I know it.'

'Then when I come back we'll talk about this matter once again.'

When Benedict the innkeeper came by I spoke about the things that bothered me. 'This boy is on his own now. You'll stand by him, won't you? Be a neighbour to him; see he comes to no harm.'

'What harm could come? He knows the secrets of the plants; he'll be all right.'

'But even so . . . if he should need a friend . . .'

'Ah, have no fear!' the innkeeper assured me comfortably. 'I'll look after him; we all will. Jesu save us – who'd have thought that Alkanet could ever die!'

And so, one morning I packed up and left.

We held each other tightly in a hard and tender kiss of parting.

'Wait here for me,' I said. 'I will be back. Don't ever go leaving this place. I need to know where to find you.'

'I will always be here. You'll find me here. I will always wait for you.'

Why was I going? It tore at my heart. I could live here with him, gather herbs and watch them grow, make up little bundles of them for the villagers of Cortle . . .

'I will be back,' I said.

I left hopefully, sure that he would think of me fondly and look forward to my return. He would remember our nights of love and he would miss me. Absent I would begin to mean more to him. But Fortune played an odd trick on me here; for the kind-hearted and well-meaning man in whose charge I left Marel, was to prove his undoing, the one who – so to speak – brought in the serpent to the garden.

IV

WALSINGHAM, AND I was a fool to be here.
I had seen too much of the world not to be wary of wonders. I believed in God's mercy and the blessings of His Saints, but I had never credited them with such piety that at the touch of a prayer they would forsake their duties to attend to the relief of a peasant's carbuncle; and neither did I think the Blessed Virgin would interest Herself overmuch in a pedlar having trouble with his arm. It would have been different if I intended to use that arm for holy works but I did not, and She would know that. So why heal a limb whose purpose was to fondle yellow-headed boys and peddle trinkets?

Desperation, however, calls for desperate remedies. Nothing that Marel had done for me in the way of poultices and incantations had had effect, and from neck to wrist I had barely any feeling and my fingers stiffened more each day. So here I was.

For a hundred years pilgrims had been coming to this

place, to worship at the spot where a widow named Rychold had been taken in a dream to Nazareth and saw Our Lady's house. She was told to learn the exact measurements and to build a house at Walsingham, her village, just the same. Our Lady told her where to build, and showed her by revealing some dry ground in a meadow, where the grass around was wet with dew. From all directions pilgrims came – up from Cambridge by the Palmer's Way, over from Norwich by the packhorse bridge. I was amongst a particularly devoted batch, who sang psalms in fervent voices as they wound their way across the grass to the wooden house where stood the shrine.

The village lay in the curve of the River Stiffkey, the priory beside it, the shrine a little to the north. We shuffled in, tightly pressed together, herded by monks.

A narrow door admitted us, into a room so dark that scented candles gave the only glow. Monks from the priory shepherded us in, another monk positioned at the statue of Our Lady was lurking to receive our offerings and to watch out for thieves. I have seen men at holy places bending down to kiss a carved stone foot and with a snake-like tongue lick up a coin or two and none the wiser. But here with me were honest pilgrims, praying, murmuring, sighing, so devout I felt all kinds of hypocrite for my awelessness. The statue of Our Lady was a mass of jewels. Carefully prodded by the monks the line of worshippers bumbled its way past, with just time enough to leave a coin, to kneel and say a prayer, to kiss a jewel. Then a kindly but severe prod in the neck from the monk, and on your way again, out into the light of day. It left me feeling most cast down; and I sat on the grass outside, under an elm, wondering if I had but made matters worse by lack of faith.

Holy music from the priory wafted on the air, and a pedlar selling drinks and cakes was hustled away by a couple of monks who told him here was food for the soul only. Besides the devout whom I had accompanied to the shrine, there was a throng of motley humanity, now lining up to enter, now emerging at the further door. As is usual at these places, one is made aware of all the ills that may befall one if one lives – there was a girl who had no hair, but a mere bald pate pockmarked with scabs and pustules; there was one hunch-backed and bearded, knocking into folk as if he could not judge his space; there was a woman with two infants wrapped in shawls, both, we were told, deformed, the mother loudly weeping. No one emerging glowed with more serenity than when he entered. It startled us all when a tall man and a little girl caused some affray as she cried that she could see. She was blind, the tall man told us, grinning like an idiot, blind all her life, and now she could see!

The pilgrims in the line now pushed and jostled eagerly, their long wait justified, their own chances increased.

'Do you believe that?' asked a young man who sat by me on the grass. 'Do you believe that miracle?'

'I know a man who earns a living getting cured at shrines. The eager people pay him with coins or food to tell his story. But I have no cause to disbelieve the couple we have witnessed. This is a holy place, though I myself felt somewhat more of holiness beside the river underneath the trees than at the shrine. But I do believe in the possibility of miracles, which is something else again.'

'Has She worked a miracle for you, Our Lady?'

I turned to see a young man with an anxious gaze and troubled eyes. I wished that I could give him grounds for faith.

'No. But I did not expect it, at heart.'

'I did. I counted on it. I thought Our Lady would understand.'

He looked hale enough, this youth, and far from having visible deformity. Indeed he was very fair of face. He was slim and of a delicate build, pale-skinned with chestnut hair and fine grey eyes. No pauper, from his clothes. And though we were a stone's throw from a place of prayer I could not help the swift glance that one man who notices maleflesh might give another. There was nothing here that did not please.

'My problem is a sin,' he told me, with a cautious look beneath his narrow eyelids.

'And were you cured?'

'Far from it. It is with me still. It is with me now.'

Slim as he was, I reckoned drily, it could not be greed; well-dressed, it was not likely to be avarice. He had made his way here on foot, which ruled out sloth.

'I have touched holy relics at Lincoln, Peterborough, Ely . . .' he continued. 'Indeed, wherever I have learnt of local saints I have asked their help. But my sin is so particular it seems beyond the power of any saint, however holy.'

208

'You surely have not killed?' I marvelled.

'Of course not!' he replied, blushing to be thought in such a company. 'My sin is quite other. It is of the mind.'

I may have had an inkling of what he meant then, and I hoped that I was right.

'Do you keep this sin there, or is it ever shifted to the body?' I enquired, as one might speak of crops and weather.

'It has been sometimes shifted to the body,' he answered gloomily. 'And since I am not cured at Walsingham it may yet trouble me again.'

'Well . . . there are other shrines . . . other saints . . .'

He brightened for a moment. 'I have heard of one on the coast – not five miles from here! What do you say? Shall we try our luck and see if we attain there what we did not here?'

I was tempted by – what? The picture he painted to me of a lonely shrine beside the wild seashore, so little known that all those pilgrims who thronged to Canterbury and Walsingham had never heard of it; a hermitage where one or two lone outcasts watched over a fragment of the One True Cross? Well, yes, that tempted me as well. The saint whose shrine it was my young friend was not sure about – one of those that fled from Rome, he thought. A splinter of the Holy Rood set into a jewel, carried carefully from Italy across north Europe, then by sea to our shores, and there in gratitude for his safe landing did this holy man make his shrine, and there we would be healed, I of my disability and he of his sin. And since we had no reason to stay longer where we were, we moved on, easterly, towards the sea.

Geoffrey his name was, this fair sinner, born and raised in Lincoln, of a merchant's family, beloved by parents and sisters, and no troubles in his life except those caused by his sin. His sin manifested itself in such great uphappiness that his parents had been glad to furnish him with money to travel on his quest from shrine to shrine, until that blessed day when the sin should go from him. Did his family know what his sin was? No, it was impossible to speak of it to Christian people. It was a sin too terrible to reveal. It would drive him to an early grave. Its burden bore him down.

Apart from his sin, he was a pleasant companion, and with a map drawn by one who had visited this shrine long ago he led us toward the coast, and in the afternoon we reached a cluster of houses on a saltmarsh, where a wide creek led towards the sea. In winter this would have been a desolate place unfit for man or beast, with wild winds off the sea bringing ice and snow in their wake. But now, in summer, it was most agreeable, the day warm, the sky blue, the air most sweet-smelling.

Confidently Geoffrey went forward with his map, and I followed leading Comfrey, along a raised grassy causeway that jutted up from a mauve-grey marsh where larks and lapwings called, ahead of us the sea. Underfoot it was firm and dry, a rough and humpy ridge speckled with windblown flowers. For maybe two miles this led seaward, though the sea was obscured by a sandy ridge, which when we reached it we found soft and white to walk upon, with thick clumps of sharp green sea-grass. Over the ridge we climbed, and there found – nothing. For there certainly was no hermitage, no holy place, nor was there anything wherein humankind could recognise itself. A flat and tawny strand stretched onward to the sea, spread lightly with flat pools that mirrored sky, and all beyond that, ocean – flat and pale and indistinct, as silent as a wall.

For several moments we stood staring, and then faced each other, somewhat at a loss.

'There *was* a hermitage,' said Geoffrey.

I believed him. About our feet there lay a heap of stones, collapsed into a jagged cairn, and even, when we rooted about, two halves of a wooden cross that must have once been bound with twine, now black and rotted. Here indeed some men might once have lived and prayed and made their little dwelling warm, and maybe they indeed guarded a relic, a splinter of the Rood set in a jewel. But not now. Whatever faith was theirs at first had been no help against the endless nothingness of sea that faced them every day but answered nothing, offered nothing, awesome in its vast indifference.

Geoffrey turned to me. I put my arm around him and he responded warmly – so fervently that for a moment I wondered whether I had been wrong about what sin he thought he carried, for he did not kiss as if he thought he was sinning.

'If the hermitage had been there,' he said, muffled in my neck, 'I would have prayed and tried to lose my sin. But the Saints always let us down; they are never there when you want them. They have only themselves to blame if we turn for

210

consolation to what does not fail.'

'They do say that when Adam and Eve were turned from the Garden the first thing they did was make love. Sometimes God's ways are too hard to understand. But Love's ways are not.'

We nestled in the soft white sand in a hollow below a line of spiky marram grass. He needed no persuasion. I felt that he was one who wished to lose himself in Love; I was the same; there was no meeting of our minds at all. So much was wrong with the world – there would always be the deformed, the lame, the disfigured, those with demons, with fevers – but in life these are mingled well enough with the beautiful and the whole. It had been our bad luck to find at Walsingham only those that merited pity, none of them healed by the shrine except the little girl, whom I believed a fraud. Disappointment lay upon us – I had not expected to be healed, and Geoffrey, I suspect, did not wish to be; either way we were as we had been, no better, and the shrine upon the strand was gone, as if the monks too had lost hope. What was there to be sure of except what you could see and touch, hold in your hand? And so we pressed against each other, not speaking, not revealing thoughts and fears, but kissing much, and sensing our warm bodies, licking with sand-flecked lips the sand-flecked skin that tasted so good. His chest was lean and boyish and his belly smooth, his prick a beauty, jutting up from curly chestnut hair and warm seed-filled balls. I sucked his cock till creamy spray came over both of us, and then he twisted round and put his lips down to my loins and took my cock into his throat. For just a few moments then, as I hung at the point of fulfilment I swear that all our disappointments did not matter – more, did not exist at all.

Ah – but afterwards . . . What was there to do but walk back from the sea, to tread the mud-dried causeway through the salt marsh, to see about a place to shelter, to find food for Comfrey and ourselves, to grapple with the old confusions? I wondered what it all had meant to Geoffrey. I tried to pass on fragments of what passed for wisdom.

'Go back to Lincoln,' I suggested. 'Live your life. You don't need to be always thinking about sin. It makes that sin much too important, and it grows with nourishing. Sin sometimes – ask forgiveness – then forget it.'

I might as well have said nothing. In the monastery where

we spent the night I heard him in the morning asking where could be found the most powerful relics hereabouts, and were they known for healing sins? I left him pondering whether to make for Norwich or North Elmham.

I honestly believe that if a man has not walked twenty miles a day he is not happy – he is restless, discontent, and does not sleep.

Following the Icknield Way towards Reading I had an odd meeting in the woodland thereabouts.

It was a fair evening, and with no wish to put up in a town I meant to sleep where chance might lead me. In a glade of birch and hazel one was there before me, with a little fire over which he crouched, frying mushrooms in a pan. He was a hunched and raggedy fellow; I thought him old at first, but he was not, though he was very bent in form. His face was of a waxen pallor and his cheek bones gaunt, but his eyes, like forest creatures' are, were bright and darting. He had no hair upon his pate but dark and wispy locks hung down his back. His hands were gnarled as twigs, and with a twig he stirred his brew, which sizzling in bacon fat smelt very good. Behind him was a covered cart, the base shaped like half a barrel, the roof of hides stretched over wooden slats. Hywel his name was. He invited me to share his meal.

We sat each side the fire, not speaking much, for as I found, he had no interest in the world, and had no news to give, nor cared to hear none. If Château Gaillard had fallen to the French what difference did it make to him? He did not know what Ghâteau Gaillard was. The only thing that caused him interest was his mushrooms.

Against his carts' wheels lay heaps of small white pear-shaped puffballs, and in an open basket a collection of fungi such as I had never before seen amassed in one place. Stinkhorns there were, a drone of flies buzzing round the dark green snouts, and those brown jellies known as Jews' Ears that are culled from elder trees. Amongst them lay some that looked like hunks of curdled cheese, others like rotten leaves in Autumn; and I recognised a hefty sprinkling of those small and shaggy knobs whose touch is like old fleece.

Amused at my surprise Hywel opened up his cart and let me peer inside. Apart from just enough space to sleep, the innards were stacked full of fungi, and the smell as can be guessed was musty with decay. Big grey shapes like sea pebbles, with fluted undersides, amber whorls ridged like woven cloth; small ones like spilt cream, and dirty yellow lumps with stems like speckled bones; others flesh-coloured, flecked with scabs like one diseased – all lay in jumbled plenty. More, from threads that hung from the slats of the roof lumps of mushroom hung to dry. There was not space to move without a chunk of the stuff nudged you as you turned.

He swore that every one I saw was wholesome and that he had no dealing with that ugly crew which poisoned, sickened, killed. He made his living gathering the plants and he knew ways to cook them which had made him praised of ladies, knights and barons, so he said. I bought a choice of them to sell down south, and we struck up a friendship firm enough for him to shift some mushrooms so I could sleep inside the cart.

'You think that there are many here? You should see my cart in Fall; it's stacked from guts to roof, there are so many. In a good year . . . that's a warm slow Summer and a gentle Fall with rain . . . but you mustn't pick them in the wet, and you must pick 'em softly, so they leave the ground without a cry . . .'

As night came on he was more forthcoming in his talk and he admitted that he had a mushroom there that caused odd dreams. He showed me it, a little yellow-brown thing with a pointed tip. 'Will you try it, pedlar?' he asked curiously. 'They do say that whatever you do see in the mushroom dream you put it there yourself.'

'How do you mean?'

'You see your fears or your desires.'

'And afterwards, do you remember?'

'Some do. Some hurry to forget.'

I questioned him some more and he convinced me. I thought I would see Màrel; so I took some mushroom brew before I slept.

I woke with a jolt for something was outside shoving the cart, pushing it to and fro. When I clambered out to look I saw nothing, but from further off came a most unearthly shriek and it was clear to me that just beyond the trees I would find trouble. We could not go back to sleep with that nearby, and so I took a few steps onward to where beside a hazel clump I had heard the sound.

It was night-black now, the trees were smudges of darkness. Underfoot I felt the ground grow boggy and my steps sank in a mire. An eerie glow now showed above the marsh, green it was, a green glimmer, and the shriek again. And now a wispy mist rose from the slime with a vile smell of decay that sickened me. My feet sank further in the mud, I felt the slime ooze into my boots. I had thought the night dark enough, but now it blackened as completely as if one had tipped hearts-blood over all. The whole bog shifted, slurped, and from its depth arose a shape, bog-black, its only colour one red eye, a glinting bullseye that looked this way and that, and paused on finding me. I heard the monster's breathing, rough and rasping, as it put out a wing as big as a boat sail, the bones within as hard as metal and its tip a claw the size of a fistful of sword blades. It bore down on me, a venomous bulk, the Worm of ancient tale, mightier than Grendel, and I drew my knife and drove it into that black bulk now overwhelming me. It felt like just a pinprick in that oozy skin. The creature being better built for fighting raised its claw. My face looked up; I saw the claw descend. Clamped in the mire I could not move and all the while the claw came down I stabbed and thrust into the heaving shape with no effect; the claw tips raked my face, my neck. I sat up, my hand across my head, and Hywel's arm upon my shoulder.

'What – would you turn the cart over?' he enquired.

'Have I – marks upon my face?' I gasped, and as he lit a candle he was chuckling. Lit by its shadowy glow he squinted at me, and I felt my face which unbelievably was as it always had been.

'I see no marks.'

'Such as a claw might make?'

'No claw is here.'

Even so I could not sleep. I lay there wide awake, all bathed in sweat, the gobbets of mushroom on the threads that dangled brushing my face, my fingers. How this cart did stink! Was that my dream? Where were the golden boys of my desire? I struggled with relief and disappointment till the dawn came. I had a headache and my guts were sore. Had I brought that grim dream upon myself? I had to laugh. How did I spend my waking hours, except with thoughts that sometimes threatened me . . . and fighting monsters of my own creation?

V

WINCHESTER IS a fair town and I did some buying and selling up and down those straight streets. This place had been a Saxon stronghold under Cerdic five hundred years ago; the Saxons of Wessex had defeated the Mercians here, and Egbert had made it his capital city. Aelfred lived here, famous for his wisdom and his learning. In the marvellous minster there is an organ so immense that it needs over fifty men to work the bellows that play its four hundred pipes. The sound of it carries all across the city, loud as thunder. It always pleased me just to walk its streets. That was the furthest west I went, and using packhorse tracks well known to sheep-herders, carters and the like I traversed southern England on my way to Canterbury, thence to London, through Andredswald. But some old familiar demon took me to Hastings on the way.

It was true that I was drawn to this place, and had many times paced the dreary field where all our hopes were lost. It is still as it was then, a sloping scrubby hillside leading to a marsh, where Bretons, Normans, French took up formation. Little streams that join the Bulverhythe and Brede course down the hill, and sedge and grasses grow where horses charged and weapons clashed, and Normans cried *Dex aïe*, and pennants trailed and gleamed. I stood on Caldbec Hill where Harold's army met, and he beneath an apple-tree, and saw again the steep cleft the Normans called Malfosse, the Evil Ditch, for in the dusk a number of them stumbled into it and all were slaughtered by the Saxons on the bank. I passed the abbey which now stands upon the spot where they say Harold fell. But no one knows if this be so; and if he was then rescued from the field, that abbey was a pointless gesture. Even so, the ghosts were here; and as I led my horse beside the abbey walls the old sad feelings were much with me.

Light rain was falling, as if this place was in a spell, condemned to gloom, a place where no sun shone and no flowers grew. I was reminded of the monster I created in my sleep; I seemed a prey to fancies. Vexed somewhat to have discovered this I stood and looked about me. To one side of me the field of battle sloped away amongst the trees, and to the other side I saw a rose-garden beyond the abbey wall, red and white roses in abundance, such as would grace any tale of

215

Love, and one robed gardener at his work, lost in his thoughts, cutting, planting.

In the long grass at my feet grew flowers of other kinds – purple vetches, clover, Lady's Tresses – and further down the field sheep grazed and clumps of thistles grew, and tufted tangled bushes. Nothing there showed what had been, indeed it was a peaceful sight I gazed upon, and all the gloom I'd been aware of was the gloom that I brought with me in my thoughts. This was a field, no more, and maybe if I had not known its story I would have crossed it without thinking, passed it by.

I went into the abbot's garden and shiftily picked a rose. Then I moved off swiftly to avoid the startled monk. I stood there in the rain and cast the rose before me on the grass. An offering, yes, to whom? The ghosts of all those Saxon lads who died in bravery and pain and to no purpose? Or to the past, with all its disappointments and its dreams? I knew that I would not come back again to this quiet place. To wander over Senlac field and dwell in bitter thoughts now seemed like the mushroom dream, as slight, as man-made, of no purpose; yet I used to think it was a pilgrimage and my part in it of the greatest magnitude, a vigil keeper at a holy grave. This new awareness left me puzzled.

As I crossed Romney marshes under lowering skies a fever laid me low. Drenched from a rainstorm I was glad enough to stagger into a priory there and receive the care of monks. A week or so I lay, thinking at times this was the end of all the roads; but I recovered, thanks to their good ministrations. I lay upon my pallet in the long cool room where the infirm were brought, and drank the brews the brothers gave me, and prayed with them before I slept. They restored health, but hardly hope.

I asked that brother who was believed to be the best at healing what he thought about my wretched arm, my chances of its strength returning.

'A fever I can understand,' he told me. 'There are remedies . . . But this . . . this is most strange.' He was a young man, narrow-eyed, pale-faced, and thin. 'I would ask you, pedlar, to consider whether you have angered God?'

'I hope not,' I said quickly, much aware of all my sins and weaknesses.

'Knowingly or unknowingly,' he continued, looking at me piercingly, 'is there anything at all which you can think of, which would mightily displease Our Lord?'

'A man who travels the roads,' I began evasively, 'lives more roughly than the villagers whose homes he passes . . . there is no other way . . .'

'Look into your heart,' the brother told me. I sensed he found me threatening – a murderer maybe, a thief? 'You will know if there is sin. This is God's judgement. You have done a wrong, and He has witnessed it. There is nothing you can do against His almighty will. That arm will wither now, and shrivel. It is beyond my little power. Your remedy is fortitude. And prayer.'

I saw beyond the tall arched windows that the rain had cleared and now the sky was blue. The sun was shining, and the bare stone walls were lightened by its beams. There was no lightness in my heart.

Liking Canterbury no more than I liked London I drew near to that walled city with no particular joy.

In high summer it was at its worst. The dusty road that led into its gate was edged with wayside stalls, piled high with food and drink of doubtful quality with which to tempt the pilgrims who came here like flies to settle on the relics in the town. For Canterbury was a treasure-house. Besides Saint Thomas' severed crown, his blood, his bones, the altar where he fell, there were in separate chapels the bodies of a host of other saints, the heads of three more, and a great number of teeth and bones; and portions of the true cross and the crown of thorns, as well as fragments of the manger and the cradle made by Saint Joseph for his infant son. In summer these wondrous lodestones drew pilgrims from all over England and beyond the seas, and in almost equal numbers came the stallholders and the sellers of remembrances and gifts. They flocked towards us as we approached, pestering those already tired and travel-stained, with tricks that I would scorn to use on those who did not speak our tongue. I saw ranks of little phials containing blood, attached to cords to be worn around the neck, and the gullible clamouring to buy. Other stalls sold bones, wrapped up in velvet, parchment, silk – this one Saint Lawrence's toe, this one Saint Catherine's finger.

I was not surprised then – in truth I was most pleased – to

find Rahere the bone-gatherer behind a stall, with Dickon helping him, and Dickon still in women's clothes, which made me smile and marvel, for with his white head-dress and cloak he looked a slim young girl – yet what a risk he took if he had been discovered! He would certainly cause affray and ribaldry, or maybe worse if anyone took offence, this being a place of pilgrimage.

Rahere yelled a welcome.

'Pedlar! Good to see you – meet me later up at the Flying Horse – all goes well for us here – and "Rowena" you already know . . .'

I was much cheered to see him and looked forward to our meeting. I gave 'Rowena' a warm kiss and set off into the town.

The streets were noisy, dusty, crowded; all the inns were full, and everywhere the trade in relics, gifts and keepsakes persevered. The ale was overpriced, the pickpockets shamelessly abundant.

It was while drinking in the Flying Horse that I first heard the news that Rouen had fallen to the French. When we lost Château Gaillard in March and Philip's forces overran all Normandy, Rouen held out, and was our one last stronghold. We thought that Philip would make straight for that, but he did not – he circled round and joined up with the Bretons, taking Caen without a fight. It seemed the Normans looked to France rather than to England as their kinfolk, and put up no resistance. We had held them down by force, and garrisoned our castles with mercenaries. One of these we had all heard about – Lupescar, the Wolf, who ravaged the lands he was entrusted to protect, and he had joined up with Philip. Our commander in Rouen, Peter de Préaux, sent messages to King John urging him to save the city with reinforcements from England. But King John who was both practical and peaceful told him he must not expect help from outside, but to make instead what terms he could. And so in June Rouen allowed the French to enter. We had lost Normandy.

The humblest thatcher, the man who brought the ale, the passing ballad singer, all had an opinion on this mighty matter. What would it mean for England?

Some reckoned they had seen it coming, because everybody knew that Philip Augustus had made it his life's work to conquer Normandy and make it part of France, and he could do it, couldn't he, since he was over there and we were over here! For years we'd left it in the hands of careless captains with no loyalty to England but only to who paid them most – the tales of that Wolf Lupescar put terror into the strongest heart; we had only ourselves to blame if the Norman gentry turned against us. Who wanted Normandy anyhow? There was enough to do in England. What would those barons do who had land in Normandy? We did not spare them much sympathy – it was a problem outside our experience; barons usually sorted out things to their best advantage. But what really riled us was the idea that across the sea stood hordes of jeering Frenchmen glutted with success, who having taken Rouen thought the English easy meat. What would they do now? The answer was obvious – they would aim for an invasion.

Someone remembered that several years ago King Philip had sworn he would invade our shores. A pedlar who had come from Paris said that it was common gossip there that England was to be attacked, and there were rowdy songs about the Conqueror's prowess sung up and down the streets. Frenchmen boasted they'd overrun us and be settled in by Christmas – look at William, he'd done it in a couple of months! But no man liked to be seen to be an aggressor – even William brought the blessing of the Pope to back his claim – so Philip would hold back. Ah, didn't we know – Philip had dug up some descendents of King Stephen and Mathilde of Boulogne. With their claim to the throne he could be seen as just a kindly friend who was helping them to regain what was rightfully theirs.

Rightfully theirs! We would be here to stop them, wouldn't we, behind our lawful king, King John, and he would lead us into battle against any scurvy Frenchman. About this point a vague and general doubtfulness crept in. He was our rightful king, true, but he was not exactly known for fighting, was he, and he was so small of stature! Now Richard, although he was a cold and heartless fellow, was glorious to behold and brilliant in war. Now *there* was a leader – remember how he went on the Crusade – the Saracens fled before him – all his enemies admired him – and he was six feet tall and very splendid. Ah, if only he were here again!

That was the first time I remember hearing Richard praised. He who all his life had done nothing for our nation was suddenly a saviour. It seems you must be dead in order to gain reputation.

Wriggling on to the bench beside me in that dark corner of the tavern Rahere downed his ale and turned to me for gossip.

'Do you remember that beggar in a cloak who used to sleep beside our fire? I did not know him well, nor did I like him very much; but he has died; I find this very sad.'

'What was his sickness?'

'No sickness. Didn't I say? Tyb slew him. What makes it worse, he did not mean to do it, but was much the worse for drink and laid about him with his fists, and afterwards was weeping like a babe for what he did. You know how Tyb was in his drinking. Well, he has left London in a hurry, and they say he made for overseas. He took Ella with him. How will they live, I wonder, thieving in foreign parts, and such a crime to weigh his soul down? But me I have a different problem, one that troubles me, and it is this: no one can tell me where the man was buried, and I am afraid now when I go about my work that I by chance might find a limb of him and all unknowing sell him as Saint Lawrence. Or worse, Saint Catherine. One bone is very like another. And though I did not like him overmuch I would not wish to show him disrespect.'

Thus Rahere's news. Such news as I could muster from my travels was too much coloured by my disability, for this left arm of mine was now a burden to me, hanging useless at my side and haunting me with images of wretches whose arms had been cut off to save their general health. I could not picture ever feeling natural happiness again, and I thought longingly of those days last year when I had taken everyday use of limbs for granted, and wondered why I had not given thanks each morning for the simple fact of being whole.

Rahere asked me what remedies I had tried. I told him, from Alkanet's to Marel's, to the many I had tried along the way. He said: 'Have you tried saintly healing?'

'You mean touching relics? That's a good jest coming from *you*!'

'Ah!' he protested, pained. 'I may peddle old bones but I believe in holy relics. *Real* relics. I believe in *them*. And here we are in Canterbury.'

I groaned. 'I have tried Walsingham. And Winchester.'

'Don't be faint-hearted. Everybody knows that for each illness there's a particular saint, and maybe Our Lady isn't interested in withered limbs. Give the blessed Saint Thomas a try.'

'Ah – I could not. I don't *believe*. You *know* I don't believe. I've peddled twigs from the crown of thorns myself in better days.'

'But what have you to lose? And much to gain!' He looked upward thoughtfully. 'You know, I always trust the English saints more, don't you? They look after their own. These foreign ones, they're not the same. They don't know our ways. Saint Marcella who was kind to Saint Jerome and suffered at the hands of the barbarians – what was she but a good-hearted Italian? Saint Sophronius – such a famous old monk – but – what would you? A Greek. Now I have nothing against Greeks. But how do they understand English prayers? You try Saint Thomas, see if I am not right – he was born in Cheapside!'

As if he was a personal spokesman for Saint Thomas, Rahere accompanied me into the great church in the morning, Dickon with us in a dress of palest blue, his hair bound into a white linen head-dress, the hem of his gown mud-spattered and his great feet protruding. We had left the tools of our trades with cronies of Rahere's, and passed as ordinary folk into the holy place, amongst the sweltering hordes that hoped to benefit from the saint's intercession. I was if anything more cynical, more dubious than I had been at Walsingham, and heartily depressed from my condition, but I made the round of pilgrimage, with Rahere blithely encouraging every step.

'Come, pedlar, this way now, and now up here . . .'

We saw the place of martyrdom and the altar which was called the Altar of the Sword's Point. The very portions of the blade which shattered from the force of the cruel blow were there for us to see. We stood before the High Altar; we touched the spot where the body had been placed after the killing, and we were duly awed in contemplation of the crime – the sacrilege – here in this fair setting, with the morning light in dusty bands between the pillars, and the jewelled smudges upon the flagstones where the sun shone through the coloured glass.

We set off to the crypt to find the tomb. A vile stench rising showed us where it was – disease and sweat and road-grimed leather, unwashed flesh and mouldy breath, bandaged limbs and festering sores, all pressed together in a small dark place. Down there was packed as dense a throng as could be found in any bee skep, pushing, struggling, buzzing, all in that weird gloom where candlelight cast looming shadows and the old carved pillar-heads smirked malevolently down.

'I can't –' I muttered irritably; but Rahere was firm, and shoved me with his bony arm, and Dickon too, and there we were tight-jammed and on our way. From the steps that led us down I peered into the wriggling gloom. The noise was deafening – believe me, this was no reverent silence. Madmen brought here in chains were screaming hoarsely, twisting in their shackles; some writhed underfoot, clutching up at limbs and hands, and were roughly shaken off; there was crying, wailing, groaning, and then of a sudden one voice or another raised an anguished wail – 'Good Saint Thomas help me – blessed Saint Thomas help me –' and all tried to shuffle further forward.

We had but been there a little while when we got trouble. Someone fondling Dickon at close quarters had suspected something, and there was a shout as Dickon's head gear was pulled off and Dickon's gawping boyish head and jutting ears exposed. With a bellow like a bull some hefty lout yelled:

'Here's a boy – a boy in woman's clothes!'

'What? In this holy place? he dares –?'

'Blasphemy – to laugh at us who suffer!'

A stupid ugly brawl was on us – there was scuffling, struggling, punches aimed, confusion. I took on the fool who had started it; there were more screams, and those already at the tomb shifted nearer to it, till somehow of a sudden we lurched forward in a heap and all of us went plunging downwards in a jumbled mass, still fighting; and I landed heavily upon my back against a pillar's base which dug into my neck and made me yell. I felt a bone move somewhere at my shoulder, heard a crack; I scrambled up, the man and I still grappling, legs and arms about us, cripples, madmen, lepers, whirling wildly by.

I stood stock still, and took a buffet in the chest from that assailant, till he saw my face and paused himself, fist raised.

'I'm cured,' I said. I lifted my left arm.

All around me stared in shock, a point of calm inside a raging pool.

'I had a useless arm; now I can move it.' Like an idiot I spoke; I could not help it, I must say the words. And then the cries went up:

'This man is cured!'

'A miracle!'

'We've seen a miracle!'

Aghast at this unwanted fame I pushed my way out, shouldering all aside. Excited arms grabbed at my ankles, elbows, shirt, my hair; I came out bruised and ragged, shaken, disbelieving. At the top of the steps a monk grasped both my arms and held me.

'Somebody is cured? There has been a miracle?'

Speechless I gestured over my shoulder to the pit below. I left the monk to work out what had happened. I disentangled myself, fled into the nave. Rahere and Dickon, hiding behind a pillar, claimed me.

'Pedlar – what –?'

'Don't speak to me –' I shook them off and wandered in a daze amongst the thoughtful pilgrims by the altar. You would have thought me mad to see me clench and unclench my fingers, bend my elbow, pick up candles. But it was true – I could do all those things. Something had shifted in me, and whatever had entrapped my arm's life had sprung free and I was cured. There in that bright place of martyrdom I lit candle after candle and I said some fervent prayers. I would swear henceforth only by Saint Thomas, and on his feast day in December I would always light a branch of candles, as many as I could afford.

And then I ran from there, and shortly after from Canterbury itself, for fear I should be recognised, and prove to be a miracle.

VI

AT ROCHESTER near the walls of the great turreted fortress by the Medway I did a good trade with the things I had garnered on my travels, and I there acquired some pleasing woven mats and baskets from the Sheppey marshes, which would sell well in Cheapside.

Watling Street then led me on to London.

I travelled with a pilgrim who had been to Rome, a sun-tanned grey-haired fellow with his thread of cockleshells about his neck to show he took his pilgrimages seriously.

'A strange place, Rome,' he said reflectively. 'All ruins. Great stone palaces with crumbling arches, and there between them the ordinary folk live out their lives – buying, selling, drinking, in the shadow of those monstrous heaps. Vines you see growing on the broken walls . . . but it's a noisome place and dirty – underneath the town's a maze of tunnels where they buried their dead in days gone by. In damp weather a pestilent vapour rises out of this labyrinth and brings fever. But they've got wonderful relics there – ah! all from the apostles! You would not believe . . .' he shook his head and marvelled. 'The things that I have seen! All set into their jewelled caskets – rubies, emeralds, wealth indescribable. And when the Pope goes forth on his white horse, his banners flying, all the people throng the streets, and kiss his feet and weep with rapture.'

London seemed a tense and edgy place. All were unsettled by the misfortunes in Normandy; no one knew what it would mean. There were rumours that each man above the age of twelve must take an oath of fealty to the king and we would all be expected to take arms, either in foreign fields, or on the English shores.

Some professed their wish to fight and swore we must regain Rouen; others thought we were better off without it, for now we could be Englishmen. Wulfstan with his fine ideas said Norman and Saxon must be a thing of the past now and we must all band together. This seemed likely with an invasion threatened, for what choice would we have except to join together against our common enemy the French? The idea was strange – folk who yesterday were foes, uniting for a cause we shared, Saxon and Norman welded into English, a race that lived upon an island others coveted, all strong together, differences forgotten.

My own reaction to this jumpy situation was a simple one – I would go north. You wouldn't find me fighting overseas, no chance! Straight up to Cortle would I go, and there collect that golden-headed boy whose image had been in my heart upon my travels. This time I would not be gainsayed. I fancied that his time alone would sober him somewhat, and I was sure that I could lead him to the paths of love.

I knew that London was awry and out of joint, for on the streets the ballads were all of King Richard – Richard our good king he now was called, he who had done nothing for our country, whom folk had hated, feared, ignored; he now was Lion Heart, saviour.

Within our wharfside hideout Wulfstan made up songs to sell and some were written down. Though the sentiments were not my own I bought some, for those who read are pleased to buy such when I travel, particularly if they know they are the latest songs from London; I knew that I could sell them. I wished that I had a good voice; but Marel had, and maybe I could teach him how they sounded, to show our hearers when we travelled the roads together, as I believed one day we would.

One sweet song concerning King Richard's captivity touched the hard heart of Henry the Sailor:

'Ce sevent bien mi honme et mi baron
Englois, Normant, Poitevin et Gascon,
que je n'avoie si povre conpaignon
cui je laissasse por avoir en prixon
je nel di pas por nule retrason
mes encor sui ge pris.

They know well enough these barons of Normandy that if I had a friend however poor I would not leave him in prison, and I don't want to blame anybody, but I am still held captive.'

It was beautiful when Wulfstan sang it, and better than the ones he made up himself, with a haunting melody, and his voice like autumn wind sighing, anyone would have been moved. Henry was; but what we had to suffer was the voice of Henry who could not speak French nor sing in tune, but would render that same song in his own way:

'See seven beans me hommy me baron
On glar Norman Pointervinny Gascon
Jernaldy pass por new lay retrasson
Maids and corn soup huger peas.'

'Poor man, how he must have suffered there in prison in a foreign land,' said Henry, 'all alone with rats and mice and thinking himself forgot.'

225

'I don't believe that he was in a dungeon,' Wulfstan said. 'Captivity for a king is often lack of liberty, no more, but yet good food is brought and servants do attend. Even so, it must have been a difficult time for him, till Blondel found him and sang the song that Richard knew, below his turret window.'

'It was lucky it was a song he knew,' Sparrow chortled. 'Or he would have still been there! Was it that song you have been teaching us?'

'No – how could it have been? That one was composed in prison, by the king himself, and so Blondel would not know it.'

'Which song was it then?'

'I don't know; it could have been one of many. The important thing is that the minstrel found our king, and our king sang a line of song, and there in that far away country of high mountains and steep valleys, the two were close and felt great happiness.'

Sparrow sniggered. 'It was lucky Blondel came riding by then and not Henry. If Henry sang the song, King Richard would have covered up his ears and hid!'

Henry clouted him. It was his favourite song, and he would sing it when and how he chose. I heard his monstrous singing with its vegetable refrain waft over the Thames between the boats as he and Sparrow plied their trade and gathered scraps from ships.

With Tyb gone, Guy the other street boy, Osbert's crony, showed his face again and Fortune played an odd twist of a game with him.

A dark-haired pouting lad with lashes thick as brushes, thin-waisted and big-thighed, he had always seemed to me a hard-skinned heartless youth with plenty of belief in his own loveableness. The rips and rents in his rough gear had not occurred by chance, but were best placed to show off all that lay beneath.

One day he said he might be leaving us. 'I've found this fellow who says he can teach me to be a dancer.'

Who should that prove to be but Simono, whom I had met at Cortle castle over Christmas! That troupe of dancers and musicians had wound up in London just as all of us did sooner or later. I felt great misgiving. I remembered how they fled the castle suddenly, the night that young Pietro was found murdered. Simono had spoken to me much of jealousy's torments, and what could I do but understand that torments such as those had proved too much for him and his dread exploded in a violent rage.

'What do you know of this man?' I warned Guy. 'Go off with these wanderers — who knows what you are letting yourself in for?'

Guy sniggered at such advice coming from one in my trade. He brought Simono back to our lair so we could all see for ourselves that Simono was trustworthy. I greeted him cautiously. He sat down by me, sure of his welcome.

'You know, ever since I lost Pietro I've been looking for a lad to take his place. It won't be easy, because Pietro was so special, wasn't he? You thought so — I thought so — and somebody high up thought so, as we all learnt to our cost. I often wonder if it was Audran de Bonnefoy himself who sent for him — they said he had a taste in boys as well as wenches . . . what do you think? Who do you think killed him? You were there — did you see anything?'

Swiftly shifting round my jumbled thoughts I muttered: 'I don't know anything. I didn't even hear of his death till I was leaving. What happened? Why did you all take off?'

'For our own safety! Why else! They sent a guard to tell us Pietro had been found stabbed on a staircase. They'd hustled him outside wrapped in a blanket. They told us to be off or it would be the worse for us; and we believed them! They reckoned if we stayed one of us would be accused of murder. They hushed it up, and we went along with it to save our skins. Lord knows what the boy was up to when they got him. I've thought about it night and day. I can't say it surprised me. That boy was doomed. The very beautiful often are. Don't you agree?'

'I haven't thought about it — beauty's not a problem I've been troubled with myself!' I laughed uncomfortably, somewhat chastened.

Well! I thought guiltily, that puts me nicely in my place. And all this time I'd never doubted but that Pietro had been killed because of jealousy, yet poor Simono knew no more than I did as to how the boy had met his end.

'He used to tell me Lady Berenice had set her sights on him

– but I thought he was boasting . . . Would you think a fine lady like that, one who could have her pick of knights and lords, would bother with a dancer? No! It's unbelievable. And now we'll never know. I cried myself sick at the time; but now I can't help thinking it was for the best. I've never slept so well as I do now, free from the pangs of jealousy and love.'

I felt a right fairweather friend now. A short while back I had been warning Guy about Simono; now I had to give a word of caution to the player.

'Are you sure Guy is the one for you? You say that you know peace now. Why not stick with that?'

'We need a dancer for our troupe, a boy to take the place of Pietro. Remember, I picked Pietro from the gutter – taught him all he knew. I'll do the same with Guy. I'll make him every whit as beautiful. And he'll be grateful. I struck lucky finding him.'

I said no more. I thought that Simono had as much chance of finding what he wanted from Guy as a rabbit might, who, freed from a trap at much cost to life and limb, jumps eagerly into another. But to be sure, before truth dawned, there'd be good times along the way.

I heard a sad tale of such woe one night I was in London.

We were drinking at the Pack Horse down near Dowgate on the Wall Brook, and listening to a man just back from the Crusade. Black-bearded he was, with a yellow skin, good-looking, gaunt and lined, with quick brown eyes, and arms and sinews like old Wayland Smith himself, and he was dining off his stories, for he had yarns to tell of lands that few of us would ever see.

'A blue and cloudless sky, the sun so hot, and castles upon crags, and palaces with marble walls and crimson carpets patterned all with birds and flowers, and plates of silver to eat strange fruits and every kind of flesh and fowl upon; the people dressed in silk and gold, but monstrous cruel, and always sweetly scented, always bathing in great pools dug out of marble, and the women always bathing too – and beautiful, all dressed in clothes that shimmer, rustle, and the feet all bare, and jewels on their sandals . . . it would seem a marvellous place and full of wonders; but no, I would give everything I own never to have seen those fabled places, never to have reached those shores . . .'

He had three companions with him, who sat somewhat apart, huddled in hoods, half turned away. One joined us now, to tell his part of the tale, his skin burnt like scorched parchment, shadowed beneath his hood.

'All four of us were landless knights, eager to try our luck and join the Pope's Crusade. They said he wanted no kings – just common folk, we heard, and we were glad to go. Two years ago it was – we went to Venice. Have you ever been to Venice? It's beautiful, but it's evil, as we were to find out. There this great company all gathered on an island called Saint Niccolo – as mighty a fleet as ever you saw – and it set sail for Zara, and we took that place, and spent the Winter there. So here we were, and then we heard we were to go by way of Constantinople, to put Prince Alexius on the throne. It was nothing to do with us – it was all between the Doge of Venice and the ones in charge; and some who'd come to save the Holy Land got angry and split up from us and went on by themselves. But we stayed with the fleet, and so we went to Constantinople.'

'Ah,' said the bearded fellow, Martin. 'We saw seas as blue as grapes, and islands in the sea like purple jewels, and sunsets red as blood, and mountains topped with snow, seeming to float in the air. We took Andros; and we landed to take grain aboard, and never asked for it but had all that we wanted when we chose.

'Then we saw Constantinople and dropped anchor. We saw golden domes flashing in the sunset, and the sea was yellow with it, and the pinnacles and towers all gold. And the walls were white, with stripes of grey stone, and it was all shining back out of the water. We went ashore and made a great camp there.

'We got Alexius crowned, and why we didn't pack up then and get on with what we'd set out to do I don't know, but we didn't. We just stayed outside the city, and they didn't like it much. There was a lot of trouble, mostly Frenchmen and Venetians on the rampage in the city. We kept ourselves to ourselves, we did; and we were content enough, though we could see that Ralph was getting ill . . .'

They both looked uneasily across at their two companions, who said nothing and did not turn their heads. Wulfstan passed some ale along the table to them; they did not pick it up.

'Then there was some trouble in the city,' Martin said. 'They rose up against that same Alexius and murdered him. Some baron took over the throne. He wouldn't pay out the money we were owed. Our leaders decided to attack the city from the sea. All our ships moved forward to the very walls – warships, galleys, small boats – banners streaming, waters churning, ladders flung up the walls, and fighting on the battlements. We had to retreat. But we tried again, and worked to make a breach in the walls, lashing ships together, ramming the prows forward at speed. We were not there at the front, but we were there when the gates were broken down and we poured in.

'The city was ours, they said, treat it how you want, take what you please. And that's what I thought it would be – the usual pillage, grabbing a handful of this and that, knobbling the ones that got in your way.' He took a swig and shook his head. 'It wasn't like that. It was wickedness. I pray I never see anything like it again. I never will except maybe in Hell. Three days and nights of killing – women, children – and everything smashed up and wrecked ... Thousands of heroes drunk out of their heads running like mad things in and out of houses, churches, tearing things down, burning – we had light enough to see by all night long – deeds of sacrilege you would never believe – fucking inside churches, pissing on holy relics – I know I grabbed a heap of rubies for myself and I'll be well set up for life – but I swear I never acted like a brute.'

We listened, awed. He went on: 'There are fabulous relics there! The real true Cross! A phial of the blood of Christ – the *true* blood of Christ – and a part of Saint John's arm. Teeth, nails and garments – I took a few ...'

'Have you still got them?' I enquired with interest, hoping for a sale; but he ignored my mercenary remark.

'They took horses into holy places to piss and shit on the floor; they passed round silver chalices like wine flagons; they brought whores in there to fuck on altar cloths ... And you know what, when it was all over we gave thanks to God who gave us victory ...'

Morosely he hunched over his ale. His friend said: 'We lost heart. It wasn't just the killing, see, but Ralph was ill, and now we knew what it was. We couldn't help but know.'

And then we felt uneasy. Ralph was sitting over there, not

three feet from us, hooded, bowed and silent.

'Ah!' groaned Martin, his hand clenched on his forehead. 'I brought him to Constantinople a beautiful boy. His hair was golden as the sun. I loved him dearly. We knew that overseas our very special friendship would be free to grow. A chance encounter on the quaysides of that city Venice spoilt our hopes for ever.'

'You are still together,' I observed, squinting warily at the hooded figure by the wall, hoping with some resignation that what I feared was not so.

'True, we are together, and will be till he dies. Till we all die . . .' he answered gloomily.

'Ah, come, enough of this sad talk!' cried Wulfstan standing up. Martin shoved him down again.

'Nobody leaves!' he growled and we all jumped. 'Nobody leaves till all have finished drinks – nobody leaves because of us!'

We sat there guardedly, since he was a large pugnacious fellow and a soldier who had killed and seen much killing; moreover he had pulled a knife almost as big as a butcher's cleaver, which he jerked from one to other of us. We were scared, no doubt of it.

'So we came home,' he said, as if there had been no interruption. 'We left the fleet, the army to wander where it would – Jerusalem – Outremer – Hell itself – who cares? And we came home.'

'What is Ralph's illness?' I enquired.

'What do you think?' said Martin bitterly. 'What would you say this was?'

He leaned across and pulled the hood off the young man. We all recoiled and stared. All of us had seen leprosy before of course, but not so close and not so sudden. If the figure before us was a young man, as we had been told, you would not know it, for the hair was old-man white, and coarse like nags' tails, and the space it framed was not a face, but grey and scabrous like the ashes of a fire; there were no lips nor nose but what was most disquieting, the eyes remained of startling wondrous blue. Then with a hand whose fingers were but crusty stumps, the leper shook his hood back into place.

'You should not be here amongst folk,' said Wulfstan bravely. 'You know the rules – the Church must be called in –

231

and there are proper ways of conduct.'

'I will not change my life to fit in with the Church's dictates,' Martin said. 'It was to serve the Church I went abroad. But what harm has this boy done? I brought him out to Venice as a lovely youth, with skin so smooth, and golden hair and lips that kissed more sweet than any woman kisses. I shall not desert him now. Our ways are one until whatever end shall come. And he shall not be put away with strangers to go begging and be cast away by those who once would have begged his favours. As for lazar houses I would kill him with my own bare hands before I let him enter one of those.'

I knew that when I was well clear of him I would applaud his words; but two feet from the grisly group my generosity was not so great. Ralph, his love who had been beautiful, was his main concern, but we guessed true enough the other hooded one was also diseased now, and maybe Martin too was fated in the same grim way. I leaned my chin upon my hand as if in thoughtful pose, but with my fist I covered up my mouth and nose, and noticed covertly that men known for their careless brutishness did the same, with sleeves or cloth. A grudging sympathy there surely was, but also some resentment, for he had gained our hearing and our wonder only to produce this tale with such a sting in it. He drank his ale, his knife still brandished, and he made sure his dark companions drank theirs too, and then they left; and you may well believe we left soon after, and the Pack Horse lost its trade for many days to come. The talk I heard was all of thus:

'Can you catch leprosy from cups?'

'Can it be passed by breathing the same air?'

'I hear if one should spit at you, you catch it.'

'No, you must touch the skin for it to pass from him to you . . . shake hands or embrace . . .'

'Embrace a leper! Are you mad?'

'You *can* catch it from cups – I heard this tale . . .' And these were men who cheated, stole and worse, yet they were ghostly scared that night.

VII

THERE IS not much in my tale concerning Lust at this time, and the reason is straightforward – I was hungering for Marel, and I knew that I must go seek him; for whatever this Summer's absence had done for him, for me it had shown only what I had suspected – that I loved him, that I wanted him with me. It was the awful tale of the Crusader that now made me know I must be gone. His golden-haired lad was all but lost to him; but mine was not. He lived, he breathed, he was still beautiful, and up in that abundant wilderness when the road ended and I reached that lovely place, he waited for me in a garden. Yes indeed, a mystic glow was in my head when thoughts of Marel took me over. Love Earthly, Love Divine, these joined and became one when I was near him.

To get some money for the journey I set about to sell what I had left. I took my wares set on an open tray that hung from my shoulders by leather straps, to sell in Cheapside. By chance I was near Jusson's cookshop by Saint Paul's, and I passed by to see how he fared.

His shop-board, stacked with cakes and pies and bread, hung open from its chains, and there he was within, and his assistant, red-faced in the heat, a brisk trade keeping them busy in the bustling street. Dogs nuzzled food scraps by my feet, and flies buzzed at the well-cooked pastries. When Jusson saw me he waved both his hands.

'Stay, pedlar! Wait!'

I drew near, and stood beside a great meat pie, which Jusson sliced for customers as we spoke.

'I am most pleased that you passed by,' he told me, swapping coins for pie, 'for I have a message, and no way to give it to you, as I did not know where you were or if you were in London. I asked at the cooper's, but none had seen you. It is a lucky chance that brought you here.'

'You have a message? For me?'

'Yes! And though I may not like the messenger – a man who always made me feel he was laughing at me behind his hand – it is no more than Christian to do a good turn for a fellow.'

'Please do it then. Who is the message from?'

'Your friend,' he said. 'Roger Fortunatus.'

And now I was astonished. 'Here in London?'

'On his way to France.'

'But when was this?'

'But a few days ago. He stayed barely a moment. He had left Cortle in a hurry. He said he was making for Dover and would take whatever ship would have him. He wished us well and promised us that we would never hear from him again. He said he had done all he could, and that in this hard world everyone must look after himself.'

'Did he look well?' I asked, a sharp tingling prickling my loins as I recalled those wicked eyes and dancer's limbs, the dark tones of his voice as he spoke holy words and made them sound like words of lust.

'Well enough,' shrugged Jusson. 'I never liked the man. But I pass his message on to you. You both were good to me in my time of trouble.'

'And the message?'

'Ah, the message.' Jusson paused in his slicing. A fly settled on his nose. I noticed absentmindedly that his skin was clear and smooth; I thought of Ralph and shuddered.

'The boy Marel,' Jusson muttered, leaning close to me. 'Remember him? Some dreadful crime . . . accused of murder . . . thrown into a dungeon, and condemned to death.'

I do not know how I made my way back towards the river; indeed my dazed and wayward steps led me a way I would not usually have taken, though the direction was the same, riverward. Jusson could tell me no more than that bare outline. The fool had not thought to ask what lay behind the bleak account, and had let Roger go away with none of the wild and urgent demands I would have made. I had not a moment to lose. I must leave for Cortle at once. I would not pause along the way. Even now I could be too late. Marel imprisoned? Marel like to die? I could not believe it – yet I knew it would be true, if Roger had passed on the news and told Jusson to let me know. And I so far away. A thousand miles seemed to lie between us – the road so long, the streets and houses bearing down on me like prison walls. Prison! Was Marel in some noisome cell, alone, he who knew only sunlight and the forest? Would no one save him? Had no one helped him? Where was Benedict? And murder? Marel could not commit a crime – he was too good, too pure – or had he, in his innocence? I did remember once he said his skill was such that he could kill whoever wished him ill. I feared to think what that might mean. Had he done that? Had someone troubled him? *Had he killed someone?* Oh, who could save him now?

The answer was plain enough. *I* could. It was all up to me. I alone could save him, because I loved him, and my love would give me strength. If I left London now I would not be long in reaching Cortle. I would not sleep, I would not rest, and I would save him.

These streets near the river were the better streets, where merchants lived, and wealthy folk, and not so far from Juhel de Bracy's house which I had been so used to visit just last year. That yellow-haired lad had been a weakness I could well have done without. Our times of pleasure hardly weighed against the suffering I had been through since we were discovered in the clothes' room and his father's guards had slung me out and caused that cursed disability. (Thanks be to the blessed Saint Thomas!) Even as I thought about him – as a slight and pleasant memory, no more – an entourage with a litter overtook me, horses with bright trappings, and a lady's face within the litter, looking out and seeing me.

'Pedlar!' she called. 'What have you for sale?'

Carrying my tray as I was, I could hardly deny my trade, and I walked alongside, giving her polite attention. Those woven mats from the Sheppey marshes seemed to please her, and I thought I'd make a quick sale in the street; but to my gloom and horror she remarked: 'My house is just nearby. Come with us. I intend to make some purchases.'

Her house was just nearby – how well I knew it! She was Juhel's mother! A haughty beak-nosed lady in a flame-coloured gown, she did not recognise me, even if she knew of me at all – one pedlar being very like another – and she thought to do a favour by her interest. I grimly chose to risk it; she had household guards about her, and I knew her sort – they only too readily cry Seize him! and then you're in for it.

We went in through the open courtyard gates and all was bustle as the men-at-arms dismounted. The lady was helped out of her conveyance, and then turned to me, and picked amongst the stuff I carried. To be fair, she bought it all, and paid with coins which I did not lose in the fray that followed. But as I turned to leave, her husband and son rode in from

235

the street, and saw me straightaway. I might have bluffed it out even then, but Juhel like a great buffoon blushed scarlet, thinking that my coming there was to do with him, and looked as guilty as if we had been meeting secretly in clothes cupboards once a week at midnight for a year.

His father's face too boiled bright red, and hard rage suffused him. I was like a rat caught in a trap.

'Seize him!' he cried pointing – I do find aggressors have limited use of words, and in their bluster cry out the same things. The guards responded instantly and I was seized.

'Hubert! This is but a pedlar!' cried his lady in amazement.

'I know what he is!' said Hubert darkly. 'And he knows it too. And I have warned him what he risks by coming here. Take him below!'

Below! I soon found out what that meant. It was indeed below. Below the floor of the house, below the steps that wound down into a cold dark place, below the river itself almost, a cellar underneath their house. A dank stench rose from dripping walls, a green slime slithered underfoot. A door was opened, and with that enjoyment which paid menials seem to find when carrying out their overbearing master's orders, the guards took the knife from my belt and shoved me roughly through and shut the door, which creaked and thudded into place. Wulfstan with his high ideals, his proud belief that political changes had turned us all now into Englishmen united in a common cause, would have been disillusioned, for this Norman oaf was quite clear in his beliefs and added before leaving: 'Saxon dog.'

Cellar or dungeon, this place was a vile hole and secure. Just high enough to stand upright in, it was a space some six feet square, and dark save for a window blocked by wooden bars. The walls were of cold stone, and underfoot the floor was puddled; from the window ledge a fitful drip of water swelled the oozy pools beneath. I knew the house bordered the river, and when I looked through the bars I saw the Thames itself not two feet from my nose, its heaving plashing surface shifting against the wall below my window, and with every swell of ebb and flow a further overflow into the noisome little room.

Alarmed, I wished I knew more about the rise of tides; it seemed to me that one full flow could do for me, coming through the window. And was that the intent? Did that misguided baron fear so much what I could do to his lily heir that I was to be silenced? You may well believe I heaved and pulled at bars and door, but to no avail. I scanned the river.

Beyond the window some way further off there passed at times the little boats of river trade – the fishermen, the baggage-carters – and I tried to get their notice with my shouts. I had no luck. I first supposed they could not see where the sound came from – the window was small and low down – but when I waved my arm between the bars it made no difference, and I grimly realised that nobody in daylight would be fool enough to venture his boat against the wall of the de Bracy stronghold for such a risky cause. And I had much chance to regret my sale of goods at Cheapside for there had been things which could have been useful for the whittling away of window bars. All I had was the little purse full of coins, in here worth nothing at all.

Now to my bodily dreads were added torments of the mind that I began to think would drive me mad. For this was so unlooked for, so needless – I had no interest in Juhel and I would not have used our past friendship to trouble his father or their reputation with threats to tell all for money; so it was for nothing I was here. And meanwhile up in Cortle there lay Marel, with no one to help him, no one strong enough to save him – Lord! maybe he even now was dead and hanged and I in this vile place so far from him. All day I languished there; I pounded on the door, the walls; I heaved at those firm bars and they stayed firm, the skin scraped from my fingers till they bled, and all for nothing. No one came; I was alone, the river rising nearer the window, splashing insolently as it swelled, flinging water through the window bars and down the walls. Night now began to fall.

SIX
Marel's Tale

I

HE PEDLAR left, and I turned back to my work.

At dawn and evening in these warm days, I go among my servants the herbs and gather what I need.

'Holy Mother Earth, Lady of Healing, Lady of Bounty, Source of all well-being, grant to me thy servant the gentle ways of goodness. Allow me so to take your gifts and use them only for good, so that all whom I serve with your abundance may grow whole and strong as they should be, in the joy of your sweet name.'

I kneel beside the little white stars of wuderove whose scent is like summer grass; and the heavy yellow blossoms of dabwort hang above me. The twilight-coloured flowers of chibbole bloom at my hand.

I collect five fingers' root, I harvest thyme, I pick the grey leaves of sage, I gather alehoof, and garclive with its pointed yellow flowers. I hang bunches of all these in the open air till they are dry as tinder and can be crumbled into powder and stored away in pots. And I pray to the Lady of the Elder Tree, whose blessing encourages all the other herbs to flourish.

I am in the herb room, and the sun slants on me like the dust of buttercups, when a loud voice calls me from outside. I come through into the room. There in the doorway is a man whom I have never seen before.

He is a short stocky person in a long robe. He has a reddish face and small round eyes which squint around the cottage. His neck is thick and short, his podgy hand holds a slim golden cross, which the sunlight catches in glittering rays.

238

Behind him stands a youth who gazes about him timidly, carrying in his arms a carved chest.

'Is anybody there?' demands the man. 'Answer me, in the name of the Lord.'

'I am here,' I answer. 'Who is it that needs me?'

'It is Angilbert the priest,' says he, coming further in and still looking about him.

'Yes?'

'There has been a death in this house,' says Angilbert, 'and I have come to perform my duties.'

'What duties?'

'Why, what do you think?' demands Angilbert. 'I have the sacred oils for anointing the body, the holy words to say, the burial to organize, and my fees to collect; and also the death dues which fall to me as priest,' and he looks round slily at the room and the herbs hanging in their bunches.

'But you are too late. The body is long buried. All that is over.'

'What do you mean, boy?' he asks in alarm. 'Where have you buried it?'

'But sir, what is it to you?' I cry. 'You did not know the woman. I did not even know that others knew of her death.'

'No, I daresay you tried to keep it secret,' says Angilbert, unpleasantly. 'You thought to escape the payments. But you reckoned without Ulf the swineherd, who happened to see you and the pedlar carrying the dead old woman. He knew his duty and came and told me.'

'But there is nothing for you to do. She died, I dealt with the body, and the pedlar and I laid her to rest.'

'But in unhallowed ground!' cries Angilbert. 'You may not do that in these civilised times. You must inform the Church and you must give the dead a Christian burial.'

'What do you mean, unhallowed ground?'

'I mean ground that is not blessed, of course.'

'Then have no fear,' I answer. 'The ground was blessed. Alkanet blessed it every day when she was alive, and I and the pedlar blessed it as we buried her.'

'But that is wicked!' screams Angilbert. 'Only a priest has the right to bless the ground. Without the approval of the Holy Church the blessing counts for nothing. The soul of the dead has no protection for its life in the hereafter.'

'Oh no, you are wrong,' I told him. 'Alkanet is with the

Earth Mother now, who gives us plants and seeds and rebirth. Alkanet is at one with the earth.'

'What nonsense are you telling me?' snaps Angilbert. 'Unless the soul is properly dealt with, unless the priest is called, that old woman will be damned to the everlasting fury of hell fire.'

'I don't understand you.'

'Where were you brought up, not to know these truths?' says Angilbert in disgust. 'Everybody knows about hell fire. If you have led a wicked life or if your last hours were not properly managed by the priest, then your soul is unde-fended like a leaky boat on the turbulent sea of eternity. The Devil reaches out for it with his grasping hands and tosses it down to the dreadful hordes who serve him around the blazing furnace. Monsters with flaming red eyes cast it carelessly into the everlasting flames. It will burn for all eternity, with the agonized cries of the damned souls and the hideous laughter of the pitiless fiends. And such may be the fate of the old woman you so wantonly buried without the approval of God.'

I am trembling.

'But God did approve,' I stutter. 'The pedlar spoke the names of God.'

'Rot the pedlar!' bellows Angilbert, thumping upon the table. 'He has not that right. The pedlar knows nothing of God. What does he know? Impious smatterings he has picked up in wayside inns and on the road. I have made a study of God. I devote my life to the furtherance of His works. You must listen to me!'

'But I don't want to listen to you!' You tell me only of horrible things. I loved Alkanet. I don't want her to be in a fire. The pedlar told me that God was kind and would welcome her with love, and pardon all her faults. And I believe him. The Earth Mother is like that too, benign though unseeing. I don't want to know about your pitiless fiends. It's cruel of you to come spreading such misery.'

Angilbert looks shifty now. He sees that he has somehow gone wrong, and he regrets the way he acted. This is clear to me.

'Well, enough of demons,' he says generously. 'As you say, all that is over. Wherever her soul may be it is not for us to wonder about. Let us be practical.'

240

He sits down and lays the cross upon the table.

'What is your name, child?'

'I'm not a child. My name is Marel.'

'A heathen sort of name, alas. We might perhaps change it. And you live here all alone since the death of the old woman?'

'Yes.'

'That's not very satisfactory,' he decides. 'And I am amazed that I didn't know of your existence. You grow herbs, it seems.'

'Yes; they are to cure illnesses and make people more beautiful.'

'Indeed.'

'I would be glad to offer you something to drink.'

'Thank you. It's very unpleasant to argue.'

He asks me more about myself. He has certainly decided that I am a soul in dire need of salvation and he is the one to save me. But he chooses not to rush it; he is gentle, fatherly; he treats me as he would a lamb, a puppy. Then he tells me I must come to the village.

'I think that you should come to church,' he says seriously. 'This would be entirely beneficial to you, and in your particular case, most needful.'

'Would you be there?' I ask doubtfully.

I see that he is pleased. I think that he misunderstands. I have no wish to see him further. He supposes that I ask from need of him.

'I will be there to guide you,' he says. 'You know where the church is.'

'Yes, I've seen the outside.'

'Oh my poor boy, only the outside! But it will all be different now. I shall look after you. Now the first thing I ought to mention is that with the old woman's death, you are obliged to offer me priestly dues.'

'What are they?'

'I am entitled to a choice of your goods.'

'Why?'

'Well, it's my right, you see, as priest. A selection of your best herbs would be appropriate.'

'I would have to gather some together.'

'Of course. I can come back another day.'

So Angilbert leaves, with this tempting promise, and instructions as to when to come to church.

241

His visit leaves me troubled and perplexed. But I find comfort when the tavern-keeper Benedict sits down to reassure me and explain. He visits me soon after, and I find his friendliness more spiritual than what Angilbert had to tell me.

'I am sad about Alkanet's death, but I believe she is at one with the earth. Or at least, I did, but now I wonder. I find myself troubled by the thought of demons.'

'Forget about them,' Benedict tells me. 'Nobody truly knows what happens to our souls after our bodies die, but believe me it is in God's hands and He knows what He's doing. I know that Angilbert is our priest, but I'm afraid that in some ways he's a fool. He had no business to go worrying you like that.'

'But what if he is right?'

'I'll tell you what to do. You take two pieces of wood and bind them into the shape of a cross. You place that cross at the head of Alkanet's grave and she'll be all right. She will not be forgotten by the Almighty.'

'Thank you. I'll do that.'

'Now, is there anything else?'

'What should I do about the priestly dues he says I owe him?'

'Did he say anything about the lord's share?'

'No. What lord?'

'By the same rule, the lord at the castle is entitled to a pick of the best animal or goods. The priest then takes the second best.'

'But isn't this unfair? A person may be very poor . . .'

'Of course it's unfair, between ourselves. But it's one of those things. If he insists on his priestly dues, you ask him what part of your goods you should offer to Audran de Bonnefoy. I daresay he wants to keep the whole business secret so he can have the pick of your best crops. We may be able to keep Angilbert happy with just a gift. Offer him a bunch of something that'll cure a troublesome gut; he'll be grateful for ever.'

Benedict promises to call back another day, and then adds: 'Will we still be having the meetings? There is one due, I think.'

'Oh yes. Nothing is to change.'

So Benedict goes cheerfully away. He seems to me a man

who does not fear or question, living one day as another, never doing harm. He makes me glad. Such people own a skill they do not know of.

There is another visitor, a bad one, and she comes in secretly, under cover of darkness. I am asleep in the little room upstairs and it is the horse's whinny that alerts me. Downstairs a girl's voice is calling Alkanet's name. I sling a cloak around myself and come down, half asleep.

'Where is Alkanet?' asks the visitor, hooded, and whispering.

'She is dead,' I answer. 'But I can do all that she used to do.'

The girl calls over her shoulder: 'My lady!'

The lady dismounts and comes into the cottage. She looks at me suspiciously. 'Where is the old woman?' she demands.

I stutter in explaining: 'But I can do everything she did, and I will gladly help you.' It is a lie; I say it to placate her. She is angry.

'Indeed you will not,' she cries. 'Oh this is dreadful! Who would have thought that the old witch would die, just when I needed her!'

'But I can . . .' I begin.

'Be silent!' orders she. 'My dealings were with the old woman. She knew what I wanted. I can't involve anybody else – it's bad enough already. Oh! What shall I do?'

I remember her. She has been here before. She is beautiful and haughty, like a birch tree. I do not like her. She is proud but she is frightened. Alkanet felt scorn for her and sneered about her afterwards; but I see the Thornapple in her, and I fear her.

'Let us go home, my lady,' says her maid soothingly. 'It's not this boy's fault. He has nothing to do with it.'

The lady of the castle turns on me. 'Listen! Do you know who I am?'

'No,' I say uneasily.

'Let me warn you. My visit here is completely secret. No one is ever to know that I came here. Do you understand?'

'Yes.'

'If you ever tell anyone that I have been here I will make sure you suffer. I will accuse you of casting spells, have you driven from the village. Do you understand me? I have that power.'

So they hurry outside and mount and ride away, to

disappear like shadows in the green-leaved night. I am left confused and anxious, wondering and wary, and I see her passion and her despair.

II

I GO to church for the first time on a blue and gold morning of early summer. I feel unhappy about it. I have never been to the village so openly before. I like the dawn or dusk, to go unnoticed like the deer.

I come to Cortle. The wayside is bright with flowers; the people, cheerful in the sunlight, are all making their way to church. Some of them stare and smile, but hesitantly, for while wishing to be welcoming, they are afraid of the powers they think I have – it was the same with Alkanet.

The church seems dark after the daylight but I find much to marvel at. The building is small and high, the roof raised by great rafters, the floor space narrow, crammed with villagers. They shuffle together, leaning against the walls, against each other. I ask myself how God can talk to you inside these walls.

I cannot see the altar or the priest, and bleak unhappiness comes over me. As more and more people press into the little building everyone moves closer together and the smells of sweat and fusty clothes stifle the sweeter smells at the altar. It is not clear when the prayers begin because the people chatter. Some mumble snatches of strange words, some gossip, and some discuss the chances of a good harvest. Lambert tells me that Berenice de Bonnefoy has got a strange new visitor up at the castle, a wandering priest, but what of it? It is not important. Two things cheer me – the bunch of wuderove that hangs against the wall, tied with lavender and roses; and the carved wooden panel against which I stand – some happy woodcarver has made shapes of flowers on it, almost as real as when they grow in the meadows.

Sometimes when the people's voices fall silent for a moment I hear Angilbert, but understand no word of what he says. Words certainly he uses, but they are spoken in a muttering rush, without sense or feeling, as if he is in a hurry to be done with it, and they are not words I know.

At last it's over, and the people shuffle out. I am not

touched by what should seem most holy. I feel in need of
guidance such as Angilbert has promised. I draw near him.
We are now alone.

'Ah!' says Angilbert with feeling. 'They leave such a stink!'
He hunts around for a bunch of rosemary, and buries his
nose deep in it.

'Do you remember me?' I ask uncertainly.

'Of course I do,' replies Angilbert. 'I am gratified to find
you able to benefit from divine care.'

'But I haven't!' I cry. 'I have tried, but I see nothing of the
things I expected. The pedlar told me . . . and you yourself
told me . . . I thought that it would be different.'

'Oh!' says Angilbert sternly. 'You are even further from
grace than I thought. Now, what can I do? Come with me,
and I will explain.'

He leads me slowly round the church, pointing to the
paintings which had before been hidden by the crowd.

'This, above the altar, is the figure of Christ in majesty,
ready to bless us. In your case, my child, God will be especially
interested. You have a life of sinful ignorance to make up for.
The sooner you offer yourself to God's loving care, the better
for you. He won't refuse you if your heart is pure. He will
forgive you. We will pray for it.'

We kneel down together and Angilbert shows me how to
pray. We ask God to forgive the wickedness of my ignorance
and I promise to come often to church and ask forgiveness.
Now I feel bitterly ashamed of all those sinful years.

'How can He possibly forgive me? All those years when I
did not say His name . . .' Angilbert is pleased to see me sad.

'I will help you,' he promised. 'Stand up and let us learn
more.'

We move to one of the walls. Here are to be found more
pictures – men employed in their proper tasks of toil and
planting. Story-like they told us the right way to live.

'God watches over us, whatever we do, however humble, in
the fields, in our homes,' Angilbert says. 'He watches you,' he
adds, making me uncomfortable with his closeness. 'He
watches you, in that little house that you thought lay hidden.
He watches you as you sleep. He sees everything you do.'

I lower my gaze, and Angilbert draws closer, as if he would
see inside my head. 'Now these soldiers . . .' says Angilbert.
'You see that these have pleasant holy faces; they are the

Virtues. These fighting against them, with ugly cruel faces, these are the Vices. The virtues represent our good qualities – obedience, goodness, toil, docility, attending mass, those sort of things. The vices represent our evil ways – pride, envy, laziness, anger, greed, and of course lust, the sinful pleasures of the flesh.'

'Are they sinful?' I ask horrified.

Angilbert frowns. 'Surely you have had no experience of them?' he gasps.

He breathes hot and heavily. 'Certainly!' he fumes. 'The body is sinful, sinful. Strive to master it. Never give way to it. Only the soul is pure. And you – you ought to cut your hair!' I draw back from him, astonished.

'But why?'

'It draws attention to you. Like the hair of women. Hair can be an – allurement. Do you know what I mean? An enticement to sin. It is so with women. The Devil's creatures.'

Angilbert pants somewhat, controls himself, and goes on to the great big picture of the Punishment of the Wicked.

'These skeletons represent the souls of the dead, the ones that denied God and lived bad lives. See them plunge into the flames of Hell to burn in everlasting torment! You too will suffer like that unless you own the goodness of God and obey His laws!'

'Oh, I will obey His laws!' I gasp. Oh, I am drawn to that picture. The damned souls sprawl and hurtle into the roaring flames, legs and arms splayed out, grimaces of pain upon their faces. And above it all, upon a throne, sits a fine figure of a man, with a crown on his head which does not conceal two curved horns. His face is beautiful, with green eyes and a pointed chin, a cruel smile upon his lips, long black hair framing his face.

'But that must be a king!' I marvel.

Angilbert pales. 'May you be forgiven!' he cries. 'Lord Above, have pity on this ignorant boy in his blasphemy!'

'What have I said?'

'The figure there that you admire so much is the Devil himself! The Antichrist! The fallen angel which God flung out of Paradise because of the Devil's pride. Yes! Down he fell, and there he lay, to rule the underworld, to preside over his damned crew, to terrorise the souls in torment. Oh! Pray for forgiveness!'

I know I am in need of prayer. A lifetime of prayer will not be enough to save my sins. The wicked lord must have been brave to fight against Almighty God and I admire his beauty. So I am damned. I am a sinner. There is no hope for me; it is too late. I plead with Angilbert to talk to God on my behalf and pray for me. He promises to do so. I hate Alkanet now, for keeping so much from me. And I blame the pedlar, who told me God was Love.

At last, with many warnings and commands to live a better life, Angilbert escorts me to the church door and we part in the warm sunlight. Benedict is waiting outside.

'Ah, so you've finished your little talk with Angilbert,' he says. 'Everything all right?'

'Yes,' I reply, too numb to explain. My wickedness hangs round me like a cloak. I am steeped in ignorance and sin and hardly know how to answer for fear that the newly watchful eye of God should see and darken with anger.

Now I remember what the pedlar taught me, and what we did together. The pedlar brought me pleasure but he did not say it was a sin. What kind of a friend is he to me, to act like that? I trusted him. Now who is there to trust? All I am sure of are my plants.

'We have a meeting coming up,' says Benedict, and nudges me.

'Yes,' I reply gloomily. 'But it will not be right.'

'Right? In what way?'

'God will be angry,' I blurt out.

Benedict would have laughed, but he sees my clear distress.

'No,' he says cheerfully. 'Has Angilbert been telling you about hell fire? That's one of his favourite tales. You mustn't mind him. He likes to frighten people; it gives him a hold over them. But *you've* nothing to worry about – who could be more innocent than you? You've led a blameless life, hurting no one, picking herbs, looking after that old crone. As for the meeting, Our Lord's got better things to do than peer down at a crowd of homely folk having a good time around a bonfire!'

I'm doubtful. But I remember God has allowed it before.

'We do no harm. And it's always cheering and merry,' I say hesitantly.

'Course it is!' says Benedict. 'And besides, this time it's my turn to wear the horns!'

Mention of the horns reminds me of the beautiful wicked

247

picture in the church, the king with horns and green eyes who presides over the fires of Hell, no, not a king, but the most evil one of all. Now I'm frightened and cannot bear to stay in the bright open street of the village. I run home, desperate for the green woods and secret places of the forest and the things I know, where I can try and sort my troubled thoughts. I must be by myself. I am most unwilling to see Angilbert again, God's messenger, trailing threat and menace, punishment and flames.

But as it happens, this is not to be. During the week that follows, Angilbert is taken poorly. He lies so ill that he cannot get up to take any of the prayers, and the villagers have no priest. Benedict comes in to tell me what has happened. While Angilbert lay tended by a kindly neighbour, a little group of villagers went to the castle to ask whether his lordship had a priest who might take mass for the villagers on the Lord's day.

'Idiots!' said Azo the reeve, who was lounging in the courtyard. 'Don't you know anything? You'll get no answer from his lordship, who is himself lying sick. Half the time he doesn't know who he is. No, it is her ladyship you must ask.'

Uneasily, Ralf and Lambert entered the great hall and were directed to where her ladyship sat, with Roger Fortunatus the priest. With much bowing and twitching they stuttered out their message, the two of them much overcome at being so close to such an important person as the lady of the castle. But they both recognised Roger, who stared at them most vaingloriously.

'As if he were nobly born hisself,' said Lambert indignantly.

'As if he were thoroughly at home,' said Ralf. 'He that had been drinking with us on the bench.'

The lady listened to their problem with merry eyes.

'She were not haughty at all,' said Ralf. 'But just like any woman, and smiling a lot. Though not like ordinary women in that she were beautifully dressed, and clean.'

She told them that she would send them a priest without fail.

As they withdrew, they were ignored. But, says Benedict meaningfully, Ralf was quite certain that even before he and Lambert had left the room, the lady of the castle had twined her hand in Roger's hair and said laughingly to him:

'What a joke! The poor things need a priest to inspire them on Sunday. How would you fancy the work? Shall I send *you*?'

248

Roger Fortunatus? That name means nothing to me.

It is to hear Angilbert and pray for forgiveness that I make my way once more to the village. I'm carrying a basket of dried tansy, shepherd's needle, sage and alehoof, rue, and rosemary, all for Angilbert. These are helpful for his trouble.

It is as bright and sunny a day as the last time, and yet the sun brings no gladness of mind to me as it used to do. I am not at peace. The stillness I once had has crumpled and I see it has been a false stillness. I know that I am ignorant, though I understand the seasons and the harvesting of plants. My mind was white, and now is splashed with shapes and colours, many of them dark, like stains.

So I come early to the church, hoping this time that by being at the front I will understand something of what is happening. This time it is different. It is not Angilbert who is to be our priest. It is a stranger who waits to speak to us. When the church is full he steps forward, and holding the gleaming cross, makes sure of our attention. He makes all quiet, he tells us to sit down. We are very docile and sit like children, surprised, even those who gossipped before.

His name is Roger Fortunatus. Instead of muttering strange words, he tells us a story. It is called *The Romance of Tristan and Iseult*. There is nothing of hell fire and angry God; yet God lets him tell the tale – He does not come down and punish.

I see that Benedict is startled, and Edith his wife, but they listen carefully. I watch. Folk like the part where the lovers drink the potion that binds them in spite of themselves. They gasp at the trick played on King Mark on his wedding night. They like the ways the lovers cheat their foes. They find it exciting when all is discovered and Iseult is handed over to the lepers as punishment, and saved by Tristan, and they flee to the forest. Here the life is so cruel that Tristan returns her to her husband-king, and after more disguises and suffering their trials end only with death.

Our strange new priest asks all to tell their feelings. He smiles and laughs; it pleases him to lead the flock like this. Some of the villagers think King Mark was foolishly kind with the lovers and ought to have punished them harshly; others feel sorry for them; and they argue amongst themselves about wedding-love and true-love, and what they would have done if they had been Tristan, Iseult or Mark.

249

I say nothing, but the story fills my mind. My pictures are coloured over by the figure of the man himself. As soon as I saw him standing there I knew him. He is the Devil on the church wall, come alive to Cortle. And I know he is not bad.

When I first saw the painting I supposed the Antichrist a king. Angilbert bitterly rebuked me and brought me misery for having seen beauty in the most evil one of all. Now I feel gladdened. He *is* a king. And here he is, alive, standing in God's house, holding God's cross, which shines golden in a shaft of light. He is beautiful as the day. The story he tells is full of love. Love I understand; and the magic potion – I can make those. And the enchanted forest and the bed of leaves and flowers – I know those things. How can they be evil? I feel free again. I am not wicked. He is bringing back the right way of thinking, giving me my peace again. It is Angilbert who is wrong, who tells lies. I gaze gladly up at Roger, and he sees my look of worship.

'There is just something I would like to ask,' says Benedict, 'and that is, why this story is told in the church. It does not seem to be religious to me.'

'It is the religion of Love,' says Roger in a deep and beautiful voice that made it seem so indeed. And we are to get no other kind of religion this day.

When we leave the church. Roger waits for me and takes my arm and draws me aside. 'You must be the young lad who lives in the forest.' He fingers the herbs in my basket. 'Do you mix love potions too?'

'Some people come for love potions,' I admit shyly, fearful to be close to him.

'Could *I*?'

'Oh, sir, you would have no need, I am sure.'

He smiles. I know that I have pleased him by my praise.

'But indeed I do have need,' he says. 'My beloved will not have me. The one I love has no idea of my passion, being good and pure like an angel, and never suspecting that I am racked with desire. What do you suggest?'

'But I don't know,' I say, amazed. 'Do you really want me to mix you a potion?'

'Would it be successful?' says Roger. 'Would it incline the heart of my beloved to me if at the moment this sweet person felt absolutely nothing for me?'

'Truly, sir, although I know the potions I can only mix

250

them. Hearts of lovers are known only to themselves. I am told my potions work. I hope they do. But willing them to work has a part in it. The lady should be in your company a while, and that will put you in her mind, and then if she drinks it will be more likely to succeed.'

'Yes, I see that,' says Roger seriously. 'But will it kindle her initially, if, for instance, she had not thought about me before today? Yourself, for example, being as I suppose fancy free, would such an uninvolved observer be touched at all?'

I hardly know how to reply. I know that I would need no potion to make me attracted to him – I am already so.

'I'll tell you what,' says Roger as if he guesses all my thoughts and is delighted and amused. 'You could do something for me, if you would be so kind. Just before you go to bed tonight will you mix up a love potion? Put all the strongest and most magical herbs in it and whisper all the spells you think are necessary. Tell yourself it is to make a certain person fall in love with Roger Fortunatus. Then wait till it is dark outside, and by the light of your little candle, comb out your golden hair. I think you should be naked for the spell to work, don't you? Kneel beside your bed, your limbs all bare, and touch yourself a little, particularly those parts which are to do with Love. Picture me standing there beside you, also naked. Lightly I caress your shoulder . . . a shiver passes along your skin, like a little breeze. You turn to me. Now everywhere is perfectly silent. Put the love potion to your lips and drink it. Then, next time that we meet, tell me whether that love potion worked. Of course, I am merely asking for your advice regarding love potions. What do you think of its chances?'

'I think that you should try the love potion on the lady,' I answer guardedly.

'Well, I will,' says Roger lightly. 'And thank you for your help. May I come and collect it from your home?'

'No!' I cry, alarmed at the threat to my peace which Roger's presence would bring.

'Then how . . .?'

'I will bring it to you at the church,' I promise. He looks disappointed, but he must agree.

'And now I must take these herbs to priest Angilbert,' I stutter. I tear myself away. Nothing like this has ever happened to me before – he smoulders like a fire and all my senses melt and quiver and my legs go weak – I love it but I want to run away. I'm trembling as I leave. I long to see him again – I fear him – I don't know myself – I am a stranger – ah – I must be close to him again – I need to know him and to hear his voice – what can I do? I dare not see him. How will we ever meet again?

Haymaking works it.

Hot weather it is now. In the fields they are cutting the hay.

At night I make all ready for the gathering, the first one we have had since Alkanet died. I am not afraid to take her place, to make the brew and welcome the folk; I am sure of what I do. Benedict wears the horns. He makes us laugh with his caperings and his good humour. It goes well. In summertime the gatherings are more joyful. And now it is the mid-point of the year. The Oak King dies to await rebirth; his place is taken by the Holly King, god of the waning year. We joy in the flow of things. The path will lead us from midsummer down to Winter's depths and back again, always the same thread binding, holding us in oneness. All goes well that night. Alkanet would have been glad. I feel that she is there and sees it all.

Next morning it is very hot, a shimmering heat that almost turns the grass blades dusky blue. The forest is so still that I can hear the sounds of folk approach, long before they come into the clearing. They call my name; I come out of the house.

Benedict and Ralf are here, bearing a hurdle, with lying on it one who bleeds, a wounded man. Now I see who it is and I begin to tremble. Roger . . . I look down at his lovely face, waxy pale and full of pain. He sees me and he's glad, but I can tell upon his eyes there lies a mist. Death lurks.

Now Benedict begins to tell me all that happened. I hardly hear. I only know that Roger has been wounded and has come to me. The mist clears and I kneel by him.

Roger looks up at me. 'It seems . . . only through your goodness that I am fated to be brought to you.'

'I cannot believe you picked this way by choice,' I stammer.

'I shall tell any lie . . . if it gets me what I want,' says Roger; and his head drops back upon my hand.

SEVEN
Roger's Tale

I

IF EVER a place portrayed the Garden of Eden on an ancient manuscript it was the forest home of Marel in high summer.

Marel said the Earth Mother kept all her jewels there, flung in clusters carelessly and in abundance, too many to count. The alecost bushes were waist high with clumps of tiny flowers. Slender rue thrust up its musty yellow petals. Elder trees hung low with heavy whorls of blossom. Tangled fenkel grew as high as a man, showering the face with a golden dust of downy seeds. Marigolds shoved upwards to the sun. Bushes of betony with stems like young oaks spurted split velvet petals; caraway fruits burst with amber ripeness, and foxgloves grew purple and tall. Fresh rain lay in the strange folded leaves of Lady's Mantle. Silvery wormwood, fragrant pink marjoram, and shimmering blue borage grew. There were boughs of rough comfrey and the homely hazel, and everywhere crimson poppies and shining chamomiles. And of them all, some hung like curtains, some crept along underfoot like exquisite snakes, some pushed themselves sturdily up, tough and honest, some tripped you as you walked, some teased you with an unexpected perfume, some curled their tendrils about your neck like fingers, some whispered, some boasted in showy splendour. They were like people. They were a kingdom in themselves.

But in that delightful land of mysteries, colours and fragrances, the wicked ones were blooming too. Dwayberry with its gloomy night-coloured bells; looming wolf's bane with flowers like dark heads plotting. And thornapple, thornapple

253

bloomed all summer long with its sickly-sweet white flowers and stinking leaves. The whole plant dripped with poison, that neither sunlight nor boiling water can destroy. These were the sinister ones at the beautiful court where Marel was prince.

And how did I come to be here in the first place and see all this wonder and get to know the names of all the plants? It was all thanks to Azo the reeve, who took against me from the first. Not without cause.

I strolled into the castle that May morning with my head full of thoughts of Lady Berenice. It so chanced that my first glimpse of her was as she crossed the courtyard. A great rough lout was with her, muscle and brawn, black-haired, black-bearded, every shift of shoulder, every strut a show of strength, an indication that he carried weight here and would shove from him all comers, whomsoever. I never could resist a challenge.

'My lovely lady,' I said in my most courtly tone. She turned to me.

Ah! What a beauty now! The pedlar hadn't lied. Her skin was pale, soft and white as rose petals, her lips painted, warm and generous, and her eyes deep set, the colour of April violets. There was a fragrance on her. Though she wore a head-dress I could see her hair was dark almost to black. Dark blue her cloak, edged with silver braid, her movement bold yet graceful, and her demeanour haughty. She had with her a maid, a red-haired girl in green, who eyed me frankly, with a little smile.

Not so the bodyguard. He'd have thrown me out if he had had the power. All in a moment he'd laid hands upon me, but I wriggled free.

'How dare you speak to my lady!' he cried, red-faced in his rage. 'Be off with you and know your place.'

'Gently, Azo,' Berenice said. 'Don't you see this is a man of the Church?'

'Let that not be the reason for your kindness,' I said. 'I have a package for you – brought from London by a pedlar.'

Such a change then in those violet eyes! Swift as a breeze passing, they showed craftiness and fear and sudden hope, then like a shutter closing, they showed nothing.

'I greet you, sir,' she said politely. 'We are going riding.

Would you like to ride with us?'

'I'd be honoured,' I said eagerly. 'As long as he stays behind!'

Azo the reeve he was, an ugly Saxon who had somehow acquired status and considered himself indispensable. Yet all he ever did for Berenice was hold her horse and escort her to and fro and come to her for orders concerning village labour. On such a slim cause he appeared to think himself her right-hand man. The expression on his face as he was told to go about his work gave added picquancy to my growing relish as I waited while a horse was got for me; and then lo and behold! from a vagrant plodding up the Icknield Way with throbbing feet and a companion who did not trust me and thought my road lore paltry, I was elevated into high romance, riding beside a lady in the Springtime woodland.

'So,' she said. 'You have a package for me.'

'The pedlar gave it to me.'

'I am surprised,' she frowned. 'I thought him trustworthy.'

'He was, my lady. To tell the truth, I stole it. Don't blame the pedlar. He's reliable. But when he said that you were beautiful, the loveliest lady he had ever seen, that you were like Sir Launfal's lady who was Queen of Faery and more beautiful than Guinevere, then I had to see you and find reason to be close to you . . .'

'You would be close to me? For what purpose?'

'Only to tell you that the pedlar was right – you are more lovely than the Queen of Faery – and because your beauty is so great I would need many days and nights to tell you so . . . if I am granted them . . .'

'It may be you are fortunate . .' said Berenice. 'Tell me about yourself.'

To hear the story I recounted would have made a listener cringe who knew the true account; so I pass over it. Suffice to say that I sat next to her at the table in the evening, and within the week I had attained her bed.

A man might think he was in Paradise to be where I was then – but I did not.

I woke after my first night with Berenice, and lay, propped on my elbow, to look at her, reflecting on that irony – when we achieve what we had often supposed the ultimate delight, it rarely turns out so.

255

Lovely she was indeed, the loveliest woman I had ever slept with. Her skin was of the pallor of the snow that falls over night and in the morning lies in totally untarnished purity. Against such whiteness the effect of her midnight-coloured hair was startlingly pleasing and for smoothness that pale skin was unsurpassed. The tawny velvet coverlet had slipped from her shoulders and showed her soft and perfect breasts. I watched her sleep. Why did I feel uneasy? No, it was not that I knew she hoped to prod her husband forward to eternity before his time. I half admired her courage there. Perhaps I diverted her, for all the time that I was at the castle she never opened up that package anyway. My uneasiness stemmed from something else.

Her long black eyelashes quivered and she opened them and caressed me with a slow gaze from her violet eyes. 'I love you, Roger,' she said. 'How I love you!'

And there you have it. This sinuous creature, half awake and smiling with all the innocence of a snake about to uncoil, this lady with complete power over all that she surveyed, believed she loved me. That wretched little Celtic lad I once had been was terrified!

But the Norman in me settled down to make the most of my new situation. For the first time in my life I could indulge that aspect of myself, for Berenice was very generous. She liked me to be always at her side, riding the boundaries of her lands, overseeing the workers, reading to her, anything! And I had her permission to give orders if I chose. And I did choose. I sent men hurrying here and there on errands, and I took particular joy in baiting Azo. I sent him off on menial tasks – after all, he was a peasant Saxon, wasn't he, for all he liked to lord it with the villagers? Most pleasing was to order him when I was on horseback and he on foot – this may have been because upon the ground he was a little taller and about twice as broad as I was.

Once when he growled at me I called him back to grovel his apology. The fury in his black-browed scowl was curiously exciting.

'Mind how you go, my lord,' he seethed at me. 'Remember Fortune's wheel, how some are raised up who shall be cast down later.'

I leaned towards him smiling. 'You speak from bitter experience, perhaps?'

256

'My lady finds you fair today,' he almost spat. 'But who knows what shall pass tomorrow?'

'Spare me such deep philosophy! It's not your place to wonder about the doings of your betters. Now be off with you.'

Ghislaine my lady's maid had heard our interchange. That evening Berenice told me severely: 'Don't ever talk about me to my servants.' I assured her I would not.

I sought out Ghislaine next day and caught her on the stairs. I blocked her way and pressed her to the wall. 'What have you been saying, blabbermouth?' I asked her, savouring her body.

'Nothing,' she replied, her eyes level with mine. 'What guilty secret have you?'

'Perhaps you'd like to go and tell my lady this,' I said and kissed her. Devil take me, but I think I would have been more satisfied with the maid. A pretty little thing she was, and warm and eager. But I knew myself too well – I'd always go to where the power source lay.

And power she possessed, did Lady Berenice. There was a man who angered her with some dishonesties to do with the selling of grain. We talked about it once, and I laughed saying: 'What will you do – burn his village?'

'No,' she said. 'I'll break him through the process of the law.'

It sounded chilling. I pitied anyone a victim of a court where Berenice sat in judgement.

But she was very warm to me.

I saw the husband once. I asked if I could see him. It was like visiting a fairground freak. She hated anything to do with him. She put him from her mind and tried to think him from existence. But he was very present.

He had been put into a little room that led off from the passageway. A guard stood at the door; I pitied his monotony. I went with Berenice into the room; she waited by the door. Upon the floor on a paliasse bed, with plenty of swansdown and velvets, lay Audran de Bonnefoy in a curious state of death-in-life, breathing with a rasping growl that gave me shudders. He must have been a great huge man when he was active – enormous bloated hands showed, weighted down with rings, and the bulk of him beneath the coverlet filled half the floor. There was a stink about him; he was helpless as a babe, and servants had to clean him. His face had a distorted look, with a crooked mouth that slobbered somewhat, and a sagging jawline that degenerated into wads of fat. But from this disturbing inertia he would suddenly emerge as lucid as the day, and bark his orders, make demands, and call for Berenice to fondle him. A kind wife and a caring priest would have done much for him; but Berenice and I were neither.

'You think me cruel,' said Berenice, as she lay in my arms. 'I am not cruel – but I hate him so. You know, at Christmastide there was a dancer . . . an Italian boy, exceptionally beautiful. I used to have him dance for me up here in my chamber. Audran found him on the stairs one night and stabbed him to death – with his own hands, as if there had been pleasure in it . . . and all for what? He thought he had been coming to my room. As if I would have jeopardized the boy by asking him to come by night! And even if I had – well, Audran used to bring his conquests to our very bed – so what right had he to such anger? He gave it out the boy was thieving.'

'And was he?'

'No!' she laughed ironically. 'We had some visitors with us – Sir Hugh and Lady Guillemette – I knew they did not care much for each other, but I had no idea that there was more to it than dullness. It was Sir Hugh who sent for the boy – his wife told me – and seemingly that night was not the first time! Who'd have guessed it – and he a soldier and honoured by the king!'

Of nights the lady Berenice lay close to me and unburdened years of misery. Her loneliness – her sense of wasted time – her dread of things to come – her anger to be treated so by Fortune. Her outpourings made me jittery. They always ended with: but now I have found *you*.

'I never thought that I could be this happy,' she declared with such conviction I felt ghastly wafts of guilt. 'I did not think that I would find one worthy of me – but you are, with your learning and your cleverness, and all your travels, which make you so interesting . . . you are like a knight of old romance, you come in off the road, a dusty weary hero looking for a haven. I feel as if I've waited for you all my life. Nor are you merely talented and fascinating – but handsome too, so dark and glamorous, such wicked wicked eyes . . . oh! blessed was the day we met! If ever I should lose you I would be lost. Oh horrible! Say you'll never leave me – tell me you love me as much as I love you!'

I told her. Well, with her I always did as I was told. I reckoned if I played her false she'd have me flayed alive!

Away from her – and I was that more and more often, escaping from the menace of her love – I did not think she truly loved me as fervently and deeply as she thought. She was sad and romantic and I fulfilled a purpose. She'd soon get over me, I reassured myself. She must – for I had no intention of remaining there for ever. My time there was in fact a little more than one month, a month when it was warm and sunny, when the days were very pleasurable and the nights were spent in passionate caresses.

I liked to ride down to the village, and I would have relished preaching in the church and telling tales of love even if it had not been the occasion on which I first met the pedlar's boy. The love of women can be suffocating. It left me feeling like a maggot burrowing into the whorls of a rose. When I saw Marel I thought he seemed fresh and bubbling as a little spring. I thought that clear water would revive me. I'd have had him one way or another; but Fortune intervened here, with a horrible snigger at the deal she handed me.

The villagers were haymaking, and as I was riding by I fancied helping them. I dismounted and joined in. There was all the crowd I'd drunk with at the inn – sturdy old Benedict, and what a giant he looked that day, his shirt off and his brawny arms a-ripple – skinny Lambert whom I always thought a little witless, pugnacious young Ralf and sullen Wilfred; they were glad to get some help. Women were turning over the swathes of last day's cut, and the men were forking the swathes into haycocks, downward sloping to ward off the rain. Hot work it was, but there seemed a lethargy about the workers not entirely due to heat and labour.

Lambert muttered ruefully about what he called witch's brew.

'If I had not drunk all that stuff last night I would be better than I am. Lord save me – I forget myself. I love the brew so much I swig it down and that boy made it every whit as well as the old crone did. What a night, eh, what a night!'

The others also had a certain look about them, something the worse for wear. Whatever they'd been up to last night it had left them rosy, happy, groaning and exhausted. I somewhat envied them!

A time came when they all decided to give in and take a rest. A cider flagon was passed round and we all sat down to doze among the haycocks. I felt hale and cheerful and was thinking briefly that a peasant's lot was not so bad, when up rode Azo the reeve upon a castle pony, his great booted shanks sticking out each side ungainly as two brooms.

'You can stop all that,' he shouted. 'You're wanted in the castle fields.'

We stared at him in some surprise. He never had a sweet way of putting things, and everyone's amazement seemed to spur him on to a sharper enjoyment.

'Come on when you're told,' he bellowed. 'Great sweating oxen, put a move on. You'll have to finish your own fields tomorrow.'

We stood up, and at this moment poor Lambert, heat overcome, collapsed in a faint; he lay in a heap in the sweet-smelling hay.

'Get this man up,' snapped Azo.

I stood forward. 'This man stays here. Anyone can see he isn't fit to move.'

'And what are you doing here?' cried Azo. 'What business have you with these people?' A slow smirk creased his chops. 'You put yourself with villeins and serfs? With these cattle?'

Everyone gathered round, in a sullen group. Legally Azo had the right to order them up to the castle and legally they'd have to go.

'This is all stupid,' I said wearily. 'You must have misunderstood, Azo. Wisdom was never one of your attributes. Go back to Lady Berenice and say that I'm down here with these folk and we are all too tired.'

'Oh no, Roger,' said Wilfred nervously. 'We could get punished for sending an answer like that.'

'It's nothing to do with you,' Azo told me, ignoring Wilfred. 'These are laws. The castle orders; the peasants obey. And I have been seeing to the carrying out of these orders ever since I have been reeve. And you are not going to stand in my way.'

'I certainly am,' said I, a little hampered by having to look up at the great dolt with the sun in my eyes. 'They may be laws, but in this instance it would be crazy to allow them. Berenice is no tyrant. It only needs someone to go and explain that the men are tired and can't give of their best.

260

She'll understand, and they can do her fields tomorrow.' I patted his pony's flank. 'And since you have the horse the one who takes the message must be you. So off you go now, honest Azo.'

Ralf sniggered. Azo boiled.

'Who are you to come into our village and change our laws and customs?' demanded Azo. 'How dare you speak for her ladyship! You think the Church will save you, I suppose? Well, you are far from Church and Pope now.'

'Take yourself off, windbag,' I said rashly. 'Go tell her ladyship that Roger sent you home.'

'No lady's love-swain tells me what to do!' he said and lurched at me and clouted me across the face. When my head stopped swimming I grabbed hold of him by his great leg and heaved him off his horse. He landed sprawling in the hay and as he crouched there I swear his eyes were little points of red. He seized a scythe that lay to hand and leered at me, panting.

Christ! he means to kill me, I thought, backing. Then he slashed the scythe at me and caught me from the shoulder downwards. Sheer astonishment was my reaction – no one thinks that he will ever die – but I saw the blood and felt the pain and instantly blacked out.

On the ghastly journey through the forst I came to but could not keep my consciousness and passed irregularly from insensibility to awareness. After an eternity of trees I looked up to see Marel, gold and promising, and there seemed good cause to come back to the world. I muttered something, and they left me with him. Poor lad, the sight of me must have been something of a shock.

It seems that I was carried there by Ralf and Benedict, the women in the hayfield having said I was beyond their cure. They gathered round me, muttering. But Azo, thinking I was done for, feared the wrath of Berenice, and jumped back on his horse and galloped off. They watched him go, the hooves bringing up clouds of dust on the distant road. He wasn't likely to come back to Cortle, so there was one good thing came of it. Lambert got up from his faint, and all the others went back to their haymaking.

When he had overcome the shock of seeing me pale and bleeding upon the hurdle, and when he could see that I was not god nor devil but sadly human, Marel's skill and sense

261

reasserted themselves; the forest gave him strength.

Benedict and Ralf left quickly. They told Marel what had happened, but they did not stay. They were ill at ease with Marel – he knew things they did not, and they did not know how to treat him, so they hurried away.

Marel's love for me was obvious. Shining-eyed and vulnerable to his emotions he kept nothing secret. While I lay all helpless and despondent he was comfortable in his chosen task, and in his care of me he showed his pleasure. He said it was like the story I had told in church. Which in Hell's name was it? Oh yes . . . He said I was like Tristan and he like Iseuet. Not a chance! You wouldn't find me doing someone else's courting for him. Marel didn't see it that way. He was happy in the comparison. He did not pursue it further – when Tristan is well, the troubles as well as the joys begin, and suffering comes along with the pleasures.

Balm he used, stauncher of blood, binder of wounds; burnet also, and comfrey, which is also called bruisewort and knitbone. He gave me soothing drinks, and as I healed, potions for strength and cheerfulness. I have never been so well tended in my life. I asked questions about the herbs and helped where I could, sitting up in bed with petals about me and fragrance all over my fingers.

'I am cutting the moleyn to make tallow torches for night-time travellers,' Marel said. 'Alkanet called it Hog's Taper. But it has another name, lungwort, because it stops cattle coughing. The Lady leaves Her signs on Her herbs. The leaves here are like the lungs, see. Plants with a "wort" are all healing herbs.'

'So who planted the herbs here in this place?'

'They have always been here.'

'Some haven't, you know. Some were brought over by the Romans. Alecost for one. And some came from Greece.'

'How do you know?'

'They are in old books. Belladonna was the plant that once killed Mark Antony's soldiers.'

'Belladonna . . . that's the one we call dwayberry.'

'And borage was called nepenthe and brought forgetfulness of grief.'

'Of everything.'

'Wormwood and rue, do you know why they are bitter?'

'It is their nature.'

262

'Ah, but not originally. When the serpent was driven out of Paradise they were not so, but he wriggled over them and they became sour.'

'And all these stories belong to a much older time than ours, so far back that we cannot imagine?'

'Yes,' I said. 'You think that it was an old time in this country when there were no Normans, only Saxons, who called the herbs by names of their own. But the herbs go back beyond, into the Golden Age, and people used them in countries beyond the seas, on magic islands, where the seas were warm and blue and the buildings were made of white stone and marble. Even the gods used herbs. Golden and beautiful people they were, and the same herbs grew at their feet as now do at ours.'

'Then they are even more wonderful than I knew,' said Marel.

We went out to harvest the coriander. Marel explained that the smell of the plants was the guide to the right time of culling. The leaves smelt rank and musty as the seeds formed, and eased to a softer scent when the plant was ready to pick.

'It is incredible,' I said laughing, 'that I find myself here in this exotic wilderness earnestly sniffing this green bush.'

'You are helping me with my harvest.'

'Your harvest!' I teased. What a mooncalf he was! He thought his pretty flowers important!

Before Marel gathered his crops he offered a prayer to the Earth Mother.

'Why?' I said uneasily, laughing, to convince myself that what I said was true. 'She's long gone . . . and you look a fool standing talking to a tree.'

'Because however gently I take the plant and with whatever good will, it remains that I am thieving from Her.'

'Oh, nonsense!' I said scornfully. 'Everything the earth has to offer is available for man; it's his right. Do you expect the Earth Mother to jump up and threaten you? Or perhaps She'll hold on to Her end and, tug as you might, the flower will stay fixed to the stalk?'

'You just don't understand,' said Marel. 'You tell me that the beginning of herbs goes back to ages we cannot picture. So it is with the gathering and the charms. There was a day when the Lady let Her servants know of Her presence. They say that the wells and stones remember. In that time the prayers were real, and I do think that without the prayers now, the herbs would be less good, and some magic lost from them.'

'Is there magic in them?' I said, interested. I recalled Toledo and the dark hot room where old Alfonso showed me spells with crocodile skins and the guts of murdered men, and sickly flowers with speckled petals and curious perfumes.

'Magic is belief,' said Marel.

'You think it was an old religion? With a temple and priests?'

'It must have been,' said Marel. 'Some of the herbs are special to Her. Nine of them are sacred – waybread, mugwort, stime, maythen, wergulu, crab apple, chervil, fenkel and alterlothe. On these She has laid Her hand. In these later days we see only the last glimpses of Her, like the long train of Her skirts after She has passed. But in other days She was more clear. She leaves us now with the knowledge, and with the stones and wells, where the old worship hangs in the air.'

'And now we call it magic, because we don't understand it,' I remarked. 'But would it still work? If only we had some of the secrets!'

'You make me feel uneasy,' said Marel. 'It's not for us to twist the workings of nature.'

'But you do,' I protested. 'Every time you save a life or mend a broken bone you twist the workings of nature.'

'No,' said Marel. 'Naturally the person was whole, and I restored Nature.'

'But if a man had been born blind he would be naturally blind. Therefore you should not try to heal him.'

'Roger you are being awkward,' said Marel. 'I work for good. I would always try to lighten suffering, even if I disliked the person I was helping.'

'Oh, you are too good,' I grumbled. I couldn't help it. Now I was recovering, his goodness was beginning to irritate me, and I was pleased if I could subvert it in some way. At first it was only by mild teasing and by hampering his work. But I was grateful for the skill which had cured me, and still enchanted by the secret forest dwelling. I waited an unusually long time before making any attempt to seduce him.

Our differences came to a head on the occasion of the elder blossom. His elder harvest! Elder was important to this strange, serious boy. It had a holy significance as the home of the Lady who protected all herbs and plants. And practically, the uses of elder were many. It whitened the skin. The flowers combined with bryony reduced swellings; dried with honey they cured fevers. Young saplings were used as wands to drive insect pests from barley and rye; stems were steeped in oil to make floating candles said to keep bad spirits away. Dyes could be made from berries, leaves and root. He had a point, the elder was a useful tree. But the Earth Mother? No chance!

'I must gather the flowers at the height of their bloom,' Marel said, 'and lay the bunches down. In a little while the petals can be shaken off. If I were to leave them too long they would spoil. The moment has to be just right.'

Before he went out into the sun to pick them, Marel hesitated, and I looked at him. I put my arm about him and drew him close and kissed his lips. We stood together in a deep embrace, and time went its way unnoticed.

II

I HAD had enough of looking. All this time I'd watched him, sometimes from my bed, and sometimes walking with him in his wilderness. If ever there was a plum that needed picking it was he. All he wore on these hot days was a little jerkin – barefoot, bare-legged, and nothing underneath! His legs were berry-brown and golden-haired; he had the loveliest knees – I couldn't take my eyes off them. And his bare arms were golden brown and boyish, hard and skinny. His face was fair enough and very sweet, but golden hair and big blue eyes are not with me necessity – I can love a monkey face and hair like tow if the body's good beneath it, and this boy's body was a dream. It hurt my hands to have to keep them off it!

And so when I first kissed him then, I needed more, and I would have it. My demanding hands grasped fistfuls of his hair and pulled his face to mine and while my mouth clamped him to me, my tongue locked down his throat, I wound a thigh about his leg and forced his loins to mine. I pulled the jerkin up around his waist and bared his arse and now with both hands I grabbed each plump cheek and squeezed them

265

till my nails dug into flesh. He whimpered, trapped; I bruised his lips with kisses and I would not let him go. I felt the hairy crevice of his arse and hooked my finger in between and held him there my prisoner. His arms around my neck, he kissed me passionately; I was amazed and gratified at his fervour. Attractive though I be, I had expected more reluctance. My heart was jumping with elation: I could do all I wanted with the boy, and more! I eased him gently down upon the rush-thick floor and all the time we never left off our embrace. We lay entangled there, and now I felt his prick – as hard as a knife handle – and I held it and stroked it up and down, and lay on him, my tongue exploring deep into his mouth, his ears. His legs splayed wide beneath me, I could feel the trembling of his body. My fingers groped his balls, his arse cleft, and the honey-coloured hairs that grew between. We must be naked, I thought pantingly, and eased off him. That was my mistake.

'The elder flowers!' he said, and pulled away, his hand over his mouth. I sat there, knees apart, in disbelief, and shook my head. He ran outside to pick the flowers, tearfully, where they bloomed on under the heat. He picked with all speed and no joy, the prayer forgotten.

'Let me help you,' I groaned generously, and arms full of blossom, heaved and tugged all anyhow, whatever I could pull. We put what we had gathered into the herb room, great heaps of elder blossom browning wiltingly upon the floor.

He looked distressed and wretched, like a disappointed child, his finger in his mouth. I put my arm around him comfortingly.

'Don't be sad,' I said. 'They'll be all right. You'll see. They are not spoilt; you'll put them right; I'll help . . .'

He turned to me, huge-eyed. Before I knew it I was kissing him again, and when I tasted him my unsatisfied old lechery stirred, my hands reached for his arse. He only had himself to blame, I argued, if he must go bare-arsed in a little shirt – what could I do but lust for him?

I undid his belt, the threads at his shirt neck, and loosed his shirt from him and he stood naked. I found him so desirable I nearly came just staring; time enough for gazing later. So I forced him gently to the ground, and now my hands were everywhere, and, I should add, in no way did he hinder me. We pressed into the elder flowers, I tearing off my robe in a great hurry, and lay down, flesh to flesh. I was half out of my mind with lust, I turned him this way and that, to kiss him, lick him, bite him, nuzzle him; with sweat and spittle I moistened him, my face between his arse-cheeks, tasting honey hairs and heat, and from the back I took him, slowly edging my hard shaft within him till I had him to the hilt. I thought he would resist or cry out, but he responded with the ease of any street whore, and I paused astonished.

'You have done this before. With whom?'

'The pedlar.'

'Ha! The pedlar!' Chuckling to myself I fucked him. So! The pedlar had been here before me. Sly one! No wonder he had tried to keep this boy a secret. Crafty fox! Well! It made it easier for me! I gripped his thighs and moved him for my greatest satisfaction, those plump and downy orbs against my belly, and his golden hair spread in the elder blooms, his face sunk in their bitter perfume. My balls were bursting and my prick felt hard as wood. I drove my seed within him deep; I howled like any wolf; it left me light as air. I dropped upon him, shivering.

Quietly the elder flowers blackened into sad little shapes. When Marel remembered them, shining-eyed and breathless, it was too late. The shrivelled spectres seemed to look up at him dumbly bewildered that it should have turned out so. Marel himself couldn't understand it.

'Oh Roger,' he wailed. 'When I am with you I am not myself and I don't know what I'm doing.'

'*I* know,' I told him complacently. 'Leave it all to me.'

It is true that I took advantage of the boy – but so what? I treated him well. I know the ways of loving. I gave pleasure as well as taking it. My moral stance may be a sorry thing, but I have more charm than many. Ask the pedlar. I know he fancied me. I could hardly be called wicked for what I did. And Marel wanted it. He was as passionate as I, as eager, often pleading for it, often offering love unasked. Besides, the pedlar had him first.

The little loft bedroom was dappled green, for over the tiny window grew flowers and leaves so thickly entwined that the sun had a deal of trouble to break through, and when he did his light came so diffused that it showed only green. When summer rain fell outside the air was so liquid that it could have been the water of a hidden pool, green with weed and flowing like reed. Green shadows fell so that illusions of water and light and the confused colours of dreams flooded a setting already unreal with wafts of further unreality.

We were very much alone, because not only were the villagers very busy in the fields at that time but also the need for healing herbs was not so strong. I sometimes thought about Berenice; but not often. I wondered vaguely why she did not come hot-foot to regain her errant lover, since I knew she was besotted with me – then it dawned on me that she did not know where I was. I suppose the villagers who had seen Azo strike me down decided to keep the whole thing to themselves. Maybe a misguided sense of loyalty to Azo prompted it; after all, he was a Saxon. The notion pleased me – to think of Berenice all restless in her bed, and I just nearby if she but knew it. Let the haughty dame find out that sometimes even castle folk cannot have all they want!

I reckoned I was living in as near to Paradise as man on earth could reach, alone with this delicious boy in this luxuriant place, and he as gasping for my love as I for his. We walked around all naked, like the Story of Creation rewritten to please those who liked boys best. Rain could not spoil it. In the rain we stood and kissed and licked the water drops from off each other's skin. On cool days we stayed within. And I played master, which he seemed to like. I would call him from his work – 'Enough of potions, Marel, come now, come suck my prick – at once or I will take a stick to you!' At first he did as he was told and most obedient and put down his plants and ran to kneel at my feet. But it was not long before he learnt that if you disobey and make your master angry, master comes and catches you and twists your arm and puts you across a table; then there are many ways to punish you. I slapped that round arse till it reddened and I hurt; but he disobeyed me afterwards again – you'd swear he yearned for punishment! And I would look at him reflectively, where he lay beneath me crimson-faced and breathless, merry-eyed, and it would cross my mind that in the wharves of London, Paris, Venice, in the brothels there, this boy could earn a fortune – lovely as an angel, with a child-like mind and puppy ways, half innocent, half mischievous, the stuff of rich men's dreams.

Now it happened that I became curious about a pile of old

268

manuscripts which lay in a corner of the little bedroom-loft. When Marel was downstairs mixing potions I chose my moment to unravel them. I sat and read them. I meant to say nothing of it to Marel; but I was so absorbed in them that he could come up the ladder and stand at my elbow all unseen – I was too engrossed to notice his approach.

'Roger! What are you doing with Alkanet's books?'

'Reading them, of course,' I said a little guiltily. 'They're fascinating. Have you read them?'

'I don't read,' said Marel. 'I don't need to. Alkanet passed on to me everything she knew; at least, all that I would need.'

'Did you know that flowers have a meaning? Nettles mean an unkind act, and daisies mean purity of heart.'

'Yes, I know all that.'

'Oh,' I said, disappointed. 'Well then, do you know,' and I paused, and then said carelessly, 'how to poison a man?'

Marel gasped. 'What devilment are you reading?'

'These spells here.'

'Spells? They aren't spells.'

'Oh no? What are they then? "Take a pinch of hemlock gathered at midnight . . ." What is that if it is not a spell?'

'It's just how to use hemlock,' Marel said hesitantly. 'They are only directions, as it would be for southernwood "Take a pinch of southernwood gathered when the moon is on the wane" . . .'

'Do you mean that you know how to poison a man, Marel, my daisy, my innocent?'

'Yes I do,' he replied. 'But I would never use that.'

'So you could have poisoned me! Giving me all those sweet broths with your soft hands. And I would never have known!'

'Roger, what foolishness are you talking? Of course I could not have poisoned you. Do you know me so little? Do you think I would lie with you and lay my hands on your body naked, and then feed you hemlock? What is happening to your sense?'

'Well, I was alarmed,' I laughed weakly. And it was true I looked at him with a new admiration. 'I had supposed you so sweet and good, knowing only gentle things.'

'I *am* like that,' said Marel reasonably. 'Nothing has changed. It isn't my fault that some of the herbs are powerful.'

'Have you got them growing here?'

'Yes.'

'Even thornapple?'

'Even thornapple? Why do you ask about that one?'

'Don't look so frightened. I only ask because it intrigues me. *Thornapple*, it says here, *a stranger from across the seas. Mistrust him.* I don't know,' I laughed. 'I thought he sounded much like me.'

'But you are mad to say that!' cried Marel much disturbed. 'You don't know what you're saying.'

'Perhaps you're right. But how strange it is that the bad plants fascinate us more than the good. Will you show me them?'

'Why?'

'I confess to a great curiosity. I should like to look the plant in the eye, that could kill me.'

'Roger, understand this. No plant reaches forward and kills. It is the man who stretches out his hand, who picks the leaf, who makes the powder. Hemlock, henbane, wolf's bane, they only grow. Even thornapple.'

'But you will show me one? Just one.'

'If you must. Which shall it be?'

'Thornapple.'

'That one I hate,' cried Marel. 'If ever a plant was evil it is he. We keep him encircled by good plants. I never thought I'd have to draw them aside and look on him.'

'But you will, for me,' I pleaded.

I could talk him into anything. We went together to that dark part of the forest where the circle of good plants guarded the thornapple tree. We pulled aside the green tendrils of the guards. 'It is a strange rare plant,' said Marel. 'Norsemen brought it from across the seas. Alkanet said that in our country it grows nowhere but here. It is like an evil king from another world.'

We gazed at the thornapple tree. I pulled a face and shuddered.

'His appearance is malevolent,' I agreed. 'And he stinks somewhat.'

'The flowers bloom all summer,' said Marel, staring at the large white shapes. 'If you smell them, they act upon your senses and make you drowsy and strange.'

'But the smell is peculiarly effective. I feel I want to go on standing here smelling the flowers.'

270

'Oh, come away,' pleaded Marel. 'It has you under its spell.'

He tugged at my elbow, and I stepped back, rubbing my eyes. We let the herbal screen fall back into place.

'It is all evil,' Marel shuddered. 'The leaves are like jagged teeth. With wolf's bane you can dry the poison out. But not thornapple.'

'Why is it called thornapple?'

'When the flowers have gone there are prickly seed pods that look a bit like shrivelled apples.'

'As if it meant to disguise itself as something good,' I mused. 'As if it did really have an evil intention, just like a person . . . Ugh! Let's get back to the house. It's too eerie here.'

Yet even so, from that time I could hardly bear to leave old Alkanet's ancient parchments alone. However much that Marel protested, saying that the notes were just the same as cooking instructions, I thought there would be secrets here – the answer to the mystery of the world locked in those fusty pages. The secrets of the Goddess.

'This is interesting,' I remarked. 'It's the same as in the old books I studied in France. I remember this now. Thornapple must have been one of the herbs they used at Delphi to achieve a trance. All the accounts of their strange behaviour accord with what it says here about thornapple and belladonna. There's a list here of the poisonous ones . . . aconite, or as you call it, wolf's bane . . . mix it with belladonna and you have the witches' brew. Used by Hecate herself . . . it gives you the illusion that you're flying.'

'Leave it alone, Roger,' said Marel.

'Wolf's bane, does that grow here too?'

'Yes; but it's of no use to man – not even a starving vole will eat it.'

'But all mixed in together . . . apparently the results are overwhelming. Don't you feel excited, sweetheart, at the thought of flying? You can make an ointment which stimulates the skin so that you feel you're soaring. Oh I'd like to try that!'

Marel sat quietly, more silent as as he sensed my eagerness.

'And amazing love potions,' I marvelled. 'Not the tame sort that silly virgins put under their pillows.'

Marel laughed uneasily. 'Roger, you have no need of that kind of potion.'

'I was only thinking of possibilities,' I protested. 'Why can't you join in, instead of being disapproving and severe?'

'Do you need an answer?'

'Yes; why not?'

'It seems to me that there is something evil in you,' said Marel unhappily, 'which makes you want to pervert what is harmless and good.'

So I became penitent and winsome and said no more about flying ointments.

But chance gave me the opportunity to try out some of my ideas. I had heard from the pedlar about those midnight gatherings they held here. And now villagers came, reminding Marel that one was due. I listened to it all with fascination. It was too good a chance to miss. These harmless meetings could be unforgettable, exciting, in the hands of a leader who understood the ancient ways. We could reincarnate them as they used to be!

'I will wear the horns,' I told Marel, 'and you need have no fear – I will direct everything.'

'That is what I do fear.'

'No need, no need, my sweet. You shall see how much better it is than the jolly romps of bumpkins. And you'll help me mix the brew, won't you?'

'At least that way I can be sure that you don't cause more trouble than you intend.'

'We shall recreate it in all its past splendour,' I declared. 'It shall be as religious as it ever was.'

'But you don't know the old ways,' said Marel. 'How can you recreate it? The words were not even Saxon; they go back to an age of mists. Even you can't summon them up.'

'I know that. We'll use the Church parlance. The words will be Latin, but the thoughts will be the same.'

'But they won't!' cried Marel. 'It used to be sacred. The folk went there to worship. And in the quiet of the night at the place the feeling of holiness is very strong. There has never been any need to add the words of now. It has always been enough for us to catch at a memory, a wisp of what used to be, so strong was the holiness.'

'I shall enrich that holiness,' I promised.

'The folk will never behave as you want.'

'Oh yes they will. They'll drink the magic brew and join in the Sabbat as if every single one of them were a witch.'

'What Sabbat? We have always called them meetings, or gatherings.'
'Oh, this will be somewhat more than a meeting . . .'

EIGHT
Benedict's Tale

I

I HAVE worn the horns myself; but I know well enough that I am Benedict the innkeeper, and when I wear the horns all I look like is an innkeeper with horns. With Roger Fortunatus it was another matter.

We all came to the secret place of the stone in the night, as we had done before, in small groups, keeping together for company, chattering in loud bold voices to keep away the wood sprites. The moon glowed very bright; it made the black leaves silver and lit the old stone in an eerie light. Bats flew in the glade, swooping low about our ears, so close we heard the fluttering of their wings. There was a good bonfire going, and piles of musky garlands to throw on it for luck. In the brightness of its flames the midges and gnats were golden dancing specks.

All our gatherings were full of sly excitement but the summer ones especially. The King of Elves might pass by underneath the elder trees. Some rash girls said that they hoped an elfin lover would carry them away and they tempted the green folk with bold challenges. Alys bared part of her body. We jibed at her that no elf came.

The fear of black shadows that was with us at the gatherings in Fall had lost its strength; now it was all rollicking and romping; and moreover it was warm. Even a drink of the old-time brew was cheering enough. But this time . . .

Unsuspecting honest folk we were, swigging back the midnight brew handed to us by Marel, but not hooded and shy as we had been used to seeing him. Brazen and free, with his mass of gold hair, he smiled at compliments and caused the village girls to notice him all afresh. And there was Roger, got up like a wizard, with a cloak and the antlers of a stag upon his head. I wondered much; for when I wear the horns, folk laugh and thump me on the back; but none did that with Roger. He was a wild, uncanny sight. I did not realise that the brew was different. I drank as much as ever. Before long I hardly knew what I was doing. I saw double; I saw nothing; I saw colours; I saw things that were not real. And it was the same with everyone. We did not understand. Flashing streaks of purple, orange, black, struck across our sight like twisted lightning. Stars and moons splattered across the circling glade. The sky opened, the earth opened. We plummeted down; we soared among the trees. We saw from a great height faraway fires, we burned in purple flames, we dragged heavy limbs through mists of scarlet. Sometimes we danced, but not like ourselves. We became forest folk, wraith-like, green, wavering; we were ghosts from the days gone by; we lost all sense of person, time and sense of right and wrong; we throbbed and raved and rolled upon the ground. And if we recognised our neighbours, we saw that they too were behaving in this way. It was all right; it must be; everyone was the same.

Roger made sure that everybody drank, and himself gave a cup to Marel, which the reckless boy drained. When everybody was crazed and helpless, Roger had us praying to Dianus the Shining One. Down went all us villagers upon our knees. Some of them could be heard to cry out Dianus' name, a name which they had never heard before that day. And Roger was so positioned in front of us, with his arms raised to the heavens, that it looked as if the villagers were upon their knees to him. He had in his hand a slim stick which gave the effect of a wand. The flickering firelight flecked the weird scene with shadows.

Then followed curious ceremonial happenings. It seemed like church, like something holy. We behaved as if he was our priest. Roger called out that those who had sinned should come forward and confess and receive their punishment. Mad as it may seem, there were those that obeyed. Funny little crimes they were, a mixture of ordinary sins and strange ones. Somebody confessed to a lie, someone to laziness, someone to stealing some seeds. Each one Roger beat with the stick, not so much vigorously but lightly. Then Alys blurted out that she had never guessed that Marel was so handsome, and she found that she desired him. And she was such a quiet girl before! And some said they loved other people's wives and wished to see them naked; and someone, and I'll not say who, confessed he once lay with a sow. It seemed as if, once started, we longed to admit more and more. Then Marel confessed bitterly that his wickedness had been to allow the meeting at all; and Roger beat him gently, once, and made sure that he had some more to drink.

Then he chanted a Latin prayer over us, we still upon our knees. It sounded very much like what Angilbert said in church, and may well have been for all any of us knew. Then he got us to up and dance again, in a ring around the bonfire; and we were so hot that some began to take off their clothes. Around and around we danced, and soon some had flung off every stitch. I shall not say if I was one. But we had lost all modesty and dignity and had no idea what we were doing. Or perhaps it was that the strange brew had freed us from bonds and laws and that this was what we longed to do but never dared. Soon whoever still had a garment on was helped off with it by the others. Our bodies were all red shadows, steaming with sweat. And then Roger called us to come forward for the magic ointment. He had it in a great jar, and we came and dipped our hands in and rubbed our bodies with it, and anybody else's body. It was slippery and soft to the touch. And now so tingling, many could not stop themselves but must have a love partner there and then. But such was the frenzy and confusion of it all that anybody might have whom they liked, even men with men and women with women, people who had up till now been staid and God-fearing and whom you would have sworn did not even know about such things.

That timid girl Alys who was always sneaking off to see old Alkanet in days gone by, lost all her modesty and flung herself at Roger's feet, kissing him, and imploring him to take her. And so he did, never – as I guess – being one to refuse a woman's prayer if he could grant it. Women gathered around Marel and kissed him. Everyone I have spoken to about that night sounds so besotted and confused, mixing shame and boasting so colourfully that it is hardly certain what befell. I was very glad that my wife Edith stayed at home. I saw Roger approach Marel and lead him from the women. I saw him smear more of the ointment on his naked body. The ointment and the touch of Roger's hands aroused the boy to wild desire. He went on his knees before the lover-priest and greedily slaked his thirst upon the object of his need. And Roger looked down on the beautiful bending shoulders and seized the long gold rippling hair and lifted the boy to his feet. He bent him over and took him hard in lust, satisfying himself between the boy's spread buttocks, where they say the Devil is kissed by his familiars. Their bodies slithered together, wet from ointment and passion. When he had finished, Roger flung Marel from him and strode back to the cauldron. Marel leaned against a tree, watching it all like one who is entranced. I went and stood by him, as dazed as he. I wept when I recalled how I had told the pedlar I would watch over the boy. What kind of guardian had I been! I was as much to blame as anyone, and so I make no judgement. I looked across the glade, I saw the naked bodies of the villagers, the fire and flames, and Roger lording it over them like a king. I saw that it looked just like the painting in the church, of the afterlife and the damned. The arms and legs that splayed awkwardly, the heads thrown back, the grimaces – it was all the same; and above it all, Roger, handsome, proud, omnipotent.

NINE
Roger's Tale

I

IT HAD been as glorious as I had hoped.

Power – it is a strange thing. I had been omnipotent. I had made them naked, crazed, rampant with lust, malleable in my hands, chanting words they did not know, fucking indiscriminately, telling all their hidden shames, gasping for the magic brew, in a communal stupor. I despised them as I despised that part of me that came of peasant stock. They were so easy to subdue. Who wanted to be Lord of those? My power lust was satisfied; and now it left me weary.

Now after that event, in the days that followed, there came a steady trickle of folk to our forest hideaway who sought remedies for headache and stomach ache; some were plagued by trembling hands and spots before the eyes. Marel gave them ointments, potions. And I could not help but notice that their attitude towards him had undergone a change.

'I see it too,' said Marel. 'It's how they used to treat Alkanet. They're more respectful . . . and afraid.'

They looked at him furtively and curiously, with an uneasy deference. Although they came ostensibly for remedies it was almost as if they had come to see if the boy and the place and the man with the horns were true; to see us in the warm light of day, to dispel confusion, and reassure themselves that trees were green and immobile and not a whirling frenzy of purple and red. And then they would carelessly and shiftily refer to it, as: 'The meeting now . . . that was a strange business . . . well, not so much strange, but . . . I did happen to notice that the drink . . . I suppose, young man, that you would not have a cup of that stuff to hand?'

Those foolish folk, having once seen the fires and splendours and shed their peasant skin and earthly troubles, were itching to try it again. They had discovered that the after-effects could be endured, and were willing to risk them for another flight into colours and distances and abandon.

'What a thing we have started!' I laughed. 'What a power we have here!'

Another of our visitors was the young girl Alys. Apparently she used to come by in the days of the old hag, and pester her for secrets.

'I never understood why Alkanet put up with her,' Marel grumbled. 'But she did. She sometimes used to tell her things.'

The little shrew-faced wench did not much interest me. She thought that when I fucked her at the Sabbat I cared who she was and used her out of love; it was not so. And now I found her irritating, gawping up at me with cows' eyes of devotion. Marel also did not like her. This amused me. I could see him scowling when she gazed at me. She turned up again and again, with all kinds of slight excuses. Marel humoured her.

'Was the love potion successful' he asked her.

'Oh that seems long ago,' said Alys pouting. 'Yes, it worked all right. Martin will do anything for me now. But I don't care for him.'

'But he's likeable,' protested Marel. 'And now he has good prospects.'

'Yes, he's cleverer than most,' agreed Alys. 'He goes to the abbey school like Angilbert. He can read a little now.'

'Well, this potion is ready,' said Marel.

'Tell me how it's made!' said Alys greedily.

'It's only maythen . . .' began Marel.

'Don't tell her your secrets,' I teased. 'You have to preserve your mystery, you know.'

'There is no mystery,' said Marel.

'But there is,' said Alys. 'As long as one person knows things that other people don't know, there is mystery. The folk in the village think you know secrets.'

'They're idiots', I dismissed them. 'You could tell them anything and they'd believe it. Marel, why don't we try casting a few spells? I could prove to you how simple it is to make them believe in magic.'

Alys' eyes shone. 'Oh! I would do it!' she said.

'Well, I would not,' said Marel. 'And, Alys, you won't be welcome here if you keep on with this. It's wrong talk. There aren't any spells here, and you would be a fool to think there were.'

When she had gone, I said to Marel: 'I don't suppose you'd be feeling just a little jealous, hey?'

'I don't know what you mean.'

'Yes you do. That girl can't take her eyes off me. And you don't like it.'

'All right; no, I don't. What's wrong with that?'

I kissed him. 'I love it when you're human. It pleases me that you're jealous. You can be so irritatingly holy.'

'Don't be silly; of course I have feelings like other people. But even if she didn't make her thoughts so plain I still wouldn't like her much. She wants to make trouble.'

I considered that: 'You would be wise, my sweet, to show more cunning in dealing with people like that one. I know you feel hurt that your wholesome herbs are thought to be magic by the ignorant. But don't make enemies over it.'

'I have no enemies,' said Marel amazed. 'I have never hurt anyone.'

'Oh you innocent,' I said, taking him in my arms. 'You don't need to hurt anyone if you possess what they long for.'

One morning we received a visit from Angilbert. He came, pompous and beaming, to call upon Marel, and as he sat down rather breathlessly, he said:

'My boy, there are two reasons for my visit. The first is to thank you for the healing herbs you brought me. I have felt very much better since that day.'

'I'm happy to have helped you.'

'The second reason is not so pleasant, I'm afraid. You have not been to church again. I thought we were working to save your soul. Why have you not come back to church?'

Marel had no need to answer when I appeared out of the shadows. I was tempted by the prospect of a scrap with Angilbert.

'You!' gasped Angilbert dramatically.

'I believe I was more of a success than you with my sermon,' I said easily.

'Scoundrel!' cried Angilbert. 'You contaminated my church

280

with your vile tale of lust – and you had no business to be there. And now what are you about? Have you perverted the thoughts of this innocent youth with your wicked guile?'

'Yes,' I grinned. 'And his body too. Don't you envy me?'

Angilbert went red with rage, and then pale, as he absorbed what he had just heard.

'Foul creature!' he puffed. 'It was bad enough that you spoke of love and adultery inside the portals of holy church. But am I to believe your sin goes further? Are you in so deep?'

'I am,' I sniggered. 'And very sweet it is too.'

'You pollute the earth upon which you walk. You are an evil man.'

'And even you do not know the full extent of my villainy,' I boasted. 'For besides all that you have accused me of, I am also a magician!'

Angilbert gasped.

'Yes,' I declared passionately. 'I am fully conversant with the black arts. And you have so offended me that I shall put a spell on you. After you have left here I shall mix a brew with your name on it. It will be fearful and strong. You will not feel anything straightaway, but within a week . . . Then you will remember me!'

'Oh! Don't believe him! It isn't true!' cried Marel.

But Angilbert was speechless. He had been gaping at me open-mouthed, and now he simply turned about and ran out of the door. He fled across the clearing. We watched his cumbersome figure stumbling away down the forest path.

'Oh, why did you do that?' Marel wailed.

'For a joke. Why do you think?'

'Oh Roger, how could you?' Marel said reproachfully. Then he shook his head wonderingly. 'But who would have thought he would believe you?'

'Exactly,' I remarked. 'And he a man of God.'

After Angilbert's visit the days passed very quietly, and I became restless. I was growing tired of Marel. The Sabbat had been the culmination and now I felt the situation was growing stale. I found myself thinking about the outside world and became eager for the sound of towns, for noise and wit and faces. London, I thought, and after London a ship, a voyage, Paris again, and after Paris unknown lands. Syria maybe, for

281

the Moorish manuscripts.

'If I should leave you, Marel,' I said, meaning to prepare him, 'what then?'

Marel looked downcast. 'Would you do that?'

'I think I might. Would you be sad?'

'Yes. There was a time when my garden was everything to me. But since you have been here your presence fills the forest. It would feel empty, I think, now, if you left.'

'Then take another lover. Try a girl!'

Marel smiled wrily. 'After you,' he said, 'a girl would seem lacking in something.'

I laughed. 'Yes – you do seem to like what I can give you . . . Well, then, another man. After all, there was someone you were fond of before me – a certain travelling man?'

'You mean the pedlar. Yes, he has always been a good friend to me, and with him I learned how to love. He is very dear to me, and I believe he loves me.'

'That pedlar – he's a sly one! All that talk about Lady Berenice!'

'What talk?'

'That pedlar tried to convince me that Berenice was the only thing of interest hereabouts. He tried to shut Jusson up when the fellow let it be known there was a pretty boy loose in the forest. How that pedlar did rave on about the lady of the castle! But now I see it was all a bluff, to keep me away from you, whom he had his eye on all along.'

'Why did he want to keep you away from me?'

'Why? Because the pedlar man sees through me. He knew from the first that I was a shiftless fellow who would let you down.'

'Ah, no, Roger, you aren't that.'

'Yes I am, my dear, and if you can believe it you will be happier when I go.'

'Don't talk about it.'

What would he do when I had gone? I wondered briefly whether he might come with me, and make a living in the wicked world. I had seen rich men overseas who lived in splendour and would surely take him on. He could soon be a prosperous courtesan, have anything he wanted. I pictured him in silks and velvets, jewelled. He could grace a rich man's bed. I might be doing him a kindness pointing him in that direction. This world was a cruel place; he could make money . . .

'Why not come with me?' I suggested.

He looked astonished. 'Do you mean you love me? You want me with you?'

'No!' I laughed, startled into truthfulness by this surprising interpretation. 'I mean if you came with me you would not be lonely here.'

'I have never been lonely here,' he answered. 'Although,' he added soberly, 'it may be different now. But, no, I could not come with you, although I thank you for your offer.'

I coughed. He little suspected the full extent of that offer, and perhaps he would not thank me if he knew.

'You prefer the quiet of your woodlands then,' I supposed, with some relief, I must admit.

'It's not that alone,' said Marel, lowering his eyes. 'It's something else.'

'What then?'

He looked at me. 'I told the pedlar I would wait for him.'

All shreds of guilt about my wished-for departure now quite disappeared.

'Ah – I'm glad!' I told him warmly. A surge of pleasure rose. The pedlar would take care of him – and Lord knows, someone would have to, for the world would be a wolf to eat him up if he set foot outside the garden. 'Was he a good lover to you then, the pedlar?'

'Yes, he was.'

'Better than me?' I disbelieved, but curious.

'He did not sweep me off my feet like you did,' Marel answered, frowning as he tried to be fair to both of us. 'But he made me happy, and I felt his love.'

'Marcel, shall we make the brew?' I said one night.

'What do you mean? There isn't a meeting due . . .'

'No, I mean just us two. Alone, now. Shall we? Shall we fly? It might be the last time.'

'I don't want to think about it being so.'

'Come then; I'll help you to forget.'

So we made the brew, and our excitement grew in the making of it. We laughed and planned and embraced, and when the darkness came, we drank it and we had our own Sabbat there in the clearing. I would call it the religion of Love. We undressed each other savouringly and when we

were both naked we smeared the slippery ointment all over
the flesh of our bodies. Ecstatic from the sensuous glow and
our own desire we made love hungrily all night. That magic
drink is everything the old tales tell. You drink it and your
prick goes broomstick-hard and lasts all night like that, and
when you penetrate each other's bodies you would swear that
you were flying. You seem to be astride some Pegasus, you
float above the trees, you spin in aery regions, light as a dust
speck; and you're giddy with it, lost, up in the sky somewhere
for ever. I was a god that night. My powers were not of earth.
I was more a magician than ever I was in Toledo, Marel my
accomplice. His beauty was more dazzling than the moon,
and fluid and translucent almost as if seen through water. He
shimmered in my strange distorted vision. His slippery body
now beneath me, now above me, glowed like flame and
warmed me with its heat – my hands were lost in the strands
of his hair, my lips melted into his lips and our bodies
merged, the edges blurring, flesh in flesh. Locked thus we
could see foaming seas below us, starry firmaments above, the
west wind wafted us like leaves and our ears buzzed with
music. Our kisses left a trail of sparkling lights that, like a
fireball, showed our dazzling path across the heavens.

When we finally fell asleep upon the scented bed in the loft
we were still floating, dizzy and enraptured, our eyes
unseeing, our minds crazed with colours.

It was that very morning, in the early sounds of dawn, that
the end of it came. Outside the cottage, in the rose-grey
half-light, riders came quietly into the clearing. We slept on
unsuspecting. The first discord that we heard was the angry
squeal of Lady Berenice as she put her head up into the loft
where we lay in our embrace.

II

I SAW her, through slit eyes. Suddenly with hideous
clarity I knew that I had not spent last night flying over
the earth astride Pegasus, nor had I seen stars and water,
nor been a magician. I had passed the night in swiving with a
tasty boy; I had had him up the arse and he had sucked my
prick; we had fallen asleep and we were lying where we fell.

'Roger!' shouted Berenice, sounding nothing like the lady

284

of the manor, but like an angry female who catches her beloved in the arms of a rival – more, a beloved that has disappeared without a word and left her angry, hurt and vengeful. I closed my eyes like one who waits a deadly blow.

Berenice came up into the loft and kicked me awake. Drugged as I was with the witch's brew, I could hardly open my eyes nor focus them properly and for a moment I formed a prayer that she was an apparition, the effects of drink and ointment.

'Wake up!' said Berenice, kneeling down and seizing me by the arm.

I groaned and tried to blink the unwelcome sight away. But it remained. A fold of velvet fell across my naked shoulder like a snake.

'What is the matter with them?' Berenice asked Ghislaine.

'They are asleep,' was all that Ghislaine could offer.

'No, it's more than that,' Berenice decided, sitting back on her heels. 'They've been drinking something . . . and his skin is streaked with something, a sort of cream. Pah,' she added, wrinkling her nose. 'The odour!' She shook her head. 'I can't believe it . . . That he should be here!'

I shut my eyes. Berenice turned on me.

'Oh no, you shall not go to sleep!' she said. 'I wait to hear your explanation. Let us begin by finding out why you left the castle.'

'That, at least, is simply done,' I said. 'I was helping the villagers with their haymaking when I cut myself with a scythe. So they brought me here because Marel knew how to heal the wound.'

'Indeed,' said Berenice folding her arms. 'And you have been here ever since.'

'It was a bad wound. Look, you can see the scar.'

'It's healed. You must have been well enough to send a message. You must have known I would wonder where you were. Didn't you think I would wonder, and be puzzled, and, incredibly enough, unhappy?'

'I must have lost my memory,' said I, attempting to look vacant. Berenice shot a look of hatred at Marel, who cowered beside me in a dreamy stupor.

'Yes I'm sure you did,' she snapped, 'with distractions to help you. You have treated me shamefully. You were pleased enough to be welcomed in the beginning. You won me with

285

your words and your stories. I tell you, Roger, I'm not accustomed to such careless treatment. Do you forget who I am? I could have you punished in any way I chose – legally at the manor court or secretly thrown into a dungeon. Don't you understand the extent of my power?'

'Yes,' I said. 'And I see myself hanging in chains surrounded by your villainous menials. I can picture you approaching, beautiful and cruel. Shivers of fear run up and down my spine – or is it a shiver of excitement? As you approach and put your face near to mine I burn so much that I never know if you have kissed me or branded me.'

Berenice began to soften. No doubt she did not find the idea unattractive . . .

It was not easy for me to indulge in poetic fancy. How my head did throb! I was petrified that she had men-at-arms waiting below who would be only too willing to drag me away if she were but to give the command. And here I was so placed that I could in no way deny my offence. I wished a thousand times that Marel was less beautiful, less obvious a rival. I wished he was a hundred miles away, anywhere but by my side, too clearly my accomplice, with the marks of lust upon him and a look much like the angel might have had if the men of Sodom had got to him.

Berenice scowled. 'I don't know why you flatter yourself that I would visit you in a dungeon. I would more likely have your ears cut off.'

'I am helpless,' I said, lying back and looking up at her. 'Please be merciful. I am yours to do with as you will.'

'For how you have treated me,' she said, but with less rancour than before, 'you should be flogged.'

'What could I do?' I said aggrieved. 'A wounded man – weak and bleeding.'

'You could have sent a message. Roger!' she cried. 'I thought you dead!'

'You did?' I blinked. What arrogance, I marvelled, to assume that only death could have kept me from her.

'Azo the reeve, who hated you with an unnatural venom, disappeared on the same day as yourself. We thought that he had murdered you and fled. The alternative possibility,' she added with a curl of the lip, 'that you had run away together did not seem very likely. But now, seeing you with this boy, perhaps it was not such an odd idea.'

286

'Truly I am only just recovered,' I said meekly. 'Look at my scar; I shall bear the mark for life.'

'It is well healed,' she observed. 'The boy did that?'

'He is a marvel!'

'What a pity that he does not confine his talents to healing,' said she with some acidity. 'I suppose you will say next that he bewitched you?'

'Yes,' I said thoughtfully. 'I suppose he did. For there can be no other explanation than devilment for my ever having left you for an instant. I must have been out of my head from the effects of witchery. I see it clearly now that I see you.'

Berenice looked at me, her lids hooded, her expression a mystery. Then she looked at Marel.

'Yes,' she said. 'He is a witch. How else could he have so deluded you and tempted you to sin against God and humankind, and you a priest? He must know all the old woman's secrets, and there is no doubt of her sorcery; everyone knew it. Certainly the fault could not have been yours. I understand that now. I see I must forgive you.'

Although I was immensely relieved by her conclusion there was that about her which made me uneasy. She smiled.

'Well, Roger . . . it still remains that I am glad to see you. Ghislaine, wait downstairs, will you?'

Her maid thus sent away, the lady Berenice leaned over me and kissed me – this at least did show her true nobility for I did stink somewhat . . .

'My love,' I murmured. 'Ah, my love . . .'

'Oh Roger,' Berenice sighed. 'Why did you go away? I've been in such turmoil . . . I needed you . . . if only you knew how insupportable my life has become, there at the castle.'

'So what has happened?' I asked her. 'Surely he has not recovered his health?'

'That is why I'm here,' said Berenice. 'When you brought me the spell I believed in it. I suppose that the old witch was tricking me. How she must have laughed at my naive belief! Yet I was so desperate. I would have done anything to be rid of him. But I couldn't bring myself to . . . kill him. I thought the spell would be the answer. Then if he died it would not be my fault; it would merely be the magic working.'

'But it did not?'

'No. Time and again I spoke the words and mixed the powders. He grew weaker. He just lies there, his eyes shut

287

and his breathing heavy, but . . . he will not die.'

'But, Berenice, if he is like that, he is no threat to you. You can live as you please. He won't pester you.'

'I can't go on like this,' she said firmly. 'He is like a weight around my neck. As long as he lives he is master. I have to ask his opinion and get his permission for the running of the estate. As long as he is known to be alive I am not in charge. It is an impossible position. Worst of all, I am tormented with the thought that he may recover. In his bouts of clarity he knows me. Suppose one day he were to sit up and grin and announce that he was well? It would be unthinkable. And that is why I made up my mind to come here.'

'Why?'

'I know she has poisons here,' Berenice whispered. 'Just a drop of something, I don't know which they are, but just a grain would do it. I have to have some. I can think of nothing else. I can't rest until it is done.'

'Oh my lady,' I breathed. 'You are a brave woman.'

'Yes,' said Berenice recovering her composure. 'My mind is clear. If there were any doubts about involving him, they are gone since I saw him with you. Oh Roger – how could you! With a *boy* . . .'

She then looked at Marel.

'Well, serf,' she said coldly. 'I have need of you. You are to become my herbalist. I shall require you to live at the castle. You will come there today; you will lodge with the other servants. You shall mix potions for me. You are to bring with you all the herbs I require. I want a bunch of every herb that you have. Every single one, do you understand?'

The poor lad was aghast and trembling too much to speak.

'My men at arms are waiting below,' continued Berenice. 'They will carry the herbs for you in baskets which I shall send. You are to come with them.'

'And what about me?' I asked her. 'No commands concerning my fate?'

Berenice said with a slight sigh of resignation: 'You may come or go as you please. But, so help me, you are still welcome at the castle.'

'I'll help you sort the herbs,' I said all brisk and businesslike, now I was dressed and splashed with icy water. 'There's no other way; you'll have to do as she says. Come on, Marel, move about. You look turned to stone.'

Marel had said nothing ever since Berenice's departure. I took no notice; this was no time for sulks. Now that I had recovered from my rough awakening I thought I had been let down lightly. All was for the best. If ever I needed final proof I should move on I had it now. I'd be out of here before the day was over and you wouldn't see my heels for dust.

'I suppose it had to happen,' I continued cheerfully, as I stocked up herbs and packed them. 'As I intended leaving anyway it simply forced my hand. Yes, it's time I was moving on, making a fresh start. I can't see myself having any more to do with her ladyship, though. Once inside that castle and the gates shut behind you . . . no, I wouldn't trust her an inch. She's sweet enough when she chooses to be but I can recognise a fellow spirit. That woman's completely unscrupulous, and anything in her path can begin to say its prayers . . . Mind you, I don't entirely disapprove of that. She'd be well rid of him and he was not much loved hereabouts. And if he's at death's door anyhow, what's the odds? You'll be doing her a service, and yourself too. She'll be grateful afterwards, and treat you well. You could be famous with her patronage. Come on now! Look about you! And,' I slapped his bottom, 'put some clothes on!'

The men-at-arms kept watch on us as we worked. Then they loaded the baskets and bore them away, and Marel went between them, like a prisoner.

Truth to tell, I was glad to see the back of him, as they say. He had been so vague and silent. I couldn't get a word from him; his eyes were big and empty; you would swear he was an idiot. He'd be all right. The villagers would see to him; they'd keep an eye on him up at the castle. Berenice wasn't an evil woman, no, she wouldn't do him harm; he'd be all right. And after all, the pedlar said that he was coming back. I liked the pedlar. He was tough; the road had hardened him; he moved on when he came to trouble; he knew a thing or two. And if he cared for that fool boy, well, he could take him over. Let the pedlar worry about Marel and look after him, for sure the boy could not fend for himself. But I couldn't take that kind of burden with me, to slow me down and bother me and cause me care. No one would expect it of me.

I wasn't clear of trouble yet. That girl Alys had been waiting nearby, till the soldiers went, hiding by the house. Now she emerged and came towards me, seizing both arms.

'Roger!' she said passionately. 'We must talk.'

'We must?'

'We are alone now. Marel's gone. There are things that only you can tell me.'

'What things?'

'I want to know about the herbs.'

'The herbs – why?'

'They are power. Everybody knows it. And now Marel has been taken they have no master. They need a master. You didn't know old Alkanet. She was fond of me, I know. She would have wanted me to be the master. Marel was never the one. It should go from woman to woman. The Mother works through women. I am the one to rule the herbs. I have known it all my life.'

I stared into her face. I wondered how I had ever thought her timid, dull. She had a trembling intensity, her eyes glowed as she spoke; I sensed a startling strength in her, but not, I thought, for good. And she intrigued me.

'It is true I learnt things from Marel,' I began.

'I knew it!' she hissed eagerly. 'And there are books too, aren't there? Old books, books of spells? And you can read them to me – and I will repay you, in a way that you will like . . .'

I laughed weakly. How astonishing it was – she quite disturbed me, and I had thought her foolish and of no account. I knew now that I was wrong.

'There are old books,' I said, my face now close to hers, 'and certainly I'll tell you all you want to know. I've heard about old Alkanet from Marel. Am I wrong – I feel that you are very like her?'

'I am not yet; but I will be. Show me the books and tell me all you know. There may not be much time.'

'What do you mean?'

'I don't know; but I know that it is true.'

'Then come with me.' What did it matter? Since I had betrayed both God and Goddess, what had I to lose?

And so I did not take the road that day, but turned again towards the house, and Alys with me.

TEN
Ghislaine's Tale

MY LADY instructed me to look out for the peasant boy Marel and to bring him to her chamber. I vow I did not realise her intention.

'Ghislaine,' she said. 'See that he speaks to no one on the way, and when he enters, see we are alone.'

And so the afternoon found me standing in the courtyard. How pleasant and agreeable was this castle in the summertime, framed in fields and backed by distant leafy woods beyond. Many a peasant might consider himself fortunate to have been chosen by Lady Berenice to serve her interests here within. As I waited I shared gossip with Agnes the farrier's daughter, a most diverting way of passing the time, for she had a tale to tell.

'It was not like the ordinary gatherings,' she told me, whispering behind her hand. 'Ooh, you should have been there! We were mother-naked all of us, and kissing whom we would. But I can hardly remember it at all, for we had this potion which the boy had made. Lord knows what was in it! It made you dizzy, but in a very merry way, so things were different, like green leaves were red, the sky was like a fire, the grass was colour of rich wine and soft to walk on ... it made you feel so happy, light as air, like you were flying ... and Stephen – whom I often have to coax into action – was as hard as a broomstick and he stayed as hard all night! By Saint Simeon who lived atop a pillar, I've never had such a good time in my life!'

I did not believe her, of course. These country folk are so simple, and are prone to telling tales. But she amused me, till she said more thoughtfully: 'That boy must have a secret power. He must know things we do not know. I fear him. It makes me shiver just to think he's coming to the castle!'

I could not accord with her entirely. Whenever I had seen the boy I thought him frightened and half-witted. The old crone scared me, yes, but not the boy. And when I saw him in the loft with Roger Fortunatus all I thought was what a pity such a pretty youth should smell so vile, for they lay like pigs.

Marel's arrival at the castle did nothing to change my judgement. Although he was not a prisoner, he looked like one condemned. Between the soldiers – who certainly were great brutes with the finesse of rutting oxen – he looked small and child-like and bereft. All stared, and muttered to each other – cooks and scullions gazed from the kitchen door, and servants paused; a mother hid her child behind her skirts.

I moved forward swiftly to give instructions. We brought Marel and the herbs upstairs, to Berenice's chamber.

We three, now alone, unpacked the herbs on to the floor, Marel in a trance, Berenice in a fervour of nervous intensity, and I with a stream of foolish chatter to dispel the awkward air. Why it was so I could not tell. What we were about was reasonable enough. Berenice asked for the names of the herbs and their uses, which Marel told her, and it was not until we came to thornapple that she showed anything more than desultory interest.

'Thornapple,' she repeated. 'A deadly poison.'

'Yes. That's why it's so carefully tied up.'

'I see . . . deadly, you say . . . very potent.'

'Yes.'

'Leave that one with me. I am so plagued by a family of rats. They come out in the night; I hear them scratching. It's frightening, isn't it, Ghislaine?'

'Yes, my lady,' I said, surprised but dutiful. There were no rats.

'We'll leave the other herbs,' said Berenice. 'I'm growing tired of it all.' She looked at Marel, and there was no mistaking her cold dislike. 'Your duties will be to help in the kitchens. Do everything you are told. From time to time I will send for you for any special duty.'

I must admit I felt dubious about that. He'd have a difficult time of it down there. The servants would distrust him and dislike him. Surely Berenice could see that? He would suffer

292

enormously. And for what purpose? Now that he had brought the herbs we did not need him. She could let him go. But she did not.

Whenever Berenice required him to mix potions she would send me to the kitchen for him, so I knew that I was right in what I guessed his treatment would be. A vile hot place the kitchen was, and full of bustle and activity, dead things hung up on hooks, and perspiring menials falling over each other as they stoked the fire and turned the spits and heaved the cauldrons, carried water, gutted fish, and swore and sang and cursed and laughed with their ugly raucous laughter.

'I don't know why you were brought here at all,' I heard the cook say many times. 'As if I didn't know my own work. What do you know about cooking and herbs that I don't know, perhaps someone will tell me that!'

And he would flounce about, grinding, cutting and mixing, till the table shook.

At first they regarded Marel as somewhat useless and stupid, and he gave them no cause to think otherwise. He did not speak or assert himself. They supposed that he was sullen or half-witted and gave him the simple tasks to do or the sort that no one wanted. And when they knew exactly who he was their manner changed – half fear, half hatred, veiled in caustic jollity. If he were seen at a simple task such as chopping mint leaves, someone might say teasingly: 'Are you mixing a potion to turn us all into frogs?'

And others would say warningly: 'Ssh! He can!'

It was to mix a face lotion or a hand cream that her ladyship sent for him at first, and I would bring him to her. How he had changed already from that golden-haired boy who lived in the forest, and but a few days had passed. He was like a wilted plant, all pale and drooping, and his hair less bright, and tangled now, like peasant's hair; he never said a word. It shocked me. I thought it seemed unkind to keep him here, but when I timorously mentioned it to my lady she said brusquely: 'Don't be ridiculous. It's obvious that I need his herbal skills.'

Another time Berenice asked him to carry a goblet of wine to his lordship.

'I will show you,' she said. She poured the wine out and handed it to Marel. 'He is very ill and won't know who you are, but it will be helpful to me not to have to look after him entirely on my own.'

Audran de Bonnefoy slept at this time upon a pallet behind
a screen in a separate room. He was grotesque. He did not
know us, and his rasping breathing could be heard from
outside his door.

'Just see that some wine passes his lips,' said Berenice.
'That's all you have to do. Now that I have instructed you, you
will know what to do when I ask you again.'

She did ask again. Many a time I peeped around the
kitchen door to look for him and call out: 'Marel – her
ladyship needs you to take wine to his lordship', and docile he
would follow me, out of the kitchen and across the sunny
courtyard to the great hall and up to the private chamber, to
do Berenice's bidding. I knew he hated going anywhere near
his lordship, just as I would; he would feel revolted and
afraid. You could see Marel crouching there beside the inert
bulk with the horrible raucous breathing, trying to ease wine
past the bulbous dribbling lips. Audran never spoke, except
some inarticulate gibberish. And then one morning Berenice
knelt down beside the pallet and she looked at me in wonder.

'Mon Dieu!' she whispered. 'I believe he's dead. At last he's
dead!'

Although he had been ill for such a long time the fact of his
death came as a shock to us – to everyone. No one was exactly
sure of the cause of his demise, though we were very glad
he'd gone. Inevitably, as often happens in such circumstances, there was some talk of poison. I don't know where it
started. The word associated itself fairly quickly with Marel's
arrival. Hadn't he been working in the kitchens, mixing food
and carrying wine to his lordship? Yes, but why would he
want to poison him? Well, he was a witch, wasn't he? But even
so . . . It was the village girl Alys who supplied the answer.
Didn't they know? It seemed that some months previously
Audran de Bonnefoy had attacked the boy in the forest; he
had never forgiven him, and swore to be revenged. Ulf the
swineherd had seen it all.

Well! That was the first I'd heard of that! Of course, I could
believe Audran capable of any villainy – and as for Marel,
well, I did not know him, after all. Perhaps he had laid plans.
But not as he was now.

Rumour is a strange thing. In my heart of heart I knew that
Marel had not poisoned Audran, for I truly thought his wits

were gone. His eyes were big and empty and he never spoke. I could not credit him with simple thought, let alone plotting. But such was the feeling in our enclosed space, within that wall of stone that shut the world out when it would, that I believed the rumours like the rest. For what else could have happened? The boy knew magic, he mixed brews and potions, he made people do strange things, act in strange ways. He bore a grudge against Audran for an ancient wrong. Each day he brought him wine. Now Audran was dead. What more natural? It must be so.

One evening at that time, Berenice sent me to the kitchen to tell Marel that he was to serve the dishes at the table.

'My lady, is that wise?' I gasped. 'If what we hear is true . . . oh my lady, send him away! It is not safe while he is here. If he knows poison he could destroy us all!'

'Don't argue, girl. Do as I say. I know what I am about.'

Most reluctantly I went down to the courtyard, where the evening dusk blurred buildings into shadows. I moved towards the kitchen and I noticed Marel in the doorway. But even as I looked, a figure slipped across to him from the farriery nearby. Roger Fortunatus!

I gasped. We had not seen him since that terrible moment when we discovered him in the witch's house, when he had been lying there with Marel in their disgusting proximity. What was he doing here? I must know. My lady would be very interested to hear. I crept around the back of the kitchen house and I hid behind a jutting wall. I heard it all! But only Roger spoke.

'Ah – listen, Marel; you must get away; you are in danger. Do you know what they are saying about you? It isn't safe for you here. You must get out. I was stupid; I didn't realise that Berenice would take this way out. It's obvious what her plan is. She's going to rid herself of you and the rumours. You've got to leave.'

I blanched. Could that be true? I listened, turned to stone.

Marel did not reply. I knew how he would look – wide-eyed and dazed. He would not understand.

'Oh Christ!' said Roger. 'I don't believe you have any idea what I am talking about. I can't stay here. I only came to steal a horse. Confound this God-forsaken village. I wish I'd never come here. It's no good for me either. I'll speak to someone on my way through the village, the innkeeper perhaps, and see if he can do something for you. Lord knows you need someone. You're helpless on your own.'

The cook's rough voice called Marel back into the kitchen, and Roger fled.

It was a bad moment for me. Certain conclusions seemed apparent, and I was frightened as I stood there, breathing hard, and leaning to the wall. It was Berenice, not Marel, who had planned the death. I knew it now, as I perhaps had known before. How long she nurtured this dark secret I could not guess, but all had fallen into place for her. She had never spoken to me about her feelings about Marel, but there must have been a powerful hatred for a person who could steal her dazzling lover – and a boy moreover, a peasant, who had so carelessly robbed her of the man she had so eagerly welcomed. She would suppose that Roger was waiting back at the herb garden for Marel's return. He had never been back to the castle; he had rejected its lady. She would prove a bad enemy for them both. Roger should never get Marel back. He could wait for ever. Her plan had worked impeccably. How cleverly she had arranged it . . .

Could I have saved the boy, now knowing what I knew? I doubt it, and I did not possess that disinterested goodness that does what it sees is right, regardless of the consequences.

My future must lie with her ladyship. I had no choice.

And so I went into the kitchen. Though my voice faltered slightly I said carelessly: 'Marel – tonight you are required to serve the dishes at the table. See he does so,' I told the others. 'Her ladyship wishes it.'

Marel took his place with those servants who were to carry the dishes across the courtyard to the great hall. From my seat at the dais I watched him approach. As he drew near to Berenice, her ladyship stood up, thereby causing all the people to look at her. They faced each other, Marel with child-eyes, Berenice the resplendent widow.

'So you think you shall serve me at the table,' sneered Berenice, 'even as you served my husband!'

Now every one fell silent and stared.

'Rumours have come to me,' said Berenice clearly. 'Rumours of your skill with the poisonous herbs. I am very much troubled by your presence. I think you mean me ill. And until I know otherwise, I find you suspect. You will be tried at the manor court. Until your crime is proved or no, you will be imprisoned.'

The guards approached as she beckoned, and took Marel out of the great hall, away.

The place to which Marel was taken was a small stone room built into the outside wall of the castle.

There were several such small cells in the castle wall, with thick low wooden doors, for prisoners whose stay was not expected to be long. No hideous dungeon was it, yet I could not help but feel that any place of constraint would cause more pain to one who lived out in the open air than one accustomed to four walls' security. I feared for that boy's reason.

The funeral of Audran de Bonnefoy was celebrated. Unfortunately 'celebrated' was the appropriate word, for nobody had been sorry to see him go, and once the official solemn faces had been put aside and the holy words spoken, the villagers hurried away to a jolly feast, enjoyed outside the ale house with tables set in the open air, and much to eat, and we up at the castle to a banquet such as I had never seen before. Next day the manor court was convened.

This event took place regularly in the rhythm of our life under the eye of the lord of the manor or his steward. It met in the castle hall in Winter, and in Summer out of doors, and everybody could attend. It was judged in accordance with local customs and blended in with the laws of the land, the punishments being mostly fines of money or goods, and sometimes the pillory or stocks. And the whole village would assemble to see justice done. This time, amongst the common misdemeanours, the fate of Marel was to be decided.

As I helped Berenice prepare herself for this occasion my heart was full of misgivings. How beautiful she looked, how regal and how rich! I found her terrifying. She was so calm. Her features showed no sign of all the dark emotion beneath. Was I the only one who knew? Could no one guess? But no, why should they? Even I, who watched, who lived beside her, I could not be sure. Perhaps her husband died of natural causes and I wronged her terribly by my suspicions. She was a warm and loving woman – she could not execute a cold and evil scheme – it was impossible.

But I remembered that she came up from the funeral feast with shining eyes. 'Gone!' she breathed. 'Finally gone!'

Now she had total power.

'Oh my lady!' I said, suddenly afraid. 'What will happen? What will become of that poor boy?'

She looked at me in some surprise.

'Why – he will be tried, of course. What would you?'

'But – what if he has done no wrong?'

'Then he has nothing to fear,' she answered coldly. This peasant boy, the witch's acolyte, who knew my lady's secret weaknesses, who stole her lover from her, lay with him, the necessary victim to her plot – he had nothing to fear? With Berenice as judge, with power to condemn?

ELEVEN
The Pedlar's Tale

NIGHT UPON the Thames lay black.

It was now quite clear to me that this hole wherein I lay would serve the part of an oubliette. It was so deep beneath the house that I heard nothing from above, no sounds of life and movement. All that I could hear nearby was water – river water, slapping at the window, rivulets of water trickling down the walls, water at my feet each time I moved.

Although I knew that only hours had passed I felt that I had been there years. I knew de Bracy would be in no hurry to let me out, if indeed I was to be released at all; I could well end my days here, one more rat in a hole – what did one less pedlar matter in the great scheme of things? What had so enraged de Bracy? His son's leanings – my seduction of him? My undisputed vagrancy – my Saxon blood? All of these? I thought of Wulfstan, who believed that in a common cause we must forget our differences and be Englishmen. Here we were, with France set to invade us – a second Conqueror in the offing, eager to divide our land to pacify his nobles in reward – and we were squabbling amongst ourselves, as we would always do. Ah, we had some way to go before our land was whole – if it could ever be so.

I wondered if I'd see the morning. Would a sea tide raise the river, flooding this dark cell? What use was I to Marel now – how I despised myself for my shortcomings, my unforgiveable stupidity.

Now, further off, the ships at anchor lit their lanthorns, smudging the darkness with lights. I heard the cries of sailors leaving ship to try the delights of brothel fare; I heard the laughs that carried on the wind, the snatches of their songs, more clearly to be heard at night across the water. Their freedom, their companionship made me feel yet more isolated than before, far from all humankind, forgotten and alone.

And then I heard a song I recognised. Its numbskull words brought waves of gladness.

'See seven beans me hommy me baron
On glar Norman Pointervinny Gascon . . .'

Henry the Sailor was about, somewhere out there, with boat, with hope for me. I put my face against the bars, and when the verse came to an end I yelled the chorus like a man out of his mind:

'Maids and corn soup – huger peas!'

A little silence, while I waited with a pounding heart – then Henry's voice again, the chorus. I joined in. He stopped. I finished the line. Across the watery stillness I even heard him guffaw.

I knew now I would be saved; but it took some doing. Our oafish enactment of their famous encounter would have made Blondel wince and King Richard turn in his tomb. I guided Henry to me by my singing, which at best was cracked and tuneless, and his little boat crept closer, with his hoarse conspiratorial reply. I could not see him till his boat merged from the darkness like a wedge of black slipped loose from black beyond, and then he banged the window with his oar.

'Pedlar? Is that you?'

'Who else! Who else would know your wretched verse!'

'My verse has saved your life, I shouldn't wonder.'

'You are right!'

'Sparrow, pass the axe.'

The boy held the boat steady to the window, and Henry swung his axe against the bars. His shoulders had the strength of ten, as if to make up for the lack of his legs. The bars cracked at his blows; they split. He heaved the jagged ends apart. He grabbed my arms and helped me through. I landed in the boat. It rocked as giddily as any twig in a whirlpool, but luckily it did not sink. 'I said I'd pay you one day,' chuckled Henry. 'I said I'd pay you for the boat. And did you not say that it would not be through singing!'

As Henry set about to row me clear of that dark stronghold I blessed my good fortune, and I laughed with him to think how it had come about.

'Did you know I was there? Had someone seen me taken?'

'No,' he replied. 'No one knew where you were.'

'Then this was – chance?' I marvelled.

'I set out as I always do. I sang because I like to sing – especially at night. They often throw their rubbish down at me,' he chuckled. 'That's how much they like my singing.'

'Chance!' I shuddered, awed. 'Does human life and fate hang by such wayward threads?'

'Did you not pray in there, then?' Henry asked, rowing us rapidly downstream.

'You may be sure I did!'

'Then it was prayer answered.'

I laughed wrily. 'Am I to believe that God has such a merry wit as to rescue me by your croaking?'

'There is a place for everything in this world of wonders!'

'It must be that I was rescued for a purpose then. That gives me hope.'

I started out for Cortle the next day.

The roads were dusty grey, the summer days now easing into the mellow gilded ones of autumn. In the fields the crops were being gathered and everywhere the swish of scythes, the cut of sickles. Cattle grazed amongst the stubble, and folk were hunting out good stuff for thatch.

It could have been a pleasant journey, for the weather was so mild and warm and the going easy; but I was so tormented in my mind that I could not delight in anything. I knew that it would take me several days to reach Cortle and anything might happen in that time. I travelled recklessly, not stopping for long, hardly ever sleeping, and when I reached Cortle I was exhausted.

I went straight to the herb garden.

But what a sight of desolation was there! For a moment I could not believe that I had come to the right place. It was like one of those clearings woodmen make when timber for a great house is needed – an earthen space, much trampled into hollows and heaps, strewn piles of logs and branches, a wilderness of chopped and stubby plants, too much sky and light. The whole place seemed much smaller. Was this where

301

we had come in secrecy, where Alkanet had held sway at her court of herbs, where Marel and I had walked and kissed and loved? For a long while I just stood staring in a silly kind of disbelief. Who had done this? Who had cut it down? What venom was there – what cold rage, to cause this havoc to a hidden place!

The cottage also had been knocked about. The roof was half off, the loft laid bare, birds flapping startled from the tangling boughs. I entered cautiously, disturbed and shocked to find some parts remaining, some parts gone, and all in disarray.

'Alkanet?' I said into the air.

Why had I spoken? The old hag was dead. And yet I half expected her to appear around the corner of the house, or from a birch bole, hunched and chuckling, with the answer to my questions. For I tell you what was eerie about this place – someone had chopped it down, but it was living yet. Doom there was not. This gaping wound already understood the ways of healing.

'Is someone there?' I asked.

I got no answer. So I poked around a bit, discovered nothing, shook my head and turned away. I took my weary horse and set off to the village, where the grateful beast was fed and watered, and myself the same inside the inn.

'Pedlar!' Benedict exclaimed, unchanged as ever, pleased to see me – yet I sensed he was uneasy. Was it Marel?

'Is he dead?' I blurted out. 'Where is the boy?'

'No, he's not dead,' said Benedict, in some relief, for if he had said otherwise to the haggard wild-eyed vision I presented I might well have strangled him.

'Imprisoned?' I demanded hoarsely, clutching him.

'No, no, be still,' he soothed me, patting me, placating me. 'After the judgement I brought him here, to sleep beneath my roof – be easy – no, he lives!'

'He isn't dead . . .' I breathed, and sank upon a bench, so tired and drained I nearly dropped.

'Bring ale!' cried Benedict to Edith who came running; and they bustled to and fro to make a meal. I had not known I was so tired. I could take in no more than that good news – he was alive – my golden-headed boy – I was in time. I shut my eyes, my elbows on the table, head in hands. Now I could rest.

'Did Roger find you?' asked Benedict, putting a great bowl

of soup before me. 'That was his plan when he left. You've made good time between you.'

'I hurried,' I said briefly. 'And now I'm flat out, so pour me ale and don't stop talking.'

As much as they could tell me, Benedict and Edith told. I put together all I could – the gaps no doubt I'd hear from Marel. Roger living at the castle – Roger wounded by Azo in the fields – Azo fled – Roger brought to Marel – Roger's Sabbat and its strange effects – Marel brought to the castle on Berenice's orders – the mysterious death of Audran – Marel accused – Marel locked up in a prison. Then his trial.

Blessing the life-giving properties of ale and bread and broth I tucked into the meat that followed, gnawing to the bone all I was brought.

Benedict sat down beside me on the bench, and took up the tale.

TWELVE
Benedict's Tale

IT WAS a sunny day, with all the turning leaves dancing on every tree, and the sun speckling the ground with yellow, more fitting for a feast than for a judgement. There were trestle tables set underneath the trees, and benches, and a canopied place for the castle folk, and a line of men-at-arms standing fidgeting in the heat. The word was about that Marel was to be accused of poison, and so we were all there that day in the meadow to see what happened and to make sure it was fair.

'That is never Marel,' whispered Edith to me, 'that thin scrap of a boy?'

'Oh that is,' I replied. 'It goes to show what it does to you to be taken from your home and made to live at the castle. I do hate a wall myself. If you are used to the free air, it can wither you away to be sealed up inside four walls.'

I remembered how he was at the meeting. Beautiful like an angel, laughing, and his hair all golden; and so alive, standing there by the side of that . . . that strange weird man.

'I can't get over it,' said my wife, shaking of her head. 'He looks so dirty. Just like any village lad who cared nothing for himself – his hair all wild and shaggy, and his manner like a poor boy who looks after the pigs.'

'We would all look so if we had been put in the castle prison,' said I all sober.

Well, there were some small wrongdoings dealt with – tree felling, straying animals, rowdy doings in the church porch. Fines were meted out. Folk chattered; this was everyday stuff.

Then Marel was brought forward between two guards. He

looked as alive as a sack. I thought that if the boy were to be condemned on the spot he would show no flicker of interest.

The lady Berenice's steward then stepped forward most importantly. I don't know his name – a new fellow, liked the sound of his own voice, much like most of the Normans are, think they know it all. Well, says he:

'The boy Marel whose home was in the forest, has been accused of poisoning the lord of the manor, recently deceased.'

'Who accuses him?' I interrupted loudly. This sort doesn't frighten me.

But he must play it by the book. He tells me to be quiet. 'It is not for you to speak yet,' he says.

'That is the usual question asked,' I stoutly said.

'You will be told when to speak.' The steward looked towards Berenice.

'Rumour accuses him,' she said. 'Moreover, there is evidence here of witchcraft, and witchcraft is a sin. I think we are all God-fearing people here. I think we would not deny that anyone who is not for God's ways is against God's ways. Any kind of worship which is not of God must be of the Devil. All this is quite clear. If anything of this nature, in conjunction with the crime of murder, were to be proved upon this boy, it is of course within my power – indeed, no one would expect otherwise – to order that he should be hanged. If thy right hand offend thee,' added Berenice reasonably, with a pleasant glance about her, 'cut it off.'

I saw young Ghislaine shudder. I looked cautiously about. In all my years in Cortle we had never needed to have anybody hanged. What did she have in mind? A gibbet in the castle yard or would it be a sudden thing, a rope across a branch! You'll pardon my dwelling on the matter, but I think it was only then I saw the greatness of the threat to that poor boy.

The steward, prompted by Ghislaine, at Berenice's direction, put forward the case:

'Her ladyship engaged the services of the boy because there was no herbalist at the castle. He brought his own herbs with him. He worked in the kitchen. Sometimes he took a drink to his lordship, to help the burden of care from my lady. It was after one of these occasions that Lord Audran died.'

'His lordship had been ill for many months,' I protested.

'Not so many,' corrected Berenice. 'He was on his feet at Christmas.'

'But we have heard that since then he had been ill, and since the Spring, bedridden,' said Ralf, eager to show his support. 'Seemingly his illness so came on that he would have died anyway.'

'Yet it is most odd that he should have died so shortly after the boy's arrival at the castle,' said Berenice. 'A boy who after all is known to be skilled in herbal lore, and who, according to some, is thought to be a witch.'

'It was not so much Marel, my lady,' said Edith here. 'It was more the old woman who was there before, and who has since died. Now she was a strange old dame, and being so old and as twisted as a stricken tree, there were tales about her. And she did nothing to disprove them, being awkward in her nature. But Marel, he was only a helper, like, who did the old woman's bidding. She reared him from a baby, see, and he had no other home.'

'That may have been so at first,' said Berenice. 'But since the old crone died, I believe this boy has absorbed all her knowledge. Although he is young, he knows the old woman's secrets. Isn't this so? Has no one a story to tell of the effectiveness of his cures?'

'I have,' said Angilbert, blooming like a flowerhead at the chance to speak. 'Ever since he brought me a mixture, I have not been troubled by my unfortunate stomach. But I ought to add, there is more to it than a simple healing process. There are charms . . .'

'Later,' interrupted Berenice. 'Who else has benefited from his skill?'

Other people told of cures that Marel worked, and Ghislaine the lady's maid said: 'There were the love potions too.'

'Who went for a love potion?'

'Agnes the blacksmith's daughter, my lady.'

'Is she here?'

'No, my lady. But it was a successful potion.'

'Who other has found so?'

'I have,' said Alys. 'But I know that there was magic in it. I had to say charms when I got home.'

'Was anyone else asked to recite charms?' asked Berenice.

'Yes, me,' said Hawise, Walther's daughter. 'I went for a

potion that would let me see fairies. But that was in the days of the old woman.'

'It doesn't matter,' said Berenice. 'We are setting out to prove that charms were spoken. If the old woman knew spells then the boy does too. They would be passed on. Who else feels that they were the victim of a spell?'

No one spoke. If anyone had been so, they had no wish to worsen Marel's case.

'I think you are keeping things from me,' said Berenice. 'Some of you look guilty. I can understand that you may not wish to disclose something so personal. But I think there are suspicions enough to suggest that he knew magic. In short, that he is some kind of witch.'

Angilbert jumped up.

'If that is true, oh, may I ask that he remove the spell that was placed upon me!' he cried. 'I have been telling myself that it was a cruel joke. But if you think that he is a witch, perhaps I am condemned. Marel, Marel! Take off that spell from me!'

'Sit down,' said Walther, shoving him back on to the bench.

'What spell was this?' enquired Berenice.

'That something fearful and strong would come upon me,' he wailed.

'And has it?'

'Not yet, my lady, but I was told it would come slowly.'

'This has nothing to do with the matter,' I said roughly. 'We are dealing with the death of Audran de Bonnefoy, whom this poor boy had never met, nor probably even heard of.'

Ghislaine whispered to the steward, who said: 'It seems that the boy Marel has been cherishing hatred towards the lord Audran for many months. Apparently there was an incident in the forest. The boy was molested, and swore to be revenged.'

We all looked surprised, and muttered one to another. I had certainly heard nothing of this.

'Where did you dig up this story?' I demanded.

'It was the girl Alys who revealed this. She heard it from Ulf the swineherd who saw it happen,' said the steward.

I thought then that it was all over for Marel. The row of Norman faces at the table sickened me with their smug expressions of success.

'Oh! Do something!' whispered Edith.

I stood up. Anyone knows I'll do my best whenever I can.

307

'We have heard accusations,' I said. 'But we seem to have forgotten the boy himself. Look at him, helpless as he is. See if you can really believe that such a sorry sight could be as evil as you are suggesting. No, there was never a word spoken against Marel before this summer. He was quiet and meek, almost unheard of. All we had heard of him was to his good. It was not until – why, it was not until the arrival of that suspect priest! That is when all the trouble started.'

There were mutters of agreement.

'Yes, that's so,' said Ralf. 'The very first time we saw him he so confused us with the question of whether Lambert was really there, and then he told Angilbert that he was a heretic.'

'Yes, our own parish priest accused of heresy!' I echoed then, for suddenly I saw how this could lead. You'd swear I was overcome with loyalty to Angilbert. 'Our own priest! Accused by a travelling clerk whom we never knew for certain to be really a priest or not; for his ideas were not holy.'

'He told us a story of lechery in church!'

'He told us that it was sometimes all right to break the holy vows of wedlock.'

'He said Love came before duty.'

Accusations flowed.

'Be quiet,' said Berenice painfully. 'It is neither here nor there.'

'But yes it is, pardon me,' I protested, still upon my feet. 'You see, he was taken to Marel a sick man. From that time forth, he so influenced this youth by his badness that Marel was not himself. Roger made him obey him. You cannot imagine, my lady, the strength of his charm. He would look you in the eye and you would feel bewildered. Lord knows that in the face of such, a weak vessel like this helpless boy or a woman would not know what he was doing. Is that not so, Alys?' I asked pointedly.

Alys looked thoughtful and mysterious: 'Yes – it is so. For all that I don't wish well to Marel I know how it might have been. That Roger had such a way. He could make you do anything. I could tell you some things . . .'

'That's enough,' said Edith. 'There is no call to be bawdy.'

Berenice stared, then sat forward. 'Come here, girl,' said she, and up jumped Alys not a whit afraid. 'Is this true?' said Berenice. 'Did you know this errant monk at all?'

'I did, my lady. I met him in the forest.'

'For what purpose?' said the lady.

'For love!' said that shameless girl. I did not see the point of Berenice's questions much, but Edith here said it was plain to see – a simple curiosity, like any woman would have showed, for hadn't Berenice herself admired the handsome stranger?

'I . . . see . . .' said Berenice, thoughtfully fingering her throat. She studied Alys with an undisguised surprise. 'He went with you . . . amazing as that seems – the girl is hardly what you might call a beauty! So Marel is not special to him, then?' She laughed, a nasty little laugh. 'For all we know, he laid half the wenches in the shire – Lord knows he was absent enough.'

'My lady, he truly was no virgin,' sniggered Alys. Why was that wretched girl so bold, I marvelled, to chat so frankly with her ladyship? I'm sure I would have been shaking in my shoes!

'Let me give you some advice,' said Berenice, all calm and firm. 'That monk we speak of – he was a weak man. He preys upon the weaknesses of others. I have no time for weakness. You may well believe that I have given this matter ample thought in those days when I believed him dead and Azo his murderer. You had best put him from your mind.' *As I shall do*, I guessed was in her mind.

'Yes, he was weak,' said Alys strangely. 'He was a torn man. He could follow neither God nor Goddess. I took from him what I needed; and I am not weak.'

Why did Berenice put up with this, I wondered? Weird claptrap – yet she did; she listened, with an odd look in her eye.

'What would you say to me?' she asked.

Skinny and little, Alys stood there unabashed. She answered: 'Old Alkanet – I am her daughter.'

Then there was a burst of laughter from whoever heard this boast for we knew well enough it was not so – she was a village girl, was Alys, and we knew her parents when they were alive, and Berenice would know of them, and therefore treat the girl's talk with great scorn. But she did not. She gazed at Alys very searchingly. 'I hope,' she said, 'that you are friendly towards *me*.'

I could not place her tone – it had so much of meaning in it; but it was not how you would expect a lady to speak to a wench. And Alys gives a squint for all the world like that old crone would do, and answers: 'I am no one's enemy.'

I had the feeling that my lady was not satisfied with that.

People were growing fidgety; not everyone could hear this strange exchange, and one of Berenice's men-at-arms reached out and buffeted·a culprit. The steward called for order. Then Angilbert stood up – no doubt he thought the Church had been too long silent.

'We have heard much about this wayward priest,' he cried. 'We all agree his influence was bad. It is he who should be standing here on trial, not the hapless youth who was his instrument. *He* should be judged – *he* should be punished!'

Berenice then gives a crooked little smile. 'Much as it would please many of us here to have the man in chains before us, I am not aware that he has committed any crime. Arrogance and mischief-making do not compare with the accusation of murder, which is the matter to hand. Moreover, unholy friar though he be, he is a friar, and the Church's to try, to punish, to condemn. And the Church looks after its own. They never use the law that sentences to death.' She tossed her head, as one who would be rid of nuisance. The cold look came again into her eyes. 'But we do have the boy. If Roger Fortunatus cared for him at all, we hurt him by default when the boy hangs. Thus do we punish both. And all by the process of the law,' she added, very smug.

But Alys interrupted!

'He did not care for anyone! He cared only for himself. As for Marel, he scorned him – he thought him little better than a halfwit. He told me so himself!'

'Be silent!' Berenice snapped – but I thought that she looked somewhat put out at that; and frowned and bit her lip.

'All this is true,' cried Angilbert. 'It is Roger Fortunatus who is to blame. I should tell you that Marel was once a devout lad who attended church. He listened to my words, as well he should, and he was very receptive to the word of God. But when that infamous man came it all changed. Since he went to live at Marel's house the boy never came to church. That man was the Devil's own instrument. No, more, he was the Devil himself!'

There was a great gasp. Angilbert revelled in the effect of his words.

'You have only to look at the painting in the church,' he continued. 'The likeness is clear. Yes, my friends, we have been lucky. The Devil was amongst us and wrought his evil. He would have had us condemn this innocent boy. It must have been part of his plan. We have seen the light in time.'

'The Lord be praised!' I cried, pressing home the advantage with great fervour. Why, I pounded on the table!

'In fact,' said Angilbert, 'it was he that put the spell on me, not the boy. As I remember, Marel tried to stop him. But he was completely ineffectual against him. That man could do anything he chose. After all, accusing me of heresy . . . it stands to reason he must have been the Devil come amongst us.'

We yelled agreement. Her ladyship looked strange, discomfited. Everyone was looking at her, waiting for her to speak.

'Where is this Devil now?' Berenice asked faintly.

'Where? Fled!' I cried. 'His work was done, you see. My lord dead, an innocent boy accused, there was nothing for him to stay for. Oh yes, he's well and truly away from here. He has fled the parish on a stolen horse. He has gone south. We shall not see him again.'

Berenice leaned back against her chair. She passed a hand across her forehead and looked pale and tired.

'Shall we not?' she sighed. 'Well, so be it.'

She looked across at Marel. She must have clearly seen the pointlessness of further spite against such an object. Roger Fortunatus had gone. He would comfort and disturb neither of them. Marel would be no rival to her now, thin and bedraggled as he was, so lorn and helpless that it could be thought that in the shock of it all he had lost his wits. But I suppose Berenice must make sure. There must be no further threat.

'This is my decision,' she said coolly, overcoming whatever thoughts were hers. 'I think you are right, those of you who feel that the boy Marel was weak and easily influenced. Clearly he had no idea what he was doing, and almost certainly the travelling priest polluted his character. We will assume that he was not himself – possessed even – and that whatever he did was because he was an easy prey to an unscrupulous mind. He shall go free.'

We raised a mighty cheer. But Berenice had not finished. She raised her hand and continued:

'But we cannot allow him to continue to practice his trade

of herbalist. Whether there be magic there or no, the power contained therein is too much to be in the hands of a young boy who is not responsible for his actions. Who knows what harm he may do, now that he has been influenced by the Devil? None of us would be safe . . . And so, he shall lose the herb garden. He shall not live there. And I shall order my soldiers to destroy it this very day.'

Her tone was very sharp and hard. But it was Alys that she looked at when she said it.

THIRTEEN
The Pedlar's Tale

I

BENEDICT SAT back and took a hefty swig of ale.

'Well, Edith and I brought Marel back to the inn, and there he sat in our back room away from prying eyes.'

'He said nothing,' Edith recounted. 'Not a word. I thought his wits were gone. Well, I said to myself, that's you fixed this side of eternity. And I couldn't see what the days to come might hold for him. And when I said as much to Benedict and he said you were sent for, pedlar, I still could not see what good it would do.'

I thanked her with a smile for her faith in me.

The same day as the judgement the soldiers from the castle had come riding down the village street in a gathering cloud of dust, on their way to cut down the herbs and trample them into the ground.

'It was a frightening sight,' said Edith. 'As if they were hell-bent on murder. We watched them pass by – but what could we do?'

'And you should have seen the place itself,' said Benedict. 'Enough to break your heart. All flattened it was, with great healthy plants cut clean across the stem, and leaves ground to pulp, and huge roots sticking up out of the soil, indecent like. Oh, but the scents that were laid bare! I stood there and sniffed and sniffed; I thought I should die of it.'

'And very like you might have,' said Edith, 'if all the tales be true. That's an evil place, for all its beauty, and you'd do well to stay away.'

Lambert joined us then, and Ralf, tanned and thirsty from

the fields. We greeted each other and they sat down to drink.
" 'I went to the herb garden myself,' I told them. 'It was cut down. But does she think the power in that place is gone? I do not think so. It did not seem a dead place.'

'Ah, it's dead all right,' said Lambert. 'Like any graveyard.'

'More a hospice?' I suggested.

'Well, it's over now,' said Edith comfortably. 'More ale? Things are better in the village. We have a new reeve now, pedlar, old Walther, with his aches in the joints of a Winter. He won't be pushing folk around. And Lady Berenice has gone away to visit. I daresay it will do her good to breathe a different air.'

'They say she is with child,' said Ralf.

'Folk do gossip,' Edith said severely.

'A strange business, though, wasn't it?' said Benedict.

'It's that wretched boy I feel sorry for,' said Edith. 'I never saw a person change so. Like a flower uprooted. I can't say I ever liked that woodland den and all its mysteries. I thought it wholly bad. I'm glad to see it go. But what can that boy do now? Where can he go? He can't live in Cortle, can he?'

'No; her ladyship would never stand for it,' agreed Benedict. 'You should have seen the way she looked at him. She hates him. It's something to do with Roger. Anyone can see that.'

'Not only that,' said Edith. 'But ordinary folk can't help themselves fearing him a little. It's difficult for us to feel easy with somebody who knows about magic potions and such, and who might have had a hand in his lordship's death. And then there was that Evening. Folk feel a bit funny about it, that he could have made them act so bad, and, between ourselves, pedlar, to act so bad himself. Not everybody saw, but some did. My Benedict says that there was – wickedness between him and that priest.'

'Of course, it was the priest's fault,' Benedict added quickly. 'But he had the sense to clear out.'

'But what I mean, pedlar,' said Edith, 'is, like, just after the manor court when I brought the lad back here, Angilbert came in after him. He kept pestering me to let him see him, saying Marel had got to take a spell off him. I told him Marel was in no fit state, but he kept on. He was convinced a doom would fall upon him. In the end I had to get Marel to touch him and say, "I take away the spell". He had no idea what he was doing, but it suited Angilbert, and he went away much gladdened. But you see what he would be up against.'

I did, and I said that if I had my way, he would suffer no more from such stupidity.

When Edith went out of the room Benedict said quietly to me: 'I don't like to worry Edith, but I thought you might be interested to know this, pedlar. You remember Alys yourself, don't you? – such a thin little thing who seemed so timid . . . Well, and I had this from Roger himself, it seems that after Marel was taken away to the castle, young Alys went and put herself into the cottage. Roger was still there. The girl had got a foolish passion for him. He showed her all the herbs. He told her what he could remember from the things he learnt of Marel. He showed her how to make the potion that we call the witch's brew, and there was an ointment too. It seemed there were some old books there, in the cottage, with spells in them. Well, they were not there when the soldiers came to kill the herb garden.'

'Where are they?'

'I don't know. But Alys knows. She can't read a word of them, but her young man, Martin, who was a bright lad, you may remember, has gone away to the abbey school. When he comes back he will be able to read them to her. I think Roger thought he had done a good thing there. He wanted me to know that, if we can wait a while, we can have the drink again, and meet again as we used to. It will be kept very secret, of course, but it's good to know that in spite of all, our ancient pleasures will continue.'

'Oh Benedict,' I said doubtfully. 'How can you think that? It will be nothing like it was. Unless the one who makes the brew has Marel's goodness, those meetings can be dangerous. Better leave it be; let it go. You don't know what you may be unleashing . . .'

Benedict shrugged.

'It's nothing to do with me,' he said.

I would have almost said he looked shifty. So, very gently, does corruption begin.

'Is it wise to allow Alys to go ahead?' I persisted. 'Could it not be stopped? Do you trust her?'

'Not a bit,' he said cheerfully. 'But it would give me great delight to thwart the lady Berenice even if it was only far off in the future. And truly, pedlar, it was a drink of drinks! I'd love to swig it again. You can't imagine!'

'Well,' I said. 'I hope you thanked Roger for his gift. He has certainly left his spell upon this village.'

After all, I couldn't be responsible for the future either. And so these things shift on in their own way. There will be dark magic in Cortle, things to fear. The thread is twisted. I am glad I shall not be there to see its unravelling.

Much comforted and restored by food and talk I stretched and smiled.

'So where is Marel now?' I asked. 'I'm going to take him with me and look after him. No one need fear he'll starve or pine. I love that boy, and he shall be my special care. Take me to him now.'

I thought that Benedict would lead me to the quiet back room or up the ladder to his loft, and there I'd find the boy asleep. There was a pause.

'You said you'd brought him here?' I asked, a curious quiver flickering in my chest.

'I did,' began Benedict in great unease. 'That was at first. He spent a night here, yes. I meant to nurture him and keep him here till you came back.'

'He isn't here?' I paled.

'He isn't, no.'

'Where is he then?'

'He's gone. He slipped away. I don't know where he is. Nobody knows. They say he's in the forest.'

'They say he is crazed,' said Lambert, crossing himself. 'Half wolf, hair turned to fur.'

'They say he has become old Alkanet,' said Ralf, 'and lies in wait in the magic garden, planning his revenge, his beauty turned to ugliness, fearful to behold.'

I stood up angrily, disgusted to my bones. 'Did none of you think to find out?'

They shifted guiltily.

'If what they say is true . . .'

'He could put a curse on us . . .'

'I be mortal scared of madmen.'

'I did go to the garden a couple of times,' said Benedict. 'He isn't there. If anyone is tending it, it's Alys. But not Marel. He's gone into the forest.'

'You did not search at all?'

'I meant to, pedlar. But I have been so busy . . . and the

forest is so vast . . .'

'Heaven help us,' I said, and stood up and wearily picked up my pack. 'Then my search is not yet done.'

II

AS I stood once again among the ruins of the herb garden, I thought that I had gone back in time. Bending amongst the tortured plants there was a hunched dark figure, long wild hair hanging down her back, a bony hand extended, and I saw the soft caress those fingers gave the crumpled stems, the bruised and bowed-down leaves. My old-time guilt and dread stirred, the fear of her witchery. I crossed myself. I knew that I had buried her, myself and Marel, we had buried her, so long ago. Yet she was here, and would turn round, and see me. Would her gaze be ghostly, ghoulish from the grave? Would it be a death's head framed in hair? A mortal terror froze me to the spot.

It was not Alkanet. She straightened and turned around and fixed me with a stare.

'Ah! Pedlar! What have you come to gawp at?'

'Um – Alys? I hoped that you might help me.'

'Why should I do that?'

'Your goodness of heart?' I observed drily, my fear lost in the comfortable familiarity of such a conversation, here where I had had many such before.

'Speak not of that you know nothing about. If my heart is good or bad, you'll never find it out.'

I marvelled at her. Young, Alkanet must have looked just so, the pinched and wizened face with none of that which we call beauty! Sharp-eyed, she watched me, drawing out my thoughts.

'You've come for Marel.'

'Oh! Tell me he is here!'

'And lie? He *was* here; but not now. He did all that was needed. When that was done I had no use for him. He didn't want to stay; he knows this is no longer his. I am the garden now.'

'You don't know where he's gone?'

'It isn't important. What matters is this place where we are standing. *This* time it will be all right. It will grow again,

317

because I am here to tend it. The Mother works through my hands; the link is unbroken.'

'The thornapple?' I said. I looked around as if by mentioning the name I might have called it up, as a bad spirit might be called. 'Has the thornapple gone?'

'Gone,' said Alys thoughtfully. 'The lady Berenice gave most particular instructions here. Be sure it is destroyed, she said, be sure *that* one has gone. Now why should she do that, I wonder, pedlar? Why take against that plant so? As if it meant something to her . . . as if it was a servant or an enemy who had once done her a favour and must not live to tell the tale . . . does not that suggest itself to you?'

'You are too sly; you look for trouble,' I shrugged.

'And you are too simple,' she snapped. 'I understand that lady very well, and you'll see I'm right.' She chuckled. 'I'll have that lady at my beck and call. She's in deep waters when she tangles with the Mother's wicked ones.'

'But you said the plant was gone . . .'

'But not out of the world, clodpole! The Norsemen brought it, didn't they, from across the Poison Sea? And where they brought it from, there it still grows, and all it needs are other travellers to find it and to bring it here. Next time you may not be so lucky and have Old Alkanet to guard it; next time it may spread and root and disguise itself, as a spellbinder would who wished to come amongst us and work wickedness unseen! There, pedlar! And will you be ready?'

I squinted at Alys, fighting hard to see her as what she was, a village girl with odd notions from whom I wanted help, and was not getting any. She came close to me and looked up into my face.

'The Mother will be appeased,' she told me, crooking her finger just as Alkanet used to. 'She will give life or She will lack. Then Her oppressors will lose. She must be nurtured if we love ourselves. Do you hear me, pedlar? This time it will be all right; but there will be other times, when other people come against the Mother, who do not know that in cutting down the Mother they are hacking off their own limbs one by one . . .'

I pulled away, uneasy, irritable.

'What is this talk of mothers! I see you can tell me nothing of the boy I seek, and I bid you good day.'

I tugged at Comfrey's tether and we plodded from the

glade. Behind us Alys cried after us, shrilly: 'You will see I am right – she will be appeased – all will bring a reckoning – what is taken will be paid for –'

I looked round once, to wave goodbye. She was standing, a sharp black shape against the broken doorway, pointing, as if she could see beyond me, to the end of all the roads.

A ghostly pedlar, doomed to search for his love throughout eternity, affrighting lone wanderers with his pale and haunted face – this is what I feared I would become as I trudged those endless forest paths, the gloomy clearings, the dark leafy ways. My legend would become like Marel's, one more thread of that vast tapestry that makes the forest.

I had occasion then to remember Roger's notion, that the forest takes on meaning over and above each twig and leaf and echoes what we carry in our thoughts. Of stark necessity I never had much played that kind of fancy – a man who treads the forest as a way of life might lose his wits if every day brought startling soul-truths. But now I did. What would *I* find in the forest? A terrible sadness born of unsatisfied longings? An endless journey along paths each so much like another that I learned nothing, gained nothing, got nothing? The grim philosophy of making do, false cheerfulness that hides the ache within? Or might I hope for Love and all its blessings, and its trials?

And Marel, what of him? What if for him the forest was the tangle of crazed thought, the bushes and briars, a twisted path, or worse, no path at all? What if the villagers were right, and he was in some way changed, haggard and unkempt, and witless as they said? It wouldn't have made any difference to my love for him, or my plans to take him away from what had become an unkind place. It was only for him that I felt afraid.

So I would dedicate my life to looking for him. I had never felt happy about leaving him. I knew that I was partly to blame for what had happened; I never should have gone away. And if I passed on into legend as a doomed elf-stricken seeker, terrifying travellers with my hunched and twisted shadow and the rattling of my packhorse's bridle, then so be it.

Travellers were to be spared this one terror – Heaven knows they had enough already – for I found him.

I could not say how long it took me. It seemed very long. The leaves had turned from red, gold, brown to dun grey, and the rains had mulched the sodden paths beneath my feet. It was at the hinge of the year, when Autumn turns to Winter, and the gateways to the Otherworld gape, and the nights grow long and cold. All around Cortle the forest lay, a wilderness, but I knew the ways of it, and if he were within, alive, I knew that I would find him.

There is a dark mere where the trees come down low to the water's edge. This was where I found him, with the dancing shadows of leaves upon his face, sitting on a fallen tree. Nothing so fearful as the stories would have me believe, it was only Marel. I sat down beside him and looked into his trance-filled eyes. I said: 'I am the pedlar man; you know me.'

His time alone in the wood had made him whole. He was still beautiful, his hair thick and shining. His eyes were strange and flecked with fear. So lovely was he, so unearthly, that for a moment I did wonder if it was his spirit, not himself, a wood elf, slippery and cold, who seduced the unwary, only to leave them gibbering idiots with wonderful tales of lust to tell that nobody believed.

'The pedlar!' he said, child-like, and turned to me. 'I said I'd be here. I told you I would wait for you.'

'And now I'm here. I said I would be back.'

We sat there by the pool, and the leaves rustled and the forest smelt moist and sweet.

Then we left those places far behind us. He rode upon the horse; I led. We went westward.

We have never been back. In the old days I used to think that by going back again and again I would be some kind of avenging angel to bring down the Norman family at the castle. I thought some situation would present itself in which I could be the working of doom for the de Bonnefoys. A modest ambition! I felt somewhat chastened at the thought now. Meddling with what the Almighty is working out Himself is uncomfortably risky, and I faithfully hope that what happened was bound to be. An inevitable pattern in which we all have a part, but only the kind of part that any one leaf has in Autumn, when it makes its own pattern amongst all its fellows, red and golden for a moment on its flight between branch and earth. And this way I justified the guilt that I certainly did feel in my guts.

In the days that followed, Marel told me what had happened to him since I went away. I pieced it all together, with Benedict's account between.

'And are you well?' I asked him.

'I am now. I was not; but the forest made me well, and now you are returned.'

'We shall always stay together, if that's what pleases you.'

'It does please me. It's what I'd like. I was the garden, but now another is the garden. It does not need me.'

Now, as we travelled on together there was something that I wondered. One night as we lay close, deep in the hay of some field barn, I asked: 'What happened with Alys?'

'You went back to the herb garden. What did you see?'

'It was all chopped down.'

'Completely gone?'

'Oh no, far from it. It was a mess and nothing like it used to be. But there were roots and stumps and such.'

'When I left the inn where I was sleeping and I came into the forest I went straight to the garden. I knelt down with my hands in the earth. I planted what I could. Of course, some were gone. But others – cut them and they only grow bigger and more beautiful. Wonderful new plants will rise up. Over each plant I said a prayer. Or would they call it a spell?' He laughed, almost a sneer. 'Alys came. We worked together. We knelt in the wet soil till our arms were black. We were possessed. We had only one aim. I told her what to do. She had some knowledge from Roger but it was nothing. I told her everything. She knows the workings now, all secrets, good and bad. She knows all Alkanet knew. She will be Alkanet and they will fear her.'

'Alys?' I grumbled. 'But you don't like her. How could you bear to pass on Alkanet's secrets?'

'The garden was more important. And we gave praise for what we had done. Do you know what I mean?'

Excited suddenly, he lay up on his elbow, and his eyes glittered. An owl that perched above us on a rafter flew out to start its hunting.

'No, I don't. What do you mean?'

'I mean we lay together!'

'You and Alys!' I was astonished.

'It needed to be done.'

'Did it indeed!'

'It was part of the bargain. It was understood. It set the seal upon the deed. It meant she took the seeds.'

'I am surprised, Marel, that you knew what to do,' I muttered disapprovingly.

'It's pretty much the same,' said Marel archly.

I was most peeved at his confession.

'I believe you're jealous,' he said, pleased.

'Not a bit of it,' I said stoutly.

'You need not be,' he promised me. 'It was not love nor lust. It was like a handclasp to make an agreement.'

I groaned. 'My lad,' I said, 'you are no longer innocent. I did not like your innocence; but please do not grow wordly instantly; let there be time in between.'

I thought, if he but knew it, that Marel had the power to be mischievously seductive – the mixture of that youthful face and golden hair, like some bright wayward cherub, with the skill that grew each time we lay together. Thank Heaven it was I into whose hands he'd fallen. I was no saint, I know, but yet my love was true.

We travelled on together, he astride the horse and I beside him. I was as happy as I'd ever known. It gave me joy to look at him. Something of his unearthliness had gone. He looked a peasant boy, more than common beautiful of course, but no longer like one who had strayed from faery with the knowledge of good and evil tucked beneath his belt. And he was glad to help me in my trade, useful, eager, charming all we met with his winning ways, learning songs to sing, picking out best herbs for me to buy, and skilful with folk's ailments. I bought for him a sturdy hood to cover up his shimmering hair. He would pass for my brother, son, or friend; but he was my lover.

I would like to say I cherished no bad feelings towards Roger. No so. He and I were both travellers, wandering the world's ways; and the paths of travellers always cross sooner or later. When that happens for him and for me, I intend to clout him senseless.

Beside a fire we sat, Marel and I, against a dry-stone wall, munching roasted meat, drinking ale. A tumbledown hut, deserted by some shepherd, would be our shelter for the night, its doorway glowing from the light of our burning lanthorn. Outside, the wild wind from the hills howled and rustled the thatch; but we would be warm upon the straw within. I watched the firelight shadows on his face, and I was silent, for the moment more aware of the difficulties in our life than of its joys. It was not easy on the roadways of the land to share my life with one who was a babe in the ways of the world, and I had to watch out for the things he did in ignorance which could land us into trouble. That day he stole all kinds of small stuff from the market stalls to help me fill my pack, and we had to have a little talk about the kind of things that might make other people angry – stealing their goods was one such and it was considered wrong. It often wore me out explaining right and wrong to one who had an open mind.

Then he tried to stop some who were felling trees. I thought him lucky to escape a similar felling. I could hear him yelling at the woodcutters, see him kicking logs about, shouting like a preacher: 'Take only what you need. Pray to those trees. You must not cut down without planting. You hurt the earth. The Mother is the strongest. There is fire inside, inside the earth. Hurt the earth and the flames will come. The flames will burn us all, both good and bad . . .'

I winced and gestured soothingly; I dragged him from that place, explaining in firm tones: 'He is a simpleton . . .'

Now he was sullen that I had removed him from his fray; he said that if he saw more things like that he could not help but speak about it.

'I had not realised that there was such a need for magic in the world,' he said. 'At least where Alys is, the magic will go on. The herbs will grow. There will be someone in the little house. Folk will come to her and she will give them what they need.'

'I fear that Berenice will work for her downfall if Alys grows too powerful,' I said.

'Myself, I think that she will grow to need her, as she needed Alkanet.'

'Oh Marel,' I said wearily. 'I hoped all that was over. I hoped that you would start forgetting that strange life – that Alys might never get to carry out her plans, for lack of herbs and knowledge. For don't tell me she deals with only wholesome things – I know about the others which are dark and dangerous.'

'Do you think that you can keep the thornapple down?' said

323

Marel passionately. 'Though it has gone from the garden it has not gone from the world; others will find it and bring it; it will always be.'

What chance did we stand, he with his innocence gone, a smudged page which had once been white, a place for good or bad to grow . . . and I to teach him, with my quirky way of looking at the world – no holy man, but no felon either and marred enough myself? The intensity of his voice might have alarmed me if I had not been confident of the sweet power of ordinary things. For it's with these so homely tools that we keep the thornapple at bay, every day of our lives.

With a laugh I knew what chance we stood – the chance that every sinner has to bumble his way through this world, trying to make sense of it, with hope to keep us going; and love our burden and reward.

'Come here,' I said, reaching for him. 'For you and me and the life we are going to share together, you have no need of any magic at all.'

I saw again the figure of Alys, in her torn and tangled garden; her black shape, and her finger pointing, pointing it seemed far into the days to come, further than we could ever see or know. *The Mother will give life or She will lack. She will be appeased. She must be nurtured if we love ourselves.*

But I put her from my mind.

also by Chris Hunt:

STREET LAVENDER

In the busy West End streets of 1880s London, young Willie Smith quickly learns to use his youth and beauty as a means of escaping the grinding poverty of his East End background.

'A gem of a book. Chris Hunt's done a marvellous job intertwining a solid narrative full of good humour and wit with a message of real social conscience and insight ... Really, you haven't had so much fun reading a gay-themed novel in years' - John Preston, *Gay Chicago.*

'The rhythym of salvation and perdition - from reformatory to male brothel to good works among the teeming poor, via a superb episode in Bohemian Kensington - is fearlessly sustained. The effect of this harlot's progress with a silver lining is irresistable' - Jonathan Keates, *The Observer.*

'I read all 343 pages in two compulsive sittings ... Both a funny study of a young gay's mounting consciousness and a voyeur's guide to the seamy side of Victoriana' - Patrick Gale, *Gay Times.*

ISBN 0 85449 035 3   UK £4.95/US $9.95

MIGNON

The glittering Paris court of Henri III provides Marc with ample chance to advance his fortunes, as a mignon, one of the king's pet boys. But when a threat is made on his life, he flees his native France to seek refuge in the England of Elizabeth I. Here life proves just as dangerous, when he encounters a celebrated new playwright by the name of Christopher Marlowe and is quickly drawn into an underworld of spies, crime and political intrigue.

'A rattling good read which adroitly mixes an entertaining plot with plenty of authentic historical detail' - *Gay Times*.

'A rich and detailed picture of Elizabethan London is revealed. Chris Hunt includes the minutest details of life at that time, contrasting the overcrowded squalor with the vast stretches of open space that still remained in what we now know as central London, highlighting the stark contrast between rich and poor' - *Him*.

ISBN 0 85449 066 3   UK £5.95/US $10.95

other historical fiction from GMP:

Edward Lucie-Smith
THE DARK PAGEANT

In the confusion of fifteenth-century France, with the kingdom riven between the King of England, the Duke of Burgundy and the still uncrowned Dauphin, two romantic figures stand out: Joan of Arc, whose "voices" led her king to coronation and herself to flames and sainthood, and the glittering Gilles de Rais, Marshal of France, whose dark voices led him to the scaffold and hundreds of little victims to a ghastly death. Joan is still a heroine to France; Gilles has become a symbol of limitless evil.

Gilles' story is told here through the eyes of Raoul de Saumur, his childhood companion and lifelong comrade-in-arms, impelled by curiosity to fathom his friend's secret, yet terrified himself by what he might discover.

'An historical meditation on the paralysing fascination of evil' - *The Times*.

'The novel has to cope with this ghoul and with the enigma of Joan herself and does so with a solid sense of period' - *The Guardian*.

ISBN 0 85449 006 X   UK £4.95/US $8.95

Vincent Virga
GAYWYCK

Robert Whyte is only seventeen when he is hired to catalogue the vast library at Gaywyck, the mysterious ancestral mansion on Long Island owned by the handsome yet melancholy Donough. It does not take him long to realise he is deeply attracted to his new employer. But he has to reckon with a hidden evil waiting in the background, fired by the dark sexual secrets of Donough's family past, sowing murder, blackmail and mayhem in its wake as it moves towards his destruction.

'An extraordinary tour de force that merits special praise. A well-researched historical novel that gives us rare glimpses of what gay men were possibly saying and doing eighty years ago' - *The Advocate*.

'I enjoyed Gaywyck very much. To me a fascinating mixture of Wilde, the Gothic and, above all, the souls laid to rest in New York' - Angus Wilson.

ISBN 0 85449 057 4   UK £4.95/US $7.95

David Rees
THE HUNGER

Ireland in the 1840s, where the beleaguered population fell victim to massive famine following an uncontrollable potato blight. Against this harsh background of turmoil, starvation and disease, an English landowner and an Irish peasant struggle to keep not only themselves and those around them alive, but also the love they feel for one another in a society and era that violently condemn it.

'A first class writer of enormous significance' - *Time Out.*

'Compelling and powerful. The story here is first-rate ... parts of the book offer the reader brilliant descriptions of life and death during the Famine. All round, a very fine gay historical novel' - *GTW Newsletter.*

'Intense and convincing, a fascinating novel' - *Book People.*

ISBN 0 85449 008 6   UK £3.95/US $7.50

Francis King
DANNY HILL:
MEMOIRS OF A PROMINENT GENTLEMAN

It is not generally known that the celebrated woman of pleasure
Fanny Hill had a foster-brother called Daniel. He too wrote his
memoirs, which reveal him to have been as accomodating as his
sister and as equally versed in the ways of the polite society of his
time. They have been painstakingly edited by Francis King, who
explains in his introduction how this priceless literary heirloom
came to be in his possession. If he is to be believed, these memoirs
offer a unique and intimate insight into the life of a young man in
eighteenth-century England, and his rise to prominence entirely
through the diligent application of those gifts with which he was
endowed.

'It's brilliant stuff - the wit and literary allusions cannot fail to
entertain, nor the charm and artistry to delight' - *Time Out*.

'A writer completely master of his technique. Mr King's great gift is
the ability to put himself into another person's skin' - *Sunday Times*.

'Mr King seems unable to write badly' - *The Observer*.

0 85449 058 2   UK £3.95/US $7.95

GMP books can be ordered from any bookshop in the UK, and from specialised bookshops overseas. If you prefer to order by mail, please send full retail price plus £1.00 for postage and packing to GMP Publishers Ltd (MO), PO Box 247, London N17 9QR. (For Access/Eurocard/Mastercharge/American Express/Visa give number and signature.) A comprehensive mail order catalogue is also available.

In North America order from Alyson Publications Inc,
40 Plympton St, Boston MA 02118, USA

NAME AND ADDRESS IN BLOCK LETTERS PLEASE:

Name _____

Address _____

_____

_____